Author photo: Lisa Morrison

Beryl Fletcher was born in New Zealand. In 1992, her book *The Word Burners* was awarded the Commonwealth Writer's Prize for the best first book in South Asia and the South Pacific. Her first two books, *The Word Burners* and *The Iron Mouth* were awarded a place in the Top Twenty of the NZ Listener Women's Book Festival. She has been the recipient of three grants from Creative NZ. In 1994, she was chosen as Writer in Residence for New Zealand at the International Writing Program at the University of Iowa, USA. Her third novel *The Silicon Tongue* was published in 1996. In 1999, she was selected as Writer in Residence at The University of Waikato in Hamilton, New Zealand.

for Hamish Duff and Catherine Brennan

Other books by Beryl Fletcher
The Word Burners
The Iron Mouth
The Silicon Tongue

THE BLOODWOOD CLAN

Beryl Fletcher

Spinifex Press Pty Ltd
504 Queensberry Street
North Melbourne, Vic. 3051
Australia
women@spinifexpress.com.au

First published by Spinifex Press, 1999

Edited by Barbara Burton
Typeset in Century Schoolbook by Alena Jencik
Chapter motifs by Sonia Kretschmar
Cover design by Deb Snibson, Modern Art Production Group
Made and printed in Australia by Australian Print Group

National Library of Australia
Cataloguing-in-Publication data:

Fletcher, Beryl, 1938–
The Bloodwood Clan

ISBN 1 875559 80 9

I. Title

NZ823.2

Acknowledgements

Thanks to the Australia/New Zealand Foundation for providing a grant for the purposes of research. Thanks to Hamish Duff and Catherine Brennan in Sydney, Cathie Dunsford and Susan Sayer in New Zealand, and Susan Hawthorne and Renate Klein in Melbourne. Thanks to my fellow members of the Waikato Writers Workshop for providing a useful critique of parts of this text.

I would like to acknowledge the following texts that were useful to me during the research for this novel.

'Bells Falls Massacre and Bathurst's History of Violence' by David A. Roberts. In *Work in Flux*, edited by E. Greenwood, K. Neumann, and A. Sartori. 1995. The University of Melbourne, History Department Publication.

Birds of Australia by J. D. Macdonald, illustrated by Peter Slater. 1984. A.H. & A.W. Reed, Sydney.

Eucalypts of the Mudgee District by Dean and Bob Nicolle and Malcolm French. 1994. F. and N. Eucalypt Publications.

Fear, Myth and History by J. C. Davis. 1986. Cambridge University Press, UK.

'Going Feral: Authentica on the Edge of Australian Culture' by Graham St John. 1997. *The Australian Journal of Anthropology*, 8:2 pp.167–189.

Utopia and the Ideal Society by J. C. Davis. 1981. Cambridge University Press, UK.

'Ur-Fascism' by Umberto Eco. 1995. *The New York Review*, June 22, 1995, pp.12-15.

Waterloo Creek by Roger Milliss. 1994. UNSW Press, Sydney.

The Works of Gerrard Winstanley with an appendix of documents relating to the Digger movement. Edited with an introduction by G. Sabine. 1965. Russell and Russell, New York.

The heading for chapter seven, 'All That is Solid Melts into Air' refers to a comment by Karl Marx in his book *The Communist Manifesto*. 1848.

Parts of the text are rewritten fragments from *The Fiery Flying Roll* written by the Ranter, Abiezer Coppe and published in 1650.

1

NOT A DOMESTIC MEMOIR

Eliza is alone in the trees on the top of a ridge. She peels away a patch of bark from the trunk of a tree and reveals fresh white bark beneath. A brittle gum. A twig for her pouch, a sample of old and new bark for her class.

See children, see how the pink and the grey give way to white in late summer. The seasons are revealed by the state of the bark. Trees know when to change the colour of their skin, they sense changes in the length of daylight. God is thoughtful to give the trees a secret eye that can understand the difference between day and night. He is in everything, he gives all knowledge. Look at this sample from *Eucalyptus mannifera* and know that when the white bark appears we are coming to the end of another long hot summer.

Eliza enjoys being up here in the hills. In a few weeks she will be too busy to take her solitary walks under the guise of collecting botanical samples for her class. The grapes will soon be ready for harvest and the children will have to leave their classes and work in the vineyards. She too will have to work, snipping the bunches of ripe fruit and placing them carefully in the baskets for the men to lift into the wagons.

She sits in the warm litter beneath the tree, her legs slightly stiff beneath her long skirt. There is a rustle of leaves. A snake? A bird? None that she can see or hear except for a solitary currawong groaning and flapping along the top of the ridge. The skin on the back of her neck prickles. She is sure that she is being watched. She stays perfectly still. She knows that she is close to the top border of the Digger's land. Too close. If someone has broken in, and there is trouble, she will be censored for moving too close to the outside. She has been warned before not to stray too far from the town.

A twig snaps. She draws her skirt tightly around her ankles and breathes as quietly as possible. There is a flash of metal deep in the undergrowth. She can see a man with a rifle creeping slowly through the thick tangle of foliage. He is stalking something. A bandicoot? A wallaby? Surely not. There are few native animals left up here. It has always been just her and the birds and the ants.

The man is wearing some sort of uniform. Green and brown patches, a black beret, heavy boots. Is he a soldier? Eliza can't decide. Her understanding of people who live in the outside world is limited to covert observations of the customers that come into the produce shop.

The man moves towards her. He seems oblivious of her presence. He lowers his gun and leans against a tree. He takes a leather pouch from his pocket and rolls a cigarette. A match flares, and a cloud of pungent smoke drifts slowly sideways in the warm still air.

Eliza is transfixed. She can see his profile clearly. A long but shapely nose, strong cheek bones, firm lips. No beard. He looks like a woman, pretty almost.

He finishes smoking his cigarette and rubs it against the rough bark of a gum. He puts the extinguished butt carefully into his pocket. Then he stands up straight and opens his trousers at the front. Eliza, horrified, sees a jet of yellow urine spurt out from between his legs and stream down into a bed of dry eucalyptus leaves.

She knows that she is forbidden to observe this male act.

She tries to close her eyes but they will not obey her will. She has never seen the penis of a grown man before and she is seized with an intense curiosity.

She watches him shake his penis dry and rezip his pants. He picks up the gun and disappears into the thick bush. She waits for a long time before she dares to stand up. Her legs have gone to sleep. She gathers up her pouch and her botanical specimens and rubs her legs to restore the blood flow. Then she creeps away, keeping her head down until she reaches the edge of the bush and the welcome sight of the vineyards and the gardens far below.

My first day at the Commonwealth of Diggers. Still recovering from having to leave my children at the in-laws in Canberra. Jack cried. Briony punished me by refusing to say goodbye. Hey kids, I said, trying to sound cheerful, it's only for six months. And then I'll get a job, we'll have plenty of money. I'm doing this for all of us.

I have been a widow for two years. My husband Russell was killed. He jumped from a plane with a defective parachute on his back. For fun, for recreation. His first jump, because he had just turned forty and wanted to have adventures again. I pleaded with him not to do it but he took no notice. Russell never did listen to my warnings and premonitions. Called me a *what if* woman, as in *what if* this happened or that happened, where would we be?

I saw it on television, his body twisting in the harness, spinning faster and faster as he neared the ground, the shape beneath the red blanket on the stretcher. Mad thoughts, angry thoughts. His beloved flesh falling, his familiar body, the lump beneath his right shoulder blade that he had asked me to massage the night before, a hole in his right leg where a mole had recently been cut out, his shining teeth, all the mercury removed at enormous expense and I thought why this pointless maintenance, what the hell for?

Briony thought me callous bringing up money. But I wasn't

talking about money, I was talking about how death steals meaning. Sensible action in the past becomes non-sense in the present. And Briony soon changed her tune when she had to give up all the luxuries that she had taken for granted. She has never forgiven Russell for failing to insure his life, she has never forgiven me for not providing her needs. She feels *entitled*. I spoilt her I suppose. I shielded her from unpleasant facts as a child, I created an illusion of safety. I thought this is what mothers had to do to keep their daughters safe.

I went back to university to do a post-graduate degree in my first love, urban sociology. I gained a First in my Masters Degree and a won a scholarship to study for a Doctorate. Happiness all round except for the problem of fieldwork.

It was just as difficult for anthropologists. The days of finding a friendly tribe were almost over. The natives around the Pacific had been studied virtually to death, and besides, they were writing (or rather re-writing) their own academic versions of themselves and gaining publications and prestige and the best university jobs. Briony said it was unfair. After all, we taught them how to do it.

No worries, my supervisor said. Interested in religious communes? Here, take a look at this. A request for a researcher. A live-in job, participant observation. Do you know Mudgee, in rural New South Wales? The Diggers are weird bastards but harmless. They don't believe in modern technology or communications. Cut off from the world. They've been making and selling wine for fifty years. Good stuff too. They specialise in varietal wines. Their cab. sauv. is to die for. Sociologists have been trying to get in there for years but no luck until now. Why not give it a go?

I did. And I was the first outsider chosen to live within the walls of the town who had not come specifically to join their religious congregation. I was over the moon! The story of this culture could be as big as the Amish. My luck had changed. I had been handed a wonderful opportunity, and I knew that if I worked hard and published as much as possible, it could lead to an interesting job in a prestigious university. And to the end of my financial and personal troubles.

I leave my car in Canberra with the children and travel by bus to Mudgee. I decide not to get a taxi to Digger Town. Too expensive. I tag along with a van of tourists who are doing the grand tour of the district. Only sixteen dollars. The other four people in the van are Japanese. They have their own interpreter, a rather sombre young woman.

Greg the tour leader agrees to take me along the gravel road. Not a route he usually travels. Unless he gets someone really keen to sample the Digger's wines. And then it has to be the weekend. The shop is closed during the week.

We drive along a valley chopped in two by the Cudgegong River. The land is controlled and parcelled. Vineyards, angora goats, abandoned chimneys of old houses standing next to long low farmhouses. The eucalypts are pushed back to the lower slopes of the hills that form a protective blue ring around the flats. The few trees that stand hopefully beside the road are weighed down with mistletoe and other parasites.

The land bristles with painted boards that tell old stories.

The first bushranger seen in Mudgee tethered his horse here. 'To take water from Clay Pipe Creek,' says Greg, 'before moving on to his next ambush.'

The first settler's gravestone, carved in rock. 'Poor bastard died of a snake bite,' says Greg. 'A lot of them did in those days.'

Another sign tells us that this is the spot where the first grapevines were planted in the district over a hundred years ago. They're still there, non-fruiting, either dying or dormant. The joints on the vines are like black arthritic fists. Greg says that they were planted close to the ground in European fashion to steal the last of the heat from the soil in autumn. Then they found out what a bloody hot place Australia was and had to move subsequent grafts higher up the stock.

In this place, where the sellers of history make more money than the farmers, it is clear that you only make it to the painted boards if you can prove that you were there *first*. But there is more to receiving this accolade than the simple naming of time and place and *firstness*. It must be the right sort of event.

Greg did not explain what this could be.

The hills are getting closer. We are almost at the end of the bitumen road.

'Welcome to the Commonwealth of Diggers,' says Greg. 'From now on, this road is hell. Hasn't seen a grader in a long while. Hold on to your hats!'

The interpreter repeats all this in Japanese. The tourists look puzzled.

'Corrugations,' explains Greg. 'Sorry to close the window in this heat but the dust is like fine sand and will permeate.'

We bump and jolt for several kilometres along the atrocious road. We come to a barred gate over a cattle grid. At the side of the road is a crude shelter like a bus shed with a seat inside.

'We must stop here,' says Greg. 'The Diggers do not allow cars to travel any further. If you want to buy wine, you must signal your arrival and wait for the horse and cart to come and collect you.'

He gets down from the van and lifts my luggage out onto the road. I pay him and with a cheerful wave he drives away. I ring the bell and wait. I open my black umbrella against the burning sun. Flies buzz around my mouth and eyes seeking moisture.

Soon I am riding in a horse and cart with my suitcase, made of leather as requested. One horse, two wheels. I am ignorant of the name of this antique carriage. The driver, a bearded man in white overalls, is reticent in the extreme. He grunts unintelligibly when I ask him questions. I fall silent but take note of my surroundings for recording later in my journal.

Write down everything Josie, no matter how trivial it seems at the time. This from Max, my thesis supervisor. The students held him in awe because he had once lived in a remote part of Indonesia for three months and had nearly died of yellow fever and loneliness and interference from the local witches. He brought back a giant tapeworm in his gut that had created a terrible hunger and cost him a fortune in Big Macs. But it had been great for his career. He knew how to do real fieldwork, how to strip away cultural presuppositions, how to look through the eyes of the Other. Or so he said. And he had his tapeworm preserved in formalin in one of those tall pasta jars. Caused a sensation in Social Anthropology 101.

You only get one bite at the cherry Josie, he told me. We don't know why the Diggers have asked for a researcher. You may be the first and last one allowed in. So keep your mouth shut and your eyes and ears open.

His instructions echo in my ears as we approach the town. It's incredible. Like a film set for a spaghetti western. Right down to the women in long skirts and horses tethered to wooden veranda posts and dogs rolling in the dust. Horse shit and flies everywhere. There are faded signs above the shops; Blacksmith, Assayer of Precious Metals, Baker, Grocer, the Great American Tobacco Saloon. But there are no goods displayed in the shop windows. They are shrouded in calico curtains.

Women are coming and going from a big stone building with an imposing set of marble steps leading up to a double door made of darkened wood. It could be an old courthouse or possibly a colonial opera theatre. They are carrying wicker baskets covered with red gingham cloths. Food and provisions? Hard to see.

Except for their uniform of long skirts and long-sleeved blouses and cotton headscarves, they look like any other group of healthy Australian women.

Oh for a camera! But they have forbidden anything but pencils and notebooks. Pencils! It's a wonder they didn't specify quill pens and indian ink. To hell with them, I have smuggled in a good supply of ballpoint pens. And a taperecorder and packets of double A batteries. I couldn't risk my laptop. Besides, Briony has just discovered the Internet and she insisted on taking my computer with her to Canberra.

The man in the white overalls ushers me into one of the old shop fronts. There are rows of men seated on high-backed wooden chairs. They are dressed in denim jeans and check shirts and have long untidy beards. They wear elastic-sided leather boots and hats with wide brims. Absolute silence. The rays of the late afternoon sun flood through the high window at the back of the shop. Motes of yellow dust ride down to the floor.

I stare at them. They stare at me. I flashback to a game from my childhood where you try to make your opponents lower their eyes before you do. I can feel my heart beating like a trapped bird against my ribs but I refuse to be intimidated by this silent crew. I note that they are all middle-aged or older and have those deeply wrinkled walnut faces of farmers and outdoor workers.

'Welcome Sister,' says one of the walnuts. 'You are very welcome.'

Ha! I won. I stared them out. I try a smile, I move forward to shake the hand of the one who spoke. His skin is dry and rough.

'My name is Gerrard,' he says. 'Now sit and take some wine and bread with us.'

He directs me to a long trestle table at the side of the room. A small door at the back of the shop opens and an old woman enters carrying a tray of food and some bottles of wine. I try to establish eye contact with her but she keeps her head lowered. There is silence while she unloads the tray and leaves the room.

'Now sit,' orders Gerrard.

The bread is delicious, small squares of sourdough rye the colour of burnt sugar. The red wine is rich and warm and spicy. No label. But it tastes rather like a shiraz. They watch me drink from a pottery goblet. Some of them take pieces of bread but I am the only one drinking. Untalkative lot. It is going to be difficult for me to understand this place. I feel compelled to break the silence. I ask if they have made the wine from their own grapes.

'We provide all our own needs within the community,' says

Gerrard. 'Everything you see is made by us. By working with the earth, shall we be uplifted.'

I make a mental note of his words. Very PC, very eco. Is it true? I could swear some of them are wearing Akubras and Levis.

After I have quenched my thirst they begin to speak, one after the other. A few sentences each. Words of welcome. Coded speech, religious clichés, but strangely reassuring. Each one refers to me as Sister Josie. Gerrard is the last. He speaks the same words of welcome. He wishes me luck with my doctoral studies and promises that the citizens of the Commonwealth will be instructed to co-operate fully with me. Then his tone shifts. There is a subtle change in the air. The walnut faces of the men fade beneath the shadowy brims of their hats. There is a soft scuffle of leather against wood as booted feet are pulled back beneath chairs.

What is Gerrard saying? Something about God bringing me to the Commonwealth as a vehicle, a carrier of essential knowledge. God has blessed me with an education and now I am here to educate them. An exchange of mutual benefit, he says. I'll get what I want and they will too.

In order to prove to herself that she had not dreamt his presence, she searched the ground for the butt until she remembered that she had seen him put it in his pocket. It had taken her a week to find the courage to climb the ridge to the dense patch of bush and find the exact spot where she had seen him lean his rifle against the tree and roll a cigarette. Since then, she had hardly slept, disturbed by dreams of voyages across a glassy sea in a fragile boat and journeys across rocky landscapes devoid of living plants in a wheeled ship that ran on land instead of floating in water. She tried desperately to escape from these frightening journeys but upon awakening, at once desired to return. She sensed his presence in the desert landscapes; reflections of shaven skin in waterless pools, stones rattling beneath a stumbling boot, blisters of sweat on the burning sand.

She sits beneath the same brittle gum that she had harvested for bark a week before. She takes a damp cloth from her bag and holds it against her hot forehead. Above her, a trilling bird throws down a liquid-sugar scale.

She sits very quietly, listening for noises in the bush, her hands folded neatly in her lap. In the distance, far below her, she can hear faint sounds of women's voices and children's laughter. They have been ordered to work in the vegetable field today, harvesting the last of the peppers and zucchinis and lettuces, then digging the crumbling chocolate soil deeply, double trenching, in readiness for the burying of compost and the sowing of winter greens.

Eliza feels a little guilty for not labouring with the others in her group. She had been named as a teacher by the elders three years ago and since then she had been allowed some freedom from the menial tasks and the backbreaking work of incessant agriculture. The deep cuts and grooves in her hands had gradually faded and the red gloss of sunburn on her face and neck had changed to a softer shade of pink. She had lost her thin stringy look, put on weight.

Secretly, she enjoys her new look, her plump pale face, her intact finger nails. She wonders what she looks like from the eyes of another. From the eyes of the man for instance. She tries to imagine herself as that white-throated warbler working high up in the brittle gum, trilling notes of sweetness while extracting insects from the bark. But all she can see is the top of her yellow headscarf and the spray of white-blond hair flowing down her back. A bird's eye view of herself. She could be any one of fifty fair-headed women from the town.

She looks around carefully then pulls the scarf from her head. After a few moments, she starts to shake her head from side to side, enjoying the unfamiliar looseness of her hair. There is a rustle in the leaves. A serpent sent to warn her? Hastily, she pulls her scarf back into its usual position and jumps to her feet.

But it's not a snake, it's an enormous marmalade cat with torn ears and mangy fur, and so thin that his ribs stick out like a greyhound. He is creeping along the ground very slowly, lifting his feet in slow motion, staring intently ahead. And behind him moving just as slowly is the man with his rifle cocked.

It's the women they are concerned about. There have been rumblings, the odd word of mutiny and, to give substance to their concern, three young girls have recently been 'lost to the world'. Gerrard gives me a brief overview of their history. The Commonwealth started with just ten families fifty years ago, now there are over a hundred. They are based on a movement from the seventeenth century. Their forefathers took up their spades and dug up the commons. To break apart the sinful relationship between food and money.

Taciturn bastard. A few tantalising sentences, a baited hook. He must have sensed my frustration because, after he has reluctantly agreed to me joining the single women in the dorm rather than live in the hut they had assigned to me, he takes me to one of the converted shops and hands me over to their historian, Joshua.

Another taciturn bastard. But he does give me some documents which will be invaluable to my research. A set of diaries kept by the various historians through the fifty-year life of their community, and the founding document of the original Diggers, the Book of the Sixty-Two Sacred Laws.

We are sitting down together in the history room above the shop front which was once the Great American Tobacco Saloon. I know it's the history room, because there is a hand-painted sign on the door that tells me so. There are shelves from floor to ceiling, books, rolls of paper, a large table with nothing on it except for a set of white candles in a brass holder and a bowl of tapers with waxen heads.

I ask Joshua why they have painted new signs inside the shops yet left the old ones outside intact. Ah, he intones, so that we know from whence we came. And that which we are not. This room was once a storehouse for cigars.

I imagine old smoke embedded in the timber walls. I am already in withdrawal although I had my last cigarette only two hours ago. I know from past experience that I will be literally climbing the walls by nightfall.

My son Jack said now that you are going to live with the fundamentalists you can get rid of your nicotine habit. He is so good, so pure. Won't smoke, won't drink, won't eat any fellow creature with a conscious mind. Sixteen years old and nagging his mother half to death. I thought he was meant to be the deviant one at his age. Instead of which I get these heavy lectures about the state of my lungs and the state of my karma.

There is a padlocked box in the history room. A carved wooden sea-chest. I run my fingers over the lid to feel the whorls and dents in the wood and quick as a flash Joshua is beside me and removes my hand.

'That is forbidden,' he says. 'Especially to females.'

I protest to Gerrard. 'You brought me here to help you understand the dynamics of your group. No secrets. Otherwise I can't do what I promised.'

Joshua is staring at me with his mouth open. He is one creepy guy. An enormous mouth with thick dry lips that he keeps licking. When he speaks you can see right into his mouth. Not a pretty sight.

Gerrard fobs me off with a vague promise that I will be able to look within the sea-chest later. When I am more familiar with the rules. It's nothing important. Just some old papers. Of historical interest only.

Eliza comes into the dining room late. She moves slowly as if in a reverie and barely acknowledges the reprimand from Hannah, the leader of her table. Hannah wants to know why Sister Eliza is late. She wants to know where Sister Eliza has been. This is the third time in so many days that Sister Eliza has been late for the evening meal and she has missed the blessing of the food. Again.

Eliza sits at her place and touches her slice of dark bread with the tips of her fingers. The red tapestry banner on the wall declares the vision of their founder: *Worke Together, Eat Bread Together*. She chants the words underneath her breath. She cannot look at Hannah. She is afraid of her. And the venom that Hannah manages to convey when she speaks her name.

Sarah, the young woman next to her, nudges her leg with the tip of her shoe. 'Psst, big news,' she whispers. 'Look over there.'

Eliza frowns. She does not want to provide Hannah with any more ammunition.

Sarah says, 'A stranger. Wearing my blue dress. Can you believe she came into the kitchen dressed in trousers? Celia was really shocked.'

There are ten long trestle tables in the main body of the dining room, each one seating over fifty people. Eliza tries to find the blue dress but fails.

'Not over there,' says Sarah, her voice rising with excitement. 'At the widow's table. Nobody knows who she is.'

Eliza waits until Hannah has left the table to bring the next tray of dishes. Then she turns and stares at the woman in Sarah's dress seated at the side of the hall with the old women. Too young to be a widow surely. And worldly, wearing lipstick and glittering earrings. Eliza is burning with curiosity. It has been a long time since anyone from the outside has joined their community.

She whispers to Sarah. 'She came into the kitchen? She is to live with us?'

Sarah nods. 'In our dorm. I can't wait till tonight. To see her things.'

Last year Sarah had refused the husband chosen for her by the council. There had been trouble, words of defiance, a brief banishment, then she had seemed to settle. Eliza wonders why the elders have taken the risk of allowing this strange woman to sleep in the same dormitory as Sarah and Celia and the other young unmarried women.

'I will ask her about the outside,' says Sarah.

Eliza makes sure that Hannah is still stacking the trays on the serving table at the side of the dining hall before she speaks. 'You must not,' she says. 'She has joined us to get away from the world. You will give her pain.'

Sarah is silent. Hannah brings the bowls of fruit to their table. They eat raw segments of apple and raisins soaked in liquid honey. Sarah drinks another glass of water. Eliza picks up a piece of apple in her fingers and pushes it into her mouth. The ripe flesh tastes of drowsy bees and autumn orchards. Yet beneath the sweetness, the taste of blood is still there on her fingers. Old meat. Proof of her sin.

My first night. The others are asleep now. At least they are lying in their beds with their eyes shut. They have allowed me a night light for my work, a candle in a glass lantern. And a tiny wooden table next to my bed. What the hell am I doing here? I will never get through to these women. At least the men talked a little, in words that I understood. There was some familiarity. The salivating Joshua could have been any man anywhere. But these women! Briony would freak out. Beyond geekdom Mother she would say, beyond slopes and skips and wogs. Her speech leaves a lot to be desired at times. She claims the power of irony but I am afraid that she'll say these things in the wrong place and get roasted by the politically correct brigade. Or worse. Briony gives me a lot of grief but she is mine and I love her. Most of the time. At least she is part of something I understand. These women are something else. How can I document something so distant from my own time and place?

Max warned me. He said I would feel like this. Incompetent, useless. Analyse it Josie, write it down. Record everything including your own feelings. You can learn a lot about difference by your reaction to it. Part of the fieldwork experience. Remember the diary of Malinowski; poor devil nearly went troppo. But look at what he achieved, in spite of his arsenic injections and his uncontrolled lust.

I want to go home to Sydney, I want my kids, I want my friends. But if I run from here now, I'll blow my chances of a good job in a university. And that would be the end of my dreams for security and happiness for me and the kids.

I've had a quick look around the place and I've found out a few basic facts. Digger Town is a real town but not one that you will ever find on a map. They brought it down from the North, a ghost town from the gold-rush days. They dragged it here. Literally. Shop by shop, house by house. Timber and stone, brick, iron and nails, with dents and warps and the dust of dead insects.

The vineyards cover hundreds of hectares. The town is at the centre of the land. Multiple tracks lead there like the spokes of a wheel. The wine is processed at the side of the town, behind high brick walls. No windows, no trees, just the walls with one locked wooden gate. Why the secrecy? Are they keeping something from getting out or something from getting in?

Gerrard showed me the shop where they sell their wares to the public. On the polished counter there are clean glasses for the tastings, brass spittoons for the unwanted swill, squares of plain brown bread to cleanse the palate between the whites and the reds and the golden ports.

Molasses barrels, round cheeses wrapped in muslin, wedges cut with wire, sugar sold in twists, glass, paper, cloth. Textures and smells lifted from a page of domestic memoir to give flesh to our collective memory. Pickles, jams, candles smelling of honey, soap, embroidered aprons, and coffee beans roasting on iron trays in a wood-fired oven. Red apples, with dry wrinkled skins, smelling like cider; half-chewed spinach leaves; nubbled potatoes covered with dirt, all produced by traditional methods. No sprays, no cool stores, no chemicals, no tractors. 'By the sweat of the brow,' said Gerrard. 'By plough and spade, hoe and scythe, we reap our harvest with simple God-given tools. Amen.'

I can't believe the work-worn hands and wrinkled skin on

the young women. The women in this dorm look ten years older than Briony. And yet they are all aged between eighteen and twenty-two. Except for Eliza.

If not for her I would not have learned anything. The others stood with their hands clasped together and their eyes downcast. Even after Gerrard's speech of welcome in the dining hall, requesting everyone to assist me in my work. Mrs Jocelyn Tabel, widow, has come to stay with us for a while. So that we can share in her knowledge. Show Sister Josie respect. We prayed to God and He sent her to us.

He didn't mention the fact that I am a sociologist. I am still unclear what it is they want from me. What will happen to me if I don't deliver the goods?

I am feeling rather angry with Max. He's dropped me in it. How can I get away from here if things turn nasty? No telephones, no cars. Will I have to steal a horse and gallop away in the dead of night?

My gothic imagination is getting the better of me. Midnight horse indeed! And yet there are serious tensions here. Eliza dropped a few hints. I quickly learned not to ask direct questions. All I got was blank stares. I don't know the moral rules and philosophies of this place, I don't know what is proper, I don't know what a woman is supposed to be or how she should act. I have to learn, and quickly, how to fit in so that I am accepted as one of them. Yet I must also keep myself apart so that I can retain my objective eye. A tall order.

My first meal in the communal dining room. Almost five hundred people eating together. About a hundred kids. I marvel at their organisation. And their discipline. The kids eat their food without speaking. Like little puppets. All dressed the same. Married couples together, kids together, unmarried men and women separated.

Gerrard leads me to the widow's table. The women interest me. They are dressed in bright print dresses and are altogether more colourful than the other women. Mary on one side of me, Maria on the other. Quite talkative compared with some of the others. Each speaks a few sentences of welcome, each tells me they are glad I am here. Their lives are rather sad now. They have no husbands and their children are grown and busy with households of their own. Maria has six children and Mary seven. Not like the young ones. 'Small families are popular now,' says Mary. She asks me if it is the same for women I know. I tell her I have two kids, Briony and Jack, and that some of my friends have chosen not to have any at all. 'They chose?' asks Mary. I am bursting to ask them about birth control but of course I don't. Far too early.

On the wall a large banner *Worke Together, Eat Bread Together*. This is what they chant over the food. Said with impeccable reverence. I suppress a smile. Sounds rather banal for a sacred text. Yet I suppose it illustrates their communal life.

Back on the main street, Gerrard shows me to the ground floor of what could have been an old tavern. A curved bar made of dark red timber, highly polished. Wide uneven floor boards, walls of timber and brick and hessian. I ask Gerrard if this place was once a public house and he said I should ask Joshua to show me the old maps of the town. If it was really necessary to my work. Is the past important? Maybe I should concentrate more on the here and now.

I try to pump him for some more information about what he wants of me but it's hopeless. He tells me that men are forbidden to go upstairs and that I should wait here until Sister Eliza arrives. She is the oldest spinster and has been told to nurture me. Then he turns and leaves without another word not even a goodnight.

Dusk is falling. I feel so alone. Just me and my heavy suitcase. I sit at the bar on a high stool. Strange how they have purposely kept the ambience and function of these old buildings. A musky smell of oil and leather and hops. Behind the counter are rows of thick glass bottles, brown and green and blue, a wooden barrel lying on its side, silver dishes glinting in the fading light, pewter mugs hanging on brass hooks each with initials scratched behind them on the wall. I wonder if the ghosts of barmaids in their frilly blouses are still working here. I almost rap my knuckles on the bar to order a stiff gin and tonic.

The door opens and a woman that I saw earlier in the dining room enters. She's about thirty. Her eyes are the deepest blue, her long hair is almost white. She is swathed in a long skirt gathered at the waist and a voluminous long-sleeved shirt. Over her clothes, she is wearing a striped pinafore or body apron tied at the back in a bow.

'My name is Eliza,' she says. 'Let me take your bag. Please come upstairs.'

The dorm for single women is at the end of a long hallway with many doors. All closed. Except for the door of the dorm which is wide open. As soon as I see it I wish I had taken up Gerrard's offer of the hut.

A row of single beds with woven white cotton covers. Spartan, bare. No curtains on the small high windows. Creaking floorboards. Must be a freezing hell in winter. Reminds me of a childhood horror I once experienced in my homeland across the Tasman Sea. A place laughingly called a Health Camp.

Eliza introduces me to the other women. Celia, Sarah, Elsa, Anne, Martha. They stand in a row with their eyes cast down. Not one of them says a word of greeting to me. Eliza is busy taking my things from my case and packing them in the cupboard beside my bed. I don't like her touching my things. But I am afraid to ask her to stop. I need her goodwill to survive.

I ask her where the other unmarried women are. Are there other dorms?

She shakes her head. I don't know if this is *no*, or whether she is signalling disapproval at my question. Then the other women come out of their trance, and crowd around my bed. Sarah seizes my satin pyjamas and drapes them around her waist. Eliza takes them from her and folds them into the cupboard. The other women stare intently at my make-up and toilet gear.

18

I ask them if they use toothpaste, face cream. Again, no verbal response.

Outside the windows the sky is black and cloudless and the stars stare down. I have lost the protective mantle of city lights, there is nothing between me and the vast watchful night. I feel smaller here, under surveillance.

This is the word Eliza uses after the other women have gone to bed. She takes me out of the door and down the hall with her finger on her lips. 'I have been asked to care for you,' she says. 'But first there is something I need to know. Forgive me, but have you been sent here to spy on us? Are we under surveillance?'

I am shocked. 'No no, I am here to make a study of your community.'

'Why?'

'For my doctoral studies, to write a book...'

Eliza is silent. Then she takes my hand and leads me back to the dorm. I watch her undress within a large tent-like arrangement that conceals her underwear and any stray bits of naked flesh. The others are already bundled into their bedding, eyes closed, breathing gently.

I climb into bed too, pulling my clothes off beneath the blankets down to my knickers and t-shirt. I glance at my watch. It's nine o'clock. My bed is directly beneath the largest window. The cold white stars move closer to my head.

Eliza comes to the side of my bed and offers to say my prayers for me.

I whisper back please do.

She speaks in rhymes, almost like a chant, old words I have heard in half-remembered songs. Tomorrow I will ask her to write down her prayers for inclusion in my notebook. The retrieval of oral traditions. This, I tell her, is one of the things about her community that others will find interesting.

When she has finished she leans over and kisses me on the forehead. Not a light butterfly kiss, a wet firm set of lips on my skin. I am flooded with conflicting emotions, physically invaded, angry with her, yet overlaid with a curious sense of loss.

'Good night Sister Josie,' she whispers. 'I will help you in your work. I too am a teacher.' She blows out the candle beside my bed and moves quietly to her own.

I can't believe that I am expected to go to sleep at this early hour. I wait for another thirty minutes then carefully lift my covers and creep out of bed. I find my cigarette lighter tucked into a side pocket of my suitcase and light the candle in the glass lantern.

I open my diary and write and write, while the stars turn the wheel of night, and the unmarried women cough gently and turn in their sleep, and outside there is a sound of horses snickering to each other and once a bird of prey, hooting and barking from a distant tree.

I must be careful of myself in this place.

There have been rumours of rain today and the winemakers are concerned about the grapes. School has been closed early. The children are on notice that they may soon be needed for the harvest. For months drought has gripped the district. The creek that flows into the Cudgegong River from the Digger's land has stopped flowing. All that remains are muddy pools that give sanctuary to the remnants of a once thriving yabbi population. There is some pure rainwater in the kitchen tanks. The women have been instructed to use it very sparingly. The water from the bores is brown and smells of decaying minerals. The elders speak of the dangers inherent in bringing that which is naturally below the earth upwards to the surface. Salination. The spoilage of the sacred soil.

Eliza is sad that she has been rostered into lunch preparation today. Sad that rain may come at last when it is not welcome, sad that she cannot show the class the nature-study specimens that she prepared yesterday. If she is not able to open her classroom tomorrow, her prize will have to be returned to the bush.

She grates carrot and beetroot and swedes for the salad bowls. Sarah is here too, peeling a bucket of onions with a bone-handled knife and rubbing her streaming eyes from time to time with the back of one red hand. Eliza notices that she is unusually subdued. They have worked beside each other for an hour but Sarah has hardly spoken except to ask Sister Eliza the whereabouts of the fourth soup tureen. Three are here where they should be but where is the other?

Eliza finds the missing pot behind a door. Sarah grumbles under her breath about non-kitchen girls working here who don't know anything about anything, but she is happy enough to allow Eliza to help her lift the enormous iron saucepan onto the top of the wood stove. Sarah stokes the fire with green mallee roots that have been harvested from the sandy flats near the creekbed. Eliza asks her if she is well.

'Yes,' she answers. 'Thank you. Just worried. Can I speak to you without fear or favour?'

Eliza promises reluctantly. There has been trouble with Sarah in the past and if the elders request information, Eliza must tell them what she knows.

There are ten other women working in here this morning. They are clustered around the single brass tap at the end of the long workbench, holding pannikins and pots, waiting their turn for cooking water.

'Be careful Sisters,' calls Sarah. 'Rain will come. Until then, count every drop.'

Eliza is uneasy. It is not Sarah's place to speak to the older women in this fashion. If Hannah knew there would be trouble.

Sarah motions to Eliza to come into the pantry with her. It is a large room without windows. Shelves from floor to ceiling. Jars of gherkins floating in vinegar, red and yellow jams, marmalade, honey, dried figs rich with black seeds, bottled fruit, a dusty smell of linseed and ground meal. Sarah shuts the door. A sudden darkness. Eliza's eyes adjust to the thin light provided by the skylight at the far end of the room.

Sarah pours out her woes to Eliza. She does not trust Josie, she is afraid of her. Josie has been sent to make trouble for them. 'I would rather die than go through banishment again. If Josie finds out anything about me and reports it to Brother Winstanley, I will kill myself.'

Eliza is shocked. 'Your words are blasphemous. Only God can choose the time of your death.'

'Maybe He seeks to punish me through her.'

'No no. I spoke with her, she is here to study us. That's all.'

'Forgive me, but why? Where is the benefit for us?'

Eliza is silent. She knows that Sarah is right. The elders would never have any transaction with the outside world without good reason.

She tries to reassure Sarah. 'Her intentions are innocent. She has come here to learn our ways. She has a love of knowledge.'

Sarah does not seem convinced.

Eliza opens the door to the kitchen. 'Enough. We must get back to our work.'

They labour for the next hour, taking the trays of hot bread from the bakehouse worker, stirring flavours into the soup, laying out the salad and fruit bowls on the side tables in the dining hall.

The gong is struck and the people file in. Sarah nudges Eliza. 'There she is. Writing in her notebook. I would give up my midday food to know what is between those covers.'

Eliza does not answer her. She is almost relieved when she sees their leader Hannah bustling towards them. 'Bread girls, more bread. On the back table. Not enough to feed a hen.' She laughs at her own witticism. Then she tells Eliza that she is to change tables until further notice. She is to sit beside Sister Josie.

Eliza speaks the blessing with folded hands. She does not touch the bread. She can feel Sarah's eyes boring into her back. They eat their soup and Josie comments on the taste. Herbs? 'Thyme and sage I recognise but there is something unfamiliar.'

Eliza mumbles something about cress or sorrel, but she can't really say. She made the salad not the soup. Josie continues to ask her questions. Who does the cooking, the cleaning, the gathering and preparation of food? Eliza answers as briefly as possible. She cannot lose the feeling of those eyes burning into her. To put a stop to the talk, she excuses herself from the table. To make a start to the washing-up. So that she can be free this afternoon to do some urgent work in her classroom.

'See you later,' says Josie. 'And thanks. You have been most helpful.'

Eliza works with the other women in the kitchen for another hour. Sarah is nowhere to be seen. There is some talk that she has gone to bed for the afternoon, that she is unwell. But when Eliza moves up the staircase and into the dorm for her afternoon rest, Sarah is not there. Celia and the others are already asleep. Josie is lying down on the top of her bed reading her notebook. She is fully clothed except for her shoes. She holds a pencil in her left hand. 'Eliza,' she says. 'I heard a bird with a harsh call. In the early hours.'

A bell is tolling in the street below. This is the signal for the women to rest before the start of the late afternoon work. Eliza removes her apron and shoes. She folds the cover neatly down and lies on her back. 'A barking owl,' she says. 'There are many here, they come for the mice in the grain sheds.'

Josie writes something in her notebook. 'Most peculiar noise,' she says. 'Wuk wuk or woof woof. Like a dog being strangled.'

'I must sleep.'

'Did you get your classroom work done?'

Eliza says yes and immediately feels guilty for lying. 'I must sleep.'

'Sorry,' says Josie. 'I will be quiet now...'

Eliza turns away from her and pulls the cover over her head. Tomorrow she will say a special prayer of atonement. For telling an untruth to Josie. High on the hill in the bush. Where God can speak to her through the bloodwoods and the myrtles and the stringybarks and every creature who crawls or flies or stings.

Before she surrenders to sleep, she touches the fragment of ginger fur beneath her pillow, her only link to the man who both fascinates and disturbs her. She dreams of a marmalade cat, creeping through the bush, lifting one long thin leg with a stained white foot attached, urinating in a yellow waterfall against a brittle gum. The waterfall becomes a stream becomes a river becomes a sea.

The whole world is urine, pumped out by the penis of a cat.

2

EVERYTHING IS A SIGN

It is night. Rain is drumming steadily on the iron roof. There is a persistent leak coming close to my head from above. Ting, ting, fat raindrops falling into a metal bowl beside me on my wooden table as I write.

My last sleep in the dorm. Tomorrow I move my things into the sociologist's hut. I can't wait. I did not realise what the lack of privacy could do to me. They watch me all the time. I have become the scientific specimen, the object under surveillance. Not them.

I am beginning to understand a few things. About the material culture at least. They appear to make almost everything themselves. From scratch. The labour involved is incredible. Eliza told me that they are not allowed to buy or sell goods. Candles and soap and other household necessities are kept in a central storehouse and are rationed out as required. The men in charge of the community are the only ones who have the necessary authority to order in things from Mudgee or to handle money.

There are contradictions between what they say God wants them to do and how they live. For example, buying and selling anything, especially food, is seen as a source of evil. I asked

Eliza about the wine and produce shop which appears to do a roaring trade at weekends. That is the exception, she said. We cannot live without money completely. For shire rates and taxes and certain mechanical essentials for the bores and irrigation system. Some cloth, some books and, very occasionally, medicines.

I have already seen the hospital, or infirmary as they call it. Looks like something out of the Crimean War. Iron beds, hardly any equipment, although they do have two doctors trained on the outside. One, Dr Macky, gave me the creeps. I hope I never fall ill while I'm inside this place. I wouldn't be a bit surprised if Dr Macky wheeled out the leeches. He seemed to be preoccupied with enemas the day I met him. He had a whole cupboard full of the damn things. And not the modern disposable kind. Lots of orange rubber tubing. He opened the cupboard with a flourish to show me his wares. Nature's little helpers he said in a soft voice. Especially after an invasion of bugs or a high fever. Gives a good clean out. So that the body can start afresh.

I felt my rectum clench in fear as he spoke. I couldn't wait to get away from him. I was rather relieved to meet the other doctor. He seems a pleasant enough guy. Absurdly young-looking though. I wanted to ask him about his training but did not. I have learned already that direct questioning is not a good way to proceed in this place.

Community life seems to be based on age and sex and marital status. So is our world, of course, but what we experience on the outside is a mere whisper compared with Digger Town. Women are divided into girls and unmarried women and widows. Period. Men up to the age of forty are considered youths. Between forty and sixty they are men. When they reach the age of sixty, they become revered elders.

A few of the men in the group who greeted me with bread and wine looked much older than Gerrard Winstanley. He is undoubtedly the leader, so gaining power must rest on something more than managing to stay alive for a long time.

As for the women, what a crew. Subservient, submissive, like little girls who never grew up. I find myself increasingly irritated and bored in their company. They are so professionally *nice*. So grateful to be allowed to exist. Their religion seems very basic. They have a direct relationship with God. I have heard them asking questions of him, seeking judgements and forgiveness for the most trivial of crimes. They talk to God as if he was a good-natured bloke standing face to face with them in the fields with a bloody spade in his hand.

They are the victims of symbols. Everything is a sign, a message from God. They constantly interpret signs in nature, in the sun the rain the wind the clouds, in the trees the soil the birds the fruits of their labours, in the faces of the men, in the behaviour of their children. What does the heavy rain that almost ruined the grape harvest signify? Is it because last year's vintage was bountiful and good and we made more money than usual? Did anyone see the sky at dusk last night, on fire, laced with roadways of light that flowed from the tops of the hills to infinity? The birds were silent at dawn, a horse went down with a mysterious illness, a currawong dropped from the sky on a day when the sun was cool and hidden by cloud. Are we also about to fall?

They are more pagan than Christian. Much time and energy is spent by the women in telling the signs. What a way to live. I would not be surprised to find them throwing the runes, tying cloth messages on bushes, making antlers for their heads.

This will be my first message to Gerrard Winstanley. That the women live in fear. That they constantly seek meanings, reasons, omens. No wonder some of them want to leave. Is fear a part of their religion? Or is it a form of collective madness, the result of close communal living without the input of television or movies, without being exposed to a multiplicity of ideas?

In two days time I meet with Max in Mudgee to have a meeting on my progress with the research and to get family news. A phone call to Canberra for news of Briony and Jack.

Post my mail. Coffee and cigarettes, food with taste and texture. As much as I can stuff into myself in three hours. They throw handfuls of fresh herbs into every pot here to disguise the fact that the food is hopelessly overcooked. I'll never eat stewed meat again.

I'm counting the hours. This was one of the concessions they have granted me. Three hours on the outside every two weeks. Another is something else that is strictly forbidden here. The writing and receiving of letters.

I miss the telephone. I have never written so many letters. To Lynda and George, to the in-laws, the kids, to Megan. Strange to write with a pen again. At first I could barely form the letters, my hand felt awkward and cramped. Now it flows better. And without the delete function I have to think hard before I write. Takes me back to the dark ages before I learned to use a computer.

I have lost my markers. No television, no running around in the car, no movies or Sunday morning brunches in cafés alongside the Parramatta River, no music, no long conversations with my best friend Lynda, no arguments with my sister Megan the drama queen of Ryde.

Time itself has changed, it has stretched into empty hours. There is so much of it. And a new and rather frightening form of solitude. I miss my electronic forms of comfort. I no longer have the means of turning on a switch to crowd out the thoughts that persist in filling up the vacuum. I experience Russells's death more vividly than before. I relive the life that we had together, the births of our children, the conflicts and the love between us. Sharp and clear. Like a video that I view over and over and then rewind.

I have asked to work in the fields and the kitchens alongside the women. Gerrard was reluctant at first. He seems to place me on a pedestal because I am 'highly educated'. He said that God did not bring me here to perform lowly tasks. I must follow the purpose that God has laid out for me.

I almost said hey, don't assume that I am a believer, but I

stopped myself just in time. And after I explained to him that I would learn more if I worked alongside the women, he promised to allow me on the roster both for inside and outside work.

'See Sister Hannah,' he said. 'She is responsible for the allocation of tasks. For the unmarried women and the widows.'

The married ones have their own houses and their children and husbands are their primary work. Their lives are a mixture of private and public duties. They come into the communal dining rooms for lunch and dinner and work in the fields and in the kitchens and in the clothing rooms. But because the tasks are usually allocated on marital status, it is proving difficult for me to get close to the married women. I will discuss my problem with Eliza. I think she is learning to trust me.

Her upbringing has been completely different from mine, almost a mirror opposite. I had an unsettled childhood because my parents kept moving all the time. My father was a farm worker, dairy farms mostly. He could never settle down. Always something better in the next town, the next farm. Look at this Mother, he would say, a free house and free meat. Herringbone cowshed, a week off a year, dogs provided. Maybe we should give it a go?

He would swing me up into the air and tickle me under the armpits. I was extremely ticklish to the point of pain. He would not stop until I was in tears. My mother Margaret never intervened. She was a tired woman, chronically tired, always fighting us and the demands of my father to take the time for a rest. I see her lying on sofas in twenty different dilapidated kitchens, asleep in chairs in front of dying fires, her slippered feet curled up on the same maroon candlewick bedspread in twenty different bedrooms. While me and Megan quarrelled with each other and ran around in bare feet and wet clothes, looking for hot soup and a crust of bread.

My father Jack was a puzzled man. He could never understand why he worked so hard for so little reward. He changed to sheep, to cows, and back again. We moved all around the

North Island and once, disastrously, to a high country sheep station in the McKenzie Country. My mother had to cook for the farmhands and she lasted just two days. She said that she could not bear to see all that greasy food going into all those cannibal mouths. The Manager was very angry with my father. He said that he had taken them on as a married couple, not a man and a mental case. We left soon after, just when the snow had come down in great drifts in the gullies and the peaks of the hills were sharpened with wind and ice and Megan swore she had seen starving rabbits biting off their own ears in the burnt tussock.

Hunterville, Karamu, Pirongia: these are just a handful of the names that evoke a blur of memories. School after school after country school, muddy winters, humid summers, scabby knees. And the inevitable descent of my mother towards that fatal day when she was seen walking into the corner shop at Te Kowhai wearing nothing but a pair of soiled white sand-shoes and a straw hat.

We left the farm at Te Kowhai and moved to Auckland. My father was thirty-five and his back was already ruined with heavy work. Or so he said. We lived in a grotty flat above a shop near the centre of the city. We became even poorer. He sat in a corner smoking and looking down at the cars and people on the roadway below. One day he disappeared. We came home from school and he wasn't there. We were alone for two days, keeping as quiet as mice and eating out of tins until we were discovered and dragged off to a foster home. Eventually, Megan and I were sent to live in Sydney with his sister Winifred. She was strict but kind and made sure that we went to school with lunches and books and clean hankies. We revelled in the attention.

But sometimes I missed my mother and longed to undo her knot of grey hair at the back of her head and brush it and brush it until she feel asleep beneath my moving fingers. I imagined that my father was searching for her on foot, with a pack on his back, rescuing her from the mad house, telling her that he loved her and needed her. And she ran to him with streaming hair falling down over her nakedness.

They are both long dead. My father was drowned trying to steal an eel from a trap set in the mouth of a river and my mother did away with herself.

Eliza's parents are dead too. They came to live in the Commonwealth of Diggers when she was three years old. She has never lived anywhere else. She said she does not want to leave. Ever. All is calm and comfort for her here. She loves her work, she loves the people, above all she loves the land. The land is perfection. Every tree, every paddock, every vine ordained by God, planted according to their needs and His wishes. Once it was a blackened wilderness, overgrazed, too many sheep and too many droughts. One final devastating bush fire drove the settler howling from the land. And the Diggers moved in with their portable town.

I must admit that this place has a peculiar sense of serenity in spite of the rigid rules that govern the conduct of the inmates. There is a sense that things fit together; each tree, each crop, each building seems to support someone or something else. Nothing stands alone for its own sake.

I am interested in Eliza's views. If she is content to be here, why is it that some of the other women are not? Are they less indoctrinated? I have already decided to recommend to Gerrard that the younger women at least be allowed to leave the town on a regular basis. To quell their pathological curiosity. To understand what the outside world is like. So that they can make an informed decision about whether they want to stay here as adults. Not that he'd want to hear this of course. All the decisions about the women's lives are made by the council.

I have learned that the ones who run away suffer terribly. One jumped from a bridge, one crawled back broken and humiliated, and one disappeared without a trace. Young teenagers. Fifteen and sixteen. I told Gerrard that these things happen to young people on the outside as well. He seemed relieved to hear this.

And something else I have just found out. Eliza's surname is Winstanley. Her father was the elder brother of Gerrard. I was upset at first that she had not told me. What if I had said something against her uncle to her? But she just smiled and said that Winstanley was her maiden name and hopefully she would change it one day soon.

Women are expected to be married by twenty-three at the latest. There is no rule for the men, although single men are strictly controlled. There are thirty more women than men here. Mostly widows. I discovered this by reading the history of the families here. A bland document. Dates and facts and figures, nothing to capture the struggle of the people to heal the land or persuade others to join them.

Why is Eliza still single at thirty? I wondered if it was her uncle's influence that kept her from the arranged marriages that are common here. They are very careful with their kinship lines. It is all written down in the history book. They are divided into four clan groups, each one named for a tree. Marriages are forbidden in certain combinations. For example, a bloodwood cannot marry a whipstick ash and a stringybark cannot marry a snow gum. Complicated. Because sometimes a bloodwood can marry a bloodwood if the generations are different but never a whipstick. I have yet to come to grips with the logic of this. I do know that there is a very strong fear of incest or of any uncontrolled sexual relations for that matter. Particularly between the young unmarried ones.

I am tired. The rain is still drumming on the roof. Soon I will extinguish my candle. Time to lie down once more on my narrow bed and try to sleep. I am deeply into nicotine withdrawal. Heart palpitations, skin crawling as if ants are devouring me, can't sleep, can't eat, drinking too much coffee. I am plotting to bring some fags in from Mudgee. I will check out my hut in the morning to see if there is a hiding place. A smoke at night might help me to still my thoughts. About Russell and the children. My unloved body. This difficult solitude endured within the company of strangers.

Eliza is in the meat room carrying a bucket which contains a candle, a match, and a small hammer. She strikes the wax match head against the sole of her shoe, lights the candle, and holds it aloft. The bodies of sheep, cleaned and skinned, throw headless shadows on the wall behind the rack.

She knows that she should not be here. But her need is urgent and she fears that if she does not chill her precious carcass, her work will be lost. She carefully places the candle on the floor away from the sweep of her long skirt. She chooses a block of ice that is already starting to melt and fracture. Bang! Bang! She hits the ice with the hammer but it makes too much noise. It frightens her. The ice shed is near the house of Joshua the historian and she knows from past experience that he is a light sleeper and a night wanderer. He could be outside at this very moment, waiting for her to come out.

She looks around the shed for another tool. The metal hooks that hold the meat on the rack are stacked in the corner. She takes one and attempts to use it as a wedge but the hammer slips from the curved top of the hook and she almost hits her fingers.

She regrets not stealing a crowbar along with the hammer.

She waits quietly on the floor, watching the beeswax candle burn down with a steady flame. When the candle goes out her project must be abandoned. She will leave with good grace.

She hears a big wind approaching from the south-west. She smiles with relief. God has given her noise to cover the sound of her hammer. Rain begins to drum fiercely on the iron roof. She smashes the ice from her chosen block into fragments and fills her bucket. Then she blows out the candle and waits until her eyes become accustomed to the gloom.

Minutes later she is standing beneath the bushy tree at the side of the communal kitchen where the food safes are hung up in the branches. The safes are large structures made of plywood and canvas and fine wire netting. A hose is positioned at the top of the tree to provide running water to wet the canvas sides. Eliza is annoyed to see that the hose is still trickling precious water after nightfall. Someone has not done their duty. She tightens the tap and looks around to make sure that she is not being watched.

Then she climbs the ladder high up into the tree and inspects the food. Today they churned the butter. Pale yellow lumps, each the size of a small melon, salted and slapped into shape with scored wooden bats. One safe holds tomorrow's lunch, corned legs of lamb. Another the bodies of smoked chickens wrapped in coarse muslin.

Eliza climbs further upwards into the crown of the tree. On the top branch are two more safes. One is empty. The other contains parcels wrapped in white paper.

She slides the wire door from the front of the canvas safe. She touches a few of the parcels before she hears the crackle of plastic beneath the white paper. She takes this parcel and conceals it under her skirt. She climbs down the ladder to the ground with some difficulty. The wind whips the wet branches of the tree in her face. She places the parcel into the bucket of ice and walks quickly to the schoolhouse in the next street.

The school is situated in a stone building that was once a public library. There are many small rooms and four larger rooms, two at ground level and two perched on top of a wide oak staircase. These are the classrooms where the children congregate to receive their lessons. There are fifteen wooden desks in each room, with lids for storage beneath and attached seats for two.

Eliza enters one of the small rooms near the bottom of the staircase. She makes sure that the curtains are pulled across the small window before she relights the candle. Then she unwraps her parcel on a small dissecting table topped with cool white marble. The cat is already cleaned and gutted and the bullet removed. He had insisted on doing at least that for her. She had pleaded with him not to remove the skin. He cut a small piece from the tail. To prove to his mates that he had shot another one. Usually he takes the ears. But if she wants it for a specimen, he'll leave the head intact. Prettier that way.

Especially for kids.

He asked her questions about herself and the town. She asked him not to tell anyone that she had spoken to him. He offered her a cigarette. She shook her head. He wanted to know her name and her age. She did not answer him. He threw her a plastic bag for the cat and stubbed out his cigarette against his left boot. She did not want him to leave so she said Eliza. And I'm thirty. He said well Lizzie that's a start. And he turned and walked through the trees calling back, see ya.

There are some instruments in a glass cupboard. She takes what she needs to remove the skin from the body. It is trickier than she imagined. She cuts away the tissues beneath the legs that join the skin to the underlying flesh. Then the skin comes away easily as if the cat is wearing gloves. She makes a neat transverse cut around the paws to leave the fur around the feet and claws. She opens the chest to show the organs, the heart, the lungs, the liver. The stomach and bowel and their contents are gone. The man took them. For his pigs he said. They are always hungry. But they are useful to us. Unlike this bloody mongrel of a feral bastard.

She pours some water from the jug into an enamel basin and washes her hands. Then she sponges the cat skin gently, stroking the fur, making sure that it runs the right way. She places the fur into the white paper and hides it beneath her skirt. Then she takes the ice from the bucket and stacks it around the opened body of the cat.

She holds the plastic bag near the candle and places it over her eyes and looks through it as if it were a piece of transparent glass. It is marked with dark brown stains. She crushes it in one hand and releases it so that she can watch it spring open. She takes one end in each hand and pulls on it to test its strength. She opens it out and makes it smooth and reads the warning about suffocation. Then she places some ice and the body of the cat inside the bag and ties the top securely with brown string and places it back in the bucket.

She blows out the candle and leaves the schoolhouse by the

side door. Once again she makes sure that there is no one out and about on the street. The rain is heavy now, and cold upon her face. The dorm comes into sight. Mission accomplished. Except for her wet things there will be no evidence that she has left her bed.

But then she sees a flickering candle in the high window and she knows that Josie is working over her notebooks and that she must wait downstairs in the saloon until the light goes from the window. She hides the bucket behind the bar and removes her cloak. She is soaked to the skin and begins to shiver violently.

There is a creaking noise. Someone is walking down the stairs. Eliza tries to conceal herself behind the counter. Josie appears. She is wearing a dressing gown over her blue satin pyjamas and holds a candle in one hand and a lump of wood in the other. 'Who's there?' she calls out in a frightened voice. 'Who's there?'

Eliza shows herself. Josie grins in relief.

'Sorry,' says Eliza. 'For scaring you.'

'You're wet through. Where have you been?'

Eliza mumbles something about not being able to sleep. Josie says she knows the feeling. 'But let me help you get out of your wet things. You'll freeze to death.'

Eliza allows Josie to help her out of her long heavy clothing. She is nervous about Josie seeing her underclothes and is grateful to her for turning her head away when she peels off her camisole and pants.

Eliza feels herself being enveloped in the warm dressing gown that Josie has taken from her own body. There is a smell of perfume on the collar. A feel of warm clean skin. Eliza opens her eyes. Josie ties the sash around her waist.

Outside, the rain thickens and the wind howls and the winemakers wake in their beds, fearful for their grapes.

In Mudgee, a rural town not known for its traffic jams or heavy industry, the first thing that strikes me is the prevalence of mechanical noise. Trucks, cars, the hum of fridges and air conditioners, the hiss of the coffee maker. I have been inside the Commonwealth for only two weeks and already my perceptions have changed. I see and hear everything with a new clarity. There is a brightness, a bolder texture to the light.

The rain has stopped and the early morning air is warm with the promise of a hot autumn day. I am sitting in a coffee shop in Market Street waiting for Max. I am simultaneously drinking a latte, smoking a fag and eating a blueberry muffin. Everything smells and tastes so good. The paper napkin beneath my muffin informs me that I am in the Land of Wine and Honey famous for Fat Lambs, Henry Lawson and Historical Buildings. I fold up the napkin to take it back with me. Eliza asked me to bring her a token from the outside. Something that would not bring trouble to her.

I am the only customer in the café. The woman behind the counter is busily cutting and wrapping sandwiches. She tries to engage me in conversation, she wants to know if I am passing through or staying in the district. I answer her politely without giving her any information. I open my folder of papers and begin to read.

The first thing I see is the copy of the Sixty-Two Sacred Laws given to me by the creepy historian. I have pored over these the past week. I am still in shock.

In Digger Town, this seemingly benign place, I have never heard a raised voice. In spite of their fear of omens and the grinding hard labour, the people appear to be happy. I have been in the vineyards with them, snipping the bunches of grapes and loading them into the baskets for the men to lift onto the waiting wagons. I have worked with them in the kitchens cooking and cleaning. I have been in Eliza's classroom with the children. They are very different from our children. Quiet and respectful. But they smile a lot.

So why these harsh laws? Is it the fear of punishment that makes them behave? Or do the rules define the parameters of their action so clearly that the sanctions are never required? I can hear Megan's voice in my ear. Appearances deceive dear sister. As if you didn't know. I acted happy for years, I made a bloody profession out of it. Look beneath the surface. The truth will be revealed. How could anyone be content to live in such a restricted place?

Max is here. He has just walked through the door. I am so glad to see him that I almost burst into tears. He gives me a big hug. I am taller than he is so I have to bend to kiss his cheek. He looks tired but then he has been staying with his girlfriend Fran in Lithgow and has had to get up early to get here for our ten o'clock meeting.

He has been with Fran for almost a year now. It's only because he drives to Lithgow to visit her that he can come to Mudgee to help me in my work. He would never bother to come all the way from Sydney just to see me. So I suppose I should be grateful to her for something.

Max and I were an item once. If you can call one drunken night together an item. It was a mistake. Highly unethical, a student and her supervisor. But I was raw and lonely after Russell's death and I didn't know if I could be with anyone else. I had to be drunk to try it. He met Fran soon after and became besotted with her. I was irrationally jealous. I did not want him for myself but I did not want him to be so openly in love with someone else. It seemed like a smack in the face at the time.

We drink coffee and I smoke and talk non-stop and he listens and responds now and again. He praises me. 'You're doing okay,' he says. 'But take it quietly. Don't rock the boat.'

Then I show him the Sixty-Two Sacred Laws and he reads the first page and says, 'Jesus Christ, where did you get these from?'

'From the historian Joshua.'

'Fucking hell!'

'Do you think they really do these things to each other?'

'Hardly likely. There would have been trouble before now. You can't keep things like this quiet. Especially in a small town.'

The door opens and Greg the tour driver comes in. He does not see me at first. He is busy chatting up the woman behind the counter and teasing her about the quality of the sandwiches he bought yesterday for his tourists. He suggests a lighter hand with the tomato sauce. She giggles. He orders the full English breakfast, bacon, eggs, fried bread, toast and marmalade. Then he turns and sees me.

I signal to him to join us. I can see that he has forgotten who I am.

'Josie Tabel,' I say. 'You took me across the valley to the Digger's land.'

'Of course, I remember now, sorry.'

I introduce him to Max. They shake hands and Greg sits at our table. I sense that Max is about to go into his interrogative mode.

'Good to meet you Greg.' He opens up my folder. 'Maybe you can clear up a mystery for us.'

I kick him under the table. I promised Gerrard that I would not take any documents out of the town let alone show them to outsiders.

'Have you ever heard any rumours about violence or other problems in Digger Town?'

'You name it, they're supposed to've done it.'

'Like what.'

'The usual stuff, whippings, killing and eating babies, goat worship...'

I'm becoming increasingly disturbed. This has nothing to do with the subservient yet gentle people I have been living and working with over the past two weeks.

'Very interesting,' says Max. 'Any evidence?'

'Nothing concrete, just talk.'

'They do have strict rules and harsh penalties,' says Max. He runs a finger down a page of the Laws. 'Listen to this. Anyone caught wasting food or neglecting their agricultural tools has to work for a year as a bondsman for his master.'

Greg's eyes gleam. 'Can I see?'

'No,' says Max.

'Amazing writing. What do you call it, copperplate?'

I try to divert his interest. 'Done by hand with fine nibs. A lost art.'

Greg tells us that it is common knowledge that the men dressed in white overalls are being punished for something. They sometimes drive the carts that bring visitors to and from the produce and wine shop. But no matter how you provoke them, they remain silent. 'Bondsman,' he says. 'Isn't that another word for slave?'

I shake my head. I am feeling angry with Max for talking about this in front of a stranger. Besides, apart from my first day, I have not seen another man dressed in white.

Then Greg says he would love a copy of the document. The Commonwealth is part of Mudgee history. This stuff should be in the local museum. It belongs to the district. He would be willing to negotiate a good price with us. Totally confidential of course. No names mentioned.

'No,' says Max again.

The woman brings Greg's food and a pot of tea on a tray. There is not enough room for all his plates so Greg moves to the next table. He is still chatting to us between swallowing mouthfuls of bacon and egg.

He tells us that Digger Town is a bone of contention in the district. Not because of the gossip. Most of that is bullshit. Except maybe for the stuff about ritual sacrifice of animals. No, the main thing is the loss of revenue for Mudgee. Forget the lambs and the beef. This place only survives through wine and tourists. And here we have right in the midst of the Cudgegong Valley the only authentic nineteenth-century town of its type, fully restored and functional, except for the brothels and taverns. A million-dollar opportunity lost. If only the town planners of fifty years ago had been able to look into the future. They would have insisted on public access in exchange for the necessary building permits. The Diggers are hopeless bastards. Except for their produce shop, they won't let tourists near the place. They could make a fortune.

Max is all ears. I just want to get away from here. Max can be an insensitive prick at times. Surely he can feel my unease. I refuse his offer of another coffee. At last he stands up and we leave the café.

We walk along Market Street and find a bench at the side of a park. I berate Max for his loose mouth. He seems surprised at my anger. 'But you said you wanted to look at the interaction between Mudgee and Digger Town. I was merely sowing a seed.'

'Greg will tell everyone about the Sixty-Two Sacred Laws.'

'Good. They should be given all the information that you can get hold of. You'll strike problems otherwise when you do your survey in the town.'

'I don't even know if I still want to do the questionnaire. According to Greg the Diggers are viewed as lower than the anti-Christ so what's the point.'

Max looks at me. 'Josie, be careful. Don't go native on me.'

That does it. The pompous bastard. Now I am really boiling mad. I let him have it right between the eyes, I call him for everything, fuckwit, traitor, racist. Go native indeed. I tell him what he can do with his undergraduate lecture on the ethics of research.

He takes it all without rancour. Or seems to. 'All I meant was, don't identify too closely with your subjects. Your objectivity will become compromised.'

'That could never happen. I would rather die than become like them.'

'I'm confused. One minute you want to protect them, the next you hate them.'

'Some of them drive me nuts. But that doesn't mean that I am willing to sit and listen to lies about them from one of the locals.'

'Greg said he thought the rumours were bullshit.'

I suddenly remember Greg's comment about animal sacrifice. I tell Max about finding a mutilated cat in a bucket of ice behind the bar of the saloon.

He gets excited. 'Ice. In a bucket. And you rang a bell to summon the wagon to the locked gate?'

I am impatient. 'Yes yes but what about the cat?'

'Electricity. That's what.'

'But we use candles, wood stoves, and there's no power points.'

'Any fridges?'

'No.'

'Must be hell in the summer. Find out what you can. About the ice.'

I write it down in my notebook. I think he is wrong about the electricity. Maybe they have some old kerosene freezers somewhere for the ice.

I'm still more concerned about the cat.

We walk around the park. There are many tall trees each with a brass plaque mounted into the bark. I read the names. Some are gums, some are imported from the Northern Hemisphere. All are beautiful. Ah, here is *Eucalyptus trachyphloia*, a type of bloodwood. I write down the description for Eliza: bark hanging in neat strips as if someone has systematically torn it off, pale green leaves below, darker green above, bunches of small cream flowers.

There are wooden fruits strewn below the tree. They remind me of the bottom half of acorns. I put some in my pocket.

Max asks me what I'm doing. I tell him about the clans and Eliza's love of nature. I intend to give her these. For identification. And to prove to her that a magnificent specimen of her clan totem is alive and well in a public park in Mudgee.

We walk around the pebbled paths. The gardens are well tended. The summer flowers are almost finished. Thin green spikes of bulbs are already pushing up through the soil. Max comments on the war memorial. 'I would like to discover just one small town in this country that does not worship death in war.'

I remind him that I am living in such a place. No symbols of war, no churches, no religious rituals except the blessing of food.

'Are you sure? About the churches?'

'Not a single building. They commune directly with God as individuals.'

'Hey, sounds like my sort of religion.'

We walk back to Max's car. Once again he praises me for my work. White clans named for trees in the redneck heartland of rural New South Wales? Fan-bloody-tastic. Once again he warns me to be careful. He wants to tell his girlfriend about the Sixty-Two Laws. Fran is a cop. She might have heard something to substantiate the rumours. Maybe she could make discreet inquiries.

I don't want him to do this. I point out that Fran is stationed in Lithgow, miles away from Mudgee. She wouldn't know anything about the Diggers.

'Don't you believe it,' he says. 'The police grapevine is very effective.'

'No,' I say. 'Not yet. I promised Gerrard.'

Max shrugs and gets into his car. He is about to drive away when he opens the door and hands me a scrap of paper. 'I almost forgot. Sorry. A message from your sister in Sydney. Please ring her. Urgently.'

My heart lurches. I run back along Market Street looking for a public phone.

I find one by the post office and ring Megan's number. No answer. I try again. This time she answers. She sounds flustered. 'Russell's mother rang me from Canberra. It's Briony. She's worried about her.'

I panic. I imagine pregnancy, drugs, rape, illness.

'Nothing like that,' says Megan. 'Something to do with computers, the Internet.'

I relax. 'Is that all.'

'Jeanette said she thought it was an unhealthy obsession.'

'She would.'

Megan says, 'Look Josie, sorry. I can't talk any longer. Can you ring me later?'

'No.'

Her voice sinks to a whisper. 'I've got someone with me at the moment.'

'A man!' I laugh. 'You bloody devil, I thought you'd signed off from all that.'

'Me too. But this one's special.'

'You always say that.'

'Ring Jeanette. Doesn't sound like much.'

'Briony's been a nethead for months. I gave her my laptop.'

'Bye, must go.'

'Okay. And no more dramatic messages via Max. You had me in a sweat.'

I ring Canberra to talk to Jeanette. No answer. The children must be at school. I am due back at the Digger's gate in one hour. Time to stroll around and check out the town. Max is right. To write an in-depth study I need to look at the relationship between Mudgee and the Commonwealth. But I want to abandon the idea of a questionnaire. After listening to Greg I fear that the results of my survey will merely perpetuate the stereotypes of satanic outsiders. Instead I will try to find some key informants, people who have lived in Mudgee for a long time. They are sure to have some authentic Digger stories. I can hear Max's voice in my ear. Beware of anecdotal evidence. Try to have some numerical data. Use multiple techniques. Remember you are working at doctoral level. The idea is to pass not fail the bloody thing.

I silence his voice. I walk along Church Street. Not many people about. A group of noisy adolescent boys wearing check shirts and baseball caps move towards me. I keep my eyes down. These boys are huge. Tall and plump. You can almost smell animal dung and farm chemicals on their skin. I think of my poor Jack and his short legs and thin arms. He longs to grow taller and wider. He would die if he had to mix it on the playground with these beef-fed boys.

I am invisible to them of course. I suppress a ridiculous urge to stop them and ask if they know anything about the Diggers. I consult the street directory in the Mudgee Visitor's

Guide. I turn left into Mealey Street. This connects with Lawson Street which will take me back to Market Street and the taxi rank.

There are no footpaths and some of the houses look run down. I stand in front of a tiny brick cottage. Is it an abandoned house? It looks like the house that children draw, a chimney on the right side of the tin roof, two sash windows, a front door with peeling green paint. The veranda is obviously a later addition. Four metal posts and a curved roof that someone has attempted to paint white. The grass is waist high and the gate is chained and padlocked. A futile gesture given that the fence on one side has rotted away and fallen over.

Standing in front of this house I am assailed by an urgent need to enter through that peeling door. I walk through the fallen fence and stand on the veranda. Red brick dust, leaves caught in dirty cobwebs as thick as ropes, a cardboard box, a plastic bottle containing brown liquid. A smell of cat piss and dry worm-cast earth.

Am I going mad? I light a cigarette to calm myself. An elderly woman with blue curls and a long droopy skirt walks past trying to hold onto a lead attached to a big dog. She stares at me. I pretend to knock at the front door. She calls out, 'You're wasting your time love...' The dog takes off and the woman breaks into a run.

In the midst of the rubbish and dead grass piled against the veranda step is a flowering plant, a daisy. Bright yellow petals radiating from dark centres. I pick a flower and hold it to my face. Pollen from its black eye dusts my skin. It has an unpleasant smell.

I place it within my folder and walk away from the house down Mealey Street.

Eliza longs for the class to end so that she can take a solitary walk up into the hills. Her children are well behaved as usual. But she cannot give them her full attention. She needs to be outside, breathing and walking, forming her thoughts away from the classroom. She is tiring of her work. Tracing her pupils' fingers across their books, suffering their clumsy attempts to read, warning them not to press too hard on the tips of their nibs, sharpening pencils, adding or deleting commas, teaching them how to write perfect sentences. The holy business of making spoken words into written language is beginning to pall.

Her dreams will not leave her alone at night. And then there is the problem of Josie who now sleeps in the sociologist's hut. Eliza misses her in the dorm. It brought something extra to her nights to have Josie there beside her, either writing in her notebooks or sleeping in her narrow bed.

Eliza is very curious about the notebooks. Once she almost succumbed to temptation. She had touched the red cover of a notebook. Opened it. Then immediately closed it, shocked with herself. After that, the covers of Josie's books became part of her travelling dreams. She rode a red carpet, twisting and turning, a bird, a red horse, a balloon; words changed shape, became blood, became fire, and against her will, became a cat tracing letters with a severed claw in sand, *I am nothing but a bloody mongrel of a feral bastard I am nothing but …*

At last the bell rings and the children file out to go to the communal dining room. Eliza decides to skip lunch. There are no classes this afternoon. The children have been rostered to help bring in the white grapes. There have been some losses due to the heavy rain and the winemakers are anxious to bring in the last of the semillon grapes while they are at their peak of sweetness.

The time has come to tell the man dressed as a soldier that she never wants to see him again. He must leave her alone. By now she is certain that this is what God is telling her to do. There have been too many signs; the dreams, the sexual arousal, the disappearance of her specimen. At first she had been unsure of how to read the situation. But the last few days, the desires of her body had begun to inflame her mind to such an extent that she now feels compelled to act.

Withdrawal. Penance. Punishment. This must be the order of events. But she is not yet ready to confess her sins to her uncle Gerrard and the council.

Last night she went to the sociologist's hut and stood outside watching the candle flickering in the window. She almost knocked at the door to ask Josie for help but thought better of it and silently crept away.

Now at last she is up in the trees calling softly to him, I am here, come to me.

No birdsong, no wind, no noise in the undergrowth. Just a stillness and patterns of flickering light on the drifts of dead leaves. She sits and dreams beneath the same brittle gum that she harvested for bark for her class. She cannot believe that she lives in the same body that extended a hand to this snowy trunk a few weeks ago.

He stands before her wearing the same black beret and camouflage clothes that he wore the first time she saw him. No gun this time. He asks her if she is dozing. She shakes her head. He sits beside her and rolls a cigarette.

'Your hair,' he says. 'The colour is awesome.' He begins to remove her headscarf. She sits quietly, allowing him to run his hand over her hair. She accepts the probability that bodily punishment is about to come.

Then he says, 'Don't be scared. You are not the only one who believes. Me too.'

She almost weeps with relief. He says, 'Only God could have created the blueness of your eyes and the whiteness of your skin.'

She finds her voice. 'Are you courting me?'

He laughs. 'You turn me on. Is that the same?'

Then he kisses her on the lips. He puts his tongue in her mouth.

It feels like a lump of wet meat. She touches his cheek once, with her left hand, to feel the softness of his skin and the curve of the bone beneath his eye. 'You have the skin of a woman,' she says.

She shakes the dead leaves from her long skirt. She replaces her scarf. She tells him that she will not be coming back to their meeting place again. It is too dangerous for her. Someone found the cat after she had skinned it. Hidden in a bucket of ice.

He grins at her. 'Danger adds spice,' he says. 'Thrill a minute. We should shag right here and now. In the open. You never know who or what is watching.'

She asks him to leave. He shakes his head. 'Can't. You have aroused me to the point of no return.'

She is terrified now. She touches the piece of cat fur in her pocket to give her strength. 'I am truly sorry.'

He grins again. 'No you're not. You did it on purpose. Confess.'

And he made her say it over and over, he twisted her arm up her back and made her say it. That she had led him to this impossible situation, that she had made him wild for her, that her lips said no no but her eyes said yes.

She confesses. She admits to everything. He throws her onto the leaves and tears off her clothes. He claims he understands her because he too lives in a group. A new one, young people, not like the old fools that she is cursed with. They too have a mission. God given. To rid this country of all that is foreign. They strive for purity of thought and action. They believe that everything they do is sacred. Just like the Diggers. Different methods, same mission.

He exclaims over the blondness of her pubic hair. He touches every part of her body. He says you are so beautiful so beautiful. White and gold and blue against the crush of eucalyptus leaves. Then he places her legs together and covers her body with her torn skirt. She is completely numb. She waits silently for his next move.

He rolls another cigarette and lights it. He inhales the smoke. 'I'll do a deal,' he says at last. 'I'll let you go if you'll find something for me.'

He tells her that there is an historic document that he

would give an arm and a leg for. He hands her a scrap of paper with something written on it. 'The man that wrote this in the seventeenth century lost his tongue for his trouble. Branded like a donkey.' He has heard a rumour that the Diggers have the original document. There are copies around, he got his off the Net. But he wants the original. As soon as possible.

She agrees to look for it. He stubs out his cigarette and uncovers her body again. She can feel the air moving on her skin. He leans down and sucks the tips of her breasts. It is agony for her but she keeps her face expressionless.

He helps her to dress. There is a long tear in her skirt and some buttons missing from her blouse. She tidies herself as well as she is able. He waves goodbye to her as if nothing has happened. He turns as he walks away and calls back to her.

'Don't cheat me Lizzie. Or I'll tell the old fools what we did.'

THE ROLL THRUST INTO MY MOUTH…

I'm worried about Eliza. I returned from Mudgee full of questions. But she is withdrawn from me, remote. She thanked me for the paper napkin and the bloodwood gumnut. But her eyes are smokey, less clear. The startling blueness is muted. Has she been weeping? I know better than to ask her. I resolve to watch her more closely.

After my meeting with Max, my anger with him, my confusion over the phone call to Megan, I am glad to be alone in my hut. I am losing the feelings of intense loneliness and alienation that have plagued me over the last two weeks. I am beginning to appreciate the order and simplicity of my immediate environment. One narrow bed covered with a woven green cotton bedspread, candles, matches, a cake of soap on a metal dish, a water jug and large china basin. One towel, one glass, one folded cream blanket with hand-stitched borders at the foot of my bed. And on my desk, one pad, one notebook, a set of pencils, a photograph of Russell and the children in a silver frame.

I remember the emotional stress when we left the house in Balmain. The packing up of all my possessions, Briony sulking, Jack tearful, both resentful at having to move to Canberra for six months. They tried every teenage trick in the book to make me feel bad. The withdrawal of affection, loud sighs, long silences interspersed with complaints about my cooking, complaints about having less money compared with other kids, complaints about having to live in a boring house with boring old people in Canberra. Once again, I had ruined their lives forever.

I ignored their bad behaviour. I had heard all this before. Each time we moved house after Russell's death, each time I refused their endless requests for money, for trendy clothes, for trips away, they put me through this shit. It is not their fault that we fell into poverty but I could do without the guilt trips. I can't seem to get it through to them that our future economic security depends upon my success at Digger Town.

I was glad to leave the house in Balmain. The rent was reasonable but this did not compensate for the sense of despair that hung around the building. I imagined that the same stale air had been breathed over and over again by a procession of prisoners who had been condemned to live within these dark rooms. The house meant nothing to me except for tiresome hassles with yet another real estate agency over missing sets of keys, inspection of the inventory, repayment of the bond, and yes that stain was already there on the carpet when we moved in and no I did not break that lightshade and yes I have informed the power and gas and the phone company and redirected my mail.

The worst part was packing up and storing our gear in Megan's garage. Russell's collection of science fiction books and some of his old clothes that I cannot bring myself to part with, wedding presents, broken toys, china and pots and linen that I have never used. Too many things, all endowed with past baggage of money and pain and loss. I resolve to live with fewer possessions in the future. Living here has taught me that simplicity can be a virtue.

I have cheated a little, I have not stuck to the letter of the law. My tape recorder and batteries and ballpoint pens are hidden beneath my pillow. And tonight I have secreted precious packets of fags in various spots around the hut.

Gerrard told me that my privacy would be respected. He assured me that no one would enter the hut without my permission. But I cannot take the risk. I must hide forbidden objects. I signed a paper when I arrived, I promised to abide by the rules of the Commonwealth while I live within the town. I have kept to my side of the bargain except for these few forbidden objects.

Max took the Sixty-Two Laws seriously. I had hoped that he would write them off as an anachronistic survival. This would have relieved my anxiety. But no such luck. I hope that he keeps his word to remain silent until I am out of here. If Gerrard discovers that I took the Laws out of the town, he could report me to the elders. The least that could happen to me is social banishment, the worst is a quick trip in the horse and cart to the locked gate at the entrance. End of my doctoral studies, end of my dreams of entering the academic profession, end of story.

The night is cool and clear. There is an owl barking and coughing near my hut. I am sure that it is the same one that serenaded me on my first night in the dorm. I think of it as my own personal pet, a canine creature accidentally trapped in a body of striped brown feathers and pale circular eyes. I name it Lupa.

I stand at the single window. The moon is almost full and rising and marks out the features of the land with a brush of polished silver. I can see the shape of the hills at the edge of the cultivated land, the curved rows of grapevines stretching to the base of the mallee flats. I can see the corrals and barns, I can hear the faint snickering of horses and the bleating of goats.

It is only nine-o'clock. The street is empty except for Lupa. I can see the hips and angles of roofs and verandas and woodsmoke drifting slowly upwards from brick chimneys. I pull the curtain across the window and light another candle.

Then I settle down on my bed and put a cigarette in my mouth and open my mail.

Jack has made a friend at his new school. Jack stayed over at his house and had a 'cool time' with Damien's parents and older brother. I am a little jealous. Damien's father is a lawyer and his mother is a doctor and the house is cool and the computers are cool and they have a cool boat on the lake and a high-rise apartment at Surfer's. Can he go with them in the school holidays? Jeanette has already given him permission.

Briony's letter disturbs me. I sit bolt upright. What the fuck is going on?

Dear Mother, she begins. Which is weird. She hardly ever calls me mother, she calls me Josie. *Dear Mother, I am fine, everything is fine, I don't go to school much, no need. Did you know that the Net is doubling every month? I get everything I need, more than, I am learning so much dear Mother you wouldn't believe. My eyes have opened, like really opened. Jeanette is fine Poppa is fine Jack is fine. You wouldn't believe I chat most nights to neighbours of yours in Mudgee. Small world and all that shit. Be good, see ya, love Briony.*

No complaints about living with her grandparents? About money? Her brother Jack? She sounds busy and happy, motivated. For the first time in two years. In two weeks her whole outlook has changed. Something is wrong, I know it. School is not the problem. She is almost eighteen and the truth is that she has been wagging it for the past two years. I have given up on her achieving her Higher School Certificate.

I need to talk to Jeanette. I curse the fact that she was not at home today when I rang from Mudgee. I can hear Russell's voice in my ear. Telling me that I have an overactive imagination, calling me the *what if* woman. Always imagining the worst. As in *what if* Briony is lying to me, *what if* she is only pretending she is fine.

I stifle his voice. I shuffle frantically through the rest of the mail. Ah, at last, Jeanette. *Dear Josie, We are enjoying having the children at least I am and Rowley hasn't said anything*

*negative yet so we can presume that he is too. I am busy of
course but it's a good sort of busy. Jack is adorable. So like my
poor Russell at that age. Idealistic, adventurous, raving against
the ills of the world, you know what I mean. Is it true that you
gave Briony permission to use your computer and your Internet
account? She seems to be very tied up with it, in fact we hardly
see her. She is in her room night and day tapping away. Is this
okay? You said not to force her to go to school as she is almost
eighteen and you can lead a horse to the dam but not make it
drink etc. Please advise …*

There is a sound at the door. Is it a knock? I stub out my
cigarette and keep very still. Oh hell, another knock. My candlelight will be casting a flicker on the curtain. The person
standing outside my door must know that I am inside. I go to
the door and call out, 'I'm trying to sleep.'

A woman answers. 'Sorry to disturb you.'

I recognise Eliza's voice. But there is something wrong. I
can hear muffled weeping. I open the door and she almost falls
into the room. I look around outside to make sure that we are
not being observed. She continues to sob in a hopeless almost
silent way that frightens me. Eliza has always struck me as a
very controlled person.

I sit her on my bed and wipe her face with my wash cloth.
'What's wrong? Are you ill?'

She manages to control herself at last. 'I wish I was dead.'

I am shocked but I can see that she is terribly distressed so
I hold her and stroke her hair as if she was Briony or Jack
when they were small.

'I am sorry to bring you this trouble,' she says. 'But I had
no one else to turn to.'

I get her a drink of water from the china jug. I pray that
she does not notice the cigarette butt in the saucer on my bedside table. She drinks greedily.

Then she tells me why she has come to me. She has done
something sinful, something that she can never speak about,
the words would poison the air. She berates herself verbally,

she calls herself evil, whorish, may God forgive her, she wants to die.

I get so fed up with her self-denigration that I want to shake her or slap her face but I manage to restrain myself. I am burning with curiosity. I ask her if there is anything I can do to ease her pain.

'Yes, but it will mean performing another sinful act.'

I snap. 'For fuck's sake, stop carrying on about sin! There's no such bloody thing!'

She seems genuinely surprised. 'You really think so?' She dabs at her eyes with the cloth. 'This is most interesting,' she continues. 'We often talk of the nature and truth of sin. Between ourselves of course.'

'We?'

'Me and Sarah. I am under instruction to advise her.'

Her voice has almost returned to normal. Losing my cool was the best thing I could have done to stop her from sinking further into the pit of self-hatred. I risk a question. 'When you speak of sin do you mean sexual things?'

Her face closes up.

I blunder on. 'Of course there are other important ways of breaking the moral code...'

She interrupts me. 'This particular sin will be stealing.' She tells me that she needs a document from the history room. She has never been allowed to go there. None of the women have. She is afraid to enter alone. She knows that I have been inside with Joshua and Gerrard. I can help her find her way around. A very important person has asked for the document. Someone from outside. It is a matter of life and death. Otherwise she would never have dared to come to my hut to ask for my help.

She pours more water from the jug and holds the glass to her lips. On an impulse, I drag a cigarette from my hidden packet and light up. I can't stop myself from asking her if she thinks that smoking is a sin.

She smiles for the first time since she knocked at my door. 'Maybe just a little one.' She moves to the window and holds the curtain to one side. 'The moonlight bothers me. Someone might see us.'

'Doing what?'

'Breaking into the history room.'

I suck in a deep lungful of smoke. I tell her I can't help her. Too much is at stake for me and my children. I need to play it safe while I do my research. I tell her about my recent past and she sits on my bed and listens intently with great concentration. Her eyes never leave my face. But how much does she understand of my story? Her life is so protected from the real world. She lives like a dependent child. Food and clothes and linen appear magically in front of her when she needs them. Someone else makes plans for her, someone else makes decisions. She was instructed to teach the children about the relationship between God and nature, she was instructed to watch over Sarah, she was instructed to sit next to me in the dining hall.

Learned helplessness. Just because someone whom she believes to be a higher authority over her has told her to go to a forbidden place and steal a document she has agreed to do it. Unconditionally. Even though she is suffering like hell from guilt and fear. These so-called Christians have no right to abuse her innocence in this manner. But wait, she said this person is from outside. A matter of life and death. Is she in some kind of danger?

Jesus. Greg in the café this morning. He showed an unhealthy interest in what goes on here in Digger Town. Maybe he met Eliza in the produce shop and put the hard word on her to get him a copy of the Sixty-Two Laws. But the Laws are public property inside the Commonwealth. I have seen them mounted on large posters in the dining hall and Eliza has one on the wall of her classroom. There would be no need for her to ask me to help steal a copy from the history room.

In spite of myself I begin to yawn. It has been a long day. I resolve to wait until the morning and then question her again.

If someone from outside is trying to force Eliza to do something against her will, I may have to inform Gerrard. For her own protection.

I ask her to go. I tell her that I will think very carefully about everything that she has said. I may be able to help her. But not tonight. Too tired. 'Go back to the dorm,' I say. 'And be careful. Think of possible consequences before you act.'

I toss and turn for hours, alternately dozing and waking, dreaming and thinking. It's cold in the hut. I pull on a sweater and socks and huddle beneath the cream blanket. The moonlight disappears from my window. The stars go out. Darkness wraps around my hut like a cloak. Just as the dawn begins to break I fall into a deep sleep broken by the strangled voice of Lupa who I swear is barking at me from just outside my window. Go and eat a mouse I call to her, be gone, fly to where owls hide from the gaze of the rising sun.

I hear no more from her but it's too late. I am wide awake. I gather myself together for the coming day, I wash my face in the cold water basin, I clean my teeth, I brush out the tangles in my hair.

I open my notebook to record the events of the day before.

Eliza rises early and goes to the bathhouse in spite of the fact that it is not her turn to take a bath today. She hopes that she will be allowed in again. This is the third consecutive day that she has felt compelled to immerse herself in hot soapy water.

She pushes open the door. Shirley Foster, the keeper of the number four women's bathhouse, is sitting at the bench cutting bars of soap into thin slivers. Her assistant Munna is pouring buckets of boiling water into the tin baths, grunting and groaning with effort. Munna falls within that category of person that the elders name as the chosen ones. She cannot learn to read and write. Munna was brought here as a baby and named for the district that lies southeast to Digger Town. She has no obvious kinship with any family in the town although there have been subterranean whispers. She had worked since she was twelve in the bathhouse, cutting wood for the chipeaters, carrying water to the tubs, cleaning, scrubbing, washing the towels.

Eliza told a half-truth to the bathhouse woman yesterday morning. I am getting soft in my job, too much bookwork, not enough hard work with the hoe. I am suffering from body pain, stiffness, caused by labouring to gather in the grapes. This is why I need to lie in hot water.

Eliza tells the same story this morning. Shirley stops cutting soap. She frowns. 'You should see Doctor Macky.'

'That won't be necessary.'

Munna stands in front of the bench. She is holding two empty buckets. Shirley tells her to get on with her work. Munna ignores her. Shirley tells her again, more sharply this time. Munna goes off reluctantly, banging the buckets against her skinny brown legs. Shortly after, there is crash from the chipeater room and the sound of boiling water hissing into metal.

'That girl is getting cheeky,' says Shirley. 'I hope you are doing nothing to encourage her.' She takes a book from beneath the bench.

'Do you need to record this?' asks Eliza.

Shirley hesitates, then replaces the book into its cubbyhole. 'Go on then, but this is the last time. You are not due for another five days. You'll get me into trouble.'

Eliza is grateful that Gerrard is her uncle. This sometimes wins her special favours from the older women. Especially someone like Shirley who can sometimes create mischief by needlessly repeating conversations from one woman to another. Next time she is hauled in front of the council for committing the sin of gossip she may well elicit the support of Eliza. For favours rendered.

It is six-thirty. The cubicles are empty. Soon they will be full of women washing their hair and their bodies and laughing and calling to each other over the top of the partitions. She chooses her favourite cubicle, the one right at the end of the bathhouse, well away from Shirley's bench.

Munna has already filled the tub. There is a clean white towel and a thin slice of yellow soap ready and waiting, a bucket of cold water with a tin ladle, a loofah, and, unexpectedly, a sprig of fresh rosemary speckled with pale blue florets.

Eliza removes her clothes and hangs them on the peg. She crushes the rosemary against her face and then tosses it into the water. She lowers her exhausted body into the bath and gives herself up to the pleasures of hot skin and the breathing in of fragrant steam. She closes her eyes. She floats, she swims, she hears the call of swamp birds, grass whistleducks, black swans, shovelers, and deeper into sleep, a cracking noise that she imagines to be a rifle shot.

The tips of her breasts are aflame, her body is aflame, sucking sucking… *nothing but a bloody mongrel of a feral bastard…*

She opens her eyes and is shocked to see a sweaty face hovering above her own. Munna is leaning over Eliza in the bath, naked, a bare foot jammed down on either side of Eliza's body. She is holding two magpie's feathers, one in each hand, and she is using these to stimulate Eliza's nipples. Eliza rages up from the water. Munna drops the feathers and lets out a high-pitched scream. She opens the door and runs from the cubicle and almost collides with Shirley who is standing outside with her hand poised to knock. Eliza grabs the towel and tries to cover her shame. She turns back towards the bath, speechless with shock. There in the water is soap scum, rosemary blackened with heat, two floating feathers, and a swirl of someone's bright red blood.

I am sitting at the table eating my porridge when Hannah brings me a folded note. From Brother Winstanley she hisses at me. She says his name with reverence. She is obviously dying to know what is written on the paper. I tease her a little. I open the paper, read it, then shake my head as if puzzled. She sits beside me, in the chair where the missing Eliza is supposed to be. I let her out of her misery, I refold it and hand it over to her. She tries to act as if she doesn't care. 'Maybe I shouldn't read it,' she says. 'This is not meant for my eyes.'

'It isn't much,' I say. 'Go for it.'

But I'm lying. It's a big breakthrough for me. I presented my first report to the council two days ago. I told them that the women should have more exposure to things in the outside world. The younger ones especially are restless, they won't take the restrictions that the older ones have accepted. Curiosity burns them up to the point of no return. I told the council that I am surprised that so few have run away so far, but that in my opinion, this won't last. From what I have already discovered, they are at risk of losing many members of the next generation of females.

I was in the same shop front where I had been brought just after I arrived in the town. Boots were scuffed in the dust and throats were cleared. I could sense a solid wall of resistance building up against me. Almost as if they knew what I was going to say but were fighting hard to block out my words.

I tried to reassure them. It's not the end of the world, I said. It's just a change, maybe a change for the better.

Voices were raised, passages from the bible were quoted at me. The level of noise grew higher, I could not finish my statement.

Gerrard rescued me. He told them to allow me to speak. God had brought me here to share my knowledge with them. Listen and learn.

Sometimes I wish I believed in God. He or She would come in very handy at times.

And now this note, informing me that he had given permission for Eliza and Sarah to leave the town with me and two of the men. We were to be taken this afternoon to one of the foodbanks that they had set up to distribute their surplus food to the poor. I'm pleased that they are willing to take my advice. And intrigued at the idea of the foodbank. I had no idea that they extended charity to the surrounding community.

So here we are, Eliza and Sarah and me and two young men,

Ned and Thomas, coming up to the locked gate. We are trotting along in a large four-wheeled wagon drawn by two horses. The two men are sitting in the front, we three women in the back. We are sitting on a small wooden seat, squashed together. There are nets of onions, sacks of potatoes, leeks, eggs packed in straw, lettuces, broccoli, cabbage, and a mound of rather tough-looking corncobs. Sarah and Eliza are wearing their long skirts and headscarves. The men are in denim overalls and check shirts. Sarah's face is almost cracking apart with smiles. She is babbling with questions, do you drive Josie, have you got a car? Maybe they will let us drive with you next time, maybe you could take us to the shops in Mudgee, just to look...

This is the first time I have seen Eliza for two days. She is a little subdued. She greeted me politely and thanked me for persuading the council to allow this outing.

I have given her dilemma a lot of thought. I let her down that night she came to my hut. She was obviously under tremendous stress. I resolve to find out more about her problem and maybe find a way of helping her.

We are at the border. Thomas gets down from the wagon and unlocks the gate. Then we are bowling along the gravel road at a fast clip, disturbing the dust into a choking cloud. Sarah coughs and sneezes. The wooden wheels are making a tremendous noise. I take a chance to talk with Eliza. I lean close to her ear and whisper. 'Are you all right?'

She nods. I try again. 'I'm very sorry. About the other night.'

She shakes her head. 'Later,' she mouths.

We reach the sealed road. I am surprised that we do not turn right into Wilbertree Road. This would lead us directly into Mudgee. Instead we turn left and travel north for about three kilometres. Then we leave the main road and cut across the countryside along unmarked narrow roads, both gravel and sealed. We pass vineyards and poultry farms, sprawling farmhouses, and odd little settlements of stone cottages gathered around a garage or a store.

I work my way towards the front and tap Ned on the shoulder. 'Where are we going?' I shout.

He shrugs. 'Wherever we can find them,' he says. 'We'll have to ask.'

I can't get any sense out him. I return to my seat and sit squashed between Sarah and Eliza. Sarah has removed her headscarf and her long hair is blowing across her face. She touches my arm. 'Josie, this is wonderful, thank you, thank you.'

I wish my spoiled brats could hear this. A grown young woman getting a tremendous kick out of driving in a clumsy wagon full of vegetables around the back of nowhere.

We arrive at a garage with a tearoom at the side. Ned says, 'Get out and stretch your legs. The horses need a drink. And we need to make some inquiries.'

The place looks very run down. There is a cluster of wooden sheds at the back of the main building. Some of them are without a roof. A shower of white sparks flares out from a dark cavernous workshop. Someone is using a welding torch. The two men disappear through the entrance and the sound of welding stops.

I take Sarah and Eliza into the tearoom. An old woman with badly permed hair comes to the counter. I order a pot of tea and biscuits for three. We sit at a wobbly table. Sarah is bright red in the face. Eliza is more composed. She pours the tea and bites into a chocolate biscuit as if she ate in teashops every week.

The place is empty. The floor is scarred with heel marks and the china is stained. Fly papers covered in black bodies turn slowly above us. Plastic pansies sit in dusty brown vases in the centre of each table. At least the tea is strong and hot and the biscuits crisp.

The old woman calls out, 'Want anything more love?'

'No thanks,' I answer. She shuffles off into the back room. I take out my packet of Benson and Hedges and light up. Sarah's eyes nearly fall out of her head.

I am feeling reckless. 'Want a puff?' I ask.

I shouldn't have done it. She looks as if she is about to burst into tears. I begin to say I'm sorry when I hear the noise of feet tramping into the tearoom. We have been invaded by a group of tourists. The tour leader is a woman. She is smartly turned out in a black cap and navy-blue blazer and pants, flushed with rouge and lipstick and importance. She calls into the back room, 'Come out Mrs Bray, six coffees, four teas, one vegetarian, nine carnivores, hurry please.' She consults her watch and frowns. 'Hell. We've lost twenty minutes somewhere.'

Her flock seat themselves with much scraping of chairs and opening of purses. The tourist at the table next to us shrieks, 'This place is adorable Henny, I didn't think there were any left like this.'

'More's the pity,' I mumble. 'Needs a bloody great bomb under it or the next bushfire that comes this way.'

Eliza allows herself a smile at my words. Sarah is oblivious. She is concentrating hard on the strangers around us, staring at their clothes, their shoes, their faces. It's like she's virtually undressing them with her eyes. Some of them stare back at us just as rudely. I am embarrassed. I realise once more the vulnerability of my charges.

Henny, who turns out to be the tour leader, yells back. 'Glad you approve. I promised you some history along with the wine tastings. And this place is full of it.'

Ned and Thomas come into the tearoom. There is a rustle of interest. Henny greets them by name. The two men hold a brief conversation with her in lowered voices. Then they come over to our table and ask us to come outside. They tell us that Henny is very excited to see Digger women dressed in traditional costume accompanying them on their food run. She has asked permission for her clients to take photos of us seated on the wagon. She is prepared to pay money for the privilege.

I am stunned that Ned and Thomas have agreed to this. I hiss to Eliza, 'What the hell is going on?'

Henny comes over and asks Thomas where I fit into the

picture. He tells her that I am not one of them, just a passenger along for the ride.

'Wow,' says Henny. 'So you're picking up hitch hikers now. Things must be hotting up back in the old hometown.'

We leave the tearoom. The tourists troop after us clutching cameras. Henny arranges Eliza and Sarah on the back of the wagon in the middle of the vegetables. The two men sit at the front. Thomas holds the reins.

I stand behind the snapping cameras feeling like a bloody idiot.

Then the tourists are directed by Henny to observe the battle scars in the side of one of the huts at the back of the garage. The last recorded shoot-out between soldiers and bushrangers in the district. They rush off to get their photos taken beside the historical bullet holes. Then Mrs Bray comes to the door of the tearoom and yells food's up! Back they swarm, buzzing with excitement.

I climb back onto the wagon. 'Walk on!' calls Thomas. The two big Clydesdales pull us away from the tearoom.

We travel for a few kilometres down the road until we turn into a gravel side road. We arrive at the foot of a range of steeply rising hills covered in bush. There is a picnic place set up at the side of the road. A tap, a brick barbecue with a greasy iron cooking plate, a toilet, a forty-four-gallon drum for rubbish. And at the back, a crude wooden platform with a roof made of some sort of thatched material.

The wagon stops. Ned and Thomas jump down and start to unload the produce onto the platform. There is nobody else in sight. I ask Thomas what we are doing here. He throws off a sack of potatoes and grunts, 'Help us please. They'll be here soon.'

They? The poor presumably. But who are they anyway, stuck way out here in the bush? I wonder if these guys are working some kind of scam. I saw Ned pocket some twenty-dollar notes after that hideous photo session. I don't know what to do about this. They made no effort to hide it from us.

Then I hear the noise of cars, but not from the sealed road. There is a one-way track leading from the picnic area up into thick bush. It is from here that the cars begin to arrive, lurching slowly down the rough terrain. There are four vehicles, ancient station wagons streaked with rust and making a terrible racket as if the engines were about to explode. The doors burst open spilling naked children and dogs and dirty looking people with long hair all the colours of the rainbow, dressed in flowing rags and bedecked with rings and shells and stones and bangles, so that they tinkled and spun and jangled like animated chandeliers.

I recognise them immediately. Ferals. There had been trouble in Sydney with them begging around Circular Quay. Programmes on television warning people about their predations. Earnest interviews by theologians on radio about their stolen spirituality, which appears to be bits and pieces cobbled together from celtic myths, buddhism, aboriginal dreamtime and native american lore. They're fakes. But interesting ones.

We get down from the wagon and unload the vegetables onto the wooden platform. Eliza is shy of the strangers but Sarah asks them their names, where they are from. They pay her scant attention. They are busy lighting the fire beneath the barbecue with firewood supplied from our wagon. A woman dressed in ragged brocade trousers and a sleeveless shirt places a large pot on the iron plate. She takes a knife from a pouch at her waist and begins to shuck the corn. She throws the wrinkled cobs into the water.

Thomas is lifting a sack from the wagon. 'Sorry about the corn. Bit tough. But the potatoes are good this year even with the drought.'

The woman shrugs. 'No worries.'

I hold out my hand to her. 'Hi. I'm Josie.'

'I'm Melody.'

I ask her if she is cold. She says that she's used to it. Living outdoors makes you tough. 'Shit,' she says. 'Who are ya anyway? Never seen women with these dudes before.'

I explain to her that Eliza and Sarah have come along for the ride. I tell her that I'm a sociologist. She frowns. 'Don't use that word around this mob. Amity'll have your guts for garters.'

Amity? She points him out. He's on the wooden platform, sorting out boxes of produce. A young man with a bright red mohawk and heavily tattooed arms. 'He got done,' whispers Melody. 'Like a bloody dinner.'

I am intrigued. 'What happened?'

'This bitch Barbara somebody or other came to live with us in the tipi. To write about our ways. She ate our food, danced with us, even fucked her brains out with Amity. I tell you butter wouldn't melt.' She shakes salt into the pot of corn.

'So?'

'So then she wrote lies about us in a magazine and made lots of money.'

'How do you know she was a sociologist?'

'Amity said so. And he knows about that stuff, he went to uni.' She takes a corncob from the boiling water and sinks her teeth into it. She offers me a bite but I shake my head. Amity carries a tray of eggs over to the fire and begins to break some into a bowl. Melody throws me a warning look.

Amity finishes with the eggs and wipes his hands down his dirty leather jerkin. He takes some twenty-dollar bills from an inside pocket. 'Sixty bucks,' he says.

'Where'd ya get it?' asks Melody.

He nods in the direction of Ned. 'He ripped off some tourists.'

I am so relieved that he has been given the money that I almost forgive him for his misplaced hatred of sociologists. Barbara's ethics were appalling. She was obviously not one of us. A journalist on the make more likely.

Eliza is standing at the side of the clearing beneath a large gum tree. She is examining a piece of bark that she has stripped from the trunk.

I walk over to her. 'A bloodwood?' I ask.

She shakes her head. 'An ironbark.'

'Let's go for a walk,' I say.

She calls over to Thomas. 'I want to gather some specimens. With Josie.'

He gives us permission to leave the picnic area. But he warns us to be careful. Stay together and don't go too far.

Eliza wants Sarah to come with us but she refuses. One of the children has taken a liking to her and is tugging on her long skirt and demanding to be lifted up into her arms. Besides, Amity has promised to explain to her the spiritual origins of the coloured wheel tattooed on his right shoulder and Melody has offered to braid her hair.

We climb up a steep slope alongside the rough track where the cars came down. It is cold and still up here. No wind. Eliza says that this part of the bush has not been burnt out for many years. She can tell by the type and number of small plants that live beneath the taller trees and the amount of dead branches rotting on the ground.

We climb even higher. I can hear the voices and laughter of the ferals far below us. A thin plume of smoke sits motionless above their fire. I am a little nervous. I am a city person, I have lived in Sydney most of my adult life. I roamed around the countryside during my early years but in another country with a gentler landscape, no snakes, no dangerous spiders, no fires, no droughts, just the constant sound of running water and the softness of moss and fern and the flutter of fantails.

The forest here is wild and disordered even when it is still. There is a sense of unfinished business which lies in waiting, always imbued with the possibility of revenge. In the bush of my homeland, the silence is that of something coming to an end. There is a sense of enclosure and departure. Extinct birds and weapons of mute warriors are buried beneath the cultivated textures of sheep pasture and exotic pine plantations that drift ever closer to the interior.

'I'm puffed,' I gasp. 'I need a rest.'

We sit on an outcrop of flinty rock. I light a cigarette. 'Let's go that way, towards those tall trees over there.'

Chapter Three

Eliza says we should keep the track in sight so that it can guide us back down. I bow to her superior knowledge.

Eliza touches my shoulder. 'Thanks for saying what you did in the wagon.'

'That's okay.'

'So you will help me?'

'I don't know.' I finish smoking my cigarette and extinguish the butt against the sole of my boot.

'But I must get hold of that document. It is even more important now.'

'Why?'

'I am in trouble for something that happened in the bathhouse.'

I ask her to tell me everything. I can't make the right decisions if I don't know what the hell is going on. I may as well have saved my breath. All she will tell me is that the document she needs is called *A Fiery Flying Roll* and that it was written in the seventeenth century. The copy in the history room is one of the last remaining original copies and is very valuable.

I tell her to come to my hut tonight. No promises. But I might do a deal. If she agrees to become a proper chief informant for my research, if she stops evading my questions about life in Digger Town, if she divulges secrets about her life and that of the other women, I just might play ball...

As soon as the words are out of my mouth I regret them. Blackmail. Bullying. I am no better than the unknown person who is putting pressure on Eliza to break her moral code by stealing.

I try to take back my words but it is too late. Eliza agrees at once. Gratefully.

'Nine o'clock?'

I nod. I feel like a complete shit.

'Thank you Josie, thank you.'

The next morning Eliza walks into the bathhouse and stands in front of Shirley Foster, who at this very moment is sitting at her table with her head down. She is unwrapping a brown paper parcel with careful fingers. She removes two magpie feathers. She holds them at the very end of the quill as if they were tainted.

Shirley looks up and sees Eliza standing in front of her. She thrusts the feathers beneath the table but it is too late. Eliza holds out her hand. 'I'll have those thank you. They belong to me.'

Be assertive, Josie had told her last night. Ask directly for what it is that you want.

'After much prayer,' says Shirley. 'God has finally revealed my duty to me.'

'So you have informed against me?'

Shirley is uneasy. She knows about Munna's tricks from past experience. And she does not want to alienate the niece of Gerrard Winstanley. 'I have no choice.'

'Have?'

'I have not yet spoken to the council.'

Eliza is immensely relieved. She sits down on the chair and talks to Shirley in a softer voice. 'Are you not afraid for yourself? You are responsible for Munna, you are meant to keep her under control.'

Shirley rallies. 'I saw what I saw. You were leading her on.'

'I was almost asleep. Now give me the feathers please.'

Shirley asks Eliza why she wants them. In her opinion they should be burnt.

'It is not for you to ask,' says Eliza. She believes that someone gave the feathers to Munna and what's more, showed her what to do with them. She intends to show them to Munna in order to jog her memory. Munna could never have thought it up for herself. However, Eliza has no intention of telling Shirley her suspicions. Her gossiping tongue could destroy them all. And what if Shirley herself was the culprit?

Reluctantly, Shirley hands the parcel across to Eliza. 'This is the end of the matter then?' she asks.

Eliza places the parcel into her skirt pocket. 'For the

moment, yes. Except that you must make your own peace with God. I cannot do that for you.'

She walks away from the bathhouse, jubilant, buoyant with relief. And with a new sense of respect for Josie. Say what it is that you want, she had said. You have nothing to lose.

Tonight will be the test. Josie has promised to help her to find the document. And in exchange, Eliza will speak about Digger Town into the black box. She has already heard her own voice coming out at her from the tape recorder. Last night in the hut Josie had given her a trial run. A moment of shock, then amusement. That strange twangy noise? Not my voice, said Eliza. My own is much deeper. Josie told her that everyone is horrified at first. Worse than looking into a mirror the morning after. After what? asked Eliza but Josie just laughed and refused to explain.

Meanwhile, Eliza prays that the thready clouds that have been gathering at the tops of the ridges since first light will thicken and descend upon the town before dusk falls. Just enough to cover the potential danger from the waning moon that still holds enough luminosity to cast a weak shadow.

At ten o'clock that night she is again inside the hut with Josie. They make plans to get into the history room without being seen. They decide to wait another hour to make sure that there will be no one out taking a walk.

Josie surprises Eliza by producing a key. 'What for,' asks Eliza. 'The buildings and houses are never locked in Digger Town.'

'Ah but the history room is,' says Josie. 'And there is another locked place too. The door in the brick wall that surrounds the sheds where the wine is made.'

'I already know that,' says Eliza.

'Haven't you ever wondered why?'

Eliza shakes her head. 'It's always been that way.'

The time passes slowly. Josie complains about the lack of electricity in her room to make hot water for coffee. She has a thermos which she fills from the tap on the woodstove at dinnertime but it tastes stewed and bitter by this time of night. 'Don't say it,' she warns Eliza. 'It's always been this way. Well I've broken enough rules already. May as well go the whole hog. Next time I get out I'm going to score a primus.'

'What's that?' asks Eliza.

'A tiny portable stove. Runs on kerosene.'

'How did you get the key?' asks Eliza.

'Joshua gave it to me.'

Eliza is shocked. 'But he will know that we have taken the document.'

'He won't miss it. The room is up to the roof with books and papers.'

Ten o'clock. It is very dark outside. The clouds are high enough to cover the moon. Eliza gives silent thanks. They dress in the long black cloaks with hoods that Eliza has borrowed from the unmarried women's dormitory. Josie giggles. Very Jane Austen, she says. Eliza laughs too. They are both in high spirits. Eliza because she can see an end to her troubles and Josie because she is relieved about the progress of her work. Eliza has agreed to record everything that she knows about this place into the tape recorder. Even last night, in Eliza's first tentative beginnings, the hair had prickled up at the back of Josie's neck. She feels poised at the very edge of a fundamental understanding of the secrets of the continuity and persistence of human community. But first she needs to understand what it would be like to live in a community that seeks to deny the movements of history or the brute fact that *time passes*.

They walk beside the boardwalk that runs underneath the verandas of the closed dark shops. The soil has been packed down into a hard surface by many booted feet and the hoofs of horses. The recent rain has softened the surface a little and this helps to muffle their footsteps. Neither speaks until they are safely inside the door that leads into the ground floor of the Great American Tobacco Saloon. They climb the stairs and Josie unlocks the door with the painted sign declaring this to be the History Room.

Eliza looks about with great interest. This is a place forbidden to women. It looks harmless enough. It could be a schoolroom or part of the town library. Tall shelves of books and rolls of paper. A brass candle holder and six white candles on a table of polished wood, a bowl of tapers with waxen heads.

Josie makes sure that the calico curtain is pulled securely across the single window. She removes her cloak and hangs it across the wooden curtain rail. Then she takes a candle from her pocket and lights it with a taper. The wick flares and hisses. There is a pungent smell of burning wax and saltpetre. She puts the dead taper in the tray of the brass candleholder. 'Remind me to take that with us,' she tells Eliza. 'We must be careful not to leave any evidence behind.'

Eliza runs her finger along the spines of a row of books. 'There are so many. This is going to take a long time.'

They work systematically, checking each shelf, unwrapping and rerolling scrolls and pamphlets. The books are mostly theological tracts. There is a handful of political and philosophical works. Josie is surprised to see well-thumbed copies of the Marxist classics *Das Kapital* and *The Communist Manifesto*.

'Oh,' says Eliza. She holds a book closer to the candlelight.

'The flying whatsit?' asks Josie.

'No,' answers Eliza. 'Writings of the original Winstanley.'

Josie is excited. 'Your uncle didn't tell me that was here. Give me a look.'

The book is a modern reprint of the seventeenth century broadsheets written by the first Gerrard Winstanley. Josie reads some of the titles out to Eliza: *The New-Yeers Gift, Truth Lifting up its Head, The Law of Freedom in a Platform*.

'Sounds fun stuff,' says Josie. 'I should take it with me. To study.'

Eliza tries to grab the book from Josie's hands. 'Leave it here.'

'Listen to this!' laughs Josie. '*A Vindication of Those, Whose Endeavors is only to Make the Earth a Common Treasury,*

Called Diggers, or, Some Reasons given by them against the immoderate use of creatures, or the excessive community of women, called Ranting...'

'Leave it,' says Eliza again. 'Please Josie.'

'Why?'

'Joshua will know.'

'You are panicking for nothing. I am allowed access to this room. That's why he gave me the key.'

Eliza frowns. 'I don't want you to take it.'

'But reading the original documents will help me in my work.'

'You will make mock of our ideas.'

Josie looks shocked. 'I'm really sorry if I gave you that impression.'

'You told me to ask for what I want. I want you to leave it here.'

'Point taken,' says Josie. 'But I'm puzzled. You wanted me to come with you tonight to steal something. But you won't let me take *this* book away. You realise that I can come back and get it anytime I want?'

Eliza nods. She is visibly upset.

'Is this some sort of holy book?'

'Yes.'

Josie hands the book back to her and Eliza replaces it on the shelf. They continue with their search. No luck. Except for the words of the title, the two women don't know what it is that they are looking for. A thick book? A scroll? A pamphlet?

Josie suddenly remembers the locked sea-chest. 'Hey, Eliza!' she says. 'Betcha I know where it is!'

'Shhhh,' warns Eliza. 'Don't raise your voice.'

'Joshua said it contained books that were forbidden to females,' says Josie. 'But where the hell is it?' She searches the room. The carved chest is not there. This makes Josie even more convinced that it contains what they are looking for. Joshua has removed anything that he does not want her to see. No wonder he gave the key to her without question.

'Damn damn damn,' says Josie. 'This is going to be harder than I thought.'

Eliza is stricken. Josie tries to comfort her. 'Look, maybe I'm wrong. Maybe it's not in the sea-chest. Let's keep looking.'

Eliza places a warning finger against her lips. She imagines she can hear someone creeping up the staircase. She blows out the candle and removes the cloak from the window.

Josie can also hear a rhythmic creaking noise. Is it booted feet slowly climbing towards the history room? She stands perfectly still. No, the noise seems to come from downstairs. 'Okay,' she whispers in Eliza's ear. 'Time to go.'

'But what if someone is down there?'

'We'll have to risk it,' says Josie. She places the used candle and the dead taper in her pocket. She looks around the room to make sure that all is in order. She locks the door and together they move as quietly as possible down the stairs.

In the old tobacco saloon the brass spittoons and chairs and glass-fronted cupboards look the same as before. The creaking noise is coming from behind a partially concealed door that leads into the back of the shop.

Eliza jumps back when she sees a life-size figure standing behind the counter. It is an American Indian in full headdress holding a long pipe. Josie holds out a steadying hand. They make it safely to the outside.

'I thought it was a man,' says Eliza in a shaky voice. 'Watching us.'

Josie tries to explain about tobacco shops and painted wooden Indians but gives up. 'Come on,' she says. 'Let's get the hell out of here.'

Eliza hesitates. 'Leave me here. I'll go back to the dorm on my own.'

Josie is disappointed. She wants Eliza to come back to her hut and answer some questions into the tape recorder. 'Tomorrow?' she asks.

'If I don't get hold of that document I don't know where I'll be.'

'I'll find that sea-chest, I swear it.'

Eliza stands in a shop doorway and waits until Josie has turned the corner into her own street. Then she retraces her steps back to the Great American Tobacco Saloon. She does not re-enter the building. Instead she walks the length of the block and then slips down a narrow alleyway to the back of the shops.

There is a window behind the Saloon. It is a heavy sash window and the top section has been pulled halfway down. The lower half is obscured by a muslin curtain. Eliza wedges herself in between two rubbish containers that sit side by side beneath the window. One contains vegetable matter for compost and one is overflowing with scraps of wool and cotton taken from the workplace of the textile workers. Eliza hears a scrabble of feet in the dead leaves at the side of the compost bin. A rat? She prays that it will not run across the tops of her shoes.

The moon is now riding high above a bank of thinning cloud. Eliza cannot tell if there is a lit candle within the room or not. If there is less light within the room compared with outside, her head will be silhouetted against the muslin. She decides not to take the risk. She keeps her head down low and listens to the noises coming from inside the room.

The same rhythmic creaking noise, louder and more furious. Then Joshua's voice, chanting these words: *blood blood, where where, plagues plagues upon the inhabitants of the earth, fire fire, sword sword...*

And a new sound, the voice of a young girl, saying, I finish now please, I finish...

Eliza recognises the voice of Munna. She has to find out what is going on. She clambers onto the bin so that she can see through the top half of the window.

Joshua moans, *go to London, to London, write, write, write...*

Eliza sees him sitting in a rocking chair with his head down. He has his back to the window. Munna has her hands on his face, massaging his beard.

And behold I writ, and lo a hand was sent to me, and a roll of a book was within, which this fleshly hand would have put wings to…

Eliza stands perfectly still. What is Munna doing now?

The roll thrust into my mouth, and I eat it up, and filled my bowels with it…

Munna is putting something into Joshua's mouth. Or is she rubbing his fat lips?

Where it was bitter as worm-wood…

Munna drops to her knees. Eliza can't see what she is doing.

Joshua's voice is getting louder and louder. He is rocking backwards and forwards in the chair. *And it lay broiling and burning in my stomach, till I brought it forth in this form…*

Eliza stretches her neck. Now she can see. Oh God God God. Joshua has forced his penis into Munna's mouth.

And now now I send it flying to thee with all my heart, and all…

Eliza hammers the window glass and cries, 'Get out Munna, get out!'

Joshua leaps up and turns his head towards the window, his eyes wide with shock. The rocking chair jumps across the room taking Munna with it.

Eliza almost falls through the window. She tries to scream but her throat closes up with fear and all she can do is make small choking noises.

Joshua comes across to the window. He grabs the metal handle attached to the lower pane and thrusts it savagely upward. He almost takes her head off. She manages to jerk her head backwards just in time but her hood is caught at one side. He stares up at her. Smiling broadly. This frightens her even more.

'Get down my dear,' he says. 'And come in out of the cold.'

The hood holds her head tightly against the window frame. She cannot speak.

'Do not be afraid. I'm sure that we can come to some accommodation.'

She does not know what else to do but obey him. She pulls her hood free with some difficulty and climbs down from the bin.

The back door opens and she slips inside.

4

A WITCH AND A CHEATER...

I am working in the vineyards alongside the unmarried women. A warm still day after a cold silent dawn. We are cutting bunches of ripe grapes and placing them into wicker baskets for the men to take to the wagons at the ends of the rows. Hard work. My hands are stained red and my back aches. On my first day I ate too many grapes. I spent most of the night running to and from the outside toilet. Lupa was bemused with my comings and goings. I probably disturbed the mice and cost her a meal.

The next morning, hives appeared on my skin. Something to do with the natural yeasts that breed on the surface of the grapes. I had to visit the dreaded infirmary and ask Dr Macky for calamine lotion. Pink blotches and watery itchy lumps all over my face and in my hair. Now I touch the fruit with care and never put a single grape into my mouth.

All week we have worked in the vineyards. The last of the grapes before the winter sets in. Sarah tells me that the pruning is the next big job but they cannot do this until the first frosts have set the sap in the vines. To cut before the frosts will cause the vine to wither and die. It has been good this work. I have spent many hours in the company of the unmarried women. I can't claim intimacy, there is still a wall between us that is impossible for me to climb. But at least I seem to have gained Sarah's trust.

She has described the clan system to me. The clan name is inherited from the mother. This is a problem for Sarah. She is whipstick ash and this means that she must marry someone whose mother was born into the snow gum clan. But try as she might, she cannot find anyone that she fancies from this group. The only man she wants is bloodwood and this is strictly forbidden.

I have searched the writings of the first Gerrard Winstanley but I cannot find any reference to clans or marriage prohibitions except for the usual kinship ones forbidding union between first cousins or deceased brother's wife etcetera that were current in the seventeenth century. So where did this clan business come from? A misplaced nostalgia for aboriginal clan systems that once lived and breathed on this land? A way of tying a historical community from a foreign land to something irrevocably rooted into this landscape? Or maybe it is more recent, maybe they have been influenced by New Age preoccupations with sanitised versions of tribal societies.

Sarah had no idea. She gave me the same answer that Eliza does when I ask difficult questions. *It's always been this way.*

Infuriating. But I can't blame them. They have been taught to accept everything in front of their noses as God-given. To question their world is to question God. And to do this would be to deny the worth of their personal existence.

The way that this community holds together it seems to me, is to deny the possibility of novelty, of innovation. They are only able to pay attention to things that have come from some sort of imagined golden age in the past. This goes far beyond technology. Their rules of conduct, their beliefs about the separate roles of men and women, their attitudes towards property, nothing can be allowed to change. To allow the possibility of change would be to destroy the history, and therefore, the very heart of their community.

They are frighteningly vulnerable. There is no way that they can remain intact into the next century. Perhaps their invitation to me as a sociologist was a last ditch effort to understand the dynamics of their community so that they can hold back the inevitable day when the walls come down and the world floods in. If so, they will be disappointed. All I can offer is an analysis of their group dynamics, no more, no less.

Elsa will not be working with us for much longer. She is to be married on Tuesday and then she'll be in a different work team. She is snow gum and is to be married to a bloodwood. This got me confused. I thought snow guns had to marry whipsticks. Not so, said Elsa. Depends on who your father is too. My father is not strictly speaking whipstick. Well he's called that but he is not whipstick by blood so I am permitted to cross over.

I'm lost. I wonder how they keep track of it all. I just hope that the bloodwood groom is not the same man that Sarah secretly loves. I can't ask Elsa of course. Sarah spoke to me in confidence.

The wedding is good news for me. I have been informed by Gerrard that I am to be allowed to observe the rituals that prepare the bride for the marriage service and to attend the party that follows. Weddings are very important, he told me. The only time all the citizens of Digger Town come together for a celebration.

A party? I am intrigued. Up until now I have never seen the slightest sign that these people dance or sing or let their hair down. Can't wait.

Eliza is standing in front of the blackboard in the classroom. She wishes that she was with the other women in the vineyards. The children had been helping in the harvest for part of the week but now that the grapes are almost all picked, regular school hours are back in place. She finds it difficult to concentrate. All she can think about is the meeting with her soldier tonight. And the handing over of *The Fiery Flying Roll*.

She is not afraid. Not since she looked through the back window of the Great American Tobacco Saloon. Not since she told Joshua want she wanted and he meekly gave it to her. Not since her dreams have flowed and rolled through the desert and over the cold seas in glass boats without the fear and the remorse of her original journeys. The voice of the marmalade cat claiming to be *nothing but a bloody mongrel of a feral bastard* has been silenced. She never wants to hear it again, asleep or awake.

Eliza has read the *The Fiery Flying Roll* cover to cover. And the slim pamphlets that Joshua gave her under protest. The history of the troubled relationship between the Diggers and the Ranters, a break-away sect that believed that God approves of every willful human act, and therefore the more sinful acts you commit, the more holy you become. There is no Satan, only God. There is no evil, only individual desire.

So these are the nightmare figures from the Digger's hell. Graphically described in this record from the past. She wonders why the soldier wants this document so badly that he is prepared to go to the extent of telling tales against her. Tales that could bring him as much trouble as they could to her.

She remembers every word he said. He had caught a copy in a net, but he wanted the real thing. This document. The roll that was delivered by the dismembered hand of God into the mouth of Abiezer Coppe.

A book can be humiliated and tortured in the same way as a living being. The English parliament of the day passed an Act that claimed that the book contained many horrid blasphemies and damnable opinions and that all copies of it *shall be burnt by the hands of the Hangman*. Hence the scarcity of the original book. The others had been publicly burned by the same set of hands that placed the rope around the necks of thieves and murderers over three hundred years ago.

Eliza is disturbed and excited by what she has read. She believes along with the Ranters that God dwells in her spirit and not within doctrine or an established church. But she cannot cope with the idea that all human acts are holy even when they are harmful to others. This leaves her with an unsolvable puzzle.

Who decides what is good and what is evil? And if nothing can be named evil, how can one know what is good?

Joshua thought he was doing Munna a favour. He said as much to Eliza. 'She is marked by dimness. She has committed no fault. Is she to have no pleasure in her blighted life?'

Night falls. Eliza climbs upwards into the scrub. A stiff breeze is blowing and the moving limbs of the gums release a faint smell of eucalyptus into the air. It is noisy up here tonight. A rustle of leaves and a sighing of trees and once a loud thump as a dead branch almost falls on her head.

The soldier is waiting for her. He is somewhat subdued. He tells her that he is feeling ashamed at his bargain with her. He has thought about her day and night since they last met. She is a golden girl, a honey girl, a treasure. He hopes she has not been fretting over what he has done to her.

Eliza hands over the document without speaking.

He cries out, 'Jesus wept, you did it!' He leans against a tree and switches his torch on and reads feverishly. 'Marvellous, marvellous. Thank you, thank you...'

Eliza stands beside him. She can feel the heat of his body through the cloth of his camouflage jacket. Now that he has what he wants from her he may not want to speak with her again. She doesn't know whether to stay with him or begin the long walk back to the dorm. She waits patiently

At last he closes the book. 'You've read it then?'

She admits that she has.

'So you know who I am?'

She shakes her head.

'A bad boy, one of them.'

She does not know what to say. She is consumed by an overwhelming desire to have him suck the tips of her breasts again. And this time she wants to touch him too, she wants to stroke his face and his body, to feel the bones and muscles beneath his skin, the meat beneath the fur. This time she helps him to remove her blouse and skirt. He covers her naked shoulders with his jacket and, this time, he parts her pubic hair with a cold finger and rubs her gently between her legs while he licks her nipples with his hot tongue.

She closes her eyes and runs her fingers up and down his bony back looking for the bodily sign that is one of the keys to salvation that the Ranters say lies embedded in the spine midway between the waist and the neck.

His hand stops. He lifts his head from her breasts. She opens her eyes. She looks up into the dense branches above her head, thrashing about in the wind.

He says, 'Do you want to go on?'

Somehow his words diffuse her desire. She suddenly sees herself from above, legs open, blouse open, opening herself to the hot and cold touch of this stranger. The ugly shame of her body exposed to the weather and to the gaze of all living things.

She panics and tries to stand up. He does not attempt to restrain her.

'It is not safe for me to stay here any longer,' she says.

He holds her against his hard body. She leans into him but keeps her face turned away. He grasps her chin and forces her to look at him. 'You will come here again.'

She leaves him leaning against the tree, clutching *The Fiery Flying Roll* to his chest. She runs through the bush to the lower slopes, her body aflame, raging with self-disgust, hating herself, hating the soldier. She passes a barn and a horse calls out to her from an open door. Stella, her favourite. She wonders why the door has not been closed. Stella is old and needs to be kept inside on cold windy nights.

Eliza goes inside the barn and leads Stella into a stall. She finds a blanket and fastens the leather straps beneath Stella's shuddering body. She takes a scoop of oats from a wooden barrel. The rubbery lips of the old horse suck the food gently from her open hand. She leans her forehead on the long face between the soft brown eyes. 'Help me,' says Eliza. The horse's eyelashes brush against her skin. 'My body travels one road, my head another. Tell me what to do.'

Stella, her mouth busy with the rough pleasure of oats, does not answer.

I'm in the produce store. Working with some unfamiliar people. Gerrard has given me permission to expand my work horizons beyond Sarah and Celia and Martha and the other unmarried women. This is good. Although they asked me to concentrate on studying the lives of the women, I am also interested in the men. Or at least in the interaction between the sexes. When I first came here I saw it in simple terms; women repressed, women unhappy, women run away. Empower the women, women happy, women stay. End of story. But it is far more complicated than this of course.

Now that I have read the original writings of the first Gerrard Winstanley I am beginning to understand what they are trying to do here. Food for all from the earth. Communal land, communal property, labouring for the survival of the group and not for private profit. Sounds idyllic. The trouble is that in order to keep their group intact they have constructed a tyrannical system of rule and punishment that borders on fascism.

Gerrard has assured me that the Sixty-Two Laws are more symbolic than real but it bothers me that they advocate whipping for a trivial 'crime' like gossiping.

Law Twelve: He who endeavours to stir up contention among neighbours, by tale-bearing or false reports shall the first time be reproved openly by the Overseers among all the people: the second time shall be whipped: the third time shall be a servant under the Taskmaster for three months...

Only men can be treated this way. Wives or daughters can never be whipped or become a servant or a bondsman. They can never be held responsible for neglecting the agricultural tools (Law Fifteen) or for wasting food (Law Sixty-One). This is because the household is under the rule of the husband. A man who continually breaks the rules can have his family taken away and 'given' to another man. Women are not subject to the Laws but they must obey the male who is in authority over them. Period.

And get this. Any man who preaches and prays in public with the intent of gaining control over *the possessions of the earth, shall be put to death for a Witch and a Cheater*. (Law Forty).

I challenged Gerrard about this. He denied that anyone had ever been put to death. He told me that they have their own interpretations of the Laws. There is little violent punishment except in extreme cases. Freedom can be lost but there is no grievous bodily harm. The group must co-operate, there can be no allowances made for anyone who stirs up trouble and threatens group harmony. Hence the rules about idle gossip and wastage of resources. The welfare of the group must always rise above the petty whims of individuals.

Okay okay I believe him. I think. But I will check it out with Eliza. The information she has given me up until now has been largely a matter-of-fact description of their everyday lives. Time for me to get into deeper issues.

In spite of my reservations about the nature of crime and punishment in Digger Town, I am warming to Gerrard. He actually listens to me with respect. I know that he believes that God is speaking to him through me. But even so I enjoy his interest in my ideas. My reaction to his attention made me realise how seldom this happens to me. My life was stolen by a meaningless death, I was renamed a widow, a penniless woman, a neglectful mother. Megan, Max, my in-laws, Aunt Winifred, my children, even my best friend Lynda. Constantly telling me who I am and what I should think and what I should be doing with my life.

You had it soft Josie, said my sister Megan. You had it easy. A loving marriage, money, a house. You didn't believe me when I told you what happens to lone women. All those desperate efforts by other women to pair us off with losers. We are seen as a threat. I've been there and I know.

Megan the drama queen. Taught from our bitter childhood to always look on the dark side of things. She claims to be a realist, whatever that means. She goes from one man to another, looking for what she calls a committed relationship. All she commits is an act of economic exchange. She gives her body and wants him to stay with her forever. They never do. She allows herself to get hurt over and over again. And she doesn't need the assistance of other women to pair her off with losers. She does a perfectly good job of it all by herself.

I was afraid of becoming like her when I lost Russell. I threw myself into my studies instead. Once I get my doctorate I'll have it until I die. No one can take it from me. It can never drop to earth in a failed parachute or decide to leave me.

I asked Gerrard why the Laws are necessary, why the people cannot act with the certainty of their belief rather than the threat of punishment. He sighed and talked about balance and the necessity of sanctions. But, I answered, your crimes are not in tune with our age, these are from another time and another place. Ah, he said, there is tremendous comfort in the knowledge that this religion and morality was rooted deep into the soil hundreds of years before our individual births.

It's a sunny day, deep blue sky, no clouds. The air is almost hot behind the thick glass at the front of the produce shop. I am very busy, weighing out cheese and potatoes and wrapping jars of pickles. There are many customers here this afternoon. The horses and carts are going back and forth non-stop from the locked gate. Ned tells me that there is a queue of people waiting their turn to enter within the perimeter fence. He can't understand it. An incredible crowd considering that it is not a long holiday weekend or the special day of the year when they bring out the new vintage for tasting.

Eliza is the only single woman here. She is in charge of the wine today. She polishes the glasses for tasting, arranges small squares of brown bread on plates, removes corks, places purchases in long brown paper bags. I am at the next counter,

selling fresh vegetables, eggs, cheese and bottled jams and pre-
serves. The woman instructing me is Mrs Nelson. No first
names. She pronounces my name incorrectly, adds a couple of
rrs in the middle. 'A quarter of tasty cheese please Mrs
Tarrbel.'

Strange woman. About forty, although it's hard to tell the
ages of the women here. Their skins are like cracked old
leather. She has a tiny head and a square body. Mousy colours
in her hair and skin. Almost ugly except for her intense blue
eyes. When she turned them on me I got a shock. I thought I
was looking into the face of Eliza. I wonder if they are related.
She's friendly enough but she is not interested in my life. Or
life on the outside. She has made that clear. I tried to ask her
questions but she shook her head and said that she could not
think of such things. I felt rebuked, like a naughty child. I
have to learn that I cannot gain a good rapport with everyone.

I enjoy handling the goods except for the potatoes. The
unwashed skins feel unpleasant against my hands. In between
customers I observe Eliza. She is wonderful with people. And
she seems to know everything about the wines she is selling.
The customers are asking her many questions about the cultivation and the manufacture of the wines. Oak of course, she
says. Nothing else. We make our own barrels, we have our own
coopers. Sometimes we have to buy in the timber. American
oak. Nothing but the best. Yes, we use green manures, we
plant them between the vines. Plough them into the soil in
Spring. Natural fermentation? Absolutely.

Mrs Nelson asks me to weigh out two pounds of carrots. I
try to open a new sack. It is sown at the top with brown twine.
I look for a knife to cut the string. Mrs Nelson tuts tuts at me.
'Undo it Mrs Tarrbel, please. And place it within this box. We
re-use everything here.'

I obey her, with much fumbling. At last I undo the knots
and grab a handful of carrots. I peer at the scales, a little
shortsighted without my reading glasses. I look up and there is
Max at the wine counter, asking Eliza if he can taste a 1995

Black Shiraz. She opens a new bottle and pours a little of the dark red fluid into a glass. He openly stares at her. Then he tries to engage her in conversation. He's practically salivating over her. She pays little attention to him and busies herself with another customer. Max sniffs the wine, tastes it, rolls it around his mouth then noisily spits it out into a brass spittoon. Pretentious bastard.

I am furious with him. He promised me that he would not come here while I was working with the Diggers. I decide to ignore him. Too late. He catches my eye and raises his glass to me. He comes over to my counter. 'Those carrots look nice.'

I hiss at him underneath my breath. 'I'll give you carrots.'

He places his face close to my own. 'We've got trouble,' he whispers.

I freeze. Not another so-called family drama.

'Come outside. Now,' he orders.

Mrs Nelson is giving me strange looks. I begin to explain to her that Max is my supervisor, and that I need to talk to him urgently. She interrupts me, waves her hand in front of my face. 'Go if you must. We are very busy.'

'I'm sorry,' I tell her. 'I won't be long.' I open the hinged section of the counter. Outside, another cartload of people is arriving at the store. Ned is helping people to alight. I can hear him informing them that cameras are forbidden in Digger Town.

'This better be good,' I snap at Max. I am annoyed with myself for apologising to Mrs Nelson. Rude bitch. She has no right to speak to me like that.

Fran is waiting across the street underneath a clump of gums. Now I am even more angry. What the hell is Max up to? Is she here as a friend of Max's or as a cop? At least she had the sense not to turn up here in uniform.

'Hi,' says Fran. 'Nice to meet you again Josie.'

I mumble an answer. Max looks around furtively. Then he pulls a folded newspaper from his pack. He opens it and hands it to me. I have to hold it a long way from my eyes in order to read it. The headlines scream *Slave Labour In Wine Cult Scandal*. I can't believe it. They've got hold of my name, they claim that I have been sent here undercover to find out about the *men in white who are forced to work for nothing. Local wine makers are up in arms. They have to pay award wages to their workers...*

'Who?' I ask. 'For fuck's sake who?'

'Read on,' says Max.

Mudgee tour organiser Mr Gregory Sharpe claims that the self-styled cult calling themselves the Commonwealth of Diggers is run by a small group of men who impose harsh laws upon its members. There have been allegations of whippings for trivial 'crimes' like the wasting of food. A spokesman for the local RSL says that the cult has no right to make a mockery of the name Digger...

I can't continue. I am shattered. I start to shake and shiver. 'I'm finished,' I stutter. 'This is the end of everything.'

Max tries to reassure me. 'Maybe we can retrieve something from this mess. Make it part of your research. The hounding of people who dare to be different...'

I start to cry, I can't help it. It's the fact that my name is in the article and that I am accused of being some sort of spy that really gets to me.

And now bloody Fran is putting me through the third degree. 'If there's any substance in these accusations you must tell me,' she says. 'You owe it to the people here. Especially the children.'

I lose it completely. 'The whole thing is fucking bullshit!' I'm not crying now, I'm yelling. The crowd of tourists across the street look at me with curiosity.

Ned hurries over. 'Is this man annoying you Josie?' he asks.

Max makes the peace. Explains who he is. Ned takes me aside. Asks me if I'm all right. I nod dumbly. He rebukes me for shouting and using profane words in front of strangers. 'They think that you are a resident of Digger Town. Your language puts us in a bad light.'

I nod again. God, if only he knew.

Ned goes back to the horse and cart and helps the waiting passengers to climb up into the seats for their return trip to the perimeter. I take possession of the newspaper. It is only a matter of time before Gerrard and the other members of the council get wind of the lies that have been told about us. Max thinks that we should find Gerrard and the others right now and warn them. He says that it won't stop with the papers. He saw a Channel Ten news truck driving towards Mudgee. Bristling with equipment.

I implore him to leave. Now. He will only make more trouble for me if he speaks to Gerrard. I will deal with the council alone. I will throw myself upon their mercy. I'll be completely honest with them. I'll tell them about the scene in the café last week when Max showed Greg my copy of the Sixty-Two Laws. I'll beg for forgiveness.

Fran runs across the road and signals to Ned, who has already told the horse to walk-on. He pulls the horse to a stop and gives Fran a hand up to the front seat next to him. 'Come on,' she calls over to Max. 'We can't do anymore here.'

Max squeezes my arm. 'Move carefully. See you in Mudgee next week?'

I nod. 'Same place, same time.'

'One last thing Josie,' he whispers. 'Who's the babe selling the wine?'

It is early on Sunday morning. Eliza is sleepless and troubled. Sarah is snoring close to her bed. A terrible snore, almost a choke deep in her throat. Eliza gets up and puts on her dressing gown. She creeps to the side of Sarah's bed and squeezes her nose. Sarah opens her mouth widely to take a breath. Carefully Eliza removes her hand. Success. The snores stop.

Eliza goes back to her bed. Sarah begins to snore again. Eliza gives up. She does not need to leave for another hour yet but if she cannot sleep, she might as well be on her way. She gets up again and puts on her long thick skirt and woollen blouse. The sky has begun to lighten, it is almost dawn. No work in Digger Town on Sundays except for serving in the produce shop and cooking communal meals and caring for children. Eliza is not due to work in the shop until after lunch. The pressure of work is off for a while. The winter vegetables are planted. The grapes are harvested. The leaves on the vines are changing colour and drifting down and carpeting the ground with drifts of gold.

A good year in spite of the drought. There are fewer grapes and they are slightly smaller but the sugar levels are high. The wagons have taken the last of the grapes through the locked door behind the brick wall for the processing to begin. The vats and crushers and ageing barrels are strictly out-of-bounds for Eliza and the other women. She picks the grapes at harvest time and uncorks the bottles of wine in the shop. What happens in between is kept secret by the winemakers. Eliza's knowledge about wine comes from her participation in a training group led by the head winemaker Brother Harold. She and a select group of women have been instructed by him in the history of wine, varieties of grapes, and the methods used by traditional winemakers; the pressing of residues (white) or whole grapes (red), fermentation of the must in vat or tanks, oxygen for maturation via quick oak or slow cork, Méthode Champenoise or the Charmat method...

But it's pure theory; all she has is the language and not the experience.

Eliza walks along the deserted street. No one is about. It's very cold. Thin sheets of ice cover the surface of the drinking troughs set out for the horses. She goes down a lane that connects the street with the grazing fields. There is black ice in the deep furrows at the edges of the fields. The few cows still milking walk slowly in line towards the dairy shed, breath drifting like white smoke from moist nostrils.

Eliza goes to the barn and greets Stella. She saddles the old horse and leads her away. She walks for almost thirty minutes, leading a plodding Stella through the thinning darkness. A lid is lifted from the frosty cauldron of night. The sun fleshes out the tall gums standing along the tops of the eastern hills. The blue heads of the trees are backlit by filaments of rose pearl light.

A pair of screeching magpies fly upwards directly in front of Eliza. She jumps back, startled by their harsh cries, then calls up to them to come back to their breakfast, come back. They land stiff-legged, wings held out for balance, cocky, self-assured, but watching the woman and the horse intently with eyes of unblinking black glass. They soon resume their search for insects, turning over twigs and dead leaves with their curved beaks.

Eliza waits until she is near the eastern fence alongside the largest vineyard before she mounts. There is a smooth area close to the edge of the vines that has been worn into two deep ruts by the constant passage of wagon wheels. She rides Stella gently, with reverence for the horse's age. The horse breaks into a gallop for a short distance. Eliza reins her into a walk. She is afraid for the old legs of Stella on this rutted road.

In spite of the exhilaration of the ride and the stimulation of the cold air blowing around her head, Eliza turns inward once again to her terrible dilemma. She cannot decide what to do about Munna. If she tells anyone what she saw, she will have to reveal that she made a deal with the soldier. She will have to admit to stealing *The Fiery Flying Roll* in exchange for his silence. Josie knows about the *Roll* but she doesn't know why Eliza wanted it. No one else knows anything. Except Joshua and Munna.

When Eliza entered the back room of the Great American Tobacco Saloon she was so terrified that she could barely speak. Joshua gloated and gleamed in the candlelight, Munna sat slumped in the corner.

'Oh how the mighty hath fallen,' he sang. 'Caught you at last. Gerrard will hear of this, mark my words. Quite the little night-time prowler.'

Eliza tried to apologise but she could not find her voice.

'Your prior nocturnal activities have not gone unnoticed,' said Joshua. 'Likewise your fascination with the internal organs of wild felines.'

So Joshua had been spying on her. He must have seen her take the ice from the meat storehouse. He must have seen her dissect the cat. And later stole it from the ground floor of the dorm. Maybe he followed her and Josie here tonight and staged this show in the hope that he would be overheard. But why? Had he seen her with the soldier? Did he imagine that she would find his disgusting actions attractive?

Suddenly, her fear left her. Instead she felt a rush of intense anger. How dare he do this to her, to Munna, how dare he!

Eliza ordered him to open the sea-chest and give her *The Fiery Flying Roll*. At once. Otherwise, she would be the one speaking to her uncle. And she would tell him what had she heard, Joshua's mad chanting about plagues and fire and swords and the hand thrusting the fiery roll into his mouth and burning his bowels...

Joshua opened the chest without a word and handed the *Roll* to her. He did not ask why she wanted it. He suddenly seemed incapable of speech altogether.

But she must do something more. Munna must be protected from Joshua. Urgently. Before she attacks another woman in the bathhouse. Before she is reported to the council and undergoes a dreadful punishment. Would they banish one of the chosen ones? Eliza can never remember it happening before. People who are intellectually impaired are not usually held to be responsible for their actions.

But how can she be certain? Unexpected things have been happening. Like the arrival of Josie to study their community. Like the wagon trip to the feral foodbank. Like her encounter with the soldier. Like her dreams of voyages across deserts that pitch and roll like the sea.

Eliza once thought she understood the meaning of change. Trees grew, shed bark, died for firewood; nests were built and fell derelict, eggs cracked, birds flew; red wine poured onto parched ground to bring down rain from empty skies, vines cut to the quick, lush again; a rhythm of death and rebirth. There was nothing to fear. Always the familiar shape of the land to cradle her body, always the same roads, the buildings, the sweat of horses, always the burning summer, the hot spring winds from the west, the freezing winter nights, always the same.

And now these new things within her. Naming what it is that she wants. And doing it. Like the taking of this horse without the prior permission of the groomsman.

She rides Stella to the end of the long field and then dismounts. She walks the horse into a clump of trees at the foot of the hill and tethers her to a low branch. Stella stands patiently, her breath steaming. Eliza removes the saddle and rubs her down with a small towel. She regrets not bringing some water for the horse to drink. She will go home another way, past the sheep paddocks. There will be some water there.

Eliza begins the climb up towards the trysting place. She is very early. Her plan is to hide from him. When he leaves, she will follow. He must have a vehicle nearby. She will find out which road he travels and then go back for the horse. She is confident that she will find her way, she has come prepared. On her back is a canvas pack. In it is a topographic map of the Mudgee District borrowed from the schoolroom. And a compass and a small bedside clock so that she knows when it is nine o'clock.

She tucks up her long skirt into the elastic of her petticoat and climbs up into the branches of a young tree. When she has gained enough height, she tries to grasp the lowest branch of a massive gum that is growing next to the small tree. But the gap is too wide. She is afraid of falling. She climbs down again. There is a clump of low-growing bushes forming a thick screen behind a tangle of fallen logs. If she remembers to keep her head down, this could provide a good hiding place.

Too soon yet. She plans to hide just before he is due to arrive. In the meantime, she asks God to throw her down a sign. Is she going into danger?

Show me what you want of me and I will understand.

Sunday night. I am still at the dining room table even though the plates have been cleared away and the married women have shepherded their children away to their beds. The workers are clanking the dishes and pots in the kitchen. I am still hungry. I did not enjoy the greasy mutton-flaps and boiled potatoes, the thin vegetable soup. I left most of my food on the plate, earning a frown from Hannah.

I am due at a council meeting in fifteen minutes. Some of the older men have already asked me what I have in mind. Gerrard must have told them that it is my idea to have a meeting on a Sunday night. This has never happened before so it is inevitable that they are both curious and concerned. Joshua looks particularly anxious. He sidled up to me when I was spooning soup from the tureen and asked me if I knew the whereabouts of Sister Eliza. She had not turned up for afternoon duty at the produce store.

I shrugged. I told him I had no idea. And that I wouldn't tell him even if I did.

Yesterday, as soon as Mrs Nelson had let me go from the shop, I went to see Gerrard. He would not allow me to tell him why I was upset. If there is a serious problem, he said, it should be revealed in front of the council. He, as a single individual, had no right to listen to me and form a personal opinion without the mediation of others. He wanted me to wait until the weekly council meeting scheduled for next Thursday. I told him that I could not wait that long. If he could not arrange a meeting for tonight, then it must be tomorrow. He was reluctant to ask the others to come to a meeting on the evening of the Lord's Day but I insisted. I tried to drop a hint about what had happened but he held up his hand to silence me.

I spent a sleepless night, worrying myself into a frenzy about the leak to the media and the inevitable consequences this would bring to my work. And I felt guilty too, for bringing this trouble to the Commonwealth of Diggers. I have not changed my view of them. They live in a world conceived in another time and another hemisphere, but they seem to be gentle with children and animals. And each year, they renew the land, take only what they need, give back what they take. There are some unresolved puzzles. Crime and punishment, the Sixty-Two Laws, the lack of autonomy of the women and the younger men. But even so, they do not deserve the terrible lies that have been published about them.

Early dawn brought a hard frost. Seven degrees I heard the men say. Enough to still the flow of sap in the vines. The day passed so slowly for me. I could not concentrate on my work so I wrote letters instead.

Dear Megan, How's it going with Current Male? I hope all is well with you...

Dear Jeanette, I am glad to report that my work is progressing, and thank you once again for taking care of my brats...

Dear Lynda, You must be joking! There's more chance of being laid in a monastery than in this place... Besides, haven't you heard of fieldwork ethics?

Dear Aunt Winifred, Sorry to hear that you have had another fall. Please take care of yourself, and ring Megan if you need anything...

Dear Jack, Be tolerant darling, don't try to foist your ideas on Jeanette and Rowley. They mean well...

Dear Briony, I'm glad that you have found some like-minded friends on the Net. Hope this makes up for having to leave your mates back in Sydney. Who's the group in Mudgee that you chat with...?

The afternoon turned on one of those cloudless winter skies that is so vast and high that it could be an inversion of the deepest ocean carrying motionless fish instead of stars and planets. Emptiness. A reflection of what could happen in my life if this research falls through. I rehearsed over and over what I might say to the council. Should I be contrite? Should I admit to knowing Mr Gregory Sharpe, tour organiser and chief informant for the reporter? Or should I deny everything, including taking a copy of the Sixty-Two Laws into a café in Mudgee?

No matter how I tried to twist the story, it sounded bad for me. I decided that I would read the article aloud without comment and then face up to their accusations and questions. I would give them only the information they wanted. Nothing more and nothing less.

So here we are in the council room. The candles burn with steady lights and someone has lit a fire. On the side table there are open bottles of wine and squares of bread. Gerrard pours me a drink. The wine is dark and fruity. The same shiraz that was offered to me on my first meeting in this room. He waits until each man has a goblet of wine and a piece of bread, then he leads the chant, *worke together, eat bread together...*

One of the men throws some logs onto the fire and a shower of sparks flares and spits. Gerrard sits me on a chair in front of the group. I ask him to bring a candle so that I might read. He stands behind me, holding a dripping candle high above my left shoulder.

I begin. The words fall like knives into the flickering light punctuated by the hiss of the fire and the gulps from wine-filled throats. It sounds much worse read aloud. *Mrs Jocelyn Tabel, a university researcher from Sydney, claims that men in white are forced into unpaid work as punishment for so-called crimes... a local informant, who wishes to remain anonymous for fear of retribution, has revealed that there have been public whippings and other barbaric rituals...*

I finish reading. Gerrard takes the candle away and sits in the front row next to the historian Joshua. Absolute silence. I am terrified. What will they do to me?

I can see the glinting eyes of Joshua. He's smiling! The bastard wants to see me suffer. But Gerrard is smiling too. What the fuck is going on?

He stands. Still nothing. He chews a lump of bread and sips the last of his wine. Then, incredibly, he says, 'We apologise for bringing this trouble down on you Sister Josie. It is not of your making.'

'What, what?' I gasp.

'This has happened to us many times.'

'I don't know how they got hold of my name...'

He raises his hand. 'We do not hold you responsible.'

The other men are listening to him attentively. He explains that persecution is part of the price that they pay for being a closed community. Besides, this is only a newspaper article, worse things have happened in the past, much worse. A house was burnt, a child was almost lost, the produce store was vandalised, and once, many years ago, a posse of men on horses, drunk and abusive, came riding through these streets. Cracking whips, screaming foul words, breaking windows. Some were in military uniform, some were dressed as whores with painted faces, some brandished rifles above their heads. A goat was found with its throat cut, and stock gates were forced open. But these events happened in the past. Things are quieter now, the times are more tolerant.

'But you should defend yourselves,' I say. 'Deny these horrible accusations...'

'No,' he says sharply. 'Remain silent, do not feed their crude hunger.'

I am almost weeping with relief. Gerrard takes the newspaper from my shaking hands and gives it to Joshua. He instructs him to file it away in the history room with the other cuttings. 'The meeting is over Brothers,' he says. 'I thank you for coming.'

Boots scuffle and stomp on the wooden floor. The men of the council file into the night. They close the door behind them. Gerrard recorks a half-full bottle of wine and gives it to me to take back to my hut. He pulls the fire apart with an iron poker, I extinguish the candles. I don't know what to say to him. I need to crawl into my bed and think over what has happened. I can't grasp the fact that I'm still here. I was certain that I would be at the perimeter fence by now, bags packed, shivering with cold and disappointment.

There is a knock on the front door leading to the street. Outside, there are a dozen young men dressed in heavy coats. I can hear the restless movements of horses behind them.

'Of course, you must go,' Gerrard is saying. 'We cannot wait until morning.'

They move off. I can hear the barking of dogs and the clatter of hoofs on the freezing ground. Gerrard puts on his coat and hat and closes the door behind us. We walk down the street together. The night is cold and deep and already full of stars. Gerrard comes to the door of my hut with me. He seems very distracted. I ask him what is happening.

'Eliza has not returned to the dorm,' he says. 'Her horse has been found lame and wandering. She may have had a fall. Or worse.'

I ask if there is anything I can do. I would like to help in the search.

He shakes his head. 'Stay here,' he says. 'You are unfamiliar with the area. There's nothing you can do.'

I go into the hut and lie on my bed. I am too anxious to work on my notebooks. I don't understand anything. I blunder from one situation to another. I was stupid to show Max the Sixty-Two Laws and I was even more stupid to assist Eliza in breaking into the history room. I'm sure that Eliza's disappearance has something to do with the document that we unsuccessfully looked for. What had she said? A very important person from the outside had asked for it. A matter of life and death.

I get up and pour some wine into my cup and smoke a cigarette. I drink two cups, three. The bottle is soon empty. It does not assuage my guilt. I knew that Eliza was in trouble. And I said nothing. I was more concerned with keeping her on my side so that she would continue to assist me in my studies.

If anything terrible has happened to Eliza it will be my fault.

He arrives promptly at nine o'clock. Eliza remains hidden in the low bushes. She has smothered the clock beneath a pile of dead leaves to muffle the tick. She is flat on her stomach with her head supported by her folded arms. She watches him roll up a cigarette. She prays that a snake does not crawl across her back. She reminds herself that most snakes will already be safely tucked away in their nests for winter. Not so the spiders. She could be lying on top of a deadly burrow of a specimen of *Atrax robustus* at this very moment. Small, shiny, black, filled with poison and aggression, ready to strike at the obstacle lying across the roof of its retreat. Her skin is alert to the slightest movement, the merest suggestion of disturbance in the bush detritus beneath her. Is she about to receive a mortal wound? A payback for her recent sins, a lesson from a creature that seems without purpose except to act as guardian of the bush floor. Dig here and die.

The soldier finishes his smoke. He glances at his watch and stamps his feet and flaps his arms around his chest. He hits at the trunk of a gum tree with a stick and pulls away strips of fibrous bark. He piles the bark on a bare patch of ground and breaks twigs to make a small fire. She almost calls out for him to stop. The smoke will rise and someone will come to investigate. Even in this winter of unusual rains, the sight of smoke will bring one of the perimeter watchers at full gallop. This part of the bush has not been burnt for over thirty years and is choked with undergrowth and fallen timber and deep drifts of leaves. It is more than ready to renew itself.

The soldier warms his hands over the fire. He sits and waits for about an hour, feeding the fire from time to time with dry eucalyptus leaves and small branches. He looks at his watch one last time then he stands up and pulls down the zip on his trousers and urinates profusely into the heart of the flames.

A hiss of acrid steam then silence. The last wisp of smoke detaches from the dead fire and drifts upwards through the latticed branches of the taller trees. Weak sunlight is just beginning to penetrate the canopy that holds the freezing air in suspension. He throws dry soil on the fire and walks away.

Eliza follows him from a safe distance. She creeps as quietly as possible through the thick bush until she reaches the fence high up on the steep ridge at the edge of the Digger's land. The fence is higher than the usual farm fence and has barbed wire across the top. She can see a neat hole snipped through the wire. The grass is flattened at the bottom. So this is where he has been getting in. And out.

Eliza hesitates, then climbs through. She is well aware that she is doing something far more serious than merely climbing through a convenient hole in a fence.

She moves down the other side of the ridge. Now that she is out of the trees, she can no longer conceal herself. The land is cleared and there are scrubby sheep nibbling at the dry brown grass. There is no sign of the soldier. She follows a sheep track down the steep slope until she comes to a dirt road that spirals down to the bottom of the hill. She walks to the edge of a small rock fall and peers downward. There he is, almost at the bottom. He is riding a bicycle with thick tyres, moving at an incredible speed. She watches him steering around the corners, his body jolting up and down, back curving downwards, boots working furiously on the pedals, the wheels leaping upwards, then bouncing back.

The bicycle reaches the sealed road down on the flats. There is a black van parked nearby. He opens the back door and places the bike inside. Then he drives away down the long straight road.

She remains at her vantage point, disappointed. She will never be able to follow him now. Even if she runs as hard as she can, she will never catch up with him. She cranes her neck until the van is almost out of sight, a black box moving along the sealed road. To her relief, it stops beside a thick windbreak and turns left through a set of gates. It disappears into the trees for a few seconds, then reappears, moving slowly down a driveway towards a long low farmhouse. There are at least five or six smaller buildings clustered around the main building. The van stops near other vehicles parked in a semi-circle around the farmhouse.

The sun is now high in the eastern sky. Steam rises from the black road as the ice melts. She sits on a pile of stones and watches and waits. He is either visiting the farm or he lives there. She memorises the position of the gate and the windbreak. She stays there for a while, but no vehicles move in or out. Time to make a move.

She decides to walk rather than go back for the horse. Stella would find the bush too thick and difficult and she would never get through the wire fence. There is a danger that passing motorists will see her walking in her distinctive clothes and stop and ask her awkward questions. She knows that it would be safer for her to walk through the paddocks but she decides to risk the road. The other way would take too much time. She must be back in Digger Town by lunch time.

She walks briskly, enjoying the stillness of the morning and the feel of a hard surface beneath her boots. A vehicle passes her on the other side of the road, an old man in a cloth hat driving a rusty ute loaded down with sacks of onions. She keeps her head down. He does not pay her the slightest attention. She arrives at the set of iron gates. They are securely shut. There are two signs attached to them; one states that guard dogs are on duty and the other that trespassers will be arrested. She stands there uncertain and afraid. What sort of place is this? Maybe it would be wiser for her to come back after dark.

Without warning the gates open inwards. She jumps back in shock and hides in the windbreak. Someone must be leaving. But there is no sound of a car coming down the driveway. She waits for a few minutes and then enters the property. She manages to conceal herself within the thick trees lining the front part of the driveway. She can see the turning circle and the parking place for cars. There is the black van standing next to a station wagon. She relaxes a little. There is no sign of the guard dogs.

She follows a foot track around the back of the main building and hides in a clump of bushes. A red white and black flag flies from a tall flagpole. On the flag is a three-sided figure like broken bits of triangles in motion. And another flag, lower down, with the letter M repeated three times, green satin on black, the letters joined together at the feet.

She can hear something moving towards her, a sudden rush of wind and sound. She drops flat to the ground. A group of about a dozen men appear from the side of the farmhouse. They all have shaved heads. They are running in a pack, black heavy boots, camouflage clothes, peaked caps; their feet hit the ground in the same rhythm and they are chanting something in unison that sounds more like a curse than a song.

From the distance comes the crack of rifle shot. She is used to this sound. The young men of her group are permitted to shoot rabbits for food and to stop them from raiding the vegetable gardens. Rats and poisonous snakes are dispatched by shotguns. But this is different. There is more than one rifle. The shots keep repeating over and over again in a fixed pattern. It sounds like target practice.

The soldiers are moving away from her, their chanting is getting fainter. The gunfire stops as abruptly as it started. Cautiously, she moves around the back of the farmhouse. She looks in the window. An empty room, large, with long tables and dozens of ornate wooden chairs. On the walls are many pictures, some are paintings, some are photographs, some are posters. All are of men in various military costumes both ancient and modern; sailors in frilled shirts holding cutlasses above their heads, soldiers in tin hats charging bags of chaff with fixed bayonets, five-star Generals, Americans in the Gulf War, masked, wired, anonymous.

There is a slight noise behind her. She turns, and it's him, standing behind her, smirking and holding his finger to his lips.

'Sshh,' he says. 'Come with me and keep very quiet.'

He grasps her arm and leads her to one of the small buildings behind the farmhouse. It is a bunkroom. There are nine bunks in tiers of three. He closes the door and pulls the curtain. He makes her sit on one of the lower bunks. She is weak with fright but obeys him. She is glad that it is him who discovered her and not one of the others. She tells him this.

'You were asking to be caught,' he says. 'Standing right out in the open like that. You must have wanted me to find you.'

She tries to explain but he won't give her a chance. 'I knew that you were hiding in the bush. I heard the clock ticking. And I opened the gate. As if you didn't know.'

She tells him why she has come here. She needs to talk to him about *The Fiery Flying Roll*. It has disturbed her. She cannot come to terms with the idea that the most holy people are the ones who sin at every opportunity. Without the slightest remorse. No guilt, no sorrow, no penitence. How can this be done?

He admits that remorse can be a problem. Unexpected moments of compassion can arise from nowhere. And this defeats the possibility of necessary cleansing action. He's working on it with his group. They are constantly in training to toughen the body and retrain the mind. They're planing a big event. Very hush hush.

'Talk is in itself the problem,' he says. 'Words are too weak to stand alone. There must always be a threat of anarchy and violence to give them meaning.'

Then he locks the door of the bunkroom and lies her on the floor and opens her clothes. The carpet square is dusty and gritty beneath her bare legs. And this time he does not touch her first or ask her if she wants to go on. He penetrates her almost immediately and plunges his penis up and down inside her body. She does not try to fight him off. She keeps her eyes open, watching his face. She feels nothing except an unpleasant stretching sensation within her vagina.

She watches his face contort and his body go into a frenzied spasm. He cries out, 'The key of liberty allows us to fulfil our lusts!' She observes everything with detachment, almost without interest.

And afterwards, he brings water for her to wash her bleeding vulva and offers to make her a hot drink. He looks a little nervous, he keeps asking her if she is okay. Is she still his golden girl, his honey girl, his treasure?

She dresses herself and asks him to unlock the door. He looks around outside and then ushers her swiftly down the driveway. There is no sign of anyone else. A doberman appears silently beside them and shows his teeth at Eliza. The soldier tells it to go away. It disappears as quickly and secretly as it came.

They emerge out onto the road. 'Better that you don't come here again,' he says. He tells her that it is not safe, some of the boys have communal attitudes towards women. And she belongs to him now. Exclusively. She must promise not to go with anyone else.

The gate closes automatically behind her. She walks alone down the road. The day is bright and clear and the sun is riding high in the sky. Frost-burnt grasses unravel in the sunlight and a few slow winter bees work the wildflowers and weeds on the unmown verge. A car draws up beside her. An expensive car, riding low on fat black wheels and reeking of leather and polish and perfume. A door opens and Eliza gets in.

The car purrs away, and the solidity of the air is broken apart and flows around the shining sides and drifts behind like a wake. Within moments, the gap is sealed and the road is as empty and tranquil as before.

5

A WEDDING AND A DEATH...

I miss the gentle winter climate of Sydney. Brisk mornings followed by long blue afternoons beside the Parramatta River, busy boats driving through the glittering water, slow jet streams melting in the skies. In the company of friends. Drinking coffee and laughing. Warmth, safety, familiarity. This hut is made of thin plywood timber. It looks decidedly temporary compared with the rest of the town. The air is just as cold inside as it is outside. I wonder what they will do with it after I'm gone. Maybe I'm the first in a long line of sociologists who will live here. Max certainly hopes so. He said that we have tapped into a rich vein of research possibilities here in Digger Town. We could spin it out for years. He told me that he has three other graduate students watching my progress. They will have access to my written work. My public work that is. My daily recordings, my notes and papers, my analysis of the clan system, my descriptions of rituals, my studies of the material culture. But not my personal diary.

I am creating three versions of events. One for Max and the academic community. One for Gerrard Winstanley and the council to help them understand the dynamics of their group. And one strictly private version which is nothing less than a conversation with myself. For my eyes only. Why do I want to keep doing this? Maybe it serves the purpose of keeping a grip on my own reality. A rock of reason in the middle of a river of academic jargon. Or maybe it is an antidote to my over-simplified and bland analysis that I am writing for the Diggers. It is so tempting to let my personal views into my research, and even more tempting to make disparaging judgements on the Digger's doomed attempt to create a microworld of religious communism within the technological madhouse of the late twentieth century.

My problem is that I sometimes forget which version it is that I am writing. I'm getting around this by using different coloured pens. Black for sociology, blue for the Diggers, red for me. Hope this solves my problem of mixing up the pages. I cannot allow one mode of speech to blur into the other. This can sometimes be amusing and at other times can be downright dangerous. I would die if Gerrard or Eliza or Max ever read my private thoughts about them.

I will destroy my diary after I leave here. I wonder if Malinowski's family wished that he had done the same after he came home from his fieldwork in New Guinea. At least I will not be revealing to the world that I am sick to death of mosquitoes and savages and cannot sleep for lustful thoughts and imaginary diseases. My obsessions are more to do with loss of self, and uncertainty about my ability to do intellectual work. Less dramatic than sex and illness, but they probably arise from the typical anxieties of my generation just as Malinowski's did from his.

Monday afternoon: Eliza has returned. This is her story. Fell from her horse and lay unconscious for hours. Then darkness came and it was not safe for her to move around the bush. She made a nest in the undergrowth, covered herself with her cloak, and waited for the dawn. She managed to get a few hours sleep. After sunrise, still dazed, she wandered far from Digger land. A stranger driving a big car brought her back to the perimeter fence. The wagon driver found her asleep in the shelter.

Why don't I believe her? Is it her lack of injuries? She refused to let Doctor Macky check her over. I don't blame her for that. But something does not quite jell for me. She has been reprimanded by Gerrard and the council for taking a horse from the barn without permission. She apologised profusely. Said it won't happen again. Then she tells me that Stella has been assigned to her since she was a child. They are the same age, thirty years old. She has to get permission to ride her own bloody horse? I still find it hard to believe that the women here are so obedient to those in authority over them. But when I brought the subject up, she gave the same old excuse. *This is how it has always been done.* And now Stella is lame and the groom wants to have her put down. Eliza was frantic. She begged her uncle to intercede on her behalf. Otherwise she would have the death of her horse to atone for as well…

I perk up my ears. As well as what? I pump her for information about her unauthorised journey out but all she will talk about is the car she rode in, a wonderful sleek black beast, *oh Josie, the wheel turned so fast and my stomach flew backwards into my spine and the trees blurred past and the painted line in the middle of the road unravelled and I clung to the door and a bird flew straight into my face so that I screamed and flung my hands up and it hit with a sickening thud and left a red smear of feathers stuck on the glass declaring itself to be a blue wren, Malurus cyaneus, possibly a non-breeding male…*

I believe this part of her story. It is too graphic for her to invent. And only Eliza would take note of the species of a wounded bird while simultaneously feeling horror at its fate. It is the lack of detail in the other events that make me smell a rat. But I decide not to hassle her too much. She has enough to cope with from the others as it is. Sarah in particular won't leave her alone. She follows Eliza around picking at her for little morsels of information like a hungry hen looking for scattered wheat in long grass.

Tuesday: Elsa's wedding day. Very low key so far. I am waiting on the bottom floor of the unmarried women's dorm for the bride to appear. Elsa is upstairs being dressed by her bridesmaids. Why do they bother? I cannot see any difference between her bridal clothes and her everyday dress. Oh there is one white flower made from silk. It is pinned to her head over her scarf. The flower has a dark green eye.

A wagon drives to the doorway. Elsa comes down the stairs with her attendants. The horse has an identical white flower tucked beneath its bridle. Elsa is helped aboard. I walk behind slowly with the unmarried women. They hold their heads down and clasp their hands low in front of their bodies. No one speaks. It's more like a funeral procession than a wedding.

We arrive at the assembly hall next to the dining hall. Elsa climbs down. The women I am with begin an eerie high-pitched wail. This shocks me from my boredom. Are they grieving for a lost sister? I find this hard to believe, given that marriage is seen as the most important thing that can happen to a woman.

We enter the hall. The wailing stops as abruptly as it began. There are hundreds of people already seated. I am struck once again by their physical conformity. It is more than the wearing of uniform clothes. The men are thin and stringy and sit with straight backs, feet flat on the floor. The women sit with their arms close to their sides, trying to take up as little space as possible. I wonder if the body is shaped more by the internal landscape of the mind than by the rigours of hard work and plain food. These people share identical beliefs. They share what could almost be called a group mind. Ergo, they *look* like clones.

Dull dull dull. No decorations and no children. This surprises me. So marriage is strictly the business of adults. I sit at the front next to Eliza and Sarah. Suddenly, there is a burst of singing from the back of the hall. I turn. A group of young men are leading John the bridegroom down the centre aisle. They are bedecked with flowers and are wearing brocade waistcoats.

The congregation lifts its collective voice. What the hell is this? They are singing the national anthem. The old one. God Save the King.

Elsa stands with her back to the approaching men. John takes his place at her side. At last some ritual! An old man I have never seen before comes in from a side door. He is dressed in a similar type of gown worn by academics when they are receiving degrees. Red in colour. He carries a book. He reads some simple words. Very similar to the standard Anglican wedding service. Except that when the celebrant asks who gives this woman in holy matrimony, the whole congregation shouts, we do.

There are no rings exchanged and the bride and groom do not make promises to each other. Instead the collective is addressed. They promise to stay with the community for life, in sickness and in health, for richer or poorer... whom God has brought together let no man put asunder...

One of the male attendants hands the celebrant two branches of gumleaves with silver cloth wound around each stem. The old man raises them aloft and asks if there is any one present who for any reason objects to this marriage. Speak now or forever more hold your peace.

A frozen moment. Then, Joshua the historian comes to the front of the hall. He reads some names from a large book. It seems that he is tracing the clan lineage of the bride and the groom. Elsa is snow gum and John, bloodwood. Her mother is snow gum and marriage is permitted by the matrilineal line. But not through the father's line. Elsa's father was bloodwood by birth but became whipstick ash through adoption. So although Elsa's father is really bloodwood, he is in a different generation and has the added advantage of a change of clan through adoption which is seen as equal to a clan birth. Therefore Elsa is allowed to marry John.

I get it I think. The system appears rigid but when two young people fall in love and the council approves, the rules are bent to allow them to marry. If for some reason the marriage is not approved, the rules are trotted out to make sure the union does not take place. Very clever.

The old man in the red gown holds up the two gum branches

and brings them slowly together. He binds them with white and red cloths. The bloodwood and the snow gum he chants. In these special circumstances we marry the two. John and Elsa, chants the congregation. Elsa and John! Blood and snow!

Another burst of singing. This time a hymn. And one that I know. Oh God our help in ages past... I sing the words loudly. Eliza gives me a half smile.

We move into the dining hall. The children are already seated and waiting for our arrival. Plates of food are laid out. Sandwiches and biscuits and dark moist cake heavy with fruit. Salted meats and various types of poultry and portions of cold rabbit doused in parsley sauce. I eat a chicken leg. It is tender for once. They must have killed some younger hens for the wedding. A welcome change compared with the old boilers that are usually served up to us. Many bottles of wine are opened. For the first time I see women drinking wine. And there is no holding back. Glass after glass is downed. The noise level rises. I get into the spirit of things and drink my first glass very quickly. Sarah refills it for me. I drink again. A superb cabernet sauvignon. I eat a large slice of the rich fruitcake and wash it down with wine. Bliss.

The bride and groom sit with the council at a special table. No sign of the bride's or the groom's parents. Or the old man in the red gown who conducted the wedding service. Gerrard clinks the side of his glass with a spoon and clears his throat.

'Dearly Beloved,' he begins. 'Today we celebrate the strength of our community through the union between two young people. And to remember who we are and who we are not. Remember those who came before us who did not submit. Those that are called Diggers do look upon the ranting practice to be a kingdom without the man, which must rust and corrupt and which thieves may break through and steal away. It is a kingdom that lies in objects. Community with a variety of women is the only life of the five senses which is the life of the beast or living flesh. Ranting is the resurrection of the unclean doggish beastly nature. Do not be tempted by this devouring beast, the ranting power…'

Ranters again. A preoccupation of the original Winstanley. Gerrard continues to speak, louder and louder, faster and faster. I don't understand any of it. Except the bit about the mark of the beast, the number 666, which he somehow links to numbered coins spent on wine and food and therefore intrinsically evil. 'If you touch this money the mark will come upon your hand. Buying and selling is the great cheat, that robs the earth one from the other and makes some rulers, some kings, others beggars…'

I can sense the excitement of the crowd at Gerrard's words. Someone starts to sing. Others join in. Sounds like some sort of folksong. And then some of the women get up from the table and begin to dance. It is wonderful to see them moving together, arm in arm, tapping their feet, clapping their hands. They move in graceful circles, the tips of their scarves flip up and down and their long skirts swirl around their ankles. The men and children watch. The wine flows.

Eliza and Sarah get up to dance. Eliza grabs my hand and I join in. It is hard for me to work out what to do but I try. Eliza holds both my hands. I am whirling around and around. Her long hair flows around her face like white silk, her eyes are on fire.

Suddenly a group of older women rush to the bridal table and grab Elsa by the elbows. She pretends to resist but they drag her to the cleared space on the floor. I recognise the widows who sit with me at meals. They are all there, pushing and shoving Elsa. They stand in a circle around her. The artificial daisy pinned to the front of her scarf has fallen down over her forehead. She is trembling.

There is a sudden silence. A door slams shut. A person dances in from the side of the hall. It is obviously a woman. But who? She is dressed in men's clothes, standard Digger gear; denim overalls, heavy boots, leather hat. She has a stock whip in her hand. What the hell is going on? The cross-dresser is cracking the whip around the circle of widows, flicking their long dresses around their legs. They melt away leaving Elsa and the woman with the whip together in the centre of the room. The air is electric. The whip cracks again. This time the flower on Elsa's head is the target. Crack! Crack! It lands on the floor.

Then the cross-dresser lays down her whip and grasps Elsa by the shoulders and thrusts her pelvis into Elsa's crotch, grunting and groaning in a grotesque parody of the male sexual act. Elsa stays absolutely still, her eyes closed. The cross-dresser shouts out in triumph and takes off her hat and bows to the crowd. It is Hannah. The people clap and cheer. Elsa is escorted back to her table by the widows. Hannah sits with the men of the council and they toast her with upraised glasses of red wine. The dancing and singing resume as if nothing has happened.

I am stunned. I never thought to see this here. I have seriously misjudged the Diggers. I thought them to be puritanical and repressive about everything to do with the body. But this was not about having sex, it was about rape. As if the older women were telling Elsa that this will be her fate from now on.

I'm back dancing with Sarah and Eliza. I say nothing to them of course. But I worry about the children who have witnessed this act. What sort of message does it send to them? There is nothing subtle at play here. The symbolism of the whip followed by the pelvic thrusting is crude in the extreme.

I will write up this wedding and give it to Max tomorrow in Mudgee. I'll leave out the bit about the simulation of intercourse in the women's dance. I don't trust him to keep his mouth shut. I can imagine what the media would make of it. *Ritual Abuse at Wine Cult Wedding*! The clan stuff and the words of the wedding ceremony are all that Max is getting for now. A nice safe set of notes about a nice safe wedding. I cannot afford another distorted newspaper article about the Commonwealth of Diggers. Gerrard and the council may not be so forgiving of me next time.

For days now Eliza has suffered from insomnia. In the deep of night and in the small hours of the morning, sleep has eluded her. Instead she has reconstructed over and over again what happened to her at the soldier's place. And with the woman in the car. The smell of leather and perfume and the lurch of bodily fluids when the car flew around tight corners. Then afterwards at her house. The brightness of marigolds and the smell of coffee, textures of fabric and skin, metallic blinds rattling at a double door made entirely of glass, sunlight sliced up into black and white stripes.

Eliza drank coffee from a cup with a gold rim; she saw a kitchen with shiny white machines of unknown functions. The woman who lived in the beautiful house said if you ever want to leave I would help you. You know where I am, *my door is always open*... This after she had asked Eliza a lot of questions about her life in Digger Town. Eliza resisted most of these questions. Then she asked one of her own. The meaning of the triple M motif on the flag which flew above the building where she had just been. Oh, said the woman. You should be very careful. The triple M stands for the Mudgee Militia Men.

Eliza is haunted by the death of the blue wren. She had created the fatal moment. If she had not been on that road at that particular time, if the woman had not stopped to pick her up, the bird could have chosen that precise moment to dart wildly from one side of the road to the other without suffering the fatal connection with the clear glass of the windscreen.

It is the day after the wedding. The unmarried women are taking their afternoon rest. Eliza tosses and turns. A dream begins to take shape around her. There is a sound of water. A sudden pain. Something is lost inside her body, she tries to pull it free. The sound becomes a roar. Eliza is being swept away in a sudden flood. And all the while she is tugging and pulling feverishly beneath her skirt. At last she pulls it free. It is the bloodied body of a blue wren. The beak has torn her vulva. She screams with horror and throws the bird into the raging water. Which now changes into dry sand. No water to wash the bloodied mass and take it far from her. Just the smashed body and a terrible heat and the drone of blowflies coming down in a noxious cloud to lay their eggs, winged black seeds against the red flesh of a half-eaten pomegranate.

She forces herself to leap away from the dream. The pale winter sunlight is slipping from the high window. Someone is snoring. Someone else is speaking quietly into her ear. It is Hannah's voice. Eliza is immediately wide awake. Something is wrong. Hannah's words are caught in her throat, she is barely coherent. Eliza has never seen Hannah like this before. Hannah's face is white, and she is terrified.

Eliza rises from her bed. There is a spot of blood on the sheet. She asks Hannah to turn her back so that she can tidy herself. Hannah obeys. Eliza takes a small piece of towelling from her bedside locker and slips it beneath her long petticoat.

'You must come now,' whispers Hannah. She leads Eliza down the stairs.

Outside, the air is chill. Women are gathering together in small groups. Some are carrying baskets covered with gingham cloths. A young boy leads a draught horse along the dirt road. The shafts of a wooden sledge weighted down with rocks are attached to the horse. There is a slow clop of hoofs and the clink of harness and the noise of rubble being crushed beneath the moving sledge. And behind the newly smoothed surface, a small procession of men leading a distraught Joshua by a rope around his neck. His hands are bound behind his back and his feet hobbled.

Women stare at Eliza and Hannah walking down the street. Nobody speaks a word to them. They go to the council room. Most of the men are already inside. Some of them are still in their working clothes. The air is thick with tension and the smell of sweat. Hannah and Eliza are asked to sit in the front row. Gerrard instructs one of the men to light the fire. Before the cold of night comes down. Eliza knows that he is signalling to the assembled group that there is a long session ahead.

She sits very still. She cannot meet his eyes when he comes and sits next to her and inquires after her health. 'Why am I here?' she manages to say at last.

'To give evidence. You were a witness to a serious crime.'

She is not surprised. From the moment she saw Joshua being led along the street like a roped steer she had known that Munna had reported his treatment of her to the council. Eliza's dilemma is resolved. She does not have to take action against Joshua. The council will do it for her. But under their laws there must be three witnesses to a crime before a person can be punished.

Me and Munna. Who was the third? Shirley Foster? And what if Joshua tells the council of my bargain with him? My silence in exchange for the Roll. I will be finished.

The accused is lead in. His thick mouth is hanging open and his eyes are darting around the room like a demented fox.

'There's been a dreadful mistake...' he begins.

Gerrard raises his hand to silence him. 'Hold your tongue Brother Joshua. You will be given every chance to defend yourself in due course.'

Gerrard names the jury. Twelve men come forward. Joshua is given the right to challenge any one of them. His head is hanging down and he looks dazed. He nods assent to the members of the jury. Two men come from the back of the room and undo his hands. The fetters around his ankles are freed.

Munna is brought in. She gives Eliza a big smile. Eliza does not respond in case the men of the jury are watching her. She does not want them to think that she is in collusion with Munna. Her guilt over Munna and her fears for her welfare have disappeared. Instead, she prays for her own personal survival. To be forced to leave this place, her animals, her plants, the paddocks and gardens scored with multiple imprints of her childhood feet, the people whose names are so familiar to her that they have ceased to be names, to walk through *that open door*...

She can hear her uncle's voice droning on. 'There is no such thing as an individual, we are always more than one. There can never be a true dialogue within one separate being.

By our rules and our communal love of God do we create one entity out of the many. *Worke together, eat bread together…'*

She tries to calm herself. She closes her eyes and chants silently, I am nothing, I count as nothing, if I am to be sacrificed for the good of the group so be it.

Gerrard is still speaking. He is asking the permission of the council for Sister Josie to be present. He would like her to bear witness to their justice system in action. So that there can be no misunderstanding later. Someone tells him that she is out of town, gone to Mudgee to meet her supervisor. Gerrard frowns.

'She is back,' says Hannah. 'I saw her come into the dining room after lunch.'

Josie is sent for. The fire crackles and smokes, the men scuff their boots on the wooden floor. Hannah lights candles and places them around the room. Joshua is given a chair to sit on. He is slumped and folded down like a broken wing.

At last Josie arrives. She is carrying a clipboard and a pencil. The trial begins.

I'm running late. The wagon is coming for me in a few minutes and I am still trying to get my hair dry by fluffing it out with a towel. Simple tasks take so long to do here. Eating breakfast, walking to the barns for tools, walking to the fields a kilometre away, walking back to the dining room for lunch. Going to the toilet in one place, washing bodies in another. Walking walking walking.

I enjoyed the bathhouse at first. The communal ritual of it. The smell of gum leaves burning in chip heaters, the steam flooding up into my face from scalding buckets, the shock of cold water thrown over hot skin. The harsh bristles of the scrubbing brush for the scouring of calloused hands and feet, the fresh slivers of yellow soap smelling of citronella and caustic soda. There's something about the movement of water and the washing of bodies. The women are more animated here. They laugh and tease each other over the top of the partitions.

Now I find myself becoming increasingly irritated with

everything. I am compiling an Energy Budget based on a typical day in the lives of the unmarried women. I am shocked by the waste of time and effort involved in performing basic tasks. The Energy Budget is part of the report that I am writing for the council. I want them to restructure the places where women work. Hot running water, inside toilets, washing machines. It would not change their belief system one jot yet it would make the lives of the women so much easier.

What is the point of these petty annoyances? Surely it is nothing to do with religion. Aunt Winifred is a devout Christian yet she has everything that opens and shuts in her house in Sydney. Try telling her that she is somewhat less holy than these people here just because she has a freezer and a clothes dryer. And then run for it.

I hear the noise of wagon wheels approaching the hut. Ned is knocking at my door. I throw my papers into my bag and climb aboard. I am the only one riding in the wagon today so I sit beside him on the driver's seat.

We drive slowly through the main street. The town looks shabby in the morning light. At first I thought it quaint and charming, rather like a purpose-built movie town. But now that I have experienced the frustrations of living within an inconvenient relic from last century, I have changed my mind. Quaint and charming are idle words that fall from the lips of a casual traveller, not from one who is forced to live here day after day. This town needs an urgent bulldozer through it and new dwellings with aluminium joinery and electric lights and modern plumbing fixtures. What was it Joshua said when I asked him why they did not remove the painted signs outside the history room? *To remember where we have come from, to remember what it is that we are not.* Okay, preserve the façades of old buildings at the front of the new and fill an art gallery with sepia photographs and build a couple of simulated long-drops complete with plastic houseflies if that's what it takes. But why make people suffer in the present like they once did in the past because of an outdated relationship between memory and identity?

Five days have passed since Max brought the newspaper article to the produce shop. He must be hanging out to see what reaction I got from the council. He will be pleasantly surprised.

A Channel Ten News helicopter was seen hovering over the town. No one paid it any attention. Gerrard told me that the people were used to being stared at from the air. Light planes once circled the town bringing tourists on sightseeing trips. After complaints about newly hatched poultry dying of fright and horses bolting, the tourist company had been forced to stop their activities.

I'm at the gate. I ask Ned to inform me when he goes out on the next food run to the ferals. I'm sure that Eliza and Sarah and some of the other women would like to come too. He shrugs his shoulders and says that he hasn't had any instructions about us coming with him again. Was it to be a regular thing?

I sit in the shelter. A dull day with high white stringy clouds. Not a breath of wind. Someone has scribbled graffiti on the wooden seat. *For sale hot digger chick ring... blonde babes! dying for it, email mmm@blahel.com.au ...*

I feel as if someone has cursed me to my face. I try to erase the words with spit on my handkerchief. I rub and rub. No luck. I take a lipstick from my bag and cover the words with red gloss. Good. All gone except for *ring* and *dying for it...*

The taxi arrives. It's the same driver that brought me back from Mudgee last time. A talkative man called Jonny. He's a Croat, lived here thirty years. His accent is so thick that I can barely understand him. I let him rattle on about the affairs of the town and settle back into the comfort of the back seat. He wants to know how I'm getting on in Digger Town, did I know that my name was in the papers? The pubs were full of talk...

Then he asks me if I've ever seen members of the cult eat babies or practice the black arts. He crosses himself as he speaks. I resist the urge to spin him a yarn. Instead I tell him that the only torture I've seen recently was in a documentary about the civil war in the former Yugoslavia. I saw graphic shots of skeletal Muslims being hacked to death. A camp in Bosnia I think. Or was it in Croatia? Can't remember.

He falls silent. I've acted like a racist bitch but I'm glad he's quiet. Besides, I am not paying him a taxi fare to ask me ignorant questions about the Diggers. Now that he has shut up I can enjoy the movement of the car, the smooth road, the expectation that I am travelling towards hot coffee and good food.

Jonny drops me off at the café in Market Street. I pay him and ask for a receipt. I book him to take me back in two hours time. He writes something down in his notebook. I go into the café. I'm surprised to find Max already here. He's standing at the counter ordering coffee and muffins. He turns around when I call his name. His smile, the shape of his mouth, the line of his cheek, something gets to me. A ridiculous feeling of grief and loss. I'm sure he's forgotten all about the brief night of passion that we shared. I hope so. If he ever brings it up I'll die of embarrassment.

But it's not sex on his mind today. He is agog with curiosity. He tells me he has been walking on eggs since he saw me last. Not tarred and feathered yet Josie? Run out on a rail? An end to your brilliant career?

'It was hell,' I say. 'Gerrard made me sweat it out until the council meeting, only to tell me that it's no big deal. Every few years there is a moral panic about the Diggers from the outside. He told me to add the article to the others in the history room. There are boxes of cuttings going back fifty years.'

'Wow,' says Max. 'Someone should do a content analysis.'

I am irritated with his response. He turns everything that I say about the Diggers into a possible research topic. I tell him so right to his face. With feeling.

He laughs uneasily. 'Can't help it. I've got frustrated students on my back.'

I gulp a mouthful of coffee and light a cigarette. I am being a little unfair. After all, I am taking advantage of the Diggers too. I salve my conscience by telling myself that there is some reciprocity between us. I tell Max about the report that I am preparing for the council about the difficulties in the lives of the women. He frowns when I get to the bit about the running water and household appliances.

'Don't try to change them too much,' he says. 'They'll lose their exotic appeal.'

That does it. He's making them sound like a bowl of ripe fruit. I blow my stack. I yell at him. 'You try working like they do, you try!'

The woman who works in the café comes out from the back room to see what is happening. 'Need any help love?' she asks. I shake my head. We walk out into the street and head towards Lawson Park. The high wispy clouds have melted away. Bright sunlight washes down from a deep blue sky. A cool breeze flows around my face. It smells of the river, dark, earthy, secretive.

'We can't go on like this,' says Max.

'Like what?'

'You have an anger problem.'

I am shocked. And scared. This guy is my supervisor. He can make or break me. I decide to bluff it out. 'I'm under stress. I'm not usually like this. Forgive me?'

Max sits on a bench beneath a towering gum. The Cudgegong River slides past, still running high from the unseasonable rain a few weeks ago. I throw a stick into the torrent. It turns round and round in a dun-coloured whirlpool. I light a cigarette and join Max on the bench.

'Are you angry with me or with what you're doing?' he asks.

'My work is going well. Most of the time.'

'Then it's me.'

'No.'

He hesitates. 'If it's something to do with that night in Balmain…'

I interrupt him. 'I don't know what's happening to me. Everything seemed so simple and clear in the beginning. I

121

move in, I study the inhabitants, I write it up. But now I'm starting to question the possibility of the whole exercise.'

He looks relieved. 'This happens to all of us in the field. It's normal.'

'What should I do?'

'Nothing. Except stop taking it out on me.'

I promise him that I won't attack him again. He has the grace to admit that his remark about 'exotic' was over the top. He knows that change happens in communities whether or not they have a sociologist living with them. And from what I have already told him, he suspects that the Commonwealth of Diggers is about to implode. The outside world is yapping at their heels and they know it.

I give him some pages of notes that I have written for him. He gets very excited about my description of the wedding and the speech that Gerrard made about the Ranters. 'What does this mean?' he asks. 'Community with a variety of women?'

I shrug. 'I'll have to study it a bit more.'

I'm pretty sure that Gerrard means indiscriminate fucking when he uses terms like 'the excessive community of women' and 'this devouring beast, the ranting power' but I don't want to talk about anything sexual with Max at the moment. I am still embarrassed at his mention of that night in Balmain.

We walk back to his car. He gives me my mail. I ask him to get me some books about the history of ranting. I don't mention that there is an original Ranter's document somewhere in Digger Town or that I helped Eliza in an abortive attempt to steal it from the history room. I know that this will set him off once again about the dangers of colluding too closely with my subjects.

I arrive at the taxi rank. No sign of Jonny. Instead a white tourist van pulls up with Greg at the wheel. 'Hop in,' he calls out cheerfully. 'Jonny had an emergency, he can't do the run.'

I am furious. I tell him I'm waiting at the rank for a taxi not him.

'We're part of the same company,' says Greg. 'If you don't come with me, you'll have a bloody long wait.'

I climb in. I am determined not to engage him in conversation. I take out a book from my pack and pretend to read.

'Cheer up,' says Greg. 'This is a lot cheaper than taking a cab.'

He introduces me to the other passengers. No Japanese tourists this time. A middle-aged woman with stylish hair and two young men wearing Raybans. All from Sydney. They express interest in buying honey and wine, they exclaim over coloured brochures with pictures of bee hives and oak barrels and historic stone buildings.

Greg starts his tourist patter. Once again I hear all about the settlers and the bushrangers and the planting of the first grapevines. Boring boring boring.

At last he drops me off. I sit in the shelter and ring the bell and wait for the wagon to appear. I open my letters. The first one is from Jeanette. *Briony wants to leave school and look for a job. What do you think? She's almost eighteen and can do what she likes of course. But Rowley and I believe that she needs more education. I'm a little out of my depth here Josie. Please let me know what to do. As soon as possible...*

The second from Briony. She wants to do more than leave school, she wants to leave Canberra. *I'm trapped here mother, bound and gagged. The roads go round and round, I want out from plastic city. I have somewhere to go. To people who understand me. Please please don't worry... I have never been so happy... I know that I am doing the right thing for me at this time...*

My stomach lurches with panic. Briony has suffered from bouts of depression since she was twelve years old. I have always managed to coax her out of it. The worst time was just after Russell died. She seemed to lose interest in everything, slept away the hours, couldn't be bothered to wash or eat or leave the house. It lasted about eight months. But this sounds different. She is not immobilised with depression. She is on the move, she has obviously made plans. But towards what? Who are these people who understand her? Why hasn't she told me where she is going? Is it because she knows that I will not approve?

I should never have left her with Jeanette and Rowley. If I had not been awarded the research grant, we would still be living together in Balmain. But would this have made any difference? What do I really know about my daughter? I don't know if she has ever had a lover. I don't even know if she is straight or gay. I have always given my children the option of complete privacy about their sexuality. I never ask any questions and they have never offered me any information. I did this because of Aunt Winifred. She spied on Megan and me. She would stand behind the curtains watching us out on the streets talking to boys. She would put us through the third degree when we came inside. She is one of the old school who believe that if a male and a female are physically in the same place, sex will inevitably occur. She spent a lot of time and energy making sure that this did not happen to us. We lied through our teeth of course. Megan still calls Aunt Winifred the sex cop. I would feel a complete failure if I ever heard my children saying things like that about me.

Briony is almost eighteen years old. When I was her age, I had been independent for two years. Fallen in and out of love twice, got pregnant, had an abortion. Briony has never done anything to worry me except for the brief attacks of depression.

Once her care was my duty and my obsession. Every morsel of food that passed her lips, every sheet she lay upon, every garment she wore, every moment she lived through, every comfort, every pain.

Now this control must pass from me to her. But I don't know how to do it. Do I stand by and let her spread her wings or do I rush to her side and force her to go back to school? Do I even have the choice?

The wagon lumbers up to the fence. It is driven by the same man in white overalls that came for me the first day I arrived. The bonded man, forced to be the servant of another in punishment for some perceived misdeed. I don't even know his name. He is not allowed to speak to me.

I forget how long it is I have been here. The moment shifts.

It is that same hot day and I have my black umbrella poised above my head and I can hear the droning of insects. The sun is burning through the black fabric, the flies suck moisture from my eyes. I pick up my pack from the wooden seat inside the shelter. I see my lipstick rubbed over the graffiti. *Ring* and *dying for it ...*

I go outside into the clean cool air of a winter's day.

Eliza is taken from the council room with Munna. They are tied together at the hand, Eliza's left to Munna's right. There is a clearing in the main street, a space where once stood a long low wooden building. It has long since succumbed to the depredations of white ants. This is where the people gather twice a year to hear Gerrard Winstanley read the Sixty-Two Laws. And this is where public punishment is carried out.

There are already dozens of people assembled. Some are carrying lanterns. Darkness has fallen. Gerrard calls for more light. Some pitch torches are lit. The pungent smoke stings Eliza's nostrils. Munna begins to snivel and jerks her hand away from the cord that binds her to Eliza.

Gerrard speaks to the crowd. 'Be silent friends, be still. We must wait until more people arrive. Justice will not be done unless there are more eyes to see it.'

Eliza speaks softly to Munna and tries to reassure her. She can see Josie at the back of the crowd. Josie works her way forward to the front. They are almost face to face when the ceremony begins.

A drum is beaten slowly and Joshua is led to the platform at the front. He stands next to Eliza and Munna, still with the rope around his neck.

Gerrard unrolls a long sheet of paper and reads aloud. 'Brother Joshua has committed two crimes. He is guilty of lust and the activities of the beast. He is guilty of trying to blame an innocent for his own sins.'

The drum beats and the smoke from the torches thickens and there is a rising murmur from the crowd. Gerrard raises his voice. 'To show no fear or favour, these two women were interrogated by the jury along with the accused. Other things have been said in other places about the behaviour of the accused. Let there be no rumours or gossip about these women. They have committed no crime except to keep their silence longer than was necessary.'

The bond between Eliza and Munna is severed. The women are released. Eliza helps Munna down from the platform. They stand next to Josie.

Joshua is placed face down upon a barrel. His shirt is torn from his back. A man in a black mask steps up. He has a whip in his hand. The whip is made of strips of thin leather. He dips it into a bucket of liquid and raises it up, flicking it around.

'Salt and water,' whispers Eliza to Josie. 'To make it sting.'

Whoosh! Whoosh! The murmuring crowd watches the whip move. The drum beats faster and faster. One last frenetic roll then it stops.

The man in the mask begins to beat Joshua on his back. The crowd counts aloud; one, two, three! Dark blood springs from the white skin.

Josie is quivering beside Eliza. Her eyes are closed and she is chanting something beneath her breath. Eliza grabs her arm. 'It will be over soon,' she whispers.

Munna is laughing and clapping her hands. The crowd counts; eight, nine, ten!

Gerrard holds up his arms and calls for silence. 'His punishment is over. Let there be no further mention of this matter. Go back to your homes.'

Joshua is lifted up and Doctor Macky swabs his bleeding back and helps him down from the platform. The pitch torches are extinguished. Eliza and Munna walk away hand in hand. The crowd disperses. Mice and insects and the hunting birds of prey take back the night.

I've been back in my hut for over an hour, I've smoked five cigarettes, I've drunk cold bitter coffee from my thermos.

Nothing helps. I am stupid and naive. I believed Gerrard when he told me that the system of laws and punishments were merely symbolic. What the hell was that I just witnessed? If that was symbolic, I'd hate to see the real thing. The raw meat of his back, so cruel.

They called me into the council room. Bring your notebook and pencil they said. And come quickly, there is urgent business to attend to.

I went all bright-eyed and bushy-tailed, excited, feeling full of myself as a privileged observer. Brother Gerrard wants you to make a full report, they said. So that you can document our love for our women and our protection of them.

And then to see Eliza and that poor creature Munna revealing the abuse. Horrific. It's been going on for years apparently. And to think that Eliza witnessed the final act on the same night we went into the history room to search for *The Fiery Flying Roll*. I was terrified that she would tell the council what we had done. She's clever, I'll give her that. She said exactly what they needed to know, no more, no less.

And Munna. Like a torrent it came out, what he had done to her… his penis in her mouth, the threats, the ritual stuff, the swallowing of words and paper… I found it difficult to follow.

Then the sentence. A public whipping followed by two years of forced labour.

I lie on my bed. I close my eyes but all I can see is that bloodied back. I cannot stay here any longer with these barbarians. To hell with my work, I will leave tonight. By foot if necessary. But first I will speak with Gerrard. I owe him some sort of explanation.

I walk towards his house. The street is deserted now, and the smoke from chimneys rises steadily above the roofs. I pass the place where Joshua was beaten. There is still a faint smell of pitch from the torches. A dog is sniffing around the barrel. I thought it had the lean yellow look of a dingo but it is wearing a leather collar. Just one of the mongrels that the children keep as pets. I hunt it off before it discovers the blood congealing in the dust. It runs away with its tail between its legs.

Gerrard's house is set somewhat apart from the other houses, almost at the edge of the town. A large square stone house surrounded with wide verandas, a shingled roof, outhouses, two noisy unchained kelpies. I hesitate at the gate. I wonder if the dogs are safe. Although I have never been inside the house before, I am convinced that I already know what the rooms are like, how they lie to the sun and the wind, how the furniture sits in relation to the doors and windows. In spite of my fear of the dogs, I feel an overwhelming need to get inside. I had a similar experience a few weeks ago near that abandoned house in Mealey Street.

I walk briskly past the dogs and knock at the door. No answer. The dogs have followed me up the steps and they are growling and nipping at my heels.

I knock again, louder this time. Are they already in bed? It's just after nine o'clock. I can see the light of a candle flickering at a side window.

The door opens slowly. 'Don't mind the dogs.'

It's Mrs Nelson from the produce store. She's bundled up in a long coat. On her head is a white frilled cap. 'Oh it's you,' she says. 'What do you want?'

I am taken aback by her rudeness. I tell her that I'm looking for Gerrard. I need to see him urgently.

We stand staring at each other for a few minutes. 'Well,' she says at last. 'You'd better come in. But he's not here.'

I don't know what to do. My desire to leave this town right here and now is beginning to wane. 'Maybe I should come back in the morning.'

'He will be here shortly.' She opens the door and I enter the hallway. She shows me into a musty room at the front of the house. It is cold in here. The fireplace has obviously not been used for a long time. No hint of ash. There is hardly any furniture, just two overstuffed chairs with a small table between them. An empty pottery vase on the mantelpiece and an old black wooden clock, crudely made, and minus the hands. Just a shell. But once I'm sure there was a piano over there and women stood around in long silky dresses and sang risqué music-hall songs. Laughter and music are embedded in these walls. And still a faint hint of orange cake and freshly-poured tea.

Mrs Nelson removes her coat. Underneath she is wearing a long calico nightgown. She sits in one chair and I take the other. The silence is a hostile presence. I swear I can hear the dust motes fall. I try to make conversation with her. I ask her if she was in the street tonight. She shakes her head. 'Busy,' she says. 'I have to sit with Mrs Winstanley.'

'When will Brother Gerrard return?'

'I told you. Shortly.'

I hear a hoarse voice calling from the back of the house. Mrs Nelson gets up from her chair with some difficulty. She leaves the room and closes the door behind her. I wait until she is out of earshot and then I carefully open the door. The hallway is long and narrow. Every door is closed and the darkness makes it difficult for me to see. I creep along the walls feeling my way, praying that I don't bump into anything. The door near the end of the hall shows a light beneath it. There is a murmuring of voices.

I reach the end of the hall. A heavy curtain is strung across the archway. I pull it aside and find that I am in a long kitchen attached to the back of the house. There are candles burning on a polished table, iron pots and kettles crowded together on the top of a woodstove, a rack of white and blue china plates. There is warmth here, and a smell of hot soup. I want to sink down into a padded chair and taste the contents of the steaming pot but I resist the urge. I am already regretting coming here. I can hear Max's voice in my ear, don't let your own moral code intrude. Accept what you find, document everything, keep your mouth shut.

If I am caught spying it will all be over for me.

I want to leave the house through the back door and creep

back to my own. But then Mrs Nelson will tell Gerrard that I came here looking for him. He will know why I came here, he will know that the beating has disturbed me. Better go back and face him. But I need to go to the toilet. Urgently. All that coffee has gone straight through me. I hope that there is a long drop behind the house and that I do not have to go and find a communal women's toilet closer to the town.

I open the back door and look at the partly enclosed back veranda. A bath with taps and somewhere an old fridge motor banging away. A fridge? I pull back a sacking curtain at the end of the lean-to and there it is. An ancient Kelvinator with a metal door handle. Probably runs on kerosene. I can't resist a peek. I open it. Nothing unusual in the way of food. Butter and eggs and milk and dishes of cold meat. A jug of chilled water. A plate of cold boiled potatoes. A bowl of well-chewed chicken bones.

There is a hinged screen next to the fridge. I look over the top and am astounded to see a modern toilet. For a split second I think that I am hallucinating. Make a wish and it shall appear. But it is real, and I make good use of it, sitting to one side so that the noise of my urgent pee is muted by the smooth inside of the toilet before it hits the water. I wipe myself dry with toilet paper. Pink double-sided tissue paper with a faint rose perfume. Obviously not homemade.

I don't dare use the flush but I risk washing my hands. I turn on the tap over the bath. Hot water comes out. I look behind the fridge. Kerosene my arse. There is an electric plug on the wall behind the fridge. Gerrard, I've found you out. You are a fake. You preach one thing and do another.

I am no longer afraid of being discovered, I am bloody angry. And disappointed. I respected Gerrard for his commitment to his religious beliefs. Misguided yes, but authentic. I thought he was the genuine article.

I want to rage at him, accuse him of betrayal.

Then I think about my research. This discovery could make it doubly interesting. Possible chapter headings flood into my mind; The Politics of Appearances, The False Preservation of the Past as a Form of Social Control...

I resolve to keep my discoveries to myself for the moment.

I go back into the kitchen. Still silent except for the soup bubbling away on the woodstove. I go through the curtain into the hallway. The door with the light beneath it is still closed but the murmuring voices have stopped. When Gerrard finally enters the house, I am sitting innocently in the overstuffed chair in the cold front room, my fantasies of musical evenings and silk dresses flown away up the chimney.

All mystery now reduced to its sum of parts, grounded firmly in the present.

6

THE PAST IS A COUNTRY...

Eliza is lying on his bunk when the soldier comes into the room. He is whistling through his teeth making a hissing sound. He stands in front of a mirror. It is too low for him and he has to bend his knees a little. He runs a brush through the short bristles on his head and turns his head this way and that. He opens his mouth and picks at something caught in his teeth with a matchstick. Then he removes his camouflage jacket and hangs it on a peg behind the door.

Eliza makes a small movement and he jumps around with his hands in a karate position. 'What the hell...?'

Eliza sits up. He stares at her. 'What the fuck are you doing here?'

'I'm sorry,' she says. 'I'll leave.'

He looks through the side window. 'Did anyone see you come in?'

She shakes her head. He sits beside her. He reminds her about being careful of the men here. It is not safe for her to come and go in daylight.

'I have found out about you,' she says.

He looks uneasy. 'What do you mean?'

'This place. The Mudgee Militia Men.'

'Who the hell have you been talking to?' He sounds angry.

'No one. I can't remember. A stranger.'

'What did they tell you?'

'Just that the triple M on your flag stands for the Mudgee Militia Men.'

'Just that?'

'Yes, nothing else.'

He sighs and takes her hand. 'Okay then. No damage done.'

She asks him why he is ashamed of his name. He denies that he is. On the contrary, he is bloody proud of the work that they do. She asks him what this is. He refuses to answer. Instead he begins to stroke her face and hair, gently, then more firmly.

She submits to him. She closes her eyes and prays that he does not ask her if she wants to make love.

Say what it is that you want. What does she want? She wants to make contact with his body, she wants to touch his smooth face with the sharp bones… but if he offers her a choice, her desire to touch him will cool. She will have to leave.

He enters her body and begins to thrust. This time, she does feel something, a tension in her nipples and in her vulva. She has felt this before. Munna in the bath with the feathers. The soldier sucking her nipples in the bush. She keeps her eyes closed and her lips clamped together.

He jerks and groans and withdraws. He asks her if she came. She remains silent. She tries to get up. He puts one hand into her vulva. At first she resists but soon finds herself unable to move. She is terrified. She does not know what is happening to her body. The tension is agonising. She hears herself groaning, deep, like an animal. Then there is a tremendous burst of pleasure between her legs, down her legs, through her head. She screams. He places his hand over her mouth and tells her to keep quiet. She can smell her fluids on his hand. She wants to die with shame.

She opens her eyes. He is smiling at her. 'Clever girl,' he says.

She pulls her pants and petticoat back into place. She buttons her blouse.

He sits beside the bunk on a wooden stool and rolls a cigarette. 'You are very beautiful,' he says. 'But now you must go.'

Her body feels as if it belongs to somebody else. She can't move.

'Hey, don't look so tragic,' he says. 'There's more where that came from. We can meet in the bush and fuck our brains out. It's safer than coming here.'

She says nothing. Her head is pounding. She closes her eyes again. She wants to lie very still, disappear into sleep, lose all sense of herself.

The door opens. The soldier drops his lighted cigarette on the floor in fright. The crisp fresh air of a winter's afternoon floods into the stuffy bunkroom.

Another man stands in the doorway, blocking the light. 'Well well,' he says. 'What have we here?'

'She's just leaving,' says the soldier. 'Get up bitch and get out.' He has retrieved his smoke and is puffing at it nervously.

Eliza is shocked at the change of tone in his voice. She leaps up from the bunk and pulls her scarf over her head.

'Jesus fucking christ,' says the stranger. 'You stupid prick.'

Eliza tries to block her ears. But the stranger raves on and on, accusing the soldier of breaking the rules and putting them all in danger. 'There are plenty of girls in the town dying for it. Why the fuck bring a Digger cunt in here?'

The soldier protests. 'She came here of her own free will. I didn't ask her to.'

The stranger calms down a little. His tongue flicks in and out like a snake. 'I get it,' he says. 'Forbidden fruit and all that shit.'

The soldier gabbles something about this being part of his test. Do the worst thing without the slightest twinge of remorse. That was the instruction from the leader. What could be worse than breaking in a Digger chick?

The stranger's tongue dances even more furiously. 'Did you force her?'

The soldier takes a drag of his cigarette. 'No way. I did something more devious. I turned her on. She's hot for me.'

Eliza has heard enough. She tries to push her way past the stranger and get out of the bunkroom.

The stranger bars her way. He pulls her scarf from her head and fumbles with her long white hair. Eliza stands very still. She suffers his touch for a moment, too afraid to move. The stranger drops his hands to Eliza's breasts. He squeezes them dispassionately, as if he was testing melons for ripeness. It hurts her.

The soldier puts his arm around Eliza's waist. 'Come with me,' he says in a low and urgent voice. 'Now.' Somehow they manage to leave the bunkhouse.

The stranger stands in the doorway with his arms crossed, laughing. 'Bring her over to the main house Ivan. Introduce her to the other boys.'

They walk as quickly as possible to the screen of eucalypts and twisted willows at the front of the property. Eliza pulls his arm from her waist. 'Is it true?' she asks.

'Is what true?'

'You only touched me because you were told to commit a sin.'

'In the beginning.' He leans against the thick cork of a willow trunk. He relights his cigarette butt. 'But now you've wormed your way into my head. All I can think about is your body. You're driving me crazy.'

Eliza turns her back on him. She picks at the protruding ridges of bark on the trunk. 'Ivan. So that's your name.'

He blows out a mouthful of smoke. 'Yeah.' He tries to kiss her but she resists. She walks to the gate and it opens automatically in front of her. She can feel something wet and sticky slide into her pants. 'Goodbye,' she says.

He is right behind her. 'Wait,' he says. 'Sorry for calling you a bitch. That was to protect you. So that he wouldn't know that you were special.'

She walks away. In her hand is a piece of bark from the

twisted willow. She holds it so hard that it cuts into her hand. She looks back to make sure that the soldier had gone back through the gate. She walks for a few minutes longer, then slips beneath a fence at the side of the road, using the bark to hold the top strand away from her head so that the spikes on the barbed wire do not catch her headscarf.

There is a screen of low scrubby eucalypts at the side of the paddock. She walks quickly down the slope behind them to a narrow creek. Refreshed with the recent rain, the water holes are deep and dark. She imagines that she sees the sleek body of a yabbi or at least the suggestion of an indolent claw snapping at a passing shadow on the surface of the water. She looks upwards and apologises to whomever or whatever may be watching, then removes her scarf. She dips it into the water, half expecting a blackish-green claw to tug at the other end. She removes her pants and washes between her legs with the wet scarf. Again and again she plunges the scarf into the creek and floods her vulva with the smell of wet earth and leaf mould and the sweetness of water that has flowed down a bush-covered hill.

It is sheltered on the banks of the creek. She finds a warm rock and lifts her petticoat. The fine hairs on her bare legs are turned into gold by the late afternoon sun. She sprays out her long hair around her face. The warmth of the sun makes her sleepy. She fights against it. She has formed a plan of action. She will place herself in a position of danger that will bring things to some sort of conclusion. She cannot go on like this, neglecting her duties in the schoolroom, avoiding Josie, sinning against the name and reputation of her uncle.

She will give God another chance to reveal his plan for her. Either she will surrender herself completely to the soldier, or she will never see him again.

Whips and ropes lie deep in our collective memory. I had let mine lie dormant, a glimpse of bodies swinging from eucalypts, sudden silences in country pubs when stories barely old enough to be history are told and retold; stories of charred skulls turned up by the plough, banks of rivers washed away to reveal sinister remains more recent and more terrible than the fossilised bones of giant marsupials.

The past is a country that cannot be revisited except through contemporary visions of imperfect memoir and static image. The hierarchy of the old world was strung together with beatings and hangings. Settlers thrashed their assigned servants, soldiers thrashed the convicts, and everyone beat up children and blacks and the Irish.

I had never thought that I would be confronted face to face with these fragmentary nightmares. What was once a distant archaeology of terror has become focussed on one individual human back, on fire with blood and salt.

I told Gerrard that the public beating had horrified me and that I wanted to leave at once. I turned his own words against him. Remember, I told him, remember what you said when I asked for some old maps of the town? You told me to concentrate on the present. Leave the past alone. But you don't do this. You constantly refer to the written history of your movement. Not that it works. You pretend to live as your founding group did, but you cannot duplicate the conditions. You merely skate over the surface. Why bother? What are you trying to prove?

'You puzzle me,' he said. 'Joshua committed a serious crime. I thought you would appreciate our care and concern for a helpless woman. What would you have done? What is your solution?'

I told him what would have happened to Joshua on the outside. Prison for ten to fifteen years. Ruin. Public hatred.

'Joshua has tasted pain and fear, almost equivalent to what Munna felt,' said Gerrard. 'And he did not receive the full punishment. There were only two witnesses to his crime instead of three so he did not have to suffer twenty lashes. He took ten instead. And rather than being locked away and eating money extracted from the labour of innocents he will work hard on the land and produce food for our community. Why is your way better?'

Then to my surprise he offered me the job of history room attendant for the rest of my stay. He said it was to help me with my research but I wondered if this was another way of punishing Joshua. To see an outsider in his place would be a full and final humiliation.

I promised to think it over. And let him know. I would wait until morning, see the sun come up over the hills one more time. Then either stay and do what he wants, or pack my bags and leave my cardboard hut and my brilliant career forever.

That was two nights ago. I ran from his house, away from the barking dogs, away from his treachery. Back in my hut, I started to go quietly mad. What had I seen and not seen? Pink toilet tissue? Power points?

If I was hallucinating, I had reached a low point of banality. Either that, or my longing for the taken-for-granted necessities of modern life had finally flipped my mind. I had to share this new knowledge with someone. I had to check it out, make sure that I was not losing my grip.

I went out into the night once again. It was beginning to grow cold. The damp ground was already crisp with a thin rime of frozen dew. The windows of the unmarried women's dorm were dark and empty. I crept up the stairs. Bodies tucked into beds, the gentle sounds of women breathing. There was someone in the spare bed where I had once slept. I pulled back the coverlet. Munna. Fast asleep. I sensed a movement behind me. It was Eliza, still fully dressed. She put her fingers to her lips and pointed down the stairs. We went down into the saloon below. Eliza lit a candle.

I told her what had happened. My shock at the public beating, my immediate desire to run away, my discoveries at Gerrard's house. But as soon as I had finished my garbled words, I regretted them. She went very still, I felt, or heard, something leave her body. It sounded like a lungful of breath being slowly expelled.

She guided me to a chair and sat me down beside her. She put her lips close to my ear and whispered, 'I can't help you anymore. You are on your own with this.'

'I'm sorry if I shocked you.'

'I already knew about my uncle's house. He needs help, his wife is ill.'

I was annoyed. 'Others need help too. Look at poor Munna and all that lifting and carrying of buckets. Why one rule for him and not for others?'

I was waiting for her to trot out her usual comment that things have always been done this way but she must have sensed my frustration because she said nothing.

I told her how I felt about the public beating. Word for word she gave me the same explanation that Gerrard had done. She even ended with the same question. 'Why is your way better?'

All I could say was that beating was uncivilised, barbaric, it degraded everyone, the person who had to do the whipping, the victim, the watchers.

She ignored these comments. It obviously meant nothing to her that I was deeply upset. I felt disappointed with her reaction. I thought that we had grown close in the past few weeks. Especially since that time when we went out in the wagon with the food for the ferals. The sessions in my hut with the tape-recorder had been going well. She had given me much valuable information about the community. And inadvertently herself. Her love of the land and her knowledge of birds and plants and wine, her genuine compassion for all living things.

She had set me thinking about the women I share my life with: Megan, Aunt Winifred, my best friend Lynda, Jeanette, Briony. All of them speak of difficult lives. All of them want something they cannot achieve, all of them have a quest. Megan searching for the perfect man to enhance her identity, to make her whole, Aunt Winifred trying to live up to the rigid demands of her Christian dogma, Lynda desperately wanting to get pregnant. Last year she had filled her body with hormones and her ovaries had shattered into pieces. I have been taught a lesson she told me. I wanted it too much and I have been punished for it.

This sort of logic drives me crazy. I told her so and almost lost a friend. It's all very well for you she shouted. You've got Briony and Jack. You don't understand.

I wonder what Lynda would say if she knew that my darling daughter has left Canberra for parts unknown and that I have done nothing to stop her. I was ripped apart with anxiety over Briony after I read the letter from Jeanette but this soon gave way to anger. How dare she treat me like this! She knows what this research grant means to me. She knows that our future economic survival depends on a well-paid job after my thesis is finished. I refuse to run after her. This is what she wants. But I will not. She knows where I am. She is eighteen years old, a woman. Why is she still trying to play the role of mother-hater? Why does she blame me for everything? Why does she fight against me instead of co-operating with me?

Lynda doesn't know what she's missing. Not that I would ever try to convince her. I would only get my head bitten off once again.

God, I hope no one ever reads this. One is not supposed to rage against the Sacred Child. One is meant to take full responsibility for the nature of the beast. What Briony *is* or *is not* will be inevitably laid at my door. But what if I refuse to open that door? What if I give back as good as I get?

I wonder if Eliza has a quest, a longing for something she can never have. She seems preternaturally content. But I wonder if this is a front. She does not live as the other women live. At thirty, she is the oldest spinster in the community. I want to ask her why she is not married. I want to ask her if she has ever been in love. I want to ask her what she thinks about sex. But I am afraid to broach these sensitive subjects for fear that I will upset her. I am dependent upon her as my chief informant.

She was very surprised when I told her that her uncle

Gerrard had offered me the role of historian. She was even more surprised when I accepted his offer.

'But listen,' I said. 'How can I refuse? A wonderful chance for both of us. Maybe we can find out more about the document you were looking for.'

She was silent. I didn't push the matter.

Two days have passed since this conversation. I have hardly seen her. I have been very busy in the history room. I've spent many hours reading newspaper cuttings and diaries and books. It is a different experience working here alone without the heavy breathing of Joshua over my shoulder, guiding my research, closing books that I had opened on the table, concealing documents that he did not want me to see.

I have discovered a thick book with a dark green cover. It was at the bottom of a pile of other books, wrapped in brown paper, and carefully tied with string. Hand-written in the copperplate fashion with a fine nib. Notes and comments about historical happenings at Digger Town. I wondered why this information was kept separate from the official diaries. Then I read it and I understood.

This book contains the secrets of the community, the happenings that had been deemed unfit for the eyes of school children studying their own history. Sexual secrets, names of people who had been banished, documentation of a breakaway group. Twenty years ago a group of families had challenged the theology of the Diggers and the strict rules of the community. They had left and started up a rival community in the district. The first half of the entry was a record of the time and date, a list of the agricultural tools and animals and furniture and wagons they had taken with them, the names and clans of those who had left. The second half was written in a different hand, a mad rave against those who had left.

These traitors are nothing but Ranters, brought from the past into our midst by Satan although they would deny that he exists and that he is merely another mischievous face of God. Those who preach no difference between heaven and hell, between good and evil, between sinful and holy, those who seek the immoderate use of women, those who claim that perfection comes from a profound lack of remorse, those who cry out that light is the source of all darkness, that God is indeed the sole author of all sin... that He holds the keys to salvation through the body, the key to the world (the womb), the key of authority to fulfil all lusts (the brain), the key to life after death (a small bone in the back). Evil Ranters! To bring his holy name to live within the filth of the body, within the unruly appetites of women, within the bowels as bitter as wormwood... Curb! Curb these appetites, unless families and kingdoms fall as surely as dead stars through the endless night...

I leafed through the rest of the diary. The so-called Ranters were never mentioned again. They brought this hatred down upon themselves simply because they wanted to leave the authoritarian rule of Digger Town. I was intensely curious about their fate. I had never heard of a rival Christian commune in the area. Max didn't know about them either, I'm sure of it. They seemed to have disappeared from the face of the earth.

On the last page of the green book a reference to me! The writer (Joshua?) claims that my research is part of a conspiracy lead by Gerrard Winstanley and his niece Eliza. A warning that my arrival could be the beginning of the end for Digger Town. *She will preach a private liberty that will turn wife against husband, son against father...*

I didn't know whether to laugh or cry. I admit to being a little afraid. I am not accustomed to being seen as powerful and disruptive.

The green book is a goldmine. I can't wait to tell Max about it. I took copious notes. I cursed the absence of a photocopier. I wondered why the writers felt the need to document these events in a separate book. If they do not want anyone to read it, why write it down in the first place. Then I felt a shock of recognition. This is precisely what I am doing. Except that I am writing three versions of my experiences here, one for Gerrard Winstanley, one for Max, and one for myself. But who is

the reader of my private notebook meant to be? Myself? My
children? Others after I am dead? I haven't worked this out
yet. I had thought it to be strictly an *aide-mémoire* and that it
should be burnt after I have finished my thesis. But now I am
not so sure.

One last thought. Did Gerrard want me to find the green
book? Is this why he asked me to take charge of the history
room? One thing is clear. His battle with Joshua has a much
longer history than the advent of the public beating. And in
coming to Digger Town I have unwittingly become another
bone of contention between them.

Eliza waits another hour before she makes her move. She
replaces the damp scarf on her head, and climbs up the gentle
slope towards the screen of low trees. She successfully negoti-
ates the barbed wire fence and walks along the road. But she
does not head for the gravel road that climbs up the hill
towards the boundary fence of the Commonwealth of Diggers.
Instead, she goes back to the gate at the front of the farmhouse that is the home of the Mudgee Militia Men. It is locked.
She hides in the thick scrub at the side of the fence. After a
while a ute drives up and a man in combat clothes leaps out
and operates a card in the electronic lock on the gate. It swings
open and the man gets back into the ute and drives through.
The gate remains open long enough for Eliza to slip inside.

The sun has fallen below the line of the western hills. The
air is already growing thin with the promise of a long chill
night ahead. She finds it difficult to believe that she was here
with the soldier in the shelter of these same trees a few short
hours ago. Memory folds down into smaller and smaller boxes,
collapsing in upon itself. Other events have played themselves
out in this place, acts of violence and redemption, wound and
counter wound. She feels aged, as if she has lost hours, days,
years. The present is a dress rehearsal of the past: parallel
events lie side by side with what is about to happen, each one
as historically inevitable as the other.

She does not attempt to hide herself. She walks slowly down the middle of the driveway, keeping a careful eye out for the dobermans. The late afternoon light has flattened the eucalpyts lining the driveway into a uniform mass of dull olive. She moves into a vacuum. Nothing stirs, no birdsong, no insect buzz, no human voice.

There are three vehicles parked beside the ute. She barely registers the presence of the expensive car with the leather seats. All her attention is on the veranda of the farmhouse. She has an audience; a line of men, holding beer cans, watching her every move. Some are wearing Akubras, others have caps. They are dressed in various types of combat fatigues. Some are wearing military boots, others have running shoes.

She walks up the veranda steps. The men raise cans to their lips. Some of them are smoking cigarettes. There is one familiar face, the man that surprised her and Ivan in the bunkhouse. He holds out his beer can to her and smiles. He has perfect teeth, white and gleaming and perfectly shaped. She ignores him, and walks through the line of men and enters the building. Behind her, a rush of voices and laughter and crude finger signs.

Eliza recognises the room at once. This is the shrine that she saw when she peeked through the window on her first visit to the farmhouse. Posters and photographs of soldiers, swords and knives and guns mounted on the walls, and everywhere, flags with the three-legged figure made of broken triangles running either towards or away from something.

High-backed chairs are drawn up to four long tables. Two women are rubbing one of the tables with yellow cloths. There is a smell of furniture polish. The younger one has a shaved head and a pierced nose sporting a small diamond stud. The older one has fair hair tied back into a bun and is dressed conservatively in a black skirt and white cotton blouse. She is the woman who spirited Eliza away in the expensive car, the one who said *my door is open any time* ...

They are busy with their work. Eliza shuffles her feet. They turn and stare at her. Eliza understands at once that she must hide the fact that she has already met the older woman and been to her house.

The younger one calls to her to come and help them. Eliza obeys. She takes a yellow cloth from a box of cleaning things and waits until the young woman shakes some polishing oil onto the next section of the table.

The older woman asks Eliza if she is visiting or is here to stay. 'I'm Madeline by the way. You are?'

'Eliza.'

'Where are you from?'

Eliza almost says, but you already know. She bites her tongue instead.

The young woman with the shaved head says, 'Oh shit, you're one of those fundamentalists from over the hill, I should have known... sorry.' She takes the duster from Eliza's hands. 'Sit down, I'll get you a drink. Tea or water?'

Eliza is shocked to see a piece of metal imbedded in the woman's tongue. She keeps her voice neutral. 'Water would be nice. Thank you.'

The young woman bustles off.

Madeline whispers, 'What the hell are you doing here?'

Eliza says nothing. To tell Madeline that she is waiting to see what happens next sounds ridiculous. But it is the truth.

The young woman returns with a tray of glasses and a tall jug of chilled water. Eliza drinks gratefully. She is very thirsty. She wonders how the young woman can swallow with that terrible injury to her tongue.

'So,' says the young woman to Madeline. 'This is great, like, meeting her I mean...'

Madeline is rubbing the table vigorously. She asks casually why this is.

'Saves me the trouble. She must be from Digger Town right?'

'Are you?' asks Madeline.

Eliza acknowledges this with a nod. The young woman says

excitedly, 'But don't you see Madeline, I told you that my mother is nearby and that soon I must tell her like, where I am.'

The men have begun to spill into the room from the veranda. One of them calls out to Madeline, 'Hey, Mrs Branson, you shouldn't be doing that. Sit down, sit down...'

'Fucking hell,' says Briony. 'You must be Eliza. I should have recognised you, like, the three b's, blonde, blue eyes, beautiful.' She laughs. 'Don't panic, my mother's words, not mine.'

'Josie is your mother?'

'Yep.'

'She is very worried about you.'

'Then you can tell her that I'm here and that I'm happy and safe.'

Madeline sits at one of the tables. Briony opens a sideboard and takes out tall wineglasses. Eliza helps her place them around the tables.

'What are you doing here anyway?' asks Briony. 'From what my mother told me you lot are never allowed out.'

A noise of boots at the door. The last of the men file in. Eliza looks for Ivan but he is not with them. The men take their places at the table. Trays of food are wheeled in on metal trolleys. Three men wearing white aprons place the covered food on the tables. Bottles of wine are opened. Eliza observes that the reds are from the Digger's vineyards. She helps Briony pour the wine. She comes to where Madeline is sitting.

'Say nothing,' Madeline mouths at her. Eliza asks her if she wants red or white. 'Red please,' says Madeline in a normal voice. Eliza pours her a glass. Madeline is miming something with her head. Eliza interprets it as get out, leave, but she shakes her head. Not yet not yet.

A man appears in the doorway. He is in full military uniform, his chest is covered with bars of stripes and medals. His long grey hair is pulled back into a ponytail. The men seated at the tables scrape back their chairs and stand to attention. He waves them down. 'Please continue with your meal.' He sits at the head of the table in the middle of the room. He raises his glass. 'I see we have a stranger in our midst. No, not a stranger. More like a neighbour.'

He beckons Eliza to his side. She obeys, and sits on the empty seat beside him. He raises his glass again. 'A toast brothers. To another maiden who has seen the light.'

They chant and gulp at their wine. The man takes hold of her left hand and tells her that his name is Terry and that he is very pleased that she has joined them. Did she know that some of the lads here are descended from some early Diggers? A breakaway group, years back. Maybe you have cousins here Miss Winstanley?

Eliza is surprised that he knows her name. She manages to keep her face still.

He pats her hand. 'I hope that your uncle is well.'

Again, she says nothing. The meal continues. Eliza plays with her food. It is very different from what she is used to in Digger Town. A body of a small bird covered in rich brown sauce, a green vegetable that looks like a cross between a cauliflower and a head of broccoli, mashed potatoes topped with an oily substance and unfamiliar herbs. She leaves her glass of wine untouched.

'So,' says Terry, picking his teeth with a plastic toothpick. 'How long do you plan to stay?'

She remains silent.

'Cat got your tongue?'

She chooses her words carefully. 'Ivan will decide.'

He signals to the waiter who is at that moment passing them with the dessert trolley. 'The chocolate mousse. Two bowls.' Then he taps the side of his glass with a teaspoon and the people in the room stop talking at once.

'Anyone here seen Ivan? This girlie wants to consult him. Urgently.'

The man that came into Ivan's room earlier in the day laughs out loud. 'She's already consulted him today. On the floor of the bunkhouse.'

Madeline stands up. 'I know where he is. I'll take her.'

'Thank you Mrs Branson,' says Terry. 'And thank you once again on behalf of the Triple M for your generous financial support.' The men cheer.

Briony follows Eliza and Madeline out to the veranda. Soft yellow lights are burning in the car park. There is a distinct chill in the air. Eliza shivers.

The room behind them is in uproar. The men are singing and calling out and laughing. Madeline tells Briony to go back and finish her dinner. She and Eliza are fine thank you. Briony insists on coming with them. She is like, dying to spend some time with Eliza. She wants to know everything about her mother. What has she told you about me? Is she wild with me for leaving Canberra? I had to get out. That town is the arse-hole of the universe.

They go into a long narrow building behind the farmhouse. Madeline opens the door with a plastic card. A room with a low ceiling, rows of chairs in front of computer screens that flicker and glimmer in the dim light. Plain white walls, a red and black poster proclaiming, *no war, no life ...*

Briony sits at one of the screens and taps rapidly at the keyboard. Noise, colour, moving shapes and symbols that have no meaning for Eliza. She stands in the centre of the narrow room uncertain of what to do.

'Ever seen anything like this before?' asks Briony. 'My mother told me that you lot are living in the dark ages.'

Madeline takes Eliza's arm. 'Sorry,' she says. 'I thought he'd be in here. He usually is this time of night.' She turns to Briony. 'You stay here. We'll go to look for him.'

'Hang on,' says Briony. 'I'm getting to where I want to go.'

She beckons Eliza to her side. 'This is a computer Eliza. The most important thing that has ever happened to the universe. Com-pu-ter. Ever heard of it?'

Eliza almost says I am a teacher, I can read, I am not ignorant. Instead, she shakes her head. She wants to draw as much as she can from Briony.

Madeline looks at her watch and frowns. 'I have to go. Eliza, would you like to walk out to my car with me?'

'Here we go,' says Briony. 'This is the Net Eliza. In-ter-net. And this is the World Wide Web.'

Eliza sits beside her. Music plays, images and words flash across the screen. Intense colours, starbursts of gold and red and blue, the wildness of the music banging and pulsing and screaming, a violent bombardment of all her senses. She starts at the top of the screen, she tries to link the pictures and the words together as if she was opening the pages of an illustrated book. But nothing is in front of her long enough for her to take it in. And although the language is English and she knows the meaning of some of the individual words, she cannot make sense of the logic. Why this word here? Why is it linked with this image? What is this story about? Is there no beginning and no end?

Briony places her right hand over a small oval object that is sitting on a pad next to the screen. 'This is a mouse Eliza. Mo-use. As in cat and mouse.'

'At least come to the door with me,' says Madeline.

Webs and nets, spiders and fish, cats and mice. There is a natural pattern here. If Eliza listens to Briony long enough, maybe it will be revealed to her.

'Are you coming?' asks Madeline.

The screeching music stops as suddenly as it began. Eliza is startled to see the heading unfolding on the computer screen, *The Glorious History of the Diggers.*

Madeline opens the door. 'Eliza!' Her voice is sharp.

'Go on,' says Briony. 'But come back. Like, there are heaps of other hits. Wrong Diggers anyway.' She clicks the mouse. 'These dudes are the boring old fart brigade.'

Eliza reluctantly gets to her feet. Madeline hustles her out-side. The air is freezing. 'Quick, come to the car.' Eliza obeys her. Madeline opens the car door and tells her to get in. Again, Eliza obeys. She is rewarded by the smell of polished leather and the remembered safety of the warm interior. She would like to ride within this smooth machine again.

Madeline turns the key and the car purrs into life. The motor idles.

'You must not tell Briony or any of the others that you have met me before,' says Madeline. 'And you must leave here. At once.'

Eliza promises to keep silent. But not to leave. Not yet. Madeline tries to persuade her. She tells Eliza that the people here are not to be trusted. They have an agenda, no she can't say what it is. The knowledge is too dangerous to reveal. Enough for Eliza to know that she must get out now and never return. And keep her mouth shut about this place when she gets back to Digger Town.

Eliza opens the door and gets out. She has seen a lone man dressed in combat gear appear in the soft yellow lights behind the car. He is jogging slowly and carrying a large pack on his back. She can tell by the posture of his body and the slow lift of his feet that he is exhausted. She is sure that the soldier is Ivan.

'Go then,' says Madeline through the open window. 'But be careful. And take this.' She hands Eliza a card. She releases the handbrake. The car moves down the driveway.

Eliza runs after the soldier to the edge of the yellow lights. She peers into the darkness. Nothing. A light flashes behind the screen of low trees. She moves cautiously towards it. Ah, here is the bunkhouse. She turns the doorhandle and peers inside. Ivan is sitting on his bunk, dripping with sweat. He raises his head and registers her presence. His eyes are dull and expressionless. She hands him a towel from the bedside shelf. He mops his forehead and neck. She sits beside him, not touching him, waiting for him to speak. After a while, he takes her hand. 'What do you want?' he asks.

She tells him about the dinner and meeting Terry and Madeline and Briony. He does not respond, just holds her hand and sighs.

She tells him not to worry, that she has come to no harm. Terry knows her uncle, knows the history of the Diggers and the breakaway group that came to live here many years ago. 'Are you one?'

He stares at her. He does not seem to understand her. She goes further. 'Your father? Your mother?'

'Stop asking me questions,' he says at last. 'I have just run twenty kilometres with fifty kilos on my back. I am more dead than alive.'

She takes off his boots and his socks. He closes his eyes. She pulls the rough blanket over his body and leaves the bunkhouse. She makes her way back to the long low building. She is afraid that Briony will be angry with her for staying away so long. The door is locked. She knocks tentatively. No one comes. She goes to the lighted window and looks within. Briony is still sitting in front of the same computer screen. Eliza taps on the window. Briony opens the door.

'Thought you'd fucked off in the merc with Madeline. Come quick, have a look at this.'

Eliza looks within the screen. This time, there is no sound, just moving images. There is Digger Town, in full colour, moving beneath her. It is as if she is a bird flying slowly overhead taking note of each dwelling. She is moving near the outskirts, she can see her uncle's house very clearly, the fence, the shed where he keeps his dogs. The grass is not quite right. Too luminous, too emerald. The images are clean cut, no dust, no unpainted timber, no untidy edges. A dream of what the town could look like if no wind blew or cold rain fell or firestorms raged, and people had never lived and died there, with their plants and litter and animals churning up the ground.

'Tell me,' says Briony excitedly. 'Like, where does my mother live?'

Eliza points to the street where the hut has been built for Josie. A blank space. Clumps of white marguerite daisies. But no building. Briony says never mind, we can add it later. Once we get the details. Maybe you can bring a photo next time you visit.

But Eliza has left the street. She is flying over the vineyards, loving the sweep and the curve of the rows of perfect plants, in full fruit, in full leaf. But something is not quite right with the picture. The sun is high overhead so it must be summer. There should not be so many ripe grapes at this time of year. And here, oh here, the grapes are wrong. This hill should be semillon, not cabernet sauvignon or shiraz. White grapes not red. And why are they painted so dark. Almost black. Wrong wrong wrong.

Then a cough behind them. And Terry is there, and he snatches the mouse from beneath Briony's hand and kills the town dead. Eliza falls down, she had come to believe that she really was flying over the land and buildings. There were more things familiar to her than strange, more known than unknown. And this is how it *would* look from the eye of a cruising bird; smooth, sanitised a perfect three-dimensional representation. The trees and roofs larger than life, complete with landing places for claws and feathers. And food everywhere; corn-husks, seeds and nests and feeding troughs of hens displayed openly like a well-stocked pantry with its roof removed.

Terry is talking to Briony. His voice is cold and angry. 'How dare you show her this. You are a bloody fool. Or worse.'

Briony whimpers, 'Sorry sorry sorry. I didn't know…'

Then she's gone and Terry is at the computer desk, tapping keys and staring at the screen. Eliza is sitting on the floor, nauseous and disoriented. She wants to take flight again. Terry turns the computer off. He bends over and helps Eliza into a chair.

'My apologies Miss Winstanley. She should not have brought you here.'

He asks her if she is staying here or returning to Digger Town. If she does decide to stay she must convey to her uncle that she is not being held here against her will. He does not want any trouble. No raiding parties from across the border ha ha. Particularly from that quarter. We are almost related. Well some of us are.

Eliza says, 'If Ivan wants me here, I'll stay.'

Terry says that unfortunately it isn't that simple. If she wants to join their group, there are certain conditions. A rigorous training. A cooling off period. Then she'll either be in or out. This community is not closed in the way that yours is. Our mission is an open book. There are many others like us around the world, we have an illustrious record. But there are conditions. Ideological, spiritual, rules of conduct. Eliza of all people would understand that.

She nods. She tells him that she will return tonight to Digger Town. No one knows where she is and she does not want to cause further worry. When and if she comes to Ivan she wants it to be in daylight, in the open, with the blessing of her uncle.

Terry seems to find this highly amusing. 'Hardly likely! But give him my regards anyway. And tell him that you are very welcome here given that you promise to obey our rules.'

'Ivan thinks it may be dangerous for me to come here.'

'Does he now.'

'He told me that some of the men here have a communal attitude towards women.'

'You have nothing to fear.'

Eliza stands up and walks to the door. 'I want to go now.'

'Would you like someone to walk back with you?'

Eliza thanks him for his concern. But she knows the bush like the back of her hand. There is nothing to harm her. However, she would like to borrow a coat or jacket against the cold night air. She had not intended to be out after the frost came down. Otherwise she would have brought her cloak.

Terry nods. He goes to a telephone and holds a brief conversation with someone.

'Briony will bring you a jacket,' he says.

Eliza waits by the door. Terry comes to her side. He lifts his hand as if to touch her hair. She holds herself very still.

'The thing is,' says Terry. 'We have much more in common than you know. I may as well come clean and tell you that I was born in Digger Town. That is how I know your uncle. My parents left there when I was fifteen. They taught me that there are only two things worth living and dying for, blood and land.'

Briony arrives at the door carrying a woollen jacket. She looks somewhat downcast. Terry takes the jacket from her. 'From now on,' he says. 'You are not permitted into this room unless the web master is with you. And you can hand over your cor card.'

'I haven't got one.'

'How did you get in here then?'

'Madeline.'

'Mmmm. Okay, we'll leave it for now. But remember that we must remain vigilant at all times.'

Eliza thanks Briony for the jacket and promises to return it as soon as possible.

'Now go in peace,' says Terry. 'Until we see you again.'

Once out on the road, Eliza moves slowly along the edge of the bitumen, facing the on-coming traffic. She fastens the jacket collar high around her neck and pulls her scarf closely across her face. A few cars pass her, flashing their headlights in her eyes. One car slows down but she keeps doggedly walking with her head down. To her relief the car does not stop.

A half moon gives out a little light. She reaches the fence and crawls beneath the wire. She moves slowly and carefully through the thick undergrowth and dense stands of eucalypts until she comes to the edge of the bush. This is the highest point of the Digger's land. Below her, the pruned and naked vines stand still and silent. Away in the distance she can see the town. She has no idea what time it is but it cannot be very late because the house fires have not yet been extinguished. Ribbons of pale smoke stand high above the roofs, some pulled sideways into long thin ropes by the movement of the cooler air above.

She arrives at a place where the grapes sidle up to the fire-break between the cultivated land and the wilderness. A sudden exhaustion takes hold of her body. Her feet feel heavy, her boots like lead. She wants to catch her breath in this blank space between the nurtured vines and the tangled chaos of the bush. She attempts to gather up a handful of soil but the frosts of this unusually harsh winter have hardened the surface of the ground. The soil is packed down and resistant to her touch.

She resumes her dogged plodding along the rutted clear ground at the edge of the vines. Soon she is at the edge of the town and close to her uncle's house. The grass surrounding the house is brown and frost-burnt. She avoids the gravel roadway and crosses over to the paddock to muffle her footsteps. She passes the barn where the horses have been put to bed for the night. Soon she is approaching the cluster of houses in the street next to her dormitory. She can see a candle flickering in the window of Josie's hut but she does not want to talk to her tonight. Tomorrow she will give Josie the news that Briony is close by and sends greetings to her mother.

She creeps past the houses where the married couples live. She is grateful for the cold night. There has not been a single person walking the streets. The smell of wood smoke and the barking of tethered watchdogs welcome her home.

7

ALL THAT IS SOLID MELTS INTO AIR...

Midnight, Tuesday. I am writing in my journal, my first entry for a few days. I'm tired. It's not just the hard physical work that I do. I'm worried about the progress of my work. Yesterday Ned brought me a message from Max, cancelling our next meeting which was supposed to take place today. He has put me off until next week at the earliest. Max did not give me any explanation. Is he punishing me for my anger problem as he calls it? Or has he cancelled his regular trip to Lithgow to see Fran? Is there trouble between them?

I pumped Ned for information but he just shrugged and said that it was just a co-incidence that he met up with Max. Ned was in Mudgee with a group of men buying some gear to expand the irrigation system when Max came up to them. Ned recognised him from that day when Max and Fran came to see me at the produce shop. Max said, hey, can one of you guys give this to Mrs Tabel? Terse words, scribbled on the back of a white paper bag. *Sorry, have to cancel meeting tomorrow, see you next week, same place same time, work hard, Max.*

It's a damn nuisance. I'm trying to get as much done as possible before I see him again. But I need help. I'm worried that I'm going off on a tangent. I'm playing around with community history instead of the contemporary situation. I'm too much into abstract issues like how the past informs the present instead of working out the current structure of the place.

Max warned me of this at our first supervisor's meeting. Focus on the Commonwealth of Diggers Josie. Don't try to work out the existential mysteries of human co-habitation for all time. Your study is nothing but a snapshot of a particular group of people in a particular place. A tiny fragment, albeit a very unusual and interesting one. That's all.

He doesn't know yet how this 'fragment' has infiltrated into my family life.

Eliza has accidentally found Briony for me. As well as the remnants of the so-called Ranter breakaways. Briony has joined their group. Eliza assured me that Briony is well and happy and sends her love to me. That's all I know.

Eliza told me this news at lunch yesterday. I was so shocked that I dropped my glass of water. My hand just opened and it smashed to the floor. In between Hannah fussing around with a pan and broom and the curious stares from the other women at our table, Eliza managed to whisper a few more sentences. I was bursting with curiosity but it was clear that Eliza was taking a huge risk in telling me that she had gone outside without permission, let alone visit those wicked people who are akin to the devil in Digger history. I managed to hold my tongue and keep my face blank and continue with my meal.

I feel greatly relieved that Briony has been found. Coupled with a tremendous anger with her. So these are the people in Mudgee that Briony has been corresponding with via a chat group on the Net. The ones that she has *learned so much from*, the ones who have *opened her eyes*. This is so out of character. She has never been interested in religion. Or living in a group. She's always been a loner. Until now.

I remember her last letter to me. *I want out from plastic city. I have somewhere to go ... I have never been so happy ...*

She may be but I am not. I'm furious with her for all the

worry that she has caused me and Jeanette. She could have told us where she was going. She loves to be mysterious. Is this a ploy to get attention from me? I bet she thinks that I'm going to rush to her side and say that all is forgiven. I'm not prepared to do that. Not yet. I must write to Jeanette to let her know that Briony has been located and that she is okay. But Briony can stew for a while. I want to teach her a lesson.

I'm not sure how intact the original group is. From the little that Eliza managed to tell me, only a few of the original ones are still there. And they are probably the grown children of the settlers, not the breakaway people themselves.

It is my belief that this event that took place over two decades ago has profoundly shaped the attitudes of the community here today. The sense of betrayal quivers on the page, the mad accusations of the writer in the green book: those who seek the immoderate use of women, those who claim that perfection comes from a profound lack of remorse...

The fear that there is about to be another defection, this time by the young women, is the very reason that the council asked me to come here. Yet the writer of the diatribe against the breakaways is full of dire warnings against the female body. Herein lies one of those tortuous contradictions that bedevil all fundamentalist ideologies. If women are so hated and despised, why the desire to hold them here?

I will be careful in my final report not to mention the historical conflict between the Diggers and the Ranters. I don't want to set them off again. I do intend to recommend big changes. Both in technology and in the attitudes towards crime and punishment. My message to Gerrard will be simple. Change or die.

Ten o'clock in the morning. It is still cold but there is a promise of a fine winter's day ahead. Even though it rained heavily a few weeks ago, Hannah still oversees our usage of water. She instructs me to use a small bowl inside the larger sink. Then she asks me in a quiet voice if Eliza had come to my hut last night. Or Sunday, the day before. I tell her no.

After she has bustled off to supervise the setting of the tables for lunch, I hear the others commenting on the odd behaviour of Eliza. The missing hours, the dereliction of duties. And the whispered complaint that she only gets away with it because of her uncle.

Ned and Thomas unexpectedly bring the wagon to the kitchen door. I can see Eliza sitting alone in the back. I am offered another visit on a food run to the ferals. I accept. I could do with a trip away from Digger Town. A chance to rethink some of my work problems. And besides, this is a good chance to get more information out of Eliza about Briony. And maybe to warn her about the gossip about her that I have just overheard.

Eliza tells me that Sarah has been forbidden to come with us. Sarah is treading a thin line. Last year she was banished for refusing to marry a particular man. Now she is stirring up the other younger women by suggesting that marriage itself should be an option, not a necessity. Radical talk indeed.

I made notes for Gerrard. Forbidding Sarah from going with us on the trip outside is not the right way to keep her silent. She will run as surely as the sun will rise. Is there no place for an unmarried woman within this community? And if not, how has Eliza escaped for so long?

I feel a certain kinship with Gerrard over this. Just as the Diggers are blamed when one of their group goes astray, so too will I be blamed for Briony's selfish behaviour. I am seen as yet another example of the big bad liberal mother. The Diggers are criticised for their old-fashioned authoritarian rule. Damned if you do and damned if you don't.

The wagon rattles along the gravel road outside the boundary. We turn left into Wilbertree Road and go across country as before. But the wagon does not stop at the tourist café this time. We drive straight to the clearing in the bush at the bottom of the hill. Ned unhitches the two horses and leads them to a small creek at the side of the clearing. They drink greedily. There is no sign of the ferals.

Eliza has been silent throughout most of the journey. I have learned patience since I came to Digger Town. I did not offer up any words to her. I know that if I wait, I learn more than if I deliberately pump her for information.

We help to unload the wagon. The Clydesdales are eating oats out of feeding bags that Ned has attached to their bridles. Thomas is sure that the ferals will arrive soon. Ned says we should have waited to unload. We'll give them an hour or two. Then we'll have to make tracks. Thomas leans against a sack of grain and tips his hat over his eyes and dozes.

Eliza and I head up into the bush where we walked together the first time that we came here. By the time we have climbed the steep slope, I am out of breath. We sit on the same outcrop of flinty rock and I light a cigarette. Less cloud, more sun. Otherwise everything feels the same. No wind, no birds. It's as if we never left.

Eliza reminds me of the thick undergrowth and the dangers of fire. I promise to be careful with my cigarette butts. Then she begins to speak. She explains about Sarah and the punishment that she endured when she spoke out against the rules for the first time. I ask questions. About banishment. What does this mean exactly? Was she sent away?

'Not physically,' says Eliza. 'But for three weeks no one was allowed to speak with her, or look her in the eyes, or acknowledge her existence in any way.'

'Ah,' I say. 'Social death.' She looks puzzled. A sociological term I tell her. An expulsion from the group. Devastating. Far worse than physical punishment. I ask Eliza if it had ever happened to her.

She shakes her head. 'God has not seen fit,' she says. 'But it will happen. I am by far a worse sinner than Sarah.'

'Oh yes,' I tease. 'You are so evil, I wonder you can sleep at night.'

Her face goes quite still. Damn. I've blown it. Now she won't tell me anything. But I'm mistaken. She takes my hand and begins to speak quietly but very quickly. It's as if I am looking right inside her head, I can almost hear the wheels turning.

the grass was too green all laid out and me flying over and over the buildings so far below no animals no people, the colours so green and blue and red the roofs instead of grey and me flying...

I hold onto her hand tightly, I don't want to stop her flow in spite of the fact that I don't know what the hell she's talking about.

and your hut not there but Briony said to bring a photo and she will put it on the vacant land instead of the daisies then Terry came and he pressed a switch and it disappeared and I fell down...

I have to interrupt her. 'Briony was there?'

She nods. 'She was working the computer.'

A light begins to dawn. 'Ah, you were looking at a computer screen. Were you playing a game? What did you see?'

all the land and the roads coming out from the town like a wheel and the grapes and the vines summer and autumn mixed together what should have been white was red and then far too deep...

A voice from below interrupts us. It's Ned calling coo-eee! coo-eee!

Eliza asks me if I have a photo of my hut to give to Briony.

'Cameras are forbidden.'

'Can you get one? It would make it complete.'

I ask her what she means but she's well ahead of me, hurrying down the track, and doesn't hear my question. I struggle after her down the steep slope.

It turns out that Ned wants us to come down and sit by the food. He and Thomas are going to the café to ask Mrs Bray if she's seen the feral people hanging around in the last few days. And to see if they can get some more money out of the tourists. Eliza looks nervous. She wants to go with them. Ned reassures her. 'You will be fine here with Josie. If they turn up before we get back, let them do the lifting. Those sacks are heavy. And if Amity shows up with them, ask him to wait for us to return. I have a message for him.'

Thomas has already harnessed the two big horses to the wagon. They head back down the narrow road and are soon out of sight. Eliza sits on the food platform. I light up another cigarette and smoke it right to the end and crush it out in the forty-four gallon drum. We have been here an hour already and no other vehicle has driven down this road. I strain my ears for any sign of the old station wagons coming down the track. Nothing. I wish the ferals would turn up. I'm bored. I wish that I had brought my notebook so that I could at least do some writing while I'm forced to wait here. I join Eliza on the platform and lean against a sack and close my eyes.

Suddenly there is a noise of a vehicle driving along the gravel road. Fast. A van of some sort. It slows down with a squeal of brakes and a great cloud of choking dust and turns into the picnic place. Four men jump from the vehicle. I am immediately alert. Bogans. One has a white staffordshire terrier on the end of a chain. They have shaved heads and pseudo-military clothes. One has a swastika tattooed on his face.

'Look out,' I hiss to Eliza. 'Get ready to run for it.'

But she gets to her feet and walks towards them without apparent fear. To my surprise she greets one of them by name. 'Ivan,' she says. 'What are you doing here?'

They hold a whispered conversation. I strain to catch their words. No luck. She comes over to me, 'It's all right Josie, they're here for the same reason that we are.'

I doubt it, but I keep silent. The dog is trying to get at me at the end of its chain, making ominous noises between a growl and a choke deep in its throat.

The one with the swastika saunters over to me. My blood freezes. 'Who are you?' he asks. 'And what the hell are you doing here with her?'

I refuse to answer him. He asks me again, then shrugs and goes to the side of the clearing. He turns his back on us and opens his fly and urinates noisily against the bark of a tree.

The other three men are turning over the boxes and examining the sacks of food. 'Je-sus,' says one. 'Look at these eggs and corn. We could do with this.'

The one that Eliza greeted by name shakes his head. 'Now boys, naughty naughty, stealing is wrong. This food is given in good faith, have some respect.'

'Hey,' shouts the one with the tattoo. 'We should make a donation too. How about a bag of flour, a Mudgee special?' The others fall about laughing.

'Yeah, come out come out wherever you are, guardians of the forest, people of the land, come out!'

'Yo, watch me hug this tree...'

'Look out, it might fall in love with you...'

'Cut a hole in the bark and stick it with a hot crystal...'

'Then declare it a sacred site,' the tattooed one yells. 'Tree Fuck Dreaming...'

Eliza moves beside me. 'This is them,' she whispers.

I must be stupid. I still don't get it. Eliza tries again. 'They are from the place I told you about, the computers, Briony...'

I am frozen with shock. What the hell is going on with my daughter? She is stupid or ignorant or both. These low-life bastards are from the bottom of the food chain. How has Eliza become involved with them? I must warn her. Enough of the story of the Ranter breakaway group. That should be placed in the past where it belongs. These bastards are only too contemporary.

I'm not afraid of them anymore, I'm wild.

'Get your hands off those sacks,' I shout. 'And go away. There is nothing for you here.' I am wasting my breath. One of the men is busily placing corncobs into his backpack. He does not miss a beat.

'Listen lady,' says the one who made the offensive remark about the tree. 'This is a public place, we have just as much right as you to be here.'

He's right. But I'm not ready to give in yet. 'This food is a gift. To the poor and needy. Can't you respect that?'

They fall about laughing. Ivan says, 'Those lazy bludgers never did a day's work in their life!'

I try to calm myself down. I must learn all that I can about these men. I decide to tell them who I am. 'How's Briony?' I ask. 'How's my one and only daughter?'

A puzzled silence. Ivan breaks it. 'She's fine,' he says quickly. 'Just fine.'

Obviously he already knows that I am Briony's mother. And just as obviously his three companions don't. There is a confused argument, Ivan defending himself, saying he did not think it was important. Why are they asking him? Terry knows, Mrs Branson knows. They don't have a problem with Briony. Or her mother. Why should they? 'Besides, Briony's old lady is not even a resident of Digger Town, she's there doing research. Strictly temporary. She'll be gone soon.'

I could strangle Eliza. It is clear she has told him my life story. I decide to keep them sweet, so I smile and say no worries, if Briony is happy then I am too. Tell her you saw me and that I am fine and that her grandparents and her brother Jack are fine and that my work is going to plan.

They prepare to leave. I am so relieved I feel like kissing the ground. The one who took the corncobs replaces them in the sack. The dog is taken back to the van. Eliza, who has remained silent throughout the whole performance, sits down exactly where she was before. I feel like shaking her until her teeth rattle.

Ivan comes over to us. 'Hey,' he says to Eliza. 'No need to mention that you saw us here. Say nothing to Terry when you see him again. Or to Briony.'

'Have I done something wrong?' she asks.

'No, no,' he answers. 'It's just that the boys get a bit carried away at times. You know how it is. We were just having a bit of fun.'

I bite down on my tongue to keep it silent. Ivan gets into the front seat next to the driver. The van roars away. I pray that they do not meet the wagon returning along the narrow

road. I wait for my heart to stop racing. When the dust has settled, I give it to Eliza right between the eyes. I tell her that
those men are not to be trusted, they are thugs. Why the hell
did she tell them about me? Especially after she found out that
Briony is mixed up with them. She is completely out of her
depth, she knows nothing about them.

She interrupts me. 'But I do Josie. They are Christians…'

I tell her that she's talking through a hole in her head. And
I swear to her that I'll do whatever it takes to turn both her
and Briony against them. Period.

Eliza spends the next two days dreaming, thinking, teaching
her class of little children, and doing her best to avoid Josie.
Meal times are difficult. She cannot get out of sitting next to
Josie at the table. Eliza makes sure that their conversation is
limited to questions and answers of a trivial nature. The weather, the state of the vines after the pruning, the growth of the
green crops between the rows, the fate of the winter vegetables
in the chilly ground, the budding of the fruit trees, the birth of
a set of twins to Hannah's only daughter, the ritual of a double
christening ceremony…

On the third day, Eliza leaves the classroom at lunchtime
and comes out into the open air. The children seem to be more
demanding than usual. They are used to hard physical work
and play but this winter has been too cold for much outdoor
activity. The woodstove in the classroom has been kept burning night and day. Eliza feels stifled, both by the overheated
classroom and the repetitive nature of her work. She fears that
she is losing her patience with the children; the sounding out
of words in the reading primers, the kan-gar-roo j-umps o-ver
the cr-eek and b-al-an-ces on his tail, the L-ord m-ade him so;
the scratch scratch of nibs tracing the letters of the alphabet
between two thin lines; the endless chant of multiplication
tables, two twos are four, two threes are six, two fours are
eight…

There are signs too that the adults are beginning to quarrel among themselves. Just yesterday, Ned and Sarah had waylaid her on the way to breakfast. Ned told a garbled story about a note that he was meant to give to Amity at the foodbank. Sarah was angry with Ned for not doing what she asked. A harmless thing, she said. Such a little thing to ask. Tell her Eliza, said Ned. Tell her the ferals weren't there. She won't take my word for it. Eliza told Sarah that Ned was speaking the truth. Why shouldn't he? And Sarah stalked off refusing to apologise to Ned.

Eliza let her go without comment. She cannot cope with this conflict. A few weeks ago she would have taken charge of the situation, she would have reminded Sarah that she, Eliza, was responsible for Sarah's behaviour and had been asked to report any problems to her uncle Gerrard. But ever since she had flown over the highly coloured and static image of Digger Town, something had shifted inside her. She struggled to give meaning to this shift but there were no words that could adequately describe the difference between *before* and *after*.

To possess knowledge without direct experience had always seemed to her to be a safe and comfortable territory. Planes flew high above, huge silver fish trailing white smoke in the winter, between the cities of Sydney and Brisbane. She knew the brute fact of the existence of planes, both through books and through observing them high in the stratosphere. But she did not know what it would feel like to be inside that silver fish. That is, not until she saw her familiar town and the trees and vines and curves of her home landscape from the point-of-view of a bird in flight. Somehow, this experience with the computer had worked its way into her head like a demented forester determined to slash and burn every familiar thread of meaning.

All that is solid melts into air, all that is holy is profaned...
I am losing hold of a thick and comforting rope that has
always been there for me. Fibre changes into water, hills into
clouds, blood into sand. I am still desperately holding on, but
the rope itself has changed...

Eliza sees Josie walking towards her. She stands in a doorway. Josie comes up close to her. There is an uncomfortable silence. Josie asks Eliza where she is going.

'Ah, to visit my horse.'

'Not teaching today?'

Eliza mumbles something about coming back later. Josie asks her if she is going to ride her horse outside the boundary fence. Eliza shakes her head and hurries away. She can feel Josie's eyes burning into the back of her head. She walks as quickly as possible to the barn. No sign of Stella. Her stall is empty, swept clean. Fresh straw on the floor and bridles hanging neatly on the hook. She sees Joshua in his white overalls at the end of the barn. He is leaning on the handle of a yard broom, observing her.

Eliza does not want to get close to him. She calls out in a loud voice, 'Where's Stella, where's my horse?'

He does not answer. He stands there, still leaning on his broom. She moves a little closer and repeats her question. He does not speak or move but his eyes do not leave her face. Eliza knows that he is not permitted to speak with any of the women. She looks around. The barn is deserted. She moves even closer. 'My horse, where is she?'

He makes a cutting motion across his neck with his right hand. There was no mistaking his sign. Or the triumphant gleam in his eye.

'There must be some mistake,' says Eliza. Yesterday Stella had taken oats from her cupped hands. And snorted twin puffs of condensed breath from her moist black nostrils, and whinnied and tossed her head and allowed Eliza to pick up her feet one by one to check her shoes.

Joshua does it again, he runs the side of his hand along his neck. Only this time he is smiling hugely.

Eliza cries out, 'Who did this, who!'

Joshua puts his finger to his fat lips and beckons her to come closer to him. She is in such a frenzy that she runs towards him and almost knocks him over. 'Has she been put down?'

He speaks her uncle's name. 'Gerrard Winstanley.' She can get nothing further from him. He begins to sweep the floor with long lazy strokes of the broom.

She runs from the barn and races through the paddocks. Her scarf becomes loose and falls off and her long hair flows down her back. She rushes along the streets and past the communal dining room where she can hear the hum of voices and the clink of plates and cutlery. She bangs on the door of Josie's hut. No answer. She runs back to the dining room. Hannah bustles up to her. 'You are late again Sister Eliza.'

The people are eating fried chicken and fried bread. The smell of the hot fat makes her feel ill. She asks Hannah if she knows where Josie is. 'No,' says Hannah. 'But then she is not obligated to attend meals. Unlike you and Sarah.'

Eliza looks around for her uncle. The elders are sitting at their usual table but he is not among them. She asks Hannah where Gerrard is.

'Cover your hair,' says Hannah. 'You are shaming us.'

Eliza leaves the dining room and runs along the street towards the edge of the town. She must find her uncle and ask him if it is true that her horse is dead. Maybe Gerrard's invalid wife can tell her where he is.

She hurtles around a corner and crashes into someone walking in the opposite direction. It is Josie. They are both winded, they hold on to each other and say sorry sorry sorry. Eliza tells Josie that she is going to Gerrard's house to ask him about Stella.

'Your horse?' asks Josie. 'Has there been an accident?'

'Joshua told me that she died last night. But I don't believe him.'

'Oh god,' says Josie. 'Oh shit...'

'Go on.'

'I told your uncle that you had been riding outside the boundary fence.'

Eliza knows at once that Stella is dead. 'Murderer,' she whispers so quietly that Josie does not hear her at first. 'Murderer,' she says more loudly. 'Murderer!' This time Josie recoils away in shock. Eliza runs away down the street without a backward glance.

Everything is falling to pieces. Eliza is angry with me, Sarah has disappeared, my work has degenerated into a trivial set of theories that bear little relationship to what is happening around me, and my daughter is playing a dangerous game. I feel both helpless and angry. Nobody takes a damn bit of notice of anything I say, so why should I take the blame when things spin out of control? The horse was thirty years old for god's sake. She was ready to be put down. And I did warn Eliza that I would do anything to keep her from going near those skinheads again.

I was careful. I told Gerrard that Eliza had confided in me that she had been leaving the land on her horse to have a look at the outside world. I said nothing about that scumbag Ivan or his dubious mates. I need more information about them before I make a move to get Briony out of there. I must have concrete proof before she will believe me. If I jump too soon, I stand a good chance of losing my daughter for good.

I can see the irony in the situation. I saw a television documentary about parents paying big money for professional kidnappers to steal their kids away from the Moonies so that they can be re-programmed back into the material world. Yet here I am, living in a community that some would label as a cult. If teenagers ran away from home and joined up with the Diggers, parents may well rush to have them rescued. Who would not be suspicious of a group who has such a wacky view of modernity? But for myself, I would rather have Briony living in this place than with those low-life racists.

Gerrard was very grateful for the information about Eliza. 'Of course we will put a stop to it,' he said. 'I am deeply grieved that my niece has disobeyed the rules. But we need to know why the young women are becoming dissatisfied.'

I opened my mouth to give him an earful but he stopped me.

'No. Please wait until your report is written. Then the council can study it at the appropriate time in the appropriate place.'

Appropriate indeed. The beating of Joshua haunts me. If Gerrard knew the full measure of Eliza's disobedience, god knows what he would do to her.

I must move carefully. And I must make sure that my final report to the council is couched in generalities. I could not bear Eliza to be hurt by her own people.

Before Eliza returns to her classroom she goes to the unmarried women's dormitory to fetch another scarf. She feels quite naked with her hair falling about in the open air.

She does not want to disturb any of the others who may be taking an afternoon nap. She walks quietly up the stairs and opens the communal clothes cupboard inside the door. She takes a blue scarf from the pile and fastens it about her hair. She looks around. The room is empty except for Munna who is lying on Sarah's bed. Eliza can see her dark eyelids twitching and fluttering like that of a child feigning sleep.

'Munna,' says Eliza. 'Open your eyes, it's me.'

Munna leaps up from the bed in fright. Eliza calms her down. 'Don't panic. I won't tell Sarah.'

Munna crouches on the floor with her head between her knees. 'She said I could have her bed,' she mumbles. 'She said.'

'No tall stories Munna.' She takes Munna's hands and helps her to her feet. 'Now, there is something I want to show you and I want you to tell me the truth. The whole truth. Do you know what that is?'

Munna nods eagerly. Eliza instructs her to stay exactly where she is. Then she goes downstairs and rummages around at the back of the counter of the old saloon. She is relieved to find the brown paper parcel where she had left it weeks before.

'Now Munna,' she says, laying the parcel out on Sarah's bed. 'I want you to look carefully at these feathers and tell me who gave them to you.'

Munna stares at the two magpie feathers and frowns. 'Dunno.'

'Try hard, it's important.'

Munna shakes her head. Eliza gets impatient. 'Think!'

Munna brightens. '*A roll of a book was written, it was as bitter as wormwood and this fleshly hand put wings to …*'

Eliza feels ill. 'So it was Joshua.'

Munna says Joshua did not give her the feathers but he gave her the words to say. More better he said, salt on the meat…

'Enough!' says Eliza. She folds the feathers away into the brown paper. But Munna is running away with herself now. 'He told me to give them to you.'

'What, what?'

'To tickle you…' Munna suddenly stops speaking and looks scared. 'I'm a wicked girl, I'm going to hell…' She begins to weep.

Eliza feels a little ashamed of herself for frightening Munna. But she tries once more. 'Joshua told you to attack me with the feathers while I lay in the water…' Munna screams and sobs and says no no no. Eliza tries desperately to get her to stop. Eventually, Munna allows Eliza to wipe her face and blow her nose.

'Cheer up, dry your eyes,' says Eliza. 'Sarah might come in and see you on her bed. And she'll wonder why you've turned on the water works.'

Munna says, 'Sarah's gone. Look on the shelf. All gone…'

Eliza looks at the shelf beside Sarah's bed. No candle, no bible, no water glass. She opens the drawer in the bedside table. No underwear, no handkerchiefs. Sarah's things have vanished. 'Where are they Munna?'

'She said I could have her bed. She said.'

Eliza gives up. She could not bear to make Munna cry again. She composes herself for the afternoon's work ahead. She pushes down the image of a trusting Stella being led away through the night paddocks and the sleeping vines and the rifle shot ringing out next to the deep rift in the rocks above the mallee flats where the dead farm animals are buried. Stella was a hack, ridden by women and children, never fleet of foot or strong enough for the wagons. No upright burial for her, no armour, no saddle, no trappings. They would have broken her legs to fit her body into the narrow shaft, removed her metal shoes, taken her shaggy brown mane and tail for horsehair, her shanks for dog meat. *Waste not want not, worke together eat bread together...*

Let her be covered with soil and lime, let her bones be safe from the dingoes and birds of prey, let her forgive me for what I have done to her...

The afternoon moves slowly. She tries to read a story aloud. The children giggle and Mark says please Miss, we've had that page already. She reprimands him. Firmly. But the children still giggle behind her back. She knows that she is losing control of them. But all she can think of is Stella when they were both in their younger years, and how they had ridden hard on burning summer days, their sweat running together like liquid salt, their breath pumping like bellows, riding towards the promise of shade beneath the gums and gulps of warm water from the canvas bag.

Later that night, after the moon has climbed high in the sky, she takes a candle and a glass jar and walks up the bush path to the rift above the mallee flats where the animals are buried. This is where the bones and bodies of goats, horses, sheep, dogs and cattle are tossed after they are no longer useful to the Diggers. She arrives at the deep rift. There is an irritating wind pulling at her long clothes. A dry wind from the northwest. Eliza is pleased that Stella's flesh will not freeze on her first night in the rift. There will be no frost tonight, the wind will take up the dew as it falls.

She attempts to light the candle. The wind blows it out immediately. She places it within the glass and almost burns her fingers trying to light it. But the wick catches at last and she places the light carefully at the edge of the rock. She stares down into the rift. On the bottom are dry gum leaves mixed with thin soil and yes, white patches of lime gleaming in the moonlight. She is instantly relieved.

On her way here she had crossed the winter crop paddock and had taken a handful of sorghum, Stella's favourite treat. Now she takes it from her pocket and throws it into the rift. She says a prayer, but not for the horse. This is forbidden. Animals do not have souls. The prayer is for herself, an apology, an attempt to heal her guilt. She had behaved irresponsibly, she had caused Stella to be killed before her time. Her guilt is like a high thick stone wall, unbreachable. She cannot climb over it, she cannot crush it, all she can do is acknowledge its existence.

She takes the lighted candle from the glass and throws it down on top of the sweet grass. It burns steadily for a moment. Something moves. A snake? A mouse? Please God, not a rat. Then the candle is snuffed out, and the rift is dark and silent.

She ties her scarf securely beneath her chin so that the wind cannot tangle her hair. She walks down the track through the moving trees. Goodbye goodbye.

I'm in a hurry. I must document this in my private notebook before I go to sleep. It takes so much time writing it out three ways. I've already done the version for Gerrard, bland and conciliatory as usual. I handed it to him to give to the elders in the morning. Max's version can wait. I will awake early in the morning and work on the research under the heading *Conflict Resolution in a Closed Community*. I'm going to write about the loss of control when tradition begins to break apart; the tussle between those who cling to outdated rules and those who know that their history is about to be consigned to the dusty pages of a book that nobody wants to read.

But now I take up my red pen and begin to write the dangerous version, the one that is for my eyes only. When I first came here, I made a pact with myself to destroy this personal notebook before I leave Digger Town. But now I feel differently about it. I don't know if I can ever destroy it. It comes from within myself, unstructured by the needs of others. I mix up the separate ingredients of my life that appear to cancel each other out yet it forms a dish that I willingly eat.

We were summoned to the council room before we had finished eating our lunch. The elders and some of the younger men, Eliza and the unmarried women, Hannah and the widows. Here we are sitting in the council room at one o'clock on a winter's day. A day defined by the absence of weather, no clouds, no wind, no frost. Unusually mild for this time of year. A nest of kindling wood and paper has been arranged in the fireplace but the fire is unlit. I rest my clipboard on my knees. I can't meet Eliza's eye. I am still smarting from her unfair attack on me yesterday. Murderer, she called me. Murderer! The horse died because Eliza was caught doing something crazy and stupid. It is so unfair of her to blame me.

Gerrard takes his place at the front. He places his hand on a leather-bound bible, to give him sustenance he says. To give him the strength to lead us through these difficult times. He tells us what I already know. It is the talk of the kitchen. Sarah has been missing for two days. 'No,' says Gerrard. 'She's not lost in the bush, we have information of her whereabouts. Disturbing information.'

The men lean forward in their chairs. The women sit with their eyes cast down. I wonder why they have been summoned here to the council room. To get a warning of what may happen to them if they defect?

Gerrard calls Ned and Thomas to the front. Ned takes a piece of paper from his pocket and holds it up. Gerrard commands him to read the note. Ned begins to mumble something in an inaudible voice. Gerrard snatches it from his hand impatiently. I sit up and take notice. Gerrard is usually a gentle and mild-mannered man. He's starting to lose his grip.

dear amity, I want to see you again, I cannot forget the tattoo on your arm, the flower of aphrodite you told me, six points to a cobwebbed wheel, six petals ...

A ripple of shock runs around the room. Gerrard says grimly, 'Now you know dear brethren why I have pulled you away from your lunch. We must act quickly.'

I raise my hand. Gerrard ignores me. Instead, he interrogates Ned and Thomas about the meeting that Sarah had with the ferals a few weeks ago. To my relief, the two men give a similar account to the one that I had given Gerrard. We took the food to the ferals, Eliza and I walked up into the hills to search for botanical specimens, Sarah had her hair braided by one of the women. At no time was she out of sight of the Digger men.

Ned is asked about the rest of the note. Has he destroyed it? And why in God's name did he not take it to Gerrard immediately after Sarah gave it to him? Is there something going on between Ned and Sarah that made him comply with her wishes? Ned appears bewildered, confused. He cannot, or will not, give a satisfactory answer.

An elder stands up and attacks Gerrard, reminding him that warnings were given about the consequences that would follow if women were allowed to go beyond the boundary fence. Once they taste the outside world, they become dissatisfied. Sarah saw the flower of aphrodite, the six-sided figure, and sin entered her heart.

Another weather-beaten old man gets to his feet and points at me. I brace myself, I already know what's coming. He raves on and on about my bad influence on the younger women, he accuses me of stirring them up, giving them tacit permission to come and go as they please, why even Sister Eliza has caught the rot...

Another ripple of shock. The stupid old man had gone too far. He had no right to bring up Gerrard's niece. For all the talk about Digger Town being a community of equals, there is a rigid hierarchy in this place. It is clan based. The bloodwoods are the powerful group and Gerrard is their leader. Things that can be said about the other women cannot be said about Eliza. She is protected by her kin relationship to Gerrard.

175

I raise my hand again. This time Gerrard gives me permission to speak. I defend myself. 'The purpose of my presence here is to help you understand the dynamics of your community, not to criticise you or to trigger off more disruptions and desertions. If you search your minds you will remember that there was trouble before I came here. There are many good things about your community. But you must expose the young people to the knowledge and experience of the outside world. Until this happens, they will have a naive and artificial view of what life is like on the outside.'

The old man (I must find out his name) challenges me again. 'Would you like to live here Mrs Tabel? Would you find sanctuary here?'

I do not answer his question. I am terrified that I will swear at him. Use foul words. Blow my cover as a respectable widow. Sanctuary? More like an idiot factory. Look at Eliza. Her ignorance did not protect her. Quite the opposite. She has no understanding of thugs like Ivan and his mates.

I ask Gerrard why he believes that Sarah is with the ferals. Maybe she is somewhere more dangerous. There are elements in the local community who have unhealthy thoughts about Digger women. I bring up the issue of the graffiti in the shelter at the boundary fence. Some of the men shift their feet uncomfortably. Gerrard holds up his hand. He asks me not to speak of such things in front of the unmarried women. I can provide him with the details later.

'But don't you see,' I say. 'This is exactly what I'm talking about! If you do not give them information, they will continue to make stupid mistakes.'

Not one of the women gives me any support. They are silent. Not so the men. They start yelling and shouting at me. Gerrard hits the table with his fist and calls for order. 'Enough! This is not helping us to solve the problem.'

I interject. I advise him to report Sarah to the police as a missing person. 'You must find out who she is with. Before anything bad happens to her.'

Gerrard says, 'There's no need. We know that she is with the feral band, she has been seen travelling with them.'

I am dying to ask him who gave him this information. Not a chance. He is in full flight. He is speaking very formally now, like a preacher. He reminds his audience that they *worke together eat bread together* and that God will send them a message. They must all pray hard tonight. But before this happens they have to make a collective decision. A judgement. All the women may leave. Except for Mrs Tabel.

The women file out. Eliza turns and looks at me. I avert my eyes. Then Gerrard pours himself a glass of water and drinks deeply. 'Now,' he says. 'Peruse the Sixty-Two Laws and see how many Ned has broken. We have to decide the punishment for him.'

I sit there with my knees shaking while they deliberate. I am very relieved when they decide that he has been foolish rather than evil. He has been friendly and polite to me. I could not bear to see him beaten. His punishment is four weeks labour in the fields dressed in the white overalls of servitude. And no trips outside with the horses for six months.

Could have been a lot worse. But I am still worried about Sarah. I hope that Gerrard's sources of information are correct. If she has run away with the ferals, she will probably be okay. At least she has not thrown in her lot with low-life bogans like Briony has.

Time to act. I must find out all I can about the group that Briony has joined. She found them on the Net. I can ask Max to do a search for me. But then I'll have to tell him about Briony and I am too ashamed to admit my failure with her. Maybe I can find them myself, maybe there is a cyber-café in Mudgee...

Now I *am* in dreamtime! But you never know. The Net is everywhere. I shall make discreet inquiries from that woman in the café. She knows all the town business. If there is a place where I can get onto the Web in Mudgee she will know about it.

Time for sleep. I light my last cigarette before getting ready for bed. I open the window to let the smoke out. Like the day, the night is empty of wind and cloud. Nothing moves. The half-moon stares down. The earth is in a state of suspension. Somewhere in the distance I can hear goats calling softly to each other and the lowing of cattle. I listen in vain for the harsh barking call of Lupa. No luck. She has deserted me again tonight.

Eliza goes back to the dorm. She should be in her classroom but she has told Hannah that she is ill and that another teacher will have to take over for her. She is sure that she will be well again tomorrow. Hannah says that it is very inconvenient but she will cope. There is no one else free today so she will have to do it herself. She could give the children some extra religious instruction. Some moral training perhaps.

Eliza knows that Hannah is dying to ask her questions about Stella. She has heard the women whispering behind her back, she has observed the sudden silences when she enters a room. She thanks Hannah for her help and walks away.

She sits on her bed in the deserted dorm. The crisp winter air carries afternoon sounds through her open window. She can hear the clopping of horses, the jingle of harness, and the murmur of women taking their covered baskets to the produce store. A man barks out an instruction for someone to come and help him lift a hay bale. In the distance a dog is crying at the end of a chain. A sob begins deep in its throat and then rises to a crescendo. The yowl of a melancholy wolf.

It is too early for the women to come to the dorm for their afternoon rest. She has lied to Hannah. She is not ill but she wants to be out of the sight and sound of others. For years her life has been uneventful. Years flowed into years without her paying any attention to the passing of time. Now everything has changed. Her mind is buzzing with the events of the last two weeks. She can sense a new pattern emerging. Soon all will be clear. She has only one regret. She should not have accused Josie of murder. Secrets never lie dormant in this place for long. Others had seen her, observed her comings and goings, Joshua for one. If Josie had not reported her to her uncle, someone else would have before too long. And there is some consolation in the fact that Stella is free of the infirmities of old age and is now safely buried in the rift.

When she disobeyed Ivan by walking openly into the farmhouse of the Mudgee Militia Men she gave God his chance to punish her. Nothing happened. She told Ivan so at the feral foodbank. You were wrong, she said. I laid myself open and only good things came about. Like finding Briony for Josie. Like finding out that your people and mine are linked through kinship. Like proving to myself that God has a plan for me but that I must help Him by placing myself into the centre.

She hears a noise below. Munna? One of the other unmarried women? She calls out, but no one answers. She goes downstairs. The saloon below is empty but someone was here. A bucket covered in a white towel has been placed inside the door.

She lifts the towel and looks inside. A heart, full of dark clotted blood. A note, written in pencil, *a specimen, for your children to dissect...*

There is ice packed around the heart. The meat is dark and cool. She presses it with a finger. Too large for a goat or pig. Some old steer, killed for the table. But why give it to her? The dogs usually feasted on the dead hearts of slaughtered beasts.

A terrible suspicion grips her. She peers at the note. It is smeared with old blood. It tells her nothing more. She stares at the heart in the bucket then lifts it up and folds it carefully into the white towel. What is the reason for this, what purpose does it serve? She is too distraught to think of possible connections. All she knows is compassion for the severed heart, and a feeling that a similar act of revenge has been inflicted upon her before in another place and in another time.

children, observe my scalpel cutting through the thick tissue at the base of the left ventricle, observe the diameter of the major coronary vessels, observe...

there is nothing new under the sun, wound and counter wound...

8

THE HUNTED AND THE HUNTER...

I'm in the café waiting for Max. I ask the woman behind the counter about the Net in Mudgee. She is bright-eyed and inquisitive. The Net? I explain what I'm looking for. She tells me that there is an office in Church Street that has something to do with email. Well she's heard about it, but she doesn't know where it is. 'I can make inquiries for you,' she says. 'Give us your phone number at Digger Town and I'll give you a ring.'

So she knows who I am and where I live. I'm sure that she is also aware that there are no telephones in Digger Town. She must be winding me up. I tell her not to bother, it's not urgent. 'How do you know I live there?'

'Read about you in the paper,' she says. 'Had some reporters in here sniffing around. They showed me your photo.'

I order a long black and a herb muffin, unbuttered.

'Not that I told them anything,' she goes on. 'Just the rumours, things that have been said over the years.' She fills my coffee cup and places a muffin on a white paper serviette. 'What's the real goss?'

'Ah,' I say. 'That would be telling.' I pretend to look around for eavesdroppers. I lower my voice. 'What's your name?'

She looks uneasy. 'Jennifer Waite.'

'Well Jennifer, forget the rumours, they are nothing. You would not believe what really goes on inside those walls.'

Her eyes glisten. She waves away the ten-dollar note I offer her for payment of my morning tea. 'My shout Mrs Tabel. Have I said it right?'

I nod. I tell her to call me Josie.

'Unusual name.' She follows me to my table and fusses around pretending to fill the sugar bowl. I am beginning to regret teasing her. I light a cigarette and sip at my coffee. It is hot and strong, just the way I like it.

Jennifer sits at the table. 'You can tell me anything in confidence, it won't go past me.'

'Well,' I say slowly. 'It's quite shocking but the truth is that Digger Town is the most boring place I have ever lived in.'

She stares at me, puzzled. 'But you said...'

I bite into the muffin. 'This is great. Do you make them yourself? All we get to eat in Digger Town are dogs and cats.'

'You're stirring me.'

'Couldn't help myself. That article in the paper was full of dangerous lies.'

'The thing is,' she says. 'My mother is there. I worry for her.'

I feel like a complete shit. 'Sorry. What's her name? Maybe I've met her.'

She tells me that her mother is a birth mother, a stranger. All she has is her original birth certificate and a letter from the authorities telling her that her birth mother is a member of the Commonwealth of Diggers but does not want to make contact with her. Not now, not ever.

I am instantly alert. So that's what they do with children born outside of marriage. Adopt them out into Mudgee families. Eliza denied that these births had ever happened. In that case I told her, you are the first tribe in history to ever achieve this. If I write this up in my notes you'll be famous. Or inundated with requests to tell the social policy experts how you did it.

Chapter Eight

Jennifer asks me if she can bum a fag. 'Help yourself,' I answer.

'I'm not supposed to smoke in here but what the heck.'

'Go for it.'

She takes in a lungful of smoke. 'So. There's no truth in the rumours.'

I drink the last of my coffee. 'None whatsoever.'

'What's it really like?'

I swallow the last piece of muffin. I wonder if she has told me the truth about her birth mother. Maybe she is doing a little stirring of her own. 'I can't divulge any information, it's confidential to me and my supervisor.'

'Is that the guy you have been meeting here?'

'Yep.'

'He was in here last week.'

'You must be mistaken, he cancelled his visit.'

'He was here, with two women. One of them was a cop up from Lithgow.'

Fran. What the hell is Max playing at? 'Who was the other woman?'

'Dunno. Never seen her before. But she must be rich, she drives a flash car.' She stubs out her cigarette. 'I have to get cracking on the sandwiches. Greg Sharpe will be here soon to pick up his order.'

She takes my empty cup to the counter and refills it. I thank her. 'You must let me pay for this one.' She shakes her head.

I decide to befriend this woman. She could be a useful informant for my work. She comes into contact with most of the people in this small town sooner or later. But first I must offer her something in return. 'Jennifer,' I say. 'Would you like me to make some discreet inquiries about your birth mother? I have access to some of the historical records of Digger Town.'

She places the refilled coffee cup on my table. 'That would be great.'

'Can you give me the date of your birth?'

She does so. I write it down in my notebook and pump her for more information. The name of the father was left blank. The name of the mother was June Bloodwood, Spinster. 'But this is exciting!' I say.

This time she helps herself to my cigarettes without asking. She strikes a match with a shaking hand. 'Bloody hell, don't tell me you know her.'

'No, but she must belong to the bloodwood clan otherwise she would never dare to use that name.'

Jennifer says, 'You've lost me.'

I am just about to explain the intricacies of the clan system when the bell on the door indicates that a customer is entering the café. Jennifer jumps up and stubs out her cigarette. I say to her quickly, the name is obviously false, but it makes it easier to find her. Knowing her clan I mean.

It's Max. He apologises for being late. He buys a coffee and a croissant. I inquire after Fran. He tells me that she is fine. Thanks.

I decide to keep quiet about Jennifer's information for the moment. He seems ill at ease, distracted. He gulps his coffee down and tears at his croissant. I discuss some of my findings. I offer him a smoke.

He shakes his head. 'No thanks, trying to give up. You'll have to hurry your research along Josie, time is passing. Two months, and it will all be over.'

'It doesn't help that you cancel a meeting without explanation.'

He shrugs. 'Sorry. Circumstances beyond my control.'

He does not explain these circumstances. Instead, he hands me a cardboard box. I open it. I'd forgotten that I'd asked him to find historical information about the Ranters. He has found a slim dissertation, some photocopied articles, an old book.

'Hope you find them useful,' he says.

I look at one of the photocopied articles. God. He's found a copy of the pamphlet that Eliza and I searched for in the history room, *The Fiery Flying Roll*.

'Any good?' asks Max.

'Fantastic.'

'Am I forgiven?'

'Now you've given me this, yes.'

He smiles. And changes his mind about the smoke. He lights one up. We finish our coffee and food. Jennifer comes and refills his cup. I wait until she is at the back of the shop then decide to show Max the green book that I have borrowed from the history room. I ask him not to tell anyone about it. Then I show him some of the stuff about the Ranters and the breakaway group. He reads a passage aloud: *those who preach no difference between heaven and hell, between good and evil, between sinful and holy, those who seek the immoderate use of women, those who claim that perfection comes from a profound lack of remorse ... God is indeed the sole author of all sin ...*

I am nervous that someone will come into the shop. I take the book from his hands. Max begs for its return. 'Later,' I say. 'I have made a lot of notes about the breakaways. And now that you have provided me with some historical information, I will be able to expand them further.'

'I wonder what happened to them?' he asks. 'I've never heard of another group of Christians living together in this area.'

I am silent for a few moments. The burden of information is beginning to overwhelm me. I lose my earlier resolve not to talk about Briony. I am afraid for her and Eliza and I must talk about it with somebody. Out it all comes, the bogans at the feral foodbank, Eliza and Ivan, Briony and the Mudgee Militia Men, how she found them through a chat group on the Net.

Max stares into my eyes without blinking. I am unnerved at his reaction, his face is like a stone. I finish my story. Then he grabs his bag. 'Let's get out of here.'

We leave just in time. Greg's tourist van is driving along the main street heading towards the café. Max tells me to hurry, we need to go somewhere, right now, no arguments. I am mystified. Even more so when we drive a short distance to a familiar street. The one that I had walked down when I explored this small town on foot and discovered the abandoned house with the rotted fence and the black-eyed daisy with the unpleasant smell.

He drives to where Mealey Street intersects with Lawson Street and parks. He looks around carefully then hurries me out of the car. The street is deserted. He walks quickly back down Mealey Street, dragging me with him. He holds my arm so hard it hurts. I want to fight him off. Is he dragging me towards the empty house? My feet stumble on the gravel strip that serves as a footpath. I ask him what the hell he thinks he's doing. He does not answer. He stops at a cottage three houses down on the same side as the abandoned house. A thick hedge and a high wooden gate. A locked and bolted garage door set into the hedge. Max knocks at the wooden gate. He still holds my arm. I can feel him trembling. I realise that he is the terrified one, not me.

He knocks again. Heels click towards us. An eye peeks out of a spy-hole in the gate. It opens and closes behind us. A woman confronts us. She is in her late forties, expensive hair-cut, very smartly dressed. She is obviously angry with Max. 'What the hell are you doing here? Come inside quickly before someone sees you. Where is your car?' He mumbles something about Lawson Street.

We follow her along a concrete path. Dead leaves thick around the trunks of bare fruit trees, a lone eucalypt with shredded bark and one dispirited bunch of brown winter flowers hanging at the end of a branch like a dying finger.

She opens the front door and ushers us into a dark hallway. The cottage is well furnished but has an impersonal feel to it. I am reminded of motel rooms. There are no books or magazines. The surfaces of the polished furniture are bare. The only ornament is a vase of pink proteas rising from tall spikes of dried grass.

The woman does not offer us any refreshment. Instead, she asks us to sit and we do so, Max in a stuffed chair and me facing him in another. The woman perches on the edge of a wooden chest that serves as a coffee table between the stuffed chairs. 'Okay Max,' she says. 'This better be good.'

Max introduces me. 'This is Jocelyn Tabel, Briony's mother.'

The woman jumps to her feet. She goes to the window and stares out into the garden. She closes the curtains. 'Are you sure that you were not followed here?'

I've had it with this cloak and dagger stuff. This is Mudgee for god's sake, not Berlin or Moscow. I jump to my feet. Max looks uneasy. I tell them that I'm going, I have ordered a cab to take me back to Digger Town and I need to be at the rank in thirty minutes. The woman thrusts a mobile phone at me. 'Cancel,' she orders.

That does it. 'Who the hell are you to give me orders,' I shout. 'I don't even know your name.'

She tells me that she is sorry that I have been brought here, it was not her idea. But now that Max has blown her cover there is no alternative but to bring me into the picture. 'I'm Madeline,' she says. 'I have been sent to investigate the Mudgee Militia Men and I have to warn you that your daughter Briony is in serious danger.'

My heart lurches. Max says, 'Tell her everything you told me Josie. Tell her about Ivan and Eliza at the picnic place, tell her how Briony found them on the Net.'

'Wait,' I say. 'How do I know who you really are?'

'She's an undercover cop,' says Max. 'Fran can vouch for her.'

Madeline flashes a shiny card in front of my nose. I am still dubious. Maybe she is someone from a newspaper or television trying to stir the dirt on the Diggers. I remember how nosey Fran was about the Sixty-Two Laws and the rumours of unusual punishments that take place in the town.

Then Madeline begins to speak. It seems that my initial judgement of the men at the foodbank was off beam. I had seen their type hanging around in Sydney; Westies, unemployed no-hopers, out of it on glue and dope and booze.

Ignorant young males flexing their muscles to give the appearance of menace. I had thought that this lot were just more of the same. But Madeline is using words like conspiracy and treason and terrorism. 'They are planning something big,' she says, 'but we don't know what it is. I have infiltrated their group as a financial backer representing a group of anti-migrant nationalists. One of those rich and respectable one-people-one-nation outfits. This is why you must never come here again. You could put my life in danger.'

I can't come to grips with her information. It doesn't seem real. 'Are you sure?' I ask. 'Sounds like something out of a B grade movie.'

Madeline agrees. She tells me that they trade on this sense of unreality. She has also had trouble believing evidence even when it landed right in front of her eyes. How could this be happening in Australia? But it is. Right now. The Triple M believe that there is a secret group running the world, the One World Order, run by Jews and non-whites. And the Triple M does not work alone. They have affiliations with neo-nazi groups all over the world. The Norsemen in Europe, the Fourth Reich and Unit 88 in New Zealand, the Attilas in Britain and hundreds of militia groups in America. Some of them are fundamentalist Christians but their real religion is racism. They are convinced that whites are being treated like second-class citizens inside their own countries.

So this is the group that my daughter has joined. How could I have reared such a monster? I did not take it very seriously when she called people names. Asians are slopes and anyone from Southern Europe is a wog or a dago. So what, she said when I challenged her. They call us skips. Right to our face. What's worse? Being named for the shape of your eyes or for a bloody talking kangaroo?

But I never heard her refer to the One World Order, I have never heard her make derogatory remarks about Jews. Where was I when she was developing these ideas? Was it possible that I was too bound up in my grief over the loss of Russell to see what was festering under my nose?

I attempt to make excuses about her to Madeline and Max. She is young I tell them, young and impressionable. Since my husband died she has felt as if she did not belong anywhere. Once she finds out the truth about her newly discovered friends she will leave at once, I know it.

Madeline cuts me short. 'I can understand your concern but there are bigger things at stake. Besides, they don't let anyone leave without a fight.'

'What do you mean?'

'They persecute anyone that tries to leave.'

'So if I get Briony out, they might try to kill her?'

'There is no evidence of murder but they do get severely harassed. We know of two men who have left. We paid for everything they needed. They have become useful informants.' She sneezes into a tissue. 'Sorry. Winter bugs.'

'Did you have to get them new identities? Plastic surgery, passports, that sort of stuff?' asks Max. He sounds excited. I hate him for that. Can't he see that I'm in agony?

Madeline sneezes again. 'No comment. You already know too much.'

I don't know what to do. I am out of my depth. This dark-haired woman, a stranger, has become my lifeline. I don't want to leave her. She alone can help me to get Briony out. She must have read my mind. She takes my hand and asks me to trust her. She will do everything in her power to protect Briony. And Eliza. Did I know that the leader of the Triple M is related to Eliza and her uncle?

I shake my head. But I am not surprised. I tell her about the breakaway group of Diggers that took place twenty years ago. This is news to her. She is very interested. I promise to write up notes about the Ranters. This is my ploy to see her again. 'How can I find you?' I ask. 'I may need to talk to you urgently. With new information.'

She shakes her head. 'Sorry. I cannot give you a contact number. But I will be in touch with you soon. I will find a way.

Meanwhile, say nothing to anyone. Especially Eliza. She has become sexually involved with Ivan and I don't know yet where her loyalties lie. Get what you can out of her. But for god's sake be discreet.'

Sexually involved? This is impossible to contemplate. Surely Madeline must be mistaken. Then I remember what Eliza had said to me in the bush just before the bogans arrived. I was pumping her for information about the practice of banishment. Eliza had claimed to be a far worse sinner than Sarah. I had joked with her, called her too evil to sleep at night. And that had sent Eliza into that peculiar soliloquy about harsh colours and birds and flight. When I had written this up later in my journal I thought that Eliza had been referring to her forbidden indulgence in contemporary technology as the ultimate sin. But now I wonder if it was a sin of the body rather than the mind.

I ring the taxi company on Madeline's mobile phone and apologise for my lateness. I reorder my taxi for twelve-thirty. Madeline lets me out of the gate after checking that the street is deserted. The plan is that I walk from here along Church Street and from there to the taxi rank. Max will go the opposite way. Just in case his car was followed.

The sun is partially obscured with streaky clouds that hang like winter rags across an otherwise faultless blue background. The temperature has dropped several degrees since we left the hot coffee comfort of the café. I shiver, and button my coat close to my neck. I'm so paranoid I swear that observers are standing behind twitching curtains at every window in the street. I stop at the abandoned house. Once again, I am drawn through the broken fence and up to the front door. The cardboard box and the plastic bottle filled with dark liquid are still on the veranda. The clump of yellow daisies at the bottom of the steps has been cut back by frost and now resembles a bunch of blackened sticks.

I check behind me. No sign of the elderly blue-haired woman with a large dog who disturbed me last time. I push

against the door and it opens. I walk in and close the door
behind me. I don't know what it is that I want to find in here.
Or not to find. I move quietly through the hall and into each of
the four rooms. Not a single stick of furniture except for an old
kapok mattress on the floor. The lean-to at the back smells
damp. The stove has been ripped from the wall. A brass tap
drips into an enamel sink.

I want to go home.

Eliza goes into the little room at the bottom of the staircase in
the school building. She takes the heart of the horse from the
bucket. There is a large white cloth on the marble-topped dissecting table. She places a smaller embroidered one in the
centre. The heart is laid on this. Small drops of brown fluid
creep through the fine linen weave. She lifts it for a moment.
The shape of the heart is crudely sketched on the cloth. She
folds the cloth away and strips the larger cloth from the table.

She gets her instruments from the cupboard and begins to
dissect the heart. Most of the aorta has already been removed.
But the stump that is left is thick and tough. She places two
fingers inside the aorta and touches the smooth sides of the
interior. She thinks about the rivers of blood that have
pumped from the left ventricle into this great arterial vessel to
power their youthful rides.

She touches her own heart through the smooth cotton of
her smock. She wants to put this part of Stella back into the
earth. And she wants some appropriate words and a song to
accompany her. She knows that it is forbidden to mourn animals but something overrides her, the refrain that Josie has
taught her, say what it is that you want. At first it was just
words skimming over the surface, without depth, without
meaning, but now, they had begun to burrow into her brain.

Within this stilled temple was once the life of a rose, a cup, a
spring, a furnace ... She stops, fearful that she is moving too
fast, too loose. But why? If the heart of a man can be sacred
why not that of a horse?

Look within this heart. Same chambers, same vessels, longer, thicker, but there is a kinship here. Who would deny this heart a ring of thorns, an umbel of flowers, a spray of leaves?

She finishes her work. She folds the pieces of flesh and gristle into the white towel and places it back into the bucket. She washes her instruments and her hands. The candle is snuffed out, the small cloth is folded neatly and hidden within her cloak. She closes the door quietly and leaves the room.

I have been immobilised for two days. I waver between horror, rage and disbelief. Sometimes, when I manage to get involved in my work, I forget for a few hours. Then it comes back to me, Briony and the neo-nazis, Eliza and Ivan.

Terrorism? This is the stuff of fiction. Madeline must be exaggerating the danger. Things like this don't happen to people like us. But then I remember my arrival in Digger Town and my sense of disbelief. I had not known that such a place existed. I could not have imagined it. So why can't I believe Madeline's story?

I have deliberately kept away from Eliza. And I think that she has been avoiding me too. But now I must speak with her. I want to tell her everything that Madeline told me. I know that Madeline warned me against this. But what choices do I have? I can't allow Eliza to get any more involved with the group than she already is. I am not without compassion for her. She irritates me at times with her complacency and her submissive behaviour. But how could she be any different given the circumstances of her upbringing in this place? She has been deliberately kept in a state of ignorance. The marvel is that she has ever strayed outside at all.

Maybe Eliza could take me to the Mudgee Militia Men. Or arrange a meeting between me and Briony outside the commune. I don't know what to do for the best. I have an urgent need to talk to somebody. I got so desperate last night that I toyed with the idea of speaking with Gerrard. Spilling out the whole story of the merging of the remnants of the Ranters and the neo-nazis, the relationship between Eliza and Ivan, my discovery that Briony has joined them. And then asking him for help. Absurd of course. He wouldn't have a hope of understanding the contemporary phenomenon of the neo-nazi. I'm not even sure that he knows much about the original ones.

In the stillness of dawn, lying cold and sleepless on my hard mattress, I heard the last harsh bark from Lupa before she hid away from the emerging light. It struck me that the Diggers and the neo-nazis have more in common than I first thought. They are both borrowed communities. The Digger's ideas come from another century and another country; a form of brute religious communism that attempts to place all forms of commerce and usage of land beyond individual control. They invented strict laws to force people to conform to a narrow conception of the common good. The neo-nazis too have borrowed their identities, their symbols, and their politics of hate from another country and another time. Their idea of the common good is to eliminate everyone who does not belong to the chosen race.

What the hell are these people doing here? Why can't they pack up their stolen histories and go back to the North where at least there is some remnant of their origin, some whisper of their stories in folk-tales and mythology, some relation between their borrowed lives and the dark forests that gave them birth.

I feel so alone. And resentful. If Russell had listened to me for once in his life he would not have died in that stupid and meaningless parachute accident. How dare he call me the *what if* woman? How dare he leave me alone with this terrible stress over Briony?

I always thought that I was good at fostering intimacy, I always thought I had a gift for friendship. Yet now that I am in a crisis there is no one that I can turn to. Lynda and Megan would be sympathetic and kind but I already know what they would say. Megan would roll her eyes and tell me to stop telling tall tales. You always loved a good yarn Josie, come in spinner! Lynda would do the sensible middle-class thing and tell me to go to the police. They will help you Josie, they will get Briony out for you.

No good me telling her that the police are already involved. And that all I've had from them so far is a warning to keep my mouth shut. Lynda has a naive trust in the structures of authority. Not me. How could I, after my broken childhood in New Zealand and my experiences as a woman alone, renting in a run-down part of Balmain? If Lynda walked the streets like a poor person her perspective would soon change.

Today is the day. I must do something. I have been left suspended, immobile, without a plan. I cannot bear it any longer.

I get up and pour cold water from the china jug into the wash bowl. I splash water over my face and neck and scrub my hands with a nailbrush. The air is freezing. There is a thin layer of ice on the bottom of the window frame where the condensation has gathered during the night. I feel incredibly resentful that I am forced to suffer like this. I want to smash the hut apart, or set fire to it.

Hold on, I tell myself, get a grip. Maybe Max is right about my anger problem. Since Russell died I do get enraged over little things. But then I always did. The difference now is that I allow myself the luxury of expressing my anger out loud. Once I denied it, buried it, squashed it down. Aunt Winifred made sure of that. Now, the rage is open and visible, a part of me, always at the ready, like an overheated volcanic lake. The truth is that I enjoy feeling angry, I like the heat rising up through my body to my mouth, I like the words that come into my mouth like choleric stones. *Say what it is that you want.* But I must be frugal with the expression of it, I must parcel it out where it can have the desired outcome. I must be particularly careful with Eliza.

There is a soft knock at my door and there is Eliza, as if I have conjured her up merely by thinking about her. I tell her this and she smiles uneasily. I invite her to come in out of the frost. I tell her that it is just as cold inside but I can make her a hot drink on my primus. She watches with interest as I flood the wick with meths and light it with my cigarette lighter. I pump kerosene up into the wick from the holding tank. The primus makes a soft purring noise and gives an illusion of warmth. Soon we are drinking hot coffee and I am trying to make toast on a small enamel plate that I have positioned over the flame.

I remind her of the early hour. She sits there with her head and body covered in her long cloak, holding her coffee cup with mittened hands. Then I notice that she has a small leather bag with her. Is she doing a runner?

She wants me to come with her. Something about a heart, a grave. That's all she would tell me. I ask her if she is leaving. She says she doesn't know.

We finish our coffee and abandon the toast which has gone as hard as a board. Eliza asks if she can take it for the hungry magpies. I turn the primus off and pour the rest of the hot water into my thermos and mix in a little instant coffee. I dress in my parka and gloves and boots. I shoulder my pack and we walk in silence through the sleeping town. A few fires have already been lit. Woodsmoke stands above the chimneys in white threads. There is a sound of coughing and the high-pitched wail of a newborn child. The tall gums on the top of the ridge have lost their heads in a chilling mist. Water forms at the end of my nose. I wipe it off with my woollen glove. We walk for what seems hours without speaking. Drops of moisture cluster around Eliza's hair at the side of her hood. She leads me to a place high above the mallee flats, a place that I have never been to before.

We come to the foot of a rise. Layers of rock with straggly gums and small wattles caught halfway up within a narrow band of soil. Eliza identifies the specimens of wattle as *Acacia doratoxylon*. It has close-grained timber, she says, good for fencing and buggy-poles. Alas, these lovely dwarfs will never amount to anything. Seeded by passing birds or carried here on the spring winds, they can never grow larger than the rocky soil allows.

I almost laugh. She can't help herself. Once a teacher always a teacher.

She climbs up the rocks. I follow her, putting my hands and feet in the same spaces that Eliza found. By the time I get to the top of the rise she is sitting patiently beside a deep rift in the rock. This unexpected climb so early in the morning has almost done for me. My legs are shaking and I am breathing hard. I sit down with a thump and take a sip of coffee from my thermos. The early sunlight has worn away the mist to a few smokey patches loitering in the gullies. I can see the vineyards spread far below me, rolling in concert with the shape of the land, the winter crops lying like fresh green carpets between the rows of dormant vines.

Eliza is taking what looks like little pieces of red meat from her bag, and throwing them down into the rift. She is whispering something about roses and springs. What on earth is she up to? Does she think there is a living beast down there who requires sustenance?

I attempt a weak humour, I mock her schoolteacher's voice. I tell her that the ancients fed the sea with burnt meat and poured wine upon the ground so that they would not die in battle. Shall I pour a libation of coffee from my flask?

She looks at me as if I'm stupid. Then she tells me that this is the place of dead animals, the dogs and goats and horses. Stella is here. Except for her heart which was unlawfully stolen from her.

I look more closely into the rift. There is a pearly gleam at the bottom. Bones?

And then I understand. She is performing a ritual of mourning for her horse. A symbolic return of the heart to the body, a reconciliation of spirit with flesh.

I must write this up in my notebook. I have no idea if this is a community practice or if Eliza is doing something new and secret. I can't ask her yet, it would break the moment apart. I sit in silence until she has finished.

She stands up and throws piles of dried gum leaves into the rift. She invites me to join her. I do so, feeling a little self-conscious. She says goodbye to Stella in a calm and matter-of-fact voice. She takes a damp cloth from her bag and carefully wipes her hands. She pulls on her knitted mittens. I offer her coffee from my thermos. She shakes her head. Then she tells me that she is going to the Triple M compound. Would I like to accompany her to see if Briony is still there?

I am completely thrown. I make a fuss over packing the thermos into my pack and the retying of bootlaces. I ask her if I can have a think about it. Can she give me five minutes? I move away from the edge of the rift and light a cigarette. I watch her put the hard toast that she has allegedly brought for hungry magpies at the edge of the rock. 'I have changed my mind,' she says. 'I have decided to put this here for the rats. To lure them up from the rift.'

I feel sick. And scared. Madeline warned me not to trust Eliza because she is involved with Ivan. But what choices do I have? I might not get another chance to confront Briony. I will be very careful not to react to anything that I might see or hear. Whatever happens, I will not allow my rage to surface. I will play the guileless bystander. Just a loving mother coming to see her young daughter.

What could be more innocent than that?

Eliza leads Josie to the cut wire beneath the high perimeter fence. They move under the fence to the cleared paddocks beyond. Eliza points out the gravel road that winds down to the sealed road below. She takes an old-fashioned spyglass from her bag and telescopes it out to its full length. She applies the telescope to her right eye. The farmhouse swims into close vision. A couple of utilities are parked in the clear area at the back of the main building. No sign of the black van.

Josie wants to take a turn. She mumbles something about her fascination with antique technology. Eliza hands her the spyglass. Josie looks through it for a long moment, turning it in all directions. Then she hands it back. 'Let's go,' she says.

The two women walk together down the side of the road. A four-wheel-drive passes them on the opposite side. Eliza pulls the hood of her cloak down over her face. At one point Josie removes her gloves and scarf and places them into her backpack. Eliza remarks that it is getting warmer by the minute.

They arrive at the cluster of trees in front of the Triple M compound. There is no sign of life. Eliza tries to open the gate but it is securely locked. Two dogs race down the drive towards them, leaping and frothing and growling deep within their throats. Josie jumps back. Eliza tells her not to be afraid. She knows them. Once they recognise her smell, they will accept her.

A voice comes from a security intercom at the side of the gate. *State your name and business.* Eliza is puzzled. She looks around for the source of the voice. Again, the box crackles out, *state your name...*

Josie taps Eliza on her arm and motions her to keep silent by placing a finger on her lips. She points out the intercom. Eliza is intrigued. She goes up to the box and states her name slowly and emphatically as if she is speaking to a child.

Josie catches a glimpse of a partially hidden security camera mounted on the other side of the gate. She wants to hide in the trees. Too late. The box answers Eliza with a question. *Who is that woman with you?*

Once again Josie tries to mime *say nothing* to Eliza. But Eliza either misunderstands or ignores her. She speaks into the box again. 'This is Briony's mother. She has come to visit her daughter.'

Silence from the box. Minutes pass. The two women keep their distance from the agitated dogs, who in spite of Eliza's reassurances, are trying to get through the iron bars to attack them. All at once, the dogs turn as if they are obeying a secret signal and disappear back into the trees.

Silence. More minutes pass. Then the gate swings open. The box crackles into life. *Eliza may enter alone...*

Eliza does not know what to do. She regrets bringing Josie here on a false promise. She wants to reunite mother and daughter. A small gift from her to Josie who has given her so much over the past few months.

Josie takes control. 'You go,' she says, 'I can find my own way back.'

All bags must be left at the gate for security reasons …

Eliza hands her leather case to Josie and walks through the gate. It swings shut behind her. She moves through the trees beneath a lifting sun and a cloudless sky that promise a mild winter's day ahead. There is a certain familiarity in the tilt of the light upon tessellated bark and the scrunch of woody fruits and pungent leaves reeking of eucalyptus oil beneath her boots. Once again, she is assailed by the feeling that she is about to relive something frightening that has already taken place here.

She walks onto the driveway. The dogs reappear, even more aggressive than before. Memory deserts her, makes her a prisoner of the present. She stands absolutely still, terrified. There is a man standing at the end of the driveway. It's Terry, dressed in a khaki uniform and long leather boots. He whistles to the dogs and they run back to him and sit beside him, so that he is flanked by two black heaving bodies. He beckons to Eliza to come forward. She obeys him, thankful that he has rescued her.

'Now come,' he says. 'Come with me. Time to eat breakfast. And talk.'

She follows him into the dining hall. It is warm inside and there are good smells of food and coffee. Briony is serving the men at the next table. She looks pale and tired. She brings a plate of toast and places it in front of Terry. Eliza longs to tell her that her mother is outside the gate but manages to restrain herself. There will be time for that later, away from the buzz and the clatter of breakfast.

Eliza eats toast and drinks coffee and listens to Terry. He is very interested in her life he says, and that of her uncle. How is Gerrard? Keeping well I hope. Any plans for new buildings, expansion of the vineyards? How many people live there now? Oh good, good. Thriving by the sound of it. Tell me Eliza, do you still have guns? For the snakes and the rats, yep. Just single-barrelled shotguns and twenty-twos? Good, good. Nothing ever changes in old Digger Town ha ha.

Briony refills Eliza's coffee cup. She seems subdued, out of sorts. Eliza tries to catch her eye, give her a signal. She wants to go into the computer room, she wants to fly once more over the strangely coloured paddocks and houses of her town. And this time she will tell Briony that changes must be made; dark red grapes into white, green grass into brown, and here, rub out the picture of the white daisies and put this building in. I drew it myself. There is a barking owl on the roof. It sounds like a dog but your mother prefers to name it for a female wolf.

But the breakfast lingers on, and Terry seems intent on asking her more trivial questions and Briony leaves the room wheeling a trolley of dirty dishes. Eliza waits for her to return. Or for Ivan to appear. Nothing happens.

She makes her apologies to Terry and walks back up the driveway and through the trees. She hopes that Josie is still waiting for her so they can move through the perimeter fence and the bush together. But when she comes to the gate, there is no sign of Josie. She turns left instead of right and walks along the verge of the road. In the distance is a lone tree, a tall eucalypt. When she reaches it, she notices that it is choked with mistletoe and road dust. She sits beneath its sad head. A middle-aged man driving a station wagon draws up beside her. He asks her if she needs any help. She thanks him for his concern. He offers her a lift, but she shakes her head, and he drives away.

She resumes walking. The morning wears on.

I go back the way that we came. I sit on the rise at the top of the gravel road and survey the scene below. The air has that peculiar transparent quality that follows after sunlight subdues a heavy frost. I can see the farmhouse and the compound of the Triple M quite clearly. They must have at least a hundred hectares of land. That's if they own the thick bush that goes from behind the farmhouse to the hills above. On either side of their property are treeless pastures and vineyards. Eliza said nothing about grape cultivation. Are the vineyards part of their land?

I want to use the spyglass to get a clearer view. I open Eliza's bag. A curious collection of things. A folded linen cloth with brown smudges in the centre, a stained white towel, a small hard-bound book, a red velvet drawstring bag holding the spyglass, and a map of the Mudgee district. It's one of those topographic maps that mark the names of homesteads and draws the boundaries between them. I read it with interest. It's a very old map. Who knows if Buckeroo Station or Claybrick or Billwillinga are still there? Digger Town is not marked. The boundaries of the land are similar though. Haysheds, pumps and dams are scattered around. And in the middle is a dot labelled Lilly-Pilly. This must be the name of the original settler's house, long since demolished.

Ah, here is the road below marked as a track with a loose surface. And the Triple M farmhouse is labelled with the innocuous name of Belfall Downs. The place must be decades old. Like this map. I have no way of knowing if the boundaries are still the same.

Now that I am so close to Briony I am reluctant to leave. Even though the savage dogs and the tight security scared me, I am glad that I came here. I can place her within a real landscape now. Before this, my visions came from television news. I saw her joining demonstrations in some unknown northern city, running along wintery streets dressed in black and yelling slogans in a foreign tongue. I lose sight of her in a stinging cloud of tear gas. All I can see are policemen hiding their faces behind plastic masks and shields. Then I catch sight of her face again, at the window of a burning cabin somewhere in the mid-west of America, trapped between survivalists and the avenging FBI.

Say what you will Madeline. Dangerous events are far easier to understand within a familiar environment. This is Australia, my adopted home for three decades. My children were born here. Surely I know something? Briony and the other young ones are misguided rather than evil. They have been influenced by those older ones who have a political axe to grind. Briony has taken on the ideology without much thought. But what has been implanted can be peeled away. I have to believe this.

I look at my watch. Ten o'clock, three hours before lunch. I could stay and watch the road below. Check it for vehicles coming or going. But then what? There must be something better to do than to sit up here feeling useless.

Okay. I'm in my hiking boots. I don't have any food or water. But I can find a stream and fill my thermos. I have my map. And this is relatively settled country, I can't get lost. Maybe I'll go walkabout. Just for a few hours.

Then I see Eliza come out of the Triple M gate. At least I think it's her. I remove the spyglass from the velvet drawstring bag. Although I can't see the woman's face very clearly, I recognise the long skirt and headscarf. Good. I'll wait for her here and then we can return to Digger Town together. But wait, she's not coming towards me, she's moving away. What the hell is she up to? Meeting Ivan somewhere out of sight of the Triple M? Not for the first time I wonder if Eliza is as innocent as she appears.

I place the spyglass back into Eliza's bag and stash it beneath an overhanging rock. I shoulder my pack and walk briskly down the sealed road. By the time I am walking on level ground she is out of sight. I quicken my pace, enjoying the mild air around my face and the movement of my body and the fleeting company of a large flock of rainbow lorikeets swooping and screeching in a clump of gums near the road. This is the first time I have seen such a large flock of these birds since I lived, pre-grief, pre-fall, in a suburban garden in Sydney. Once I used to leave small dishes of bread and sugar lumps out for these noisy and beautiful birds and they would come each day to take food and give me joy. Now, the sight of their blue heads and multi-coloured bodies and the sound of their harsh song weaves a tapestry of loss and remembrance that comforts me. Because when Briony was a little girl, she loved them too. She would hold up a bowl of dark thick treacle and these wild parrots would fly like demented missiles towards her. Yet she was never afraid.

I want to ask her if she remembers the safety and peace of our garden and that she once fed treacle to rainbow lorikeets. I want to believe that she still has a respect for all living things.

Eliza is disturbed by a noise ahead of her in the bush. A sharp noise of a boot breaking a fragile branch. More noise, more crunching of leaves and rotting wood on the floor of the bush. She stays quite still. If she can hear them, they can also hear her. Them? She listens carefully. She is quite sure that there is more than one person. And that they are moving quickly and roughly without any thought of preserving saplings or disturbing animals and birds. It upsets her that bushwalkers treat the bush with so little respect.

Someone, a man, shouts orders to the others. She cannot distinguish the words, but something in the tone of his voice frightens her.

She is standing on the sandy bed of a small creek. There is little water except for one or two shallow water holes. She has climbed down from a great height. To her relief, the group of bushwalkers appears to be moving away from her, climbing up the slope that she has just descended. She remains quiet for several more minutes, then she tucks her long skirt into her waistband and climbs up the opposite side.

She has no plan in her mind except to remain undiscovered. Curiosity about this wild back section of the Triple M's land brought her here. She had not meant to stay so long or to climb so far but the excitement of discovering so many beautiful specimens of mature eucalypts drove her on. There must be something in the soil, or something in the way the sun falls or the wind blows that accounts for the health and size of these trees. Massive snow gums, the tallest she had ever seen, brown bloodwoods, red ironbarks, white stringybarks. Perfection.

She climbs to the top of the ridge. In spite of the shade cast by the thick heads of the trees she is hot and thirsty. She knows that it is foolish to have come so far into the bush without food and drink even though it is winter. She decides to find a place where she can rest for a while and then make her way down to cleared farmland on the boundary of the Triple M. She checks the angle of the sun glinting at her through the trees. Probably about mid-day. She calculates due west and walks a little further along the top of the ridge. She is quite sure that she is not lost.

She approaches a clear rocky outcrop that is devoid of trees. There is already someone else here, a person with a backpack sitting on the top of a slab of rock.

After a millisecond of fear, Eliza recognises Josie. She creeps up behind her and says in a low voice, 'What are you doing here?'

Josie nearly falls off the rock. Eliza puts her fingers to her lips and cautions her to keep her voice down. 'There are others around.'

'I know,' whispers Josie. 'I followed them into the bush but I lost them. Do you know where they are now?'

Eliza shakes her head. She sits beside Josie and asks her for water. Josie wants to know if she has seen Briony today. Eliza sips cool creek water from the thermos. 'Yes,' she answers. 'Working in the dining room.'

'She's with them, here in the bush. That's why I followed them.'

'With the bushwalkers?'

'They're not bushwalkers. It's Ivan and the skinheads.'

Eliza is not convinced. 'Are you sure?'

'I saw them quite clearly. The same guys that were at the foodbank. Plus two or three others that I have not seen before.'

Eliza drinks the last of the water.

'I hardly recognised Briony,' says Josie. 'With her shaved head and studs and rings piercing her ears and eyebrows and god knows what else.'

Eliza tells Josie that Ivan did not come into the dining room when she visited the compound this morning. Now that she knows that he is here, she would like to speak to him. They might be heading towards a place that she had just come from. The top of a deep ravine, with patches of damp soil and plants clinging to the sides and a smooth place down a rocky cliff that looked as if it would turn into a waterfall when the creek was in flood. If Josie wants to come with her to confront her daughter, it's fine by her. As long as Ivan is there, they'll both be safe. She's sure of it.

I nearly died of fright when Eliza crept up on me like that. My first thought was that she was with the skinheads and that they had sent her to warn me off their land. But after speaking with her, I'm certain that she did not come with them. Which begs the question of why she is here at all.

I am still shocked at the sight of Briony, clad in camouflage gear, capless, hairless, rows of silver earrings, rings through her eyebrows, a diamond in the side of her nose. Her shoulder-length black hair all gone, her bald head full of bumps and hollows that are unfamiliar to me. She was carrying a large long canvas bag. So were the others. Guns? But why not have them out in the open? Who is there to see them here except us? And they don't know that we are here. I hope.

Eliza and I walk as quietly as possible along the ridge. From time to time she points out a particularly good specimen of eucalyptus something-or-other to me until I say to her, for god's sake, please, no more. I have far too much on my mind to think about admiring a bloody gum tree. She looks a little hurt but there's nothing I can do about it.

We walk for about half an hour before we get to the ravine. It is deep and narrow. Stunted trees and bushes cling to the rocky slope. I peer over the side. It looks like an ancient riverbed. It is quite gloomy at the bottom but I can see the glint of a black water hole. And there at the edge is the sudden drop where Eliza thought a waterfall might roar down after heavy rains.

She points to a thin spire of smoke on the opposite side. I tell her to give them a coo-ee. She grasps my arm. 'Hide yourself Josie.'

I don't get it. One minute she's telling me that Ivan will protect us from the skinheads and now she wants me to hide from them. But something in her voice tells me to obey her, so I do.

I get behind a tree. A breeze is moving along the tops of the ridges and I can see tongues of flames coming from a campfire. A man comes into view. It's not Ivan or any of the other skinheads. It's someone dressed in a fringed leather coat with a mohawk hairstyle. There are others with him. Two or three women and behind them, some kids. I can't see them very clearly without my glasses.

'Amity,' whispers Eliza.

'Are you sure?'

'Absolutely,' says Eliza. 'And Sarah is with them.'

So Gerrard was right. She did run away to be with the ferals. But what is Eliza saying? Something about danger, something about praying that Ivan and the others will not discover that the ferals are on their land.

Too late. The skinheads burst out of the bush and surround the group around the campfire. They are holding weapons. Not guns, bows and arrows. I almost laugh. They are playing tricks, a bizarre game of cowboys and Indians. 'Come on Eliza,' I begin to say. 'Let's give them a yell, let them know that we're...'

The words die away in my throat, I can't believe what is happening. Amity falls to the ground with an arrow in his throat. He lets out a dreadful gurgle. The women and children take flight. And Briony is chasing them too, with her bow held high above her head. I hear her voice screaming like a banshee, over here over here!

Eliza is clinging to me, shaking and white-faced. I hold her in my arms. I don't know what to do. Maybe if I do call out, if they knew there were witnesses...

Then a primitive terror takes hold of me, and I sink to the ground still holding Eliza. Every cell of my body is racing and raging with anger and horror and fear. I want to crawl away beneath the litter on the floor of the bush and go deaf and dumb and blind. I want to banish the sound of that gurgle, I want to erase the sight of Briony in full war cry, I want to fall into a deep sleep. But I can't even close my eyes. I have to watch what is happening, I have to know.

They are hunted down like animals. The bush shakes as if a herd of beasts are stampeding through it. I can hear Sarah pleading for forgiveness, a child cry out, the swish of an arrow, a woman screeching my baby my baby my... then silence.

I put my mouth over Eliza's left ear. 'Stay calm, stay perfectly still.'

We watch as they drag the bodies to the dry bed of the waterfall and throw them over. I try to memorise as many details as I can, the time, the smell and feel of the bush, how the light falls, the number of victims, the order in which they are tossed over, the clothes they are wearing. It takes on the quality of a ridiculous dream. I have to crush an impulse to stand up and call out, okay you lot, joke's over, you can stop playing your stupid war games now.

Instead, someone seizes me from behind. And I hear a man say what have we here? Two birds in the bush... I turn my head. It's the skinhead with the swastika on his face. My hands are tied behind my back. Then he ties Eliza's hands as well and we are marched along the top of the ridge.

I trip and almost fall. He hits at my legs with a leather thong and calls me a stinking cunt. On and on he drives us. And all the time cursing and swearing, making sexual threats. We come to the edge of the dry waterfall.

Ivan and Briony and the others are waiting for us. They are as high as kites on drugs or adrenalin or both.

Ivan unties Eliza's hands. 'This is a very unfortunate business.'

'We can't let them go,' says the tattooed one. 'They've seen everything.'

I can't grasp the fact that any minute now I will be lifted like a rag doll and thrown over the edge. My body feels so alive, my heart is beating like a drum. Soon I will be falling helplessly, like Russell. How many seconds before he knew that his body was going to hit the ground? And that no matter what he did, no matter how he pleaded, no matter how powerful he was, there was nothing more that he could do...

I want it over with, finished. I cannot bear this drum, the ticking over of seconds, the look of stricken terror on Eliza's face.

So I goad them, 'You fucking bastards, you'll get yours...'

Then something solid hits the side of my head and my eyes fly out and treetops whirl and the sky rolls out a great wheel that spins me into oblivion.

9

THE UNRULY APPETITES OF WOMEN...

I'm riding in a bus to Melbourne. I'm sitting in the front seat across from the driver and I'm dressed in the garb of a Digger woman. It's raining and grey and my life is over.

There is a small child behind me, kicking aimlessly at the back of my seat. The pulse penetrates my body. A promotional video plays close to my head. Tourist delights. Electronic music, fake didgeridoos, green trams, plastic prawns, the Yarra.

I want to put my fist through the screen or at least make a strong protest to the driver, but then I remember that I am impersonating a submissive Christian woman. I did not want to wear this wig of long hair beneath my scarf, I did not want to wear this skirt or these clumsy boots, and above all, I did not want to board this bus. But I had no choice. Madeline had made this quite clear to both of us. Run or die.

'Do not labour under the illusion that we are small town boys,' said Terry. 'There are many thousands of us, in every country. Your names and faces are already spinning around the world on the Net. Wherever you go, whatever you do, someone will find you. So keep very very silent. Relegate this unfortunate incident to the past, think of it as something that happened in another place and in another time. Erase it from your memory. And carry on with your lives as if nothing has happened.'

Madeline thought it safer for me and Eliza to travel separately. And to swap identities. Eliza is now on her way to Sydney pretending to be me. We are supposed to meet up there. After that, who knows.

I have become a puppet in Madeline's hands. She convinced me that Terry meant to have both of us killed. But not there, not in the farmhouse, not in front of Ivan and Briony, who had both pleaded for us, Briony with tears in her eyes. Why does she still care about me? She might as well have thrown me over the dry waterfall with the others for all that is left of me now. She has utterly betrayed me and everything that I hold to be true. My work is in ruins, and I have been forced to abandon Jack. He will be told hurtful lies to explain my absence. He will be told that I no longer want to be his mother and that I have gone to a better and brighter life that has no place for a sixteen-year-old boy.

I feel terrible about Max too. He will never understand why I have thrown my work away after all his efforts to get me into Digger Town. He will be very angry with me. So too will Gerrard. He will blame me for the disappearance of both Sarah and Eliza. With good reason. *If* I had never gone there, *if* I had never given birth to Briony, *if* I had reared her differently, *if if if* ...

My daughter, the murderer. Who had unbelievably tried to get me on her side. God, what does she take me for? 'They steal sheep and cattle,' she said. 'They take firewood, trespass on our land, leave their campfires uncovered. They never work, they live off the sweat of others. The bush has been cleansed. The locals would do the same thing if they had the balls.'

'Hey hey,' said Terry. 'Enough of this talk. This incident should never have happened. It is a diversion, it takes us away from our true path. And no talk of the locals please. Or anything else. Silence silence silence.'

Terry instructed us to return to Digger Town the next morning and pretend that we had become lost in the bush and that I had fallen and injured my head. Madeline offered to take us back to her house for the night. Terry wanted Eliza to stay until she had recovered from the booze and pills that Ivan had fed her. Madeline was very persuasive. The sooner we get them away from here the better. What if someone comes looking for them? In the end, he agreed.

So we were bundled into Madeline's car. But she did not take us to her house in Mudgee. We drove on back roads for hours. I was too distracted to take note of the route. My head was throbbing unbearably. Eliza lay unconscious in the back seat. Madeline drove down a long and bumpy driveway to an old stone house. A woman with long untidy hair came out with a flashlight. It took the efforts of both of them to get Eliza out of the car. Madeline told me to stay put. I was to be taken elsewhere.

I sat mute and mutinous, half dead with worry and pain. I thought of sneaking away into the bush and hiding until daybreak. But I had no idea where I was. And my head hurt. I decided to go along with Madeline, for now at least.

She was gone for fifteen minutes. Then we drove on for almost another hour before we turned off the road again. This time, there was no wild-haired woman with a flashlight. The house was anonymous, cold, unlived in, similar to Madeline's house in Mealey Street. By now, it was almost three o'clock in the morning. Madeline bathed my wounds and made several calls on her mobile phone. I lay on a lumpy sofa, my stomach sour with paracetamol. I asked her why Eliza was not with us but she said the less I knew the better. She was officious, calm, very sure of herself. She chilled me almost as much as the people at the Triple M.

I could not get Sarah out of my mind. I had shown her a glimpse of the outside world and she had run away from Digger Town hungry for love and adventure. Now she lies broken at the bottom of a ravine. And it was all my fault.

I tried to explain to Madeline how I felt. She dismissed me with a shrug.

I asked her what she intended to do about the bodies. Are they condemned to be left to the predations of weather and stray dogs?

'There is nothing more that can be done for them at the moment,' she said. 'They will be attended to in due course. There are higher things at stake. Your survival for a start.'

I asked Madeline what made her so sure that I still cared whether I lived or died.

That made her pause. 'Others are at risk beside you,' she said. 'Eliza for one and me for another. Follow my orders, or you will be responsible for what happens to us.'

So here I am on the bus, grinding through an afternoon in late winter, passing hills and farms and little country towns with desolate verandas and boarded-up shop fronts and mile after mile of eucalypts standing cold and blue in the persistent rain.

I have travelled this road before in happier times. Once Russell and I drove to Melbourne in October and the hills and paddocks were covered with Patterson's Curse in full flower. An unusually wet spring had allowed the curse to form vast purple fields. The painted wilderness ran in clean lines along rows of barbed wire where the herbicide had stopped. It looked like a child's attempt to colour in a black and white sketch without going over the lines.

But today there is no sign of the deadly purple fields. Just the rain falling on the windows and the hiss of the wipers and the hectic voice-over from the video.

The bus stops at Albury. The driver invites us to help ourselves to refreshments in the café. And to please take our seats in twenty minutes.

The café is crowded. I join the queue. I'm starving until I see the food; soggy chips under lights, limp sandwiches, plastic containers of wilted salads. I wonder if Madeline knows what she is doing making me get dressed up like this. I'm getting stared at. I told her this would happen but she insisted. 'They will be looking for a young blond woman with blue eyes,' she said. 'In a long skirt and scarf. They would never guess that you have become Eliza and that she has become you. Far too bold for them to come to grips with.'

I take a greasy chicken leg and a buttered roll and a cup of coffee. I'm dying for a fag but I dare not light up in here. It would not match the costume. There are no empty tables. A group of truckies are seated near the door, smoking and cracking jokes with the waitress. I want to join them and inhale some of the side-smoke but again I remember Madeline's warning to stay in character.

I move to a booth where two elderly women are already seated. Big mistake. One of them immediately asks me in a conspiratorial whisper if I'm Closed Brethren. 'Hope you don't think I'm being nosey, but women dressed like you usually move in flocks. Are you on the run dear?'

'No no,' I answer. 'Nothing like that.'

The other one pipes up. 'My sister was Closed and she had to get out, that's how we know about it.'

'I'm not Brethren,' I say firmly. 'I'm a nun, one of those community ones.'

That shuts them up. But I'm shaken. So before I board the bus again I go into the women's room, and remove the scarf and the long skirt. I change my shoes too but not the wig. It would make me look too different. So I pull the wig back into a ponytail and tie it with a wet rubber band that is conveniently sitting on the hand basin. Then I take out my make-up and apply foundation and powder and a little lipstick and I put the gold sleepers back into my pierced earlobes.

God, what do I look like now? A little more like myself. Except for the hair which looks even more fake without the covering of the scarf.

I climb back into the bus. There is a shrouded figure sitting in my window seat. I can hear Madeline's voice in my ear. Do not be fooled. The most unlikely person is often the one you have to watch out for. Trust no one.

The woman in my seat is enveloped in a vast brown rain-coat. I touch her arm and ask her to move out. She turns two enormous protruding eyes towards me without speaking. I glance back to see if there is another spare seat. The two elderly gossips are four seats behind me. They are staring at me with beady eyes. I duck my head and sit next to the woman in the raincoat. She is looking out of the window, and grasping the metal bar in front of the seat with tight hands.

Then it starts. Her monologue, and the sour smell that emanates from her raincoat every time she shifts position. 'Is it safe?' she gasps every time we go around a corner. 'Oh tell me, is it safe?'

Her name is Grange. Christian name. Her mother was a hippy. She won't use her surname because it has nothing to do with her, it belongs to that bastard her mother married. But she'd better shut up. No one wants to hear her story anymore. Abuse is boring boring boring.

I murmur something trivial and listen politely. She is trav-elling to Melbourne to meet her brother. First time out for seven years. She's been holed up in a shack on her mother's farm. Not alone, she had her horse and cats and chickens for company. Her mother went mental just because she'd taken out a wall. Well, she had no choice. Poor Pixie could not turn around.

It looks like I'm stuck with this neurotic woman for the next six hours. Every other seat on the bus is taken. On and on she goes. It gets worse. She claims that her brother took the step-father's ashes up the Parramatta River, and the wind blew back into his mouth and he choked on the ashes and he had to have therapy because he thought the bastard was try-ing to strangle him from beyond the grave.

We stop at a roadside complex for half-an-hour. I help Grange out of the bus. Both of us sneak around the back to smoke. Then she asks me if I have a pair of thongs in my lug-gage. She wants to take a shower, she wants to be clean when she meets her brother after all these years. She is quite unable to place her feet where others have been. No thongs, I tell her. Sorry. Maybe she could hire a towel to stand on? She shakes her head.

We go inside. The food looks better in this place but she refuses to eat or drink anything. She carries on about the hidden filth in food, she swears she can see viruses multiplying in my ham sandwich, bacteria breeding inside my bottle of spring water. She's driving me nuts. The bus driver rounds us up and counts heads. Grange clings to me and thanks me for being kind. She could not have managed to get back on the bus without me. The rain stops and the sun comes out. There are signs of flooding along the motorway and cows and horses stand with steaming coats in sodden fields.

We arrive in Melbourne. I have been instructed to wait in the terminal until a young woman called Mary White comes for me. Grange sits beside me, smoking my cigarettes, until her brother arrives. She thanks me again for my kindness. I wish her all the best.

I wait for ages. I buy a coffee in a polystyrene cup and light another cigarette. Oh no, here comes the two old gossips. I thought they had left long ago.

They sit beside me. 'Enjoying your cigarette Sister?' asks the one in the powder-blue jacket. 'We noticed you changed your clothes. Are you permitted to do this?'

Now I'm getting scared. Who are these pests?

'I'm Mary,' says the same woman, as if she could read my mind.

The other one pipes up. 'And I'm White.'

They try to persuade me to come with them to a safe house. But I'm suspicious. Madeline said nothing about two old women. So I trick them. At first I'm all smiles and gratitude. I ask them to mind my bag while I go to the toilet. Then I climb through a window. Next thing, I'm in a taxi. Thank god I had the forethought to put the money and ticket into my body belt. I don't care about losing my bag. There was nothing personal in there, just some bits and pieces that Madeline put together for me.

214

I mourn the loss of my papers and journals that I was forced to leave behind in Digger Town. Madeline told me that she would try to get them out for me but she could not promise anything. Max might be able to do something. She will get a message to him through Fran. 'Listen,' I told her. 'He'll be so pissed off that I have abandoned my research without explanation, he'll tell you to get lost. Can't you tell him the truth about why I had to leave so suddenly? He already knows a lot about Briony and the Triple M. He might be able to get me an extension for my thesis if he's on my side.'

But Madeline refused to tell Max anything. 'Nobody must know. Not even Fran. Lives are at stake. Yours and Eliza's for a start. And probably Briony's too. They will never let her go after this. They will use her as a hostage to keep you silent.'

The taxi lets me off at Bourke Street Mall. I need to buy a bag and some new clothes and get rid of this long wig. I need to find a place to sleep before I board the train next morning for Sydney. I sit on a bench near the Royal Arcade, uncertain of my next move. There is something happening across the Mall. Three men in red overalls and silver helmets are abseiling down the front of Myer's. Is there a fire inside the building or is this a stunt? There are three tall women dressed in bikinis waiting below for the abseilers. They are holding balloons and flowers. Must be some sort of fund-raising event.

Okay. Time to move. I buy a tracksuit, two t-shirts, underwear, a brown jacket, make-up and shampoo, a small wheeled suitcase. An unwanted expense but I still have several thousand dollars left. I will need all of this when I meet up with Eliza in Sydney.

I spend some time in Myer's rest room restoring my appearance. I wrap the wig in a plastic bag and throw it into the rubbish bin. I brush my own short hair down flat and put on a little make-up. I try to make myself look as ordinary as possible.

Then I walk to the railway station and swap my ticket for one on the night train into New South Wales. This will save the expense of a motel. And anyone who expects me to travel tomorrow will be thrown off the scent. The clerk apologises for the extra ten dollars booking fee. I must look poor. Good. Nobody will remember the face of a cheaply dressed nondescript woman of uncertain age.

I have two hours to wait. I'm so tired I could almost go to sleep sitting up in the uncomfortable plastic seat. I would give anything to be able to lie down. There are homeless people here, two men and a woman. They have perfected the art of lying along the plastic chairs without the armrests interfering with their limbs. They have padded the seats with their bags of gear. The woman has the remnants of a feather doona wrapped around her body. I feel like one of them now. Nowhere to go. The only difference is that I am loaded with cash and the comfort of a promise from Madeline that there will be more later.

There are some weird people in this terminal. Some of them look ill or crazy or both. I must not doze off. I walk about, drink coffee, chant childhood poems beneath my breath. I watch a big brute of a security guard shake the homeless woman awake. He orders her to get lost. No sleeping in the terminal. He sends the men packing too. A few on-lookers clap his efforts and he gives a mock bow in their direction.

The train arrives thirty minutes late at the interstate platform. I notice that the homeless people have returned and have set up their beds for the night in a darkened corner of the mezzanine floor. The security guard is there too, helping the woman spread her things and giving her sips of liquid from a thermos flask. I am absurdly relieved. I clutch my money belt tightly underneath my t-shirt. This money is all that stands between me and the fate of that bag lady in her dirty doona.

I will be very careful on the train tonight. Ready for anything.

When Eliza awakes, she understands at once that she is in a strange room. It is barely dawn. There is a thin suggestion of light between the blind and the window frame. She listens intently, trying to hear any familiar noise that will enable her to place herself. Is there someone else here? She can hear the merest suspicion of a breath moving in and out. She speaks names, Sarah, Josie, Munna...

No answer. She tries to lift her head but it is heavy and pounding with pain. She vaguely recalls the night before, the drinks that they made her swallow, the white pills washed down with whisky. Who? She tries to focus her mind but all she can see is a swirl of faces and loud hypnotic music, someone crying freedom! freedom! over and over. Ivan? Yes he was there, stroking her hair, telling her she was his honey girl, his golden girl. He swears one day he will come for her. When this unfortunate incident has blown over, he will find her wherever she is. And someone else, terrifying, bending over her... Go with Madeline he is saying, go go. He gathered her hair into a ponytail with rough hands. Another man cut her hair off with a pair of scissors. Go now, said this man, leave this place and never come back or you will lose more than your hair. And ropes of white silk floating around the room, mixing with swirls of dust, adrift from her, forever unconnected to her body.

She lies perfectly still. She tries to pray, but the pounding of her head gets between her and the words she wishes to have with God. Strong words. Pleading words. But all she can do is stutter. There is a jug of water beside her bed. She tastes it tentatively, suspiciously, but it tastes pure enough. So she drinks glass after glass until she has drained the jug.

It is lighter now and she can see the heavy oak furniture in the room. The breathing she thought she had imagined earlier is coming from the wheezy lungs of a fat old tabby, who opens one eye and yawns and stretches out a paw towards her when she calls to it. The presence of the friendly cat reassures her a little.

'Carlos, where are you?' A woman's husky voice. 'Carlos, puss puss puss...'

There is a knock at the door. Eliza freezes. Another knock,

then the same voice, 'Sorry to disturb you Missus, but I'm
looking for Carlos. Is he in there?'

Eliza gets up quickly, almost collapsing with the deep pain
in her head. She does not recognise the nightwear that she is
wearing. Or the sight of her swollen face framed in spikes of
wild hair in the mirror above the oak tallboy.

The cat ambles out between her legs as she opens the door.

'Oh there you are, you bloody nuisance,' cries the woman.
'Hope he hasn't been a bother. He didn't do anything nasty in
your room did he?'

Eliza shakes her head. The woman rattles on, love 'em or
hate 'em, moggies earn their keep. Especially here. Rats, she
whispers conspiratorially, rats as big as bandicoots. And even
though Carlos is getting senile he can still bring home the
bacon.

She peers at Eliza. 'Can I make you something?'

Eliza risks a question. 'Is this a boarding house?'

The woman giggles. 'You don't have the faintest clue where
you are do you dear? You sure tied one on last night. Come
down to the kitchen when you're ready.'

Eliza investigates her new clothes in the bag that has been
left beside her bed. She struggles with the pantyhose, and the
short skirt. She panics when she cannot find a scarf to cover
her shorn head. She feels naked and exposed.

She finds the kitchen downstairs. The woman is cooking
eggs and fried bread in a heavy iron pan. Eliza's stomach con-
tracts. The woman says that her name is Mabel Baker. Good
thing I didn't marry your husband, she giggles. Then I'd have
been Mabel Tabel ha ha. Sit down Jocelyn, make yourself at
home.

Eliza obeys. She picks at the food and drinks two cups of
hot coffee. Mabel informs her that she can smoke if she likes,
in fact she welcomes it. Then she won't feel such a deviant
when she lights up. Which is quite often, seeing as how she is a
chain smoker. 'Don't look surprised, I saw the carton of B and
H in your bag when I helped your friend get you to bed last

night. I borrowed a packet, hope you don't mind. We're a long way from the shops out here.'

Eliza has already peeked out of the kitchen window and observed that she is no longer in the Mudgee district. The sun is coming up from an odd angle, and the trees look different. She can tell by the presence of *Eucalyptus oreodes*, the blue mountains ash, and the size of the *Eucalyptus goniocalyx* growing in drifts on a granite ridge that she is at a higher altitude and further south than her home in the Cudgegong Valley.

'Who left me here?' she asks.

The woman says evasively, 'Your friend left a ticket for you. And a sealed envelope.' She gives no further information and Eliza does not ask any more questions. Her head is clearing. She is beginning to remember the terror of the day before. Sarah, Amity, the little children, the wound on the back of Josie's head, the deathly colour of her face. The slow journey back to the farmhouse, Briony assisting her mother to walk, Ivan gibbering like a crazy man.

They finish their breakfast. Eliza helps Mrs Baker to wash up. She sweeps the kitchen floor and offers to wash it as well. 'Pity you can't stay for longer,' says Mabel thoughtfully. 'You're very handy.'

Eliza spends a quiet morning in her room, packing and repacking her new things and stroking Carlos who had managed once again to sneak through the half-open window. Then Mrs Baker drives a battered ute up to the veranda and calls out to Eliza to shake a leg, it's time to go. Eliza begs for a scarf to cover her raw head. Mrs Baker grumbles a little and gets out of the ute, returning after a few minutes with a black velvet cloth with greenish tassels and a musty smell of mothballs. 'Sorry,' she says. 'This is the only one I have. Hang it out the window for a bit to get rid of the pong.'

It is a long drive, over narrow winding roads, down towards flatter land below. They arrive at a bitumen road. Eliza ties the scarf beneath her chin. It still smells a little and the fabric is stiff and scratchy but she does not care. She has been taught from childhood that a woman's head must be protected from the stares and comments of others. And now that the flesh of her neck is exposed by the loss of her long hair, she feels even more naked without a covering.

Mrs Baker instructs her to wait at the side of the road for the bus to Sydney. 'Flag it down when you see it approaching. Otherwise the driver won't stop. Good luck Jocelyn, and if anyone ever asks, you never met me. Okay?'

The ute drives away. Eliza watches it turn back into the gravel side road. She feels very alone. She wonders what she'll do when she gets to Sydney. The cryptic note in the sealed envelope had told her to go to an outdoor café near ferry terminal number three on Circular Quay and wait for Josie. And to speak to no one else. But where is Circular Quay? And how will she find it? Why isn't Josie here to help her?

She has a vague memory of asking Josie for help just before her hair was forcibly cut from her head. And of Josie whispering back, courage, courage.

The bus arrives and the journey begins. It's the noise that confuses her most. The wheels on the road and the loud radio and the interminable conversation between two teenage girls sitting behind her. She barely understands a word of it.

They come into the outer suburbs of Sydney in late afternoon. An enormous plane hangs overhead, scarcely moving. Eliza wonders what prevents it from falling to the earth. The uproar of the traffic makes her head pound. Cars and trucks and buses weave in and out of traffic lanes. They seem pre-programmed, like ants buzzing around an antheap. She can't get her breath. She struggles to open a window. The bus driver barks over the intercom for Madam to desist. At once. 'You've paid your fare to travel in this air-conditioned coach,' he says. 'You can suffocate yourself for free when you get out at the terminal.'

'Silly bitch,' sniggers one of the teenage girls.

'Petrol head,' says the other.

Eliza folds herself down into her seat and closes her eyes.

She lets the rhythm of the bus and the blaring horns and the screeching of brakes wash over her. She gives in to the motion, she relaxes her body. She turns away from the winter frosts, the burning summers, the bush, the vines and fields, the children, the dwellings. Away from the architecture of love and memory laid down through the hard labour of obedience that until now has sung her life into being.

All night I have sat alone with my face pressed against the window, watching the moon ride across the sky. Once again I cross the state line from Victoria into New South Wales. I glide on wheels through small country towns; Wagga, Junee, Yass. I exist in that state of deep fatigue halfway between consciousness and dreams. My slide into sleep is constantly broken by the ding ding ding of bells at level crossings. I guide my path through the night from the memory of maps, I trace a line from town to town, I count off the kilometres.

I find it hard to believe that it was only yesterday that I was spirited away to Melbourne on a wet motorway. This night is dry and free of clouds. And I have two whole seats to myself. The dawn confronts us as we move steadily east. The bush-covered hills come into focus with the arrival of early light. Soon I'm in familiar territory; Goulburn, Bowral, Campbelltown. I am thankful that I am being pulled towards my own city and the comfort of friends. I never thought I would welcome the sight of the endless red-brick boxes in the jumbled streets of the western suburbs.

The train comes into Central. I'm stiff, and as tired as hell. I have been instructed to meet Eliza on Circular Quay but I'm eight hours early. Loose hours, loose deeds. I make plans to ring Lynda, Aunt Winifred, my sister Megan. I will say nothing about Briony of course. And Megan won't know yet that I have left Digger Town without a word to anyone. Maybe I will drop a hint to her about things not being quite as they seem. And I will ask her to reassure Jack and the in-laws that I have not abandoned them for good. Madeline will be angry with me if

221

she finds out, but to hell with her. I just can't clear out without saying something to my sister. It would create more trouble. I know Megan. She would make a big drama out of my disappearance, she would go to the media, or to the police. Out-of-character she would say, a devoted mother, something terrible must have happened to her. Which is close to the truth, but I must warn her to keep her mouth shut. I'm surprised that Madeline did not think of this. She is supposed to be the professional, not me.

I walk down George Street. I am molested by a chill wind that is being sucked down between the tall buildings. My headache is almost gone and I'm hungry. I find a café, and eat a fresh croissant and drink two long blacks one after the other. I want to stay here in the warmth until I work out my plan for the day. There is an abandoned copy of the *Sydney Morning Herald* on the table next to me. I collect it and reassemble the sections. I freeze. *Massacre* screams the headline, *Murder of Innocents*. I relax. It happened in America. Another small town kid dressed in combat fatigues going nuts in his classroom with an AK40. I go through the rest of the paper carefully. Just the usual city murders; a drunk beaten to death on the streets of Woolloomooloo, a domestic shoot-out in Glebe, a transvestite stabbed outside a nightclub at the Cross. But no mention of a mass killing in Small Town New South Wales.

Early morning Sydney unfolds before me. The traffic thickens, and droves of well-dressed people walk briskly on the footpaths with that freshly showered and important look of city dwellers on a mission. I would give anything to be one of them.

I buy a phone card and try to ring Megan. She's not there. But it is good to hear her cheerful voice asking the caller to please leave a message after the beep. She promises to ring back, a.s.a.p…

I don't take up her invitation. Not a good idea to leave a recording of my voice in her voice mail. Now what. Aunt Winifred? No, I've changed my mind. She would never understand that I am about to disappear. She is fragile now, both in body and mind. I must be careful not to frighten her. I already have enough on my conscience.

I ring Lynda. 'Hello,' she says in her soft low voice.

'It's me, your old mate Josie.'

Can she hear me? She's asking pedantically, whom did you wish to speak to? 'Oh dear no, so sorry, there's no one here of that name.'

Then the sound of a door slamming shut and a whisper, 'Josie! Don't hang up. I'm on the cordless in the other room. It's safe to speak now.'

I'm instantly on the alert. I ask her to stop playing silly buggers, why all the mystery? She tells me that Megan is spreading it around that I have left Digger Town under a cloud and that no one but no one was supposed to speak to me. Roger is in the other room. That's why she had to pretend that I was a wrong number.

So Madeline has already got to Megan. I try to reassure Lynda. 'But you know that my sister is a drama queen,' I say. 'She can make a big story out of a puff of wind.'

'Where are you ringing from Josie? I must see you, I'm dying of curiosity.'

There's something unnatural about her voice, a tightness, as if she is acting out something to impress someone else. Or reading from a script.

I hang up and almost run down George Street. I want to get as far away from the phone box as possible. I know that numbers can be traced almost instantaneously. Then I feel stupid. Lynda is my best friend. She would never believe anything bad about me, she would never work against me.

But I've learned my lesson. No more phone calls.

I decide to head towards Circular Quay and hang around until it's time to meet Eliza at number three wharf. I walk slowly through the heart of my city, down the length of George Street, past Liverpool and Bathurst Streets, past Market and King, and I struggle not to weep. I love the buildings, the hum and pace of this part of the city, the smell of the air, a mixture of exhaust fumes and an adumbration of moist air lingering in the canyons from the rain of yesterday. Sydney in winter. High clear skies, cloudless, giving forth surprising warmth on still afternoons, and days like these, when we are rudely reminded that the next continent down from us is a frozen one.

I turn into Bridge Street. A cold dry wind is beating up from the south, gaining strength, and cutting through the thin fabric of my jacket. I do not relish the thought of sitting outside for hours on the Quay waiting for Eliza.

I arrive at the Sydney Museum on the corner of Phillip and Bridge. I stand, shivering, near the sculptured poles in the forecourt. The recordings within the poles are triggered by my presence. Ghostly Koori voices chant the place names of the original clans at the time of contact. And etched on the sandstone and steel and wood the names of the first-fleeters and the dual names of trees.

This installation is called *The Edge of the Trees*. It's meant to symbolise that apocryphal moment of contact when the whites came surging through the surf in all their technological glory and the blacks stared out blankly from the edge of the bush.

I dislike museums. They presume a lofty scholarship that pretends to be superior to the crude history that is sold to tourists. But they tell similar stories of beginnings and endings. Museum curators fabricate history just like those tricksters who claim that the bullet holes at the back of the tearoom near Mudgee came from nineteenth-century weapons during the last armed confrontation between soldiers and bushrangers.

At least the tourist operators acknowledge that history is nothing but a commodity, manufactured and sold to eager consumers. The sign on Greg Sharpe's van proclaims *More Wine, More History*, and that is exactly what he delivers; booze and remembrance. What you see is what you get.

I go in. More voices from the imagined past assault my ears. A supposed conversation at the time of contact between an Eora woman and a soldier called Dawes. Astonishment at the lack of certain sounds in Koori words and the richness of English. How can you say sea without an s? Or velvet without a v? I move quickly through the foyer. At least it is warm in here. And anonymous.

I pretend to look at the exhibits; the skeleton of a dog dug from beneath Governor Phillip's house, fragments of hand-painted china, a brick bread oven. More voices, this time from a video that appears to float in the air. Actors, dressed in eighteenth-century clothes, speaking in drama-school dialects.

There are few people about. A group of schoolboys in striped blazers and navy-blue hats shepherded by two teachers. A couple of street kids sitting on a wooden bench pretending to watch the video. An attendant is observing them. I wonder what he would do if they suddenly smashed open a glass cabinet and stole some history. The thigh bone of a dog perhaps or a broken bottle.

Little chance of that. Like me they are here to gain shelter from the wind not to reclaim the past. I sit beside them. They smell of damp clothes and fags and fuggy armpits. I give them my packet of cigarettes. And a fifty-dollar bill.

Quick as a flash, one of the pair, a boy of about fifteen, folds the money into the palm of his hand. The girl takes the cigarettes. Neither of them says a word.

'No smoking,' snarls the attendant. 'And you two get out. No begging allowed.'

I curse myself for drawing his attention to me. 'Sorry,' I mumble. 'Sorry.'

'I don't mind them sitting in here. Until they annoy the patrons that is.'

The street kids disappear through the double doors to the outside without a backward glance. I retreat to a dark room that represents a colonial storehouse and the vessels that transported goods to Sydney two hundred years ago. There is a carved figurehead from an old sailing ship, ropes, a stuffed emu, boxes of stores, and haunting sea shanties of love and loss and shipwreck coming out of concealed speakers. I hear the harsh cries of seabirds and the roar of wind in the rigging.

This is the only part of this museum that I enjoy. I gain a sense of comfort from the solidity of the tea chests, the heavy sails and beams. I experience the tangible presence of past journeys, I dream that I once rode a sailing ship laden with spices and salted meat to an unknown land.

I sit there in the dark for what seems hours. My need for nicotine finally drives me out. Is it my imagination or does the attendant give me the once over? I ignore his parting command to have a nice day. I slink through the double doors.

A miniature whirlwind whips up dead leaves and scraps of paper into a circular dance, then drops them abruptly at my feet. Tables and chairs have been placed on the open space in front of the café next to the Museum. Maybe someone is expecting the wind to drop. If so their optimism is misplaced. The southerly is even stronger than before. And although there is little obvious cloud, the sky seems to be lower, heavier.

Twelve-thirty. Cigarettes. And coffee. In that order.

I walk into the café. It's packed with well-dressed people. I have to stand in the queue for ages. Exhaustion is taking hold of me. I feel as if I have been travelling for weeks. If I can't lie down soon and sleep I will die.

I buy cigarettes, coffee and a huge slice of fudge cake. I find a spare seat in the smoking section and I pump nicotine and caffeine and sugar into my failing system. They collectively provide an immediate lift. Then I hear someone calling my name. Josie, Josie… No, this can't be. Megan's voice. I must be hallucinating.

But it is her, and she's standing right beside my table, looking very serious and hissing at me, what the hell are you doing here?

'Same to you,' I say. 'Tried to ring you…'

'Are you alone?'

'Grab a spare chair, and sit with me and share my cake…'

'No no, I'm with someone. Over there.'

She points. A man, of course. Probably the current Mr Right. He looks quite ordinary, small build, neatly dressed. Nice head of grey hair. Older than her usual lovers. Bet he's married. She never learns.

I ask her if I can join them. She looks shocked. 'Absolutely not. How can you even think of such a thing?'

Megan is more than angry with me, she's downright hostile. Someone has got to her. But what cock-and-bull story has she been told? Please god not the truth. About Briony, and what she did.

I choose my words carefully. 'Can I speak with you? Outside?'

She shakes her head. 'I'm supposed to ring this number. If I see you that is.'

I flash her what I hope is a reassuring smile. 'Please help me Megan, I have nowhere else to turn.'

She hesitates, then whispers, 'Come to the Ladies with me. You go first.'

I check the cubicles. No feet beneath the doors. Good. I stand at the mirror and pretend to comb my hair. I half expect her to do a runner but she comes in a minute or two later, looking flustered and red in the face.

I ask her if she's given lover boy the push.

'Don't call him that. It's disrespectful.'

I bite my tongue. It is not the right time to get into a fight with my sister over her disastrous affairs.

She fishes through the junk in her handbag and hands me a scrap of paper. A phone number. Probably Madeline's. I ask Megan if she has a mobile phone on her. She shakes her head. 'I need to pee,' she says. 'You stay here.'

She's in there for ages. Then she comes out of the cubicle, complaining that her period has come early. 'Stress,' she says. 'It's a killer on my cycle.'

I almost hit her. She's probably about to blame me for causing her hormones to fluctuate. She always was self-centred. Can't she see that I'm almost off my head?

'Now listen,' I hiss in her ear. 'Forget yourself for once and concentrate on something really important. I need to know exactly what you've been told.'

She looks scared. 'That you've been driven out of Digger Town, and that the police are looking for you.'

I try to keep my voice steady. 'For what reason? What am I supposed to have done?' We are interrupted by a woman coming into the Ladies. I take Megan by the arm and lead her outside. She comes with me meekly enough. We sit at one of the wind-swept tables and she begs me for a cigarette. Lover boy forbids her to smoke, apparently. We both light up but only after she has had a good look behind her to make sure he is not still around.

So Megan, with her smudged lipsticked mouth sucking ravenously at her smoke, tells me what she knows. Not the truth, thank god. Nothing about Briony. But it's bad enough. Megan was phoned by a woman who claimed to be a detective. She did not give her name. But it had to be Madeline. No one else knows that Eliza and I are on the run. This woman said that Megan must phone her if I contact her. The police want to ask me some questions. Something to do with sexual misconduct at Digger Town. Something that I was supposed to have done to Eliza. Feathers in a bath or some such nonsense. Megan is very vague. She asks me if it's true that I have run off with Eliza, fallen for her, changed sides.

I am sad that Megan believes that I could have sexually abused a woman. And that she's obviously wasted no time in repeating this nonsense to Lynda. I ask her if she has told anyone else. She is evasive. I wonder if she has been stupid enough to tell lover boy. I challenge her.

Megan stubs out her cigarette and fills her mouth with a handful of tiny peppermints. 'Not the point,' she mumbles. 'Did you really do that stuff?'

I am speechless. Madeline had better be ready for me when I see her again. This malicious gossip will ruin me. And Megan is sure to spread it around even more now that she's seen me.

She can't help herself. I try to stop myself from weeping but I fail. Tears pour down my cheek, almost soundlessly. This gets Megan going. She hands me a tissue and tells me that people are staring at us. And that she's sorry. For everything. Especially for listening to that woman on the phone. 'But what really did happen, Josie? Why are you here in Sydney looking like death warmed up, if you don't mind me saying so. What am I supposed to believe?'

I stem the flow of tears with her scented tissues, furious with her, angry with Madeline, and deeply frightened. At last I gain a measure of control over myself.

'Now listen to me carefully,' I say. 'This is one time when you must trust me and not anybody else. I am telling you the truth. Something terrible has happened, no, don't ask me what it is. It's not safe for you to know. But get one thing straight. It has absolutely nothing to do with sexual abuse.'

She takes another smoke from my packet and lights up. 'I hope I didn't accidentally tell that fake cop anything important,' she says in a trembling voice.

I reassure her. I tell her that I must leave now. She must not tell anyone that she has seen me. Or telephone my in-laws in Canberra. I lie through my teeth about the kids. 'Fine fine. Both doing well at school. No worries.'

Megan tells me she loves me and we hug each other. I promise to get in touch with her as soon as it's safe. I walk away, leaving her there alone at the table.

I arrive at the Quay. The sea around the wharves is deep green and there is a high swell running. The water taxis are tossing up and down at their moorings like toy boats in a turbulent bathtub. A ferry is coming into the Quay, dancing sideways through the troughs in an awkward waltz. The engine reverses, and ropes are thrown around the bollards on the wharf. People move gingerly down the heaving gangway.

I fight an urge to buy a ferry ticket and sail into the throat of the southerly. Just go where the wind leads me, disappear into the North Shore, or ride the ferries to and fro, become an eternal traveller, always on the move.

Instead, I buy a filled roll and a bottle of spring water and sit on a damp wooden bench watching the boats on the harbour and the gulls battling to stay aloft.

There are few buskers working the Quay today; an old man playing bush tunes on a musical saw, a living statue covered in gold paint, a bearded Koori blowing bird calls through his didgeridoo. He's the only one doing any business. His upturned Akubra is rich with coins. Giggling Japanese schoolgirls sit next to him one by one and have their photos taken by their minder.

Hours pass. The old man on the musical saw has a limited repertoire, he plays the same tunes over and over again. The only ones I recognise are Walzing Matilda and The Road to Gundagai. The living statue gives up. He sits on the seat next to me, discouraged at the lack of patronage. He eats a sandwich and swigs a bottle of beer through gilded lips. The paint on his arms is roughened with goose bumps.

There is a disturbance behind me. It's the two street kids from the museum being frisked by a cop. He holds up a fiftydollar bill. 'Who did you pinch this from?' he wants to know. 'Been rolling derros again?'

He gets the young boy in an armlock. I want to call out, it's okay, I gave it to them but I dare not call attention to myself. The girl turns and looks at me but she does not show the slightest hint of recognition. She must think that I'm a thief too. I'm grateful to her but I feel angry at having to hide the truth. Madeline had better come up with a good plan for my immediate future. I can't keep living like this.

The cop pushes the boy towards a police car. The girl insists that she go with him but the cop waves her away. She starts to make a fuss, swearing and yelling. To make her point, she kicks the cop in the shins. Next moment, she's in the car too, and they are driven away. I relax a little.

Then I see Eliza getting out of a bus across the street. I watch her for a couple of minutes, unobserved. Her hair is short, she is dressed in modern clothes, yet she looks like a refugee from another time and place, or perhaps an amateur drag queen, one newly arrived from a country town. She is obviously having trouble with her high-heeled shoes. And what the hell is that thing on her head?

Poor Eliza. I can't begin to understand what sense she is making of the city. She is becoming an exile in her own land. And yet like me, she has done nothing wrong.

I greet her quietly and invite her to sit next to me on the bench. I place a sheet of newspaper over the gold smear left by the living statue. The thing on her head reminds me of the cushion covers at Aunt Winifred's house. Tasselled black velvet. All that's missing is a lurid painting of the Sydney Harbour Bridge.

I tell her to take that smelly thing off her head pronto. It will draw attention to us. Even in this place where eccentrics are thick on the ground. I take her to a nearby clothing stall and buy her a proper headscarf decorated with a map of Australia and a kangaroo wearing boxing gloves. Good. Now she can pass as a regular tourist.

I buy her sandwiches and an orange drink. She eats a little but gives most of it to a flock of sparrows and two dishevelled seagulls who are pestering each other around our feet. She is very quiet. She does say that she has never been so pleased to see anyone in her life. Meaning me.

I pull up the collar of my jacket against the cold wind. I'm desolate and confused. Briony has taken the lives of innocents. Has she, by her actions, lost the right to my protection? The old code of blood loyalty, mothers weeping in courts, claiming the essential goodness of their rapist sons. I don't know where I stand on this. I don't even know if Briony wants my forgiveness. There was no sign of it two nights ago. She helped me to walk back to the farmhouse, she bathed my head wound. But she was not sorry for what she had done to the ferals. Quite the contrary. It was almost as if she expected me to praise her for her actions. She must know that she has committed a serious crime. So why isn't she scared out of her wits? And why isn't she looking to me, her mother, to help her in her time of need?

Now I'm saddled with another child, a devout advocate of an archaic religion that has about as much relevance to modern life as flat earth theory. She's landed up in my city. I will have to become her informant, her translator. The timing could not be worse. I don't know whether or not I'm up to this new responsibility. I need all my wits about me. Briony should be the one asking me for help, not this pale and lost woman, who can only be considered normal within the context of the closed community that formed her.

I'm freezing. I wish Madeline would hurry up. She's already half-an-hour late. If she's not here in another fifteen minutes, I'll disobey her again and make other plans. I'll book us into a motel for the night. The only reason I've waited this long is to quiz her about the phone call to Megan. And she'd better have a good story to tell me.

A damn good story.

Eliza and Josie are in the economy section of a Qantas jumbo half way across the Tasman Sea. The plane is packed and they have seats in the middle of the centre block. Josie is reading an airport paperback. Or at least she is turning the pages. Josie has hardly spoken a word except to say that the book is a load of crap and that she is dying for a cigarette. Eliza is glad of this. Since the unpleasant confrontation between Josie and Madeline on Circular Quay yesterday, she has not sought conversation with Josie.

She is finding that words once familiar to her are now like small stones on her tongue, an impediment to speech. But there is little else to replace them. She has not been provided with a language to describe the events around her, she can't think beyond the crude words flying machine, moving, *outside*. She wishes that she was closer to the window to gaze unobstructed at the layers of fine white clouds beneath their machine. Fine spun sugar, layers of cotton with a wide weave, higher than any bird could ever fly. She is comforted by this. And by the sight of the enormous grey wing jutting out into space, dipping and shuddering, holding them up, driving them forward.

She obeys Madeline's instructions. Watch and learn. Do not draw attention to yourself. She observes how the elderly man next to her opens the little packages of food, lifting the tab on a minute serving of butter, tearing the silver cover from his orange juice. She copies his actions. Perfect. No one watching her would know that this was her first time. She is surprised that her body can still function while moving at this incredible speed above the earth, surprised that she is able to swallow the water brought to her in a plastic glass and to sip the white wine served with lunch.

Here, sitting in this cramped uncomfortable seat next to Josie, she undergoes again that peculiar sensation of memory folding down into smaller and smaller boxes, collapsing in upon itself, so that she feels aged, as if she has lost days, hours, years.

Yesterday she had seen a side of Josie that disturbed her. Madeline had arrived late with a stranger in tow. Josie was hostile towards Madeline, accusing her of telling lies to someone called Megan. She started to yell. Madeline and the man accompanying her had taken hold of Josie's arms and marched her away from the ferry terminal.

'Are you mad?' hissed Madeline. 'Not here, not now…'

They walked along the path towards the Opera House. Madeline gave them money, plane tickets and passports. Josie said, 'You've got to be joking. I haven't been there since I was ten years old.'

Madeline told her that there had been no choice. No visa required, and you both have legitimate birth certificates. In your maiden names. Eliza becomes Megan Hathaway and you become your former unmarried self.

Josie went crazy. She raved. She accused Madeline of double-dealing and hypocrisy. 'You knew what those bastards were capable of…'

Madeline said, 'I am not responsible for your daughter's actions.'

Deathly silence. Madeline must have noticed the stricken look on Josie's face because she tried to take her hand. Josie resisted her overture. They walked to the steps of the Opera House. In spite of the cold wind, there were quite a few people watching the boats riding through the choppy sea and promenading along the walkways. Madeline and her male companion pretended to window-shop.

Josie eventually quietened down. Especially when Madeline promised to ring Josie's sister Megan and tell her that her original phone call was a decoy and that Josie had done nothing wrong. She said that it was partly Josie's fault that she'd had to tell lies, because Josie had disobeyed orders and come into Sydney on a different train. Madeline thought that she had been kidnapped. If Josie had managed to get to a phone, her sister would be the obvious one to call. Contacting Megan was all that Madeline could think of doing under the circumstances.

'Let me say it once more loud and clear,' she said. 'When the Triple M discover that you and Eliza have not returned to Digger Town, you will be hunted down. You must not tell anybody what you saw. Briony's life is at risk if you go to the authorities. And so is mine.'

Half-way back to the Quay, Eliza had asked a question. 'Will they ever be punished for what they did?'

'Of course,' replied Madeline. 'When we have finished our investigations, we will move in.'

'So we can come back to Sydney,' said Josie.

'Eventually.' She gave Josie a strange look. 'You do realise that when this happens, Briony will be arrested and charged with murder.'

A car arrived at Circular Quay and took the two women to a motel near the airport. Josie had chain smoked and watched television throughout the night. Her face was swollen and her eyes tight with unshed tears. Eliza was too afraid to ask if she could open the window to allow some fresh air into the choking haze.

Now, the plane begins its descent and Eliza is having trouble with her ears. She asks Josie if this is normal. Josie rummages around in her pack and finds some chewing gum. Eliza thanks her. The ice is broken.

Eliza cranes her neck to see the land below. The plane banks to the right. She has a sudden clear view of grassland of the brightest green that she has ever seen. For a moment, she imagines herself to be looking within the same computer screen that showed a similar unnatural colour in the paddocks around her town, but then she sees the bright threads of sea-water lacing the green land with tidal channels. The plane banks once more and all she can see is the empty sky again, and she hears the engines racing and then dying down to an almost soundless purr and she is a little afraid.

'Hold my hand,' says Josie. 'We're nearly there.'

The plane lands with a loud bump and they race along the tarmac. The intercom tells them that it is ten degrees outside and damp. It's fine at the moment but more rain is forecast for later this afternoon.

'That's what I remember most,' says Josie. 'The endless drizzle, and the grey skies.'

Eliza asks her for help with her migration and customs forms. They get through the barriers with no trouble. Nothing to declare. The computer at the immigration desk accepts their electronic passports. The customs official waves them through without opening their bags.

Outside, Josie finds a taxi and they drive away down a long four-lane road buzzing with traffic. Everything is alien to Eliza, the smell of the air, the unfamiliar trees, the talkative driver wearing a long colourful dress and carved bone earrings.

Josie has a great conversation with the driver, asks her where she is from, and seems to know everything about the Pacific island that the woman named.

Eliza has never heard of it. She does not understand much

of the conversation either. She has known for days that she cannot return to her home. But until this moment, it has not hit her how dependent on Josie she has become. She must be careful not to fall out with her. Without Josie, she would not survive.

And survival is now a fervent desire. She wants to witness for Sarah. She wants to tell the story of how she held a little boy close to her body so that he would not see the wound on his father's neck and the deep chasm awaiting them. She wants to confess to her uncle about Ivan, take her punishment. She wants to erase the last few months, start again.

They arrive at a large wooden house somewhere in the inner city. Josie pays the driver and they carry their bags inside the foyer. She rings a brass bell on the counter. Nobody comes. She rings it again, more loudly this time.

They sit side-by-side on a sofa and wait for attention. Josie takes an envelope from her pocket and consults a list of instructions that Madeline had given her last night. She frowns and looks at her watch.

Outside, a soft rain begins to fall.

SAINTS AND LIARS

For three weeks Eliza has risen early and prepared herself for work. At first it was difficult for her. Time was the main problem, working out how long it took to arise and eat her breakfast and do her household chores and choose her clothes. She had to leave the flat at exactly seven o'clock in order to catch the first of two connecting buses that she took across the city. Each morning she waited for Josie to check her clothes and make-up and hair. And each morning, Josie recommended fewer and fewer changes, so that for the past week, Eliza had passed the morning muster with full approval.

Jones had suggested that they both get jobs in order to meld into the landscape. Remember that you are sisters, returning after many years in Australia. Have a story ready. Say that you have just buried your mother or whatever. And that you need to stay for as long as it takes to sort out the family estate.

Jones has become an important figure in their lives. He brings them money, and advice, and sometimes news. Two nights after they had arrived in Auckland, he took them a few streets away from the boarding house to a rambling single-storeyed house turned into four flats. Eliza and Josie have the largest one, two bedrooms, a combined kitchen and living room, and a bathroom the size of a broom cupboard. There is a communal laundry in an open-sided shed at the back.

A telephone, a television, a microwave. A wardrobe of clothes, both new and second-hand. Dishes, groceries, fresh fruit in a hanging wire holder. Chequebooks, CVs complete with fake job and personal references. And a set of written instructions. How to pay rent and phone and electricity and a set of do's and don'ts. Make casual acquaintances only, no visitors to the flat. A toll bar is in place on the telephone. No calls to Australia from here or any other telephone. No Internet connection allowed. Do not register your names on the electoral roll. No medical visits or dental treatment. Answer job advertisements from the newspaper only. No signing on at any employment service, private or public.

Eliza had followed these instructions to the letter. Within days of moving to the flat she had an interview for a job in a wine and health food shop in Mt Eden. She dazzled the elderly couple who owned the store with her knowledge of wine. They hired her on the spot. For a low wage. And afterwards they had asked her if she was a Christian. 'Not that we are bigots,' said Mr Temple hastily. 'But Miss Hathaway, what a pleasure to meet someone such as yourself, a believer in this godless age.'

The weeks went past in a flash. Each morning, just as the first light lifted the weeping skies above the iron roofs and telegraph poles, she climbed into a crowded bus. Bodies in wet coats crushed against her, strangers who never looked into her eyes. Once she became disoriented and failed to ring the bell and went past her stop. She arrived late, much to the amusement of Fiona, the morning assistant. 'Sleep in did you? Go for it!'

Her response bewildered Eliza. She had expected a reprimand from Fiona, not this flippant comment. She was a little afraid of Fiona, a young woman with metallic silver hair and a diamond in her nose. Fiona was an arts student, and she hated the Temples. She was always complaining about them to Eliza. 'They pay shit wages so serve them right if we fiddle things a bit.'

Her speech was peppered with expressions like bloody hell, and holy shit and fucking jesus. She claimed that the Temples would burn her and her kind at the stake if they could get away with it. Eliza did not want to talk negatively about the Temples. They had been kind to her. But she did not want to confront Fiona either. So she nodded from time to time and tried to look vaguely sympathetic. Fiona must have read her response as agreement, because she never let up.

In a way, it was easier for Eliza to give Fiona her head over her hatred of her job and her bosses and, it seemed at times, her entire life. It took the pressure off Eliza to talk about her own past experiences. And she soon learned to switch off Fiona's dirty tongue and not allow it to penetrate her mind. Initially, Fiona had been very inquisitive about Eliza's prior life in Australia but Eliza and Josie had practised their lies over the kitchen table and Eliza had no problem reciting them back to Fiona.

Eliza much preferred Norah, the afternoon assistant. Norah was just twenty, quiet and hard-working. Engaged to be married. Still living with her parents. Norah described herself as old-fashioned by name, and old-fashioned by nature. And she accepted Eliza as Megan Hathaway and her story about coming to live in New Zealand without question.

Jones had been a little uneasy over Eliza's report about Fiona. He said that she was too nosey for his liking. Josie was worried too. Or at least she said as much. Eliza doesn't know if Josie really meant it. Ever since their arrival in New Zealand, Josie has been distracted, moody, melancholic.

Eliza is worried about Josie. She haunts the public library, reading all hours of the night and day and making endless notes. Eliza had discussed this privately with Jones over coffee. He had formed the habit of popping in after work and drinking their wine and eating their food. Josie had half-joked with him about not having a home to go to and when he said you're right about that, she had looked sad, almost as if she was on the verge of tears.

One night, Josie was particularly ill-tempered. She snapped Eliza's head off when asked if she would like a cup of tea. She claimed to be coming down with a cold. Jones asked Eliza if she would like to take a walk along Ponsonby Road and drink coffee with him. Eliza had checked with Josie. 'Do what you like,' she answered in a rude voice. 'You don't need my permission.'

So Eliza went with Jones to a place called The Atomic Café and they had coffee and cake and talked about Josie and her problems.

Jones said when he was first assigned to be their protector, he would have put money on Eliza having a harder time adjusting than Josie but it just goes to show you can't predict anything when it comes to human behaviour.

Then he pumped Eliza about the books that Josie was reading. Eliza thought that they were mostly history, old stuff, religion, politics, that sort of thing. Then he asked if she had ever peeked into her journal. Eliza was mortified. 'Certainly not,' she said.

He laughed. 'You are either the most moral person I have ever had the pleasure of meeting, or the biggest liar. Which is it Megan?'

Eliza, remembering her falseness with the Temples and her fake CV, almost said a liar of course, but instead she repeated a phrase that she had often heard Fiona using during her interminable personal telephone calls. 'That's for me to know and you to find out.'

Which for some reason sent Jones into hoots of laughter so that he almost choked on a piece of chocolate cake and had to gulp huge mouthfuls of hot coffee to recover his breath.

I can't believe that Eliza's got a job already. There is high unemployment here, especially as Jones so delicately put it, for someone of my age. Nonsense. Nothing to do with age. I'm too highly qualified for the temporary shit work that Jones advised us to go for. Who would believe that a woman with a Masters

Degree wants to work in a shop or as a cleaner or waitress? And come to think of it, why put the truth about my educational achievements on my CV? I've been sabotaged before I even begin.

Eliza's personal documents are a pack of lies. Mine are too close for comfort. Does this mean that the powers that be don't care if I am easily traced? Is it more important for them to protect Eliza? And why the insistence that we seek work? It would be safer for us to stay in the flat. Especially Eliza. She is like a fish out of water. It's only a matter of time before she makes a big mistake and blows our cover.

Jones claims ignorance. He says that he takes his orders from across the Tasman. I can't make him out. I don't know if he approves of me or not. One minute he blows hot, the next cold. I never know what to expect. Last night, he sat drinking and joking with us and just for a moment, I got the impression that he's got the hots for Eliza. Or Megan as he calls her.

Eliza's appearance is changing. The shoes, the pantyhose, the clear red lipstick. She's leaner, harder. Jones insisted that she go to a hairstylist. And lose the headscarf. I have to admit that her hair does look spectacular now that it has been styled. Thick and pale and shimmering. Sometimes in a particular light, I imagine that she is beginning to look like her namesake, especially those years when Megan was going through her obsessive search for the perfect bleach. Something that would turn her dark hair snow white. She never completely achieved it of course. The colour ranged from unripe corn to a malignant shade of orange.

Yesterday Eliza came home with pierced ears. Two tiny gold studs. I was shocked. It's against her religion to defile the holy temple of the body. She said something about Fiona making her do it. Has she no will of her own? I asked her what she would have done if Fiona had told her to put her fingers in the ham slicer. No answer. But later I saw her turn her head from side to side in the mirror admiring the flash of gold in her lobes.

Chapter Ten

I am beginning to reconsider the theoretical base of my thesis. I had thought that people brought up in rigid and conservative communities could never adapt to freer worlds. I believed that these communities produced a group mind, that their structure negated the very possibility of the emergence of a true individual.

Even though Eliza does what she is told, she is coping well. Who would have believed that she could get a job in a city in a strange land and work with ordinary women? This gives me hope for Briony. If I can get her away from the destructive influence of the Mudgee Militia Men, I might be able to get her to see reason.

As for me, I've never had such leisure. If that's the right word. I'm like a rat caught in a maze. Each time I think I've found a way out for Briony, I come up against the brutal facts of her terrible crime.

I hate living here. Our flat is on the southern side of the house and there is a suggestion of mould in the walls. The shower is disgusting. A flat metal rose with green muck stuck in the holes. And Tongan neighbours, one of whom works all night and snores all day through the thin walls. I can hear him turning his bulk right next to me where I sink exhausted on the sofa after returning each afternoon from the library. There are three enormous people living in the tiny one-bedroom flat. The two men work at a local seafood-processing factory, one during the day and one at night. The woman Mele stays at home and cooks and cleans. She is married to one of the men and the other one is her brother. She has an old-fashioned washing machine on her doorstep with the extension cord running through the kitchen window. Each day she prays for a child. I know this because I have to walk past the churning machine to get to the street frontage. She feeds thick clothes through the wringer and asks after my children. Are they good boys, she wants to know, do they work hard, send you money?

I have told her lies about my past. I have claimed the ownership of three sons, all in their twenties. Wish I hadn't. After eight years of marriage she is desperate for a son and keeps asking my secret recipe for such success. I asked her if she had thought of going to an infertility clinic. 'No no,' she cried. 'My husband say leave it to God. But Mrs Josie, please pray for me.'

The irony of it. Asking me, the mother of a killer, to intercede with a higher authority to produce a pregnancy. One day, when she was particularly sad, I wanted to tell her the truth about motherhood. But my words had barely stuttered into life before they died away. I almost ran out to the letterboxes to get away from her.

I could have been brutally honest with her. I could have told her that once you have given birth to a child, the love is almost too fierce to enjoy. Any hurt, any illness, the merest slight, is outrageous to you. War is declared. Over and over. When Jack was continually bullied by a group of bigger boys, I could have taken a chain saw down to the school and cut them off at their knees.

But these savage thoughts of revenge are a logical part of motherhood. What to do when your *own* child is the bully? Chain saw or forgiveness?

I kept my side of the unspoken pact that exists between women. The pretence that children are an eternal treasure and that I would not be without them. Mele was kind though. She brought mugs of coffee to my door and biscuits and once some taro sent to her from her family garden back in Tonga.

I didn't have the heart to tell her that I loathe the stuff.

She's lonely. And I would like to spend more time with her. I've never been to Tonga and she is eager to talk about her lost home. Although I have never been into the South Pacific, I have always liked the idea of small islands. I would like to live surrounded by sea in a small but utterly familiar landscape, where every pathway and rocky outcrop had the dignity of its own narrative.

A romantic view no doubt. But I remembered what Jones had told us. Don't get too close to anyone. Be careful, be careful.

It's easier to avoid Mele now that I have started work at the public library. I have wrenched myself away from the sofa and the horror of daytime television. I have a quest, a reason to get up in the mornings. I am simultaneously researching three histories; Diggers and Ranters in seventeenth-century England, the rise of militia groups in the West, and my own past and that of my ancestors in New Zealand.

I have been gathering documents. Certificates of birth and deaths, names on electoral rolls. I have already found the address of the house where I was born forty years ago. The same house where my father and Aunt Winifred were born. An unexpected sign of family stability. I intend to go to this place with a camera. If the house is gone, I will gather soil. Or take leaves from a tree or a hedge. Anything.

My mother's past is silent. She was adopted. I don't know her date of birth or her birth mother's name. There are blank spaces on my birth certificate where these should have been. Aunt Winifred once wrote my mother's real name down for me. After weeks of pleading. But it's long gone. I have tried all the tricks to recover the name from my memory. Meditation, word association. All I can see is black scribble on a yellow page. Nothing else has surfaced. I will keep trying. I will not return to Sydney empty-handed.

Early spring in the Cudgegong Valley. In her waking dreams Eliza follows the plough that crushes the green crops into the dry soil between the sleeping vines. The birds lie in wait for the warm September winds that come in from the west. And the sun, a burning yellow eye. The indoor fires are stilled. The wood stove in her schoolroom scoured and blacked ready for the summer retreat from the necessity of artificial heat. Day after day of almost cloudless skies that grow higher and higher above the expanding skin of land floating away from the cramping frosts of winter. The children in fresh summer shirts, coming out into the sweet air with upraised arms, flesh swelling brown and warm. Thready clouds drifting in seas of colour. Variations on the theme of blueness; the delicate tint of eggshell, the shriek of peacock tails, the moody cobalt of dusk.

All this, while she stands in a speeding bus with rainwater leaking from her clothes. Drip drip, the tops of her suede shoes are pitted with drops of dirty water falling from the ferrule of her folded umbrella. She presses the bell. The bus lurches to a halt. A stiff breeze is blowing. After a brief struggle, she gives up trying to open her umbrella. She is surprised to find Mr and Mrs Temple at the shop. They look anxious. Fiona has been sent away. The accountant has discovered that there are discrepancies in the cash reconciliation. Mr Temple makes no bones about the fact that for a time Eliza was also under suspicion. But he and the wife, after careful consideration, had come to the conclusion that Eliza is probably innocent. The cash problems started before she came to the shop. Besides, there's more to it. Fiona broke other rules. She knew that she was not supposed to have personal phone calls at work. And there have been complaints from the customers about inappropriate language.

Mrs Temple says, 'We're sorry Miss Hathaway.'

'Yes yes, but can you cope?' asks Mr Temple.

It takes Eliza a few minutes to realise that they are asking her to take sole charge in the mornings. And do the ordering from the bakeries and other suppliers. She panics. The wine is no problem. It's the food that bothers her. So much of it is strange. There are at least twenty types of bread. Fiona knew all about them, the types of flour, gluten-free, rye, foccacia…

She is too afraid to reveal her ignorance to the Temples. She smiles. 'No problem,' she says. 'I'll do my best for you.'

'See,' says Mr Temple to his wife. 'Told you so. We did a good thing when we hired her.'

Mr Temple phones a few bakeries and tells them that Miss Hathaway will be placing the orders until further notice. He allows Eliza to help herself to a free bottle of lemon juice and spring water. But only after warning her not to make a habit of it. All stock uplifted must be paid for. He gives Eliza their private phone number just in case she needs to contact them. Mrs Temple invites Eliza to attend church with them next Sunday. That's if she hasn't already found a place of worship.

Eliza declines with thanks. 'I have been accepted into a congregation,' she lies. 'Close to where I live and with wonderful singing.' A villa at the end of her street has been transformed into a church by replacing the finial with a wooden cross. Polynesians go there every Sunday accompanied by flocks of children dressed in formal clothes. They sing in polyphonic style, harmonising lines of notes that seem to be chosen at random yet fit in perfectly with the basic melody. Old tunes dressed up in a new language. Sometimes she walks past the gate and peeks through the open windows at the sea of white hats decorated with shells and flowers. And here and there she recognises a familiar hymn, sung with rising top notes and joyous shouts, more like love songs than the pious music of her lost home.

In Digger Town, a settlement without churches, the singing could break out anywhere and for any reason; as a warning or a punishment, to mark a wedding or a death, or beneath the breath, a tonic prayer, a one-to-one communion with God. Sometimes she finds herself singing one of these sub-vocal dirges, an incantation against the fragmentation and complexity of the city. Everything that was once familiar to her is now set within mysterious contexts and she constantly stumbles, misreading the intentions of others. Her only defence is her rigid training in obedience. Here is the one who knows. Follow him. Or her. Jones is a lifeline, Fiona too until she was sacked.

That night Eliza dreams that the Temples are hiding in the bush at the foodbank near Mudgee. After the food has been unloaded and the horses have pulled the wagons away, they emerge like clattering ghosts, carrying empty sacks. Eliza watches them steal the food intended for the ferals. Then she comes out from behind the bushes and demands that all uplifted stock be paid for.

'Ha!' says Mr Temple. 'Caught you. Sinning against God's

intention. Fruit of the land must never be bought or sold.'

'And besides,' chimes in Mrs Temple. 'There's nobody here to eat it. The bloody mongrel of a feral bastard's dead. They all are.'

And Eliza, crushing fresh eucalyptus leaves into her face, floods her hungry body with aromatic oil to wash away the foul matter in the bush.

I'm standing in front of a house in Queen Street, Onehunga. Is this the right place? The clerk at Land Information warned me that the numbers had been changed at least twice since it was built at the turn of the century. The house certainly looks large enough and old enough to be the private maternity hospital where we were born. Aunt Winifred is seventy and my father would be sixty-five now if he had not drowned while stealing from an eel trap at Port Waikato. He fancied an eel, so Aunt Winifred said, and the river was in flood. Such a trivial death. Unlike my mother's. She died because she could no longer endure the pain of living. Was it us? Did we drive her to it?

When I was eight years old, my father Macca took Megan and me to a place called a Health Camp. This happened after the school nurse had looked into our eyes and ears and down our pants and tut-tutted; skin infections, runny noses, waxy ears. Something called failure to thrive, a case of chronic neglect. My mother Margaret claimed that the nurse was a liar. 'School sores Macca, that's all. Nothing to worry about. Bring me the calamine lotion and some cotton swabs, no need to take my girls away.'

But we were taken. For months. And Macca left us there in anger, worried sick about the failure of his current farm job, and the mysterious illness of our mother. I remember him leaving us at the door of the Camp, too embarrassed to come in. I asked him why Mum spent so much time lying in bed, or slumped in front of the fire, doing nothing. I blamed her for sending us to this cold and hostile place, I accused her of not wanting us. And Macca lost his temper and said you girls have made her ill, she was fine before… and then he cried, which frightened me to death because I had never seen a man shed a single tear before. I thought that weeping was something reserved for women and babies.

For once the sky is clear of rain. Am I imagining a hint of spring in the air? Maybe it's just the shock of seeing the sun again. The old house looks a little sad. The roof is rusting and the paint around the windowsills is blistered and peeling. There are three letterboxes outside so it's obviously met the same renovative fate as the house where I'm living in Ponsonby. I take a couple of photos for Aunt Winifred. She calls this place The Home. And she told us how my mother gave birth to me and Megan here, long labours, no doctors in attendance, just the two women who ran the place. Mildred the midwife, Penny the nurse aide.

I'm not sure of my next move. I want to try and work out the original layout of the house. Have new walls been added, old doorways blocked? I need to get inside. The pattern of light and dark on varnished floors may show changes in the structure. I walk slowly around the building, wary of dogs. But there's only an elderly cat who catches sight of me and rises stiff legged from a bed of flattened primulas.

The lawn around the house is uncut and damp underfoot. I climb the steps to Flat A and knock on the door. A young women answers, releasing a strong smell of marijuana into the outside air. Her voice is slow and her eyes half shut. She knows nothing, nothing. 'But, hey, cool that you were born here, cool as.' She closes the door.

Flat B is empty. I peek through a gap in the net curtains. A bed-sit by the look of it. A long wide room with a bed, a sofa, a sink and stove at one end, and what could be a door leading to a bathroom at the other.

Flat C is occupied. A woman opens the door. There is a baby bawling in her arms, and toddlers tugging and pulling at her long skirt. Behind her, I can see several other adults sitting around a table holding coffee mugs and smoking cigarettes. The woman draped with children provides helpful information. Oh yeah, she knows about this place. Born and bred in Onehunga she was.

I ask about the maternity hospital. 'Yeah,' she says. 'That's the trouble.'

'The trouble?' I parrot.

'Flat B used to be the labour ward. Nobody stays in there for long.'

I get the name of the landlord from her. She says he's an Indian, you know, one of those who come down here and buy up all the dairies and flats? From Fiji. He's okay though, doesn't mind kids...

She closes the door with a friendly wave. Then I see the row of stunted trees with small dark green leaves growing in a straight line at the back of the house. I walk over to them and yes, I see the berries clustering at the end of the twisted branches and I know that I have come to the right place. I take a dark red berry into my mouth and crush it to release the astringent juice deep into my throat. The guava hedge. Aunt Winifred often talked about the picnics here with Mildred and Penny to gather the berries in late winter and how they made guava jelly by suspending the cooked fruit in muslin bags draped across the backs of kitchen chairs. The thin red juice would drip slowly into the bowl below. A delicacy.

Mildred was Aunt Winifred's best friend before Winifred moved over to Sydney. Mildred owned The Home and had delivered both me and Megan. Mildred's mother was a midwife before her, and had delivered Aunt Winifred and Mackenzie my father. Two generations born in the one house. And now, all that's left of us are Aunt Winifred, my divorced sister Megan, and me, with two children, one of whom has already ruined her chances of living a good life.

But The Home survives, and by the look of Flat C, is still in the business of producing babies. I steal a small branch from a guava tree with a cluster of fruit attached. And I walk through the streets of Onehunga in the weak sunlight, clutching my pathetic memento and feeling a hypocrite or an idiot for attempting to link myself to past events through the means of a souvenir. The memories of the guava picnics and the rituals of jellymaking are not even mine. They belong to Aunt Winifred.

I throw the guava branch into a skip and wait for the next bus into the city. But before it arrives, the wind picks up from the west, bringing low dark clouds and the salty smell of the harbour and fat raindrops that clatter on the roof of the bus shelter. Eventually, a bus beats up the hill through the increasingly heavy rain and I climb the steps. We drive up Queen Street. I can still taste the guava in my mouth. I take one last look at the old house through a curtain of water.

Eliza has already eaten her dinner and is waiting for Josie. The pasta she has so carefully prepared is cold. She has had a frustrating day at work. A customer had complained that her loaf of rosemary and garlic bread was undercooked and demanded a refund. A minute later, someone else had returned a half-empty bottle of red wine claiming that it was corked. Eliza, flustered, had dropped a large jar of preserved peppers and gerkins onto the floor. It had smashed to bits and she had cut her finger on a shard of glass. The shop reeked of spicy vinegar. And she could not stem the bleeding. Norah arrived soon after and found the first aid kit. She insisted that Eliza write down a full report of what had happened and sign her name to it. Norah could not afford to be blamed by the Temples. Any breakages were deducted from the offender's wage. And the cost of things taken from the first aid kit. So Eliza stands to lose thirty bucks. Thirty-two actually, if the cost of the sterile dressing is included.

Eliza turns on the television set and just as quickly turns it off again. She is slowly becoming accustomed to the speed of the images and the puzzling movement between the reality of the news and the make-believe of drama. But tonight, she sees black children with flies in their ears and eyes, starving, too weak to weep. She does not want to know the whereabouts of this place of suffering.

Where is Josie? Jones had given them strict instructions to telephone each other if there had been a change of plans. They should know exactly where the other one was at all times. This morning Josie had said that she would be home at six. On the dot. She's already over an hour late.

In the last week, Eliza and Josie have been talking, really talking. About Eliza's relationship with her uncle Gerrard, with Ivan, and with God. Eliza has discovered many things about herself during these conversations. Emotions and beliefs took on an entirely new life when she put them into words. At first she was hesitant to transform certain notions into speech but Josie encouraged her, led her on. And in return, as if exchanging gifts, Josie had divulged secrets about her own past.

Fiona came to the shop yesterday. Eliza had felt very uncomfortable at first but Fiona made it clear that she did not blame Eliza for taking her job. She had come, she said, to see how Eliza was making out without her. And to pick up a few bits and pieces that she had left in the lunchroom. Which turned out to be a coat and an umbrella and two boxes of goods that she swore she had paid for ages ago. One box contained heat-sealed packets of fine ground coffee, the other expensive Swiss chocolates wrapped in Christmas paper.

Eliza asked Fiona what she should tell the friends who telephoned and Fiona shrugged and said tell them I've been sacked for having too many personal calls. 'That'll give them a laugh. Blame them. Say what you like. Except that I fiddled the till. The old bastards lied about that to get rid of me.'

Eliza covers the bowl of pasta and puts it into the fridge. She sits on the sofa, then gets up and paces around the small living room. She can hear Mele's voice coming through the wall. She sounds agitated. A man's voice answers her from time to time in a low rumble. Eliza is thankful that she cannot understand a word of what they are saying. Silence for a few minutes, then it starts again. Mele's voice is getting louder and louder. Suddenly, a loud crash, as if furniture is being overturned.

Then Mele is hammering at the glass door, she wants to borrow the phone to ring her sister, urgent urgent, please Mrs Josie, please open ...

Eliza goes into her bedroom and closes the door. She finds a card that Jones has given her and rings a mobile phone number. Jones had made it clear that no one was allowed inside the flat, not for any reason. Eliza does not want to break the rules.

Within minutes, Jones is there. Mele has given up and gone around the side of the house to the next flat. Eliza, immensely relieved, opens the door to Jones and does not object when he puts his arms around her and praises her for not interfering with the domestic situation next door. 'Stay quiet, stay calm,' he counselled. 'Keep yourself to yourself. And don't worry about your neighbour. She can take care of herself. It was probably her beating up on him if the truth be known.'

The lights begin to go out in the library. Surely it can't be closing time already? I had become so absorbed in my reading that I simply forgot to check the time. I replace the thick tomes of the electoral roll circa 1950 to 1953 back on the shelves. My watch is on the blink but the clock in the foyer tells that it is just after eight o'clock. God, Eliza will be frantic. I race outside and look for a public telephone. I find one but it's out of order. Jones would not allow me a mobile phone. Not secure enough he said. I run for a bus but the driver slams the door in my face before I reach the bottom step.

The night is fine and cool. A brisk wind is blowing clouds high above the tall streetlights. Not rain clouds I hope. I walk up the steep hill towards Karangahape Road. I am raging with that peculiar elation that I can only describe as the thrill of the chase. Primitive maybe, but my blood lust is up. I am honing in on my personal past. I have my mother's name. I have it!

And this one simple statement, Margaret Hathaway nee Brophy, led me on to a welter of other names. I have her birth date and the names of her parents and the fact that she was one of eight children. This means that somewhere out there I have a huge undiscovered family of aunts and uncles and cousins. I can see them, moving towards me, their faces flashing colour in the flickering neons, calling to me, Jocelyn, Jocelyn...

My three quests are moving forward together. The search for my mother's family is almost complete. I use the Internet to get as much information as I can about the rise of neo-nazis. Terry was not lying when he told us that groups like the Triple M are everywhere in the West. I have found hundreds of web sites and forced myself to listen to their hideous music and read their hate words. I have to try and understand the lure that pulled Briony so far from me. And I'm reading as much as I can about the Diggers and the Ranters. At first I thought that these three areas were discrete. But now I am beginning to create a synergy. Whether it is an historic Christian community, or a twisted version of racial superiority, or the naming of those linked by family blood, they all come down to the same entity.

I am terrified. Why do we keep on reinventing ourselves as members of a group? Why can't we stand alone? For a group to exist, it must say what is good and what is evil, it must say who is one of us and who is the hated stranger. Is the promise of personal freedom and choice the biggest lie of our age? I am very resistant to this.

Look at Eliza. She can't do anything unless someone in authority over her tells her what to do. The whole business with Ivan was like this. She has been taught to obey men, they are a god-given authority. So when Ivan wanted her, she obeyed. She did not say it like this, she is quite clever. She told me that when she is confronted by choices, she does not have the right to go her own way or follow her own desires. She places herself in a particular place where either *this* or *that* can happen and then leaves it to God to make the final decision. What a cop out. It means she never has to take any responsibility for her own actions.

I am walking briskly along Karangahape Road into the unfolding night. Sleaze. Naked dancers, massage parlours, transvestites with big hair and tight glittering clothes. The sickness of sex. Or the joy of it. I know that some people say that paid sex is the most honest form. But I've never been able to understand the erotic nature of commercial sex. Like history, it becomes a packaged commodity divorced from its original purpose and its original desire.

Does history arise from a genuine desire to understand the present? Or is it primarily a refuge? I am painfully aware that I have been hiding in the past because I cannot bear to confront the future. The dilemma of Briony. What to do what to do.

I can't understand why Madeline has not contacted me. She promised that when certain security issues had been worked through, action would be taken against the Triple M for the killing of the ferals. But we have been here for weeks and nothing has happened. I don't know how long I can remain silent.

Briony will not leave me alone, she comes to me in my dreams, crying Mother save me save me, her face swollen with weeping and bites which may or may not be of animal origin and I rush to her crying I'm here, I'm here! And when I am almost near enough to hold her in my arms she drives a deadly arrow up into the air and breaks the bow over my head and throws me down into the deep ravine. Night after night I hear my bones crack against the skull of a fallen child.

And I wake and lie rigid with grief and try to console myself with the fact that she pleaded for my life, persuaded Terry not to kill me, just as Ivan had pleaded for Eliza. Then inevitably, my grief turns to rage. Eliza and I were only spared because we were seen as belonging to someone in the neo-nazi group. Me through blood and Eliza through lust. But membership of a group is fickle. *One of us* can just as quickly be turned into *one of them.*

I have no doubt that if Eliza had been found in the tipi with Sarah and the ferals, she would have instantly crossed over from being Ivan's honey girl into his prey.

I arrive at the flat to find a police car outside. I can see Mele sitting in the back seat with a woman cop. Has she been arrested? I creep around the side of the building in case Mele calls out a greeting and the cop decides to interrogate me.

I let myself in. Jones is here. He starts in on me, wanting to know where the hell I've been, Mele tried to get into the flat, Eliza was frantic etc. etc. etc.

I am anxious about Mele. Is she hurt? 'Just a domestic,' says Jones. 'The two men had a fight and Mele tried to stop them and they both turned on her. Or something like that. You never really know with these people.'

And then I know I have come to the end of a line. It's a strong physical feeling, like a box snapping shut in the centre of my brain. Within the closed box lies the remnants of my collaboration. I will never open it again.

I run outside and tap on the window of the police car. Mele tells me of the quarrel between her husband and her brother. Her face is badly bruised. She is very upset. The cop asks me if I am willing to answer some questions. 'Have you heard arguing through the walls? Any prior incidents?'

I demand that Mele be taken to a medical centre. At once.

The cop climbs into the front seat. I tell her that I am happy to help in any way I can. But only after Mele has been attended to.

The car takes off. I glance back and see Jones waving his mobile phone at me from the side of the house. I think he is sending me a signal to ring him as soon as possible. Fat chance. He's finished, or more truthfully I'm finished with him. And the bloody charade of the past few weeks. From this moment on, I will do as exactly as I please.

I will never obey orders again.

11

THE EYE OF THE BLOODWOOD

Eliza is finding the hours lonely and empty. This past week has dragged. She has never lived without a routine before. Jones swore she would enjoy her enforced leisure. Indulge yourself Megan, he had said. Josie has told me what it was like for you in Digger Town. They worked you like a slave. Time to be self-indulgent. Go for it.

She asked him not to call her Megan when they were alone. She wanted him to use her real name. He refused. He claimed that it would be unsafe for him to get into the habit of using it in private in case he accidentally called her Eliza in front of someone who could do her harm.

She is becoming increasingly uneasy in his presence. She does not like the way that he fondles her hair, exclaiming over the purity of the colour. She does not like the way that he leans into her when they pass through doorways or where he puts his hands when he fastens her seat belt in his car.

Now that she is forced to spend long hours alone in the flat, her desire to return home is becoming stronger than ever. Homesickness. A trivial word that cannot describe the sense of loss that inhabits her body at almost a cellular level.

She had not wanted to leave her job but Jones had insisted

on it. He went to the Temples behind her back and spun some fantastic yarn about serious family illness in Australia that necessitated her immediate return. Eliza had begged him to let her stay at the shop but Jones said no way, too risky. 'And don't look at me like that, Josie blew your cover not me.'

When she arose at dawn, rain was falling. Gentle rain, thin and soft. A whisper of moisture on her window where a few drops had strayed in beneath the eaves. Now the sun is out and grey clouds are scudding away in front of a brisk westerly breeze. Steam rises briefly from the asphalt pathways at the side of the house. The sun appears for a short time, then is hidden once again, this time with fat white clouds.

She finds it difficult to read the weather here. Within the space of one day, the wind rises and dies away or changes direction. Black clouds, white clouds, grey clouds and every shade in between, coming and going, and always the threat of rain. The rain is wispy and indecisive compared with the heavy rainstorms that come to Mudgee in the spring. And there is little heat in the sun here. She finds herself avoiding the shadows and seeking the warmth. She deliberately exposes her bare face and arms to the sun, something she could never do at home. Her white skin would have become flayed into the colour of the internal juice of her clan totem. Scratch the bark of a bloodwood, pierce the dark flesh beneath. Can a tree weep? If so, the eye of the bloodwood sheds blood instead of salt.

Eliza opens the oven door. She searches for any spots of burnt fat that she did not pick up yesterday when she cleaned it. But the speckled navy-blue enamel surface is sparkling. She sighs. She must find some work to do. The shower cubicle then. Or maybe the plastic shower curtain. When she pulls it aside, it gives off a sour smell. There is mould embedded in the seams. But she is uncertain of the correct cleaning method. Does plastic melt in a washing machine? Mele would know but she can't ask her. Eliza does not want to look like an ignorant fool.

Josie has changed. Her melancholia has left her. She seems almost happy. Eliza feels more comfortable with her than ever before but Jones is suspicious. Every afternoon he comes to the flat and takes Eliza out for what he calls a walk and a talk. And every afternoon he asks her the same questions about Josie. Has she said anything to anyone? Has she been back to the police? Has she made any phone calls to Australia?

Eliza had made Josie breakfast at seven o'clock this morning but Josie had refused to eat anything. She had gulped down a cup of tea and then walked off with her bag of books and papers. 'Off for the day,' she said. 'Be good. And thanks for the tea.'

Eliza abandons the idea of doing any more cleaning. She decides not to wait for Jones to come. She needs to be outside, in the freshly washed air, away from the possibility of interrogation, away from questions she cannot, or will not, answer.

She walks as quietly as possible past Mele's door. The washing machine on the front porch is unplugged and the windows are closed. There is no sign of life coming from any of the flats except for the crying of a puppy somewhere from deep within the building. Eliza hesitates. She tries to work out where the noise is coming from so that she can go to the appropriate window to call out soothing words in an attempt to calm the puppy's distress. But the crying stops as abruptly as it started.

Eliza makes it out to the street unnoticed.

Since the incident last week, Jones has cautioned Eliza to be on her guard. 'Be extra careful,' he said. 'Just because the police think that Josie's a paranoid liar doesn't mean that others will share their view. People crave stories of death and disaster, they want to believe the very worst and people like Josie feed this obsession.'

Eliza said nothing. She did not bother to point out that Josie had told the truth about the scene of terror in the bush. She knew from experience that he would launch into one of his mini-lectures on how people often have very different versions of the same event. Then he would proceed to tell her how she felt about things. This, he claimed, was part and parcel of his obligation to her. He was being paid to be her minder, not just of her body but of her mental health as well. 'Just think of me as your personal translator,' he said. 'Let me carry you from your closed community to the ways of the real world.'

She goes to the park nearby. There is a lone dog, mustard-coloured, running free with a chain attached to his collar. He runs with his big feet flung sideways, leaping with joy. She whistles to him but he pretends he has not heard her.

At the other side of the park is a small pond. A small flock of mallard ducks has taken possession of it. She watches them dipping their heads beneath the brown water. She sits on the damp ground and leans her back against a strange tree that consoles her a little for the absence of eucalypts in this park. She has noted a heavily pruned bottlebrush with a few crimson flowers poking through the chopped branches. Possibly *Callistemon citrinus*. The only other familiar face is an immature specimen of *Banksia marginata* holding up a solitary yellow cone. They are crammed into the middle of a collection of unknown shrubs. She can't tell if they are native to this country or if they have been brought down from the Northern Hemisphere.

She wants to tear the flowers of her homeland from their sad branches and hide them away within the folds of her clothing. She wants to take them back to the privacy of her room and hold the crimson brush up to the light to marvel at the richness of the pollen. She wants to shake loose the warm honey smell from the yellow cone of banksia. But it would be wrong of her to cause harm to these plants in order to assuage her hunger for the known. Besides, there are too many people around.

Hours pass. Children come and go with pieces of bread for the ducks. And she sees the mustard dog again, recaptured, and being pulled along on the broken chain by an old man. He is clearly angry with the dog and jerks the chain whenever the dog wants to stop and sniff. The dog pays no attention to him. He seems to understand that his owner does not have the strength to control him.

The wind is picking up and the rain is thickening. Drops of rain spit down through the canopy of the tree onto her uncovered head. People are running for the bandstand. A woman struggles with the plastic cover of her child's stroller.

Eliza stays where she is, holding her face up to the wetness, her coat opened to the weather. Then she sees a familiar-looking elderly couple walking along the path towards her, huddling beneath a large black umbrella. Eliza does not attempt to hide her face. Let them see her, let them see her still here in this country of rain and stolen trees. And know that lies have been told about her.

But at the last minute, the umbrella shifts in the wind and the woman's head is revealed. It is not Mrs Temple.

Eliza gets to her feet. Her blouse is wet and clinging to her skin. She wraps her coat securely around her damp body and walks out through the park gate to the busy street beyond.

I was naive. I should have known that my story would be impossible to believe. Mass killing, Mrs Tabel? We have not been informed of anything of this nature from New South Wales. Evidence? Oh there was another witness beside you. Your sister Megan, the one who came into New Zealand with you? Oh she's not your sister. Mmmm… What is your relationship with this woman then? You were studying her. In a closed community. Mmmm…

I was left alone for a long time in the interview room. Every five minutes or so someone in a uniform would come and stare at me through the glass panel. Eventually, a cheerful young woman came back into the interview room and told me I was free to go. And thanks for the help with your neighbours. Things should be okay there from now on but if there's any further trouble ring this number.

She handed me a card. Constable Annette Summershill, Domestic Violence Unit.

I left. There was no point in repeating my story to any more cops. Jones must have got to them. He probably told them that I was mentally unstable and to take anything I said with a big pinch of salt.

I did not mention Briony or the fact that I am her mother. I intended to, but three minutes into the interview I knew that I was not going to be believed. The look on the faces of the two officers interviewing me told me that it was hopeless. So in the end I said okay, okay, I know it sounds implausible but please ring the New South Wales police and tell them to go up into the hills behind the Triple M compound and find a ravine. Yes yes one man with tattoos and hair teased up into a mohawk and three women, two dressed as hippies, and four children. I think. There may have been three, no I remember now that Sarah tried to hide a toddler in her clothes. So that would make four. Her name? Yes yes I knew her, I was studying her too but the others were strangers. No I can't draw you a map they hit me on the head which fuddled me a bit but I know what I saw.

These New Zealand cops live in cloud-cuckoo land. I tried to tell them about the survivalists and the neo-nazis and the black helicopters of the apocalypse and the One World Order but they just stared at me as if I was mad. But the relief I feel is amazing. I spoke into a tape recorder, I told the story of the massacre. I have turned it from a private hell into a public matter. And I know that when I get back to Australia, I will get some action.

It's almost five o'clock. My last day working in this library. I feel almost sad that my work here has come to an end. The librarians here have been very helpful. One of them told me this afternoon that I have become almost part of the furniture and that they will miss me. I have spoken with several of them today. About my studies here, and about my triple quest. I asked the one who made the comment about furniture if she had ever seen bodies fall from a great height like sacks of meat breaking apart on rocks. She backed away uncertainly so I quickly explained to her that I had seen my own husband fall from the sky, in a parachute that did not open. Did she remember ever seeing it? Oh it went around the world on Real TV, a famous amateur video, I saw it many times.

I begin to pack my bag. Tonight I will present Eliza with this thick folder. Within are papers and notes that signal a return of pre-modern terror, couched in pious religious speech, transformed, but still recognisable. I check to make sure that I have made two other copies of the contents of this folder, one for Madeline and one for Briony. I have been searching all week for a title that catches the intent of my argument against the misuses of history and the inherent deception within borrowed communities and today I found it.

I write *Ranters Redux* on the front of the manilla folder in thick black letters.

The naming of the other two folders is, by comparison, a simple task. I label one *Identity through Bloodlines*. This contains official certificates of my mother's family and some of the names and addresses of people in New Zealand who could be related to me. This is for my sister Megan.

I call the last folder *Stuff*. Because that is exactly how I look at it. *Stuff* off the Internet about the forms of fascism that exist today. I have not written a single word. I have photocopied and printed out the ideas of others. This collection is brief, succinct, and necessarily superficial. I will insist that Briony read every single word. And because it is not my voice, my language, my ideas, she may just listen. There is always the possibility of redemption.

Eliza arrives back at the flat. There is a wet, striped umbrella opened out on the back porch. It has a broken rib. Eliza hesitates. Jones? She had hoped that he had given up waiting for her. But then she recognises the umbrella as the one that Josie had brought back from the library yesterday. 'Just borrowed,' she had said cheerfully. 'I'll return it tomorrow. Or when it stops raining.'

Eliza opens the door. Josie is sitting at the table, unpacking her papers from her bag. She exclaims at the rain running down from Eliza's coat onto the carpet. 'Get out of your wet things, you'll freeze to death.' Then she laughs and says that she remembers saying these exact words to Eliza once before. 'Remember? I came down the stairs of the dorm carrying a club, I thought that you were an intruder.'

Eliza showers and comes back into the living room wrapped in a towel. Josie insists that Eliza borrow her dressing gown. Not the same one that Josie had lent her on that other occasion when she had arrived soaking wet from one of her wanderings. That one had been left in Digger Town along with the rest of her things.

Eliza tells her that on that same night she had hidden a dissected cat in a bucket of ice behind the old saloon bar. The next morning when she went to get it to take it into her class for a nature-study lesson, it had gone. She had often wondered who had removed it. Did Josie know anything about it?

'A dissected cat, for your class?'

'Yes. Did you take it?'

Josie confesses that she had. And that she had got the wrong idea. She saw it as mutilated, not dissected. A sacrifice of some sort. She admits to a feeling of relief. Now that Eliza has told her the truth that is.

'What did you do with it?'

'I buried it at the side of one of the paddocks. I felt sorry for it.'

'It was a wild cat, a predator, a killer of native birds and lizards.'

Josie asks why Eliza had hidden it. 'The ice,' she answers. 'You were not meant to know about it. Only the butchers knew about the ice.'

Josie jumps in. 'Well then I may as well come clean about a few more technological marvels that were not supposed to be in Digger Town.'

Eliza says, 'But I told you that my uncle was allowed to have a generator and plumbing because Aunt Hilda is very ill.'

'No no,' says Josie. 'I mean about the wine.'

Chapter Eleven

Eliza is genuinely puzzled. She listens in amazement as Josie tells her about a night two months ago when she, Josie, had broken into the locked door of the high wall surrounding the sheds where the wine was made. Josie did not exactly break in, a certain key was extracted from a certain person by placing certain threats. But never mind. What she saw behind that locked wall shocked her so much that she was unable to write it up in her notebooks or even think about the consequences until now.

'You have been lied to Eliza, all of you have. Organic and traditional methods? Bullshit. The place is full of huge stainless steel vats and automatic machines. I wouldn't be surprised if the whole operation is run by computers.'

'But I have seen the oak casks being made...'

'There were a few empty ones stacked up along one wall with some rusty hand-bottling machines and other devices but they were strictly museum pieces.'

Eliza is stunned. She wants to call Josie a liar, a fabulator, a troublemaker. But why would Josie make this up? What is her motive?

Josie says that she's sorry for upsetting Eliza but given their present situation, the truth must be told. Not just about the wine. Everything. Like Eliza's relationship with Ivan and what she intended to do about it. 'Information is survival. For both of us.'

Josie goes to the table and takes a manilla folder from beneath a pile of papers. She insists that Eliza take it and read it. Now. Tonight. From cover to cover.

Eliza doesn't want to look at it. She has collapsed onto the sofa, shivering and shaking inside the warm dressing gown.

Josie says, 'You don't believe me do you? I can't prove it of course. But didn't you ever wonder why so few people were permitted to go beyond the locked wall and why the wine-making process was kept so secret?'

Eliza fights back. 'We sold the finished product in the shop. That was our job. We did not need to know.'

'Who's we?'

'Me and some of the other women.'

'So. A few select men produced the wine and the selling was left to women.'

Eliza hates Josie at this moment. She gets up from the sofa and fills the kettle to make tea. She asks Josie if she would like some food.

'Can't eat,' says Josie. 'Too wound up.'

'You're working too hard.'

'Not any more. It's over with, finished.'

Eliza pours the tea. They drink from large white cups. Eliza nibbles on dry salty crackers. Josie wants to know if Eliza has seen Jones today. Eliza shakes her head. 'I had to get outside, I went to the park and stayed longer than I intended.'

'If he doesn't come tonight, I'll ring him in the morning. I must speak with him.'

Eliza pulls some more crackers from the packet. 'Please don't tell him about the wine.'

'What do you take me for? It's not my intention to poke fun at you or your community. Besides, that's private information. I'm not telling him anything except that we're leaving.'

'Are we going to move house?'

'Better than that. We're going home.'

Eliza leaps up and throws her arms around Josie. She could weep with joy.

Josie laughs uneasily and tells her to hang on, it's all up in the air. Money is the problem. A small matter of nine-hundred dollars. That, and getting past security at Auckland Airport. That's why she wants to clear it with Jones first.

Eliza pours another cup of tea and drinks it down quickly. The salty biscuits have made her thirsty. 'He will not allow us to leave.'

'But his job as our protector is finished. I spoke up over a week ago but nothing has happened to us. Madeline must have exaggerated the danger.'

'He will never let us go,' says Eliza. 'We will be silenced.'

'You know something,' says Josie. 'What has he said to you?'

'Nothing. It's just a strong feeling that I have.'

'Do what you want. I'm going back to Sydney, either with you, or without you.'

Eliza knows that she will leave with Josie. In spite of her fear of Jones. Or maybe because of it. She knows that he wants to have sex with her. The thought of it makes her flesh creep. And it puzzles her. She has never given him any encouragement, not the slightest sign. The sexual passion that drives him to touch her has nothing to do with her will or her desire. It is entirely his own invention.

Eliza cooks poached eggs on toast. Josie once again refuses to eat but accepts the offer of a cup of freshly brewed tea. Outside, the rain has eased to a drizzle and the wind has died away. Josie is preoccupied with her papers. She tries to give Eliza the manilla folder again. Eliza refuses. She announces that she wants to go to bed. To sleep first and then think things over with a fresh mind. She already has an idea about getting the money for their fares. Josie cries tell me tell me! but Eliza refuses. She closes her bedroom door on Josie's stricken face.

Eliza takes off the dressing gown and folds it neatly at the end of the bed. She puts on her short satin nightgown. She longs for a return to her familiar clothes. Like the chaste calico tents that she and the other women wore in Digger Town at night. Textures, of rough cloth, and soil clinging to the skins of vegetables, and the crush of eucalyptus leaves beneath the soles of her feet. Sounds, voices of children, and water bubbling in chip heaters, and the clatter of plates in the dining room.

Deep sleep must come, deep enough to deny the possibility of dreams.

The Qantas jet is lurching around in severe turbulence and Eliza is hanging on to my arm, pale and sweating with fear. I have explained that these huge planes are built to withstand fierce winds and thunderstorms and changes in air pressure. Imagine that we are on a sailing ship on the Tasman Sea, I tell her. Forget that we are high above the sea. Imagine that this is a fast clipper from last century, running cargo to Sydney Town. Three tall masts ballooning out with studding sails, riding up the side of green canyons, then dropping down into the troughs. Ride the waves, listen to the song of canvas and rope and timber, feel secure within the strength of the hull.

I'm still amazed at Eliza's cleverness. She has certainly learned the ways of the world in a few brief weeks. Either that, or she found out a long time ago that her beauty can be used as a weapon for getting exactly what she wants.

Jones' credit card did not stand a chance. She had asked him for some cash to buy a new dress. One she had seen in a boutique window on Ponsonby Road. So lovely, floating blue panels falling from a daring white bodice, did he think that it would suit her? 'Oh yes,' he had said. 'The colours will echo your eyes and your hair. I will give you the money right now. But only if you wear it for me tonight. And say that you'll drink a bottle of red wine with me. In candle-light.'

She promised so sincerely. And she memorised the exact position of his fingers on the console of the automatic teller machine. She took the cash he gave her and then stole his credit card from his hip pocket. And all the while gazing into his eyes and pretending to flirt with him.

I was all for taking the whole amount in his expense account, three thousand and two hundred dollars. But Eliza would not let me. She said that we should take just what we need for the fares. She would not budge even after I explained to her that morally this money belongs to us. We are the expenses. Eliza hoped that Madeline will give us more when we get to Sydney.

I thought this very unlikely. She'll be so angry with us for disobeying her orders and giving Jones the slip that I doubt that she'll willingly open her wallet for us again.

Until this moment I had given little thought to where to turn for help after we arrive. But now, strapped into my heaving seat, riding a mean westerly storm, my plans fall into place. I decide to go straight to Megan's house, tell her everything, throw myself on her mercy. I need a safe place to stay, a few days to get things sorted out before I make a move. I am determined to approach the Sydney police with more preparation than I had done in Auckland. I need to get some evidence first. Either find myself a good lawyer or go to someone reliable from the media. I could not bear to be treated like a mad fool again.

Meanwhile, there is the problem of Eliza. I don't know what to do with her after we arrive. She seems to be suffering from the delusion that she can just turn up at Digger Town and resume her life as if nothing has happened.

The cabin crew are strapped into their seats and the captain has just announced that the serving of food and alcohol will be delayed until the turbulence is over. I am hungry and thirsty and I need to get to the toilet urgently. I was so tense at the airport, I forgot to buy snack food and a bottle of water. I had been deprived of caffeine for days and all I could think of was coffee coffee coffee. So I had three large cups at the airport café, one after the other. And now my kidneys are going berserk and I'm dying for a pee.

It took us three days to get a booking on this plane. Three days on the run from Jones and anyone who vaguely looked like a cop. We waited until just before Jones was due to arrive to take Eliza out for the candle-lit dinner. I wrote a note and pinned it to the door of the flat. *Have taken Eliza for urgent treatment to the hospital, sudden asthma attack, will ring you a.s.a.p. ...*

We walked from Ponsonby to Onehunga, and it took hours. Especially since Eliza insisted that we bring all our things. I wanted to leave most of our clothes but she could not bear to leave anything behind. We rumbled our wheeled suitcases along uneven pathways. I had the added burden of my heavy case of papers and folders.

I decided that we should walk for safety reasons. A taxi driver might remember us. And I had no doubt that Jones would move heaven and earth to try and track us down. Especially when he discovered the missing money. He is clever enough to work out that nine-hundred dollars is about the standard economy fare and departure tax, times two, from Auckland to Sydney.

I had obtained a key to the empty flat at The Home on the pretext of a possible tenancy agreement. After viewing the accommodation, I went back to the real estate office and told the receptionist that I had decided that it was too small for my needs. But only after I had taken the key to a busy kiosk in the Onehunga Mall and had a copy made.

I don't know why I did this. I had no intention of breaking into the place. I desperately wanted to see inside and this I did by pretending to be a prospective tenant. Then after I had seen the interior, I felt that I had to have a copy of the key. There is something about the retracking of my past that is bringing out the souvenir hunter in me. I regret this new and unexpected side of my personality. I know that I have clung to certain things that belonged to Russell but I excuse myself by seeing his things as remnants of a shared past that I had willingly helped to shape. This key business has me rattled. I pretended that I was walking through the same door that my labouring mother entered forty years ago. But how could it be? The whole building has changed radically since the conversion into flats.

Eliza stayed within the walls with the curtains pulled the whole time we were there. The power had been disconnected but there was cold water in the taps and we managed to wash ourselves with damp cloths. We resorted to such tricks as flushing the toilet only when the peak hour traffic was grinding up Queen Street or the mob of children next door were yelling and fighting. I crept out after dark and bought bread and tomatoes and cakes and fresh fruit. Each night I ranged further, each night I went to a different Superette or dairy. I missed coffee the most. In the mornings, I could smell it wafting through the cracked louvre window from the flat behind us, the one where the children lived. On my second night out, foraging for food, I discovered some chocolate-covered coffee beans and brought them back to Eliza in great delight. She ate one but found it too bitter. She suggested that I eat the rest. Which I did with great enjoyment.

I can't make Eliza out. She did not ask me any questions about the key or why I had chosen to come to this house or why we had to keep our presence here secret from the other tenants. I was going to tell Eliza about the significance of this room but in the end I didn't. I have no idea how she would have reacted to the news that this was the room of my birth. I am a little shocked myself, both at the sentimental motive that took me there, and the stained and battered appearance of the place.

There was just one bed, a single one. Eliza insisted that I take the bed and that she sleep on the sofa. The days were long and silent; Eliza creeping around in her socks and me prostrate on the bed, sometimes reading my notes, but mostly lying with my eyes shut. The room smelt of something. It caught me at the oddest moments, flooding into my nostrils when I lifted my head from the pillow and then disappearing when I took my next breath. Not unpleasant. But I raged to give a name to it. Not quite blood, not quite water, not quite semen.

I asked Eliza if she could smell anything. She shook her head. She asked me to describe it to her.

What could I say? That the birth fluids of hundreds of women including my own mother had somehow leached into the floor and the walls? In the end I told Eliza to forget about it. Maybe I was just reacting to the stuffiness caused by the unopened windows.

I wanted Eliza to take the opportunity of reading the folder that I had so carefully assembled for her while we were stuck here with nothing to do. I tried to explain to her what *Ranters*

Redux meant but she stared at me with a blank face. Sometimes I could hit her. She shuts herself off when there is something that she does not wish to hear. At times she reminds me of teenagers that I have known. Briony especially had turned *no see no hear no speak* into an art form.

The seatbelt sign goes off. The severe turbulence has stopped as suddenly as it started. The cabin crew race to the galleys to prepare the delayed meal. I jump over Eliza in the aisle seat and make for the lavatories aft. Too late. There is already a queue. I'm almost wetting myself. Then I hear someone vomiting behind a half-closed lavatory door and it makes me want to throw up too. I manage to suppress the urge but I must have turned green because the woman in front of me offers to give up her place to me and I'm too desperate to say no you go first.

I pull my knickers down just in time. I hold onto the safety rail in case the turbulence returns, peeing gallons.

Then I return to my seat and eat and drink in comfort.

I watch the diagram on the screen that shows a picture of a plane approaching the East Coast of Australia. Four hundred kilometres to go. So far so good, but if Jones has tipped Madeline off, there may be a reception committee waiting for us.

Eliza asks me how long to go before we get to Sydney. About thirty minutes I tell her. She has not touched her meal. I ask her if she feels okay. She nods but I can see that the rough ride has really frightened her.

Over the last month I have learned a bitter lesson. In my frantic search for family names and the links between communities like the neo-nazis and the Ranters and the Diggers I came to understand that I was uncovering the same set of truths over and over again. The differences between these modes of belonging are superficial, they are all variations on the theme of fascist community. Invented, stolen, rewritten, transported to a different place and a different time, but underneath, the same stern warning.

There can be no individual morality. Members must act for

the good of the group. Failure to do so results in banishment or death.

This was the downfall of Briony. She acted out the rules of the group that she joined. Her misguided loyalty, her fierce desire to belong, overrode her own morality.

The plane begins to descend. I can see the land appear below, and although I'm apprehensive of getting safely through Customs and Immigration, I feel a sense of relief, a sense of coming home.

From now on I will act alone, I will make my own decisions. And these will be based on my logic, my needs, my desires. Any other path will lead me to a state of irretrievable breakdown from which I can never return.

Eliza is pleased to be back on firm ground. They sit in the transit lounge and Josie smokes two cigarettes one after the other. Eliza points out the *no smoking* sign but Josie seems oblivious. That is, until a woman traveller approaches them and complains about the smoke and Josie says quick! let's move! as if it's Eliza who is calling attention to themselves. They hide for fifteen minutes in the women's toilet. Then they split up and sit in different sections of the transit lounge. The crowd thins out. Two more jumbo jets land in quick succession and suddenly there are hundreds of people milling around.

Josie appears at Eliza's side. 'Time to pick up our bags,' she whispers. 'It's over an hour since we landed, they won't wait for us forever.'

They line up for Immigration and present their New Zealand passports. Eliza had suggested that it might be safer for them to join different queues but Josie reminded her that they are supposed to be sisters. Why would they not be together? The official asks them if they are coming for a holiday. They both answer yes. She checks their entry forms. Josie had put Megan's address as her contact. So too had Eliza. The official does not question the fact that one Megan Hathaway coming from New Zealand had given her own address in Ryde as a contact. This is because Josie had taken the precaution of using Megan's married name on the forms. If the official thought it co-incidental that one Megan was visiting another, she did not say so. 'Have a great time in Sydney,' she says. 'Half your luck to be on holiday...next please!'

Eliza and Josie walk away, pulling their suitcases towards the *Nothing to Declare* doorway. They pass through unchallenged.

They join the line of people waiting for the shuttle. Eliza revels in the scorching heat radiating upwards from the pavement and the high cloudless sky but Josie is worried. 'I smell a rat,' she says. 'That was too easy, by far.'

The bus arrives and the door springs open. Josie pays for two fares to Circular Quay. They sit at the back. Josie is looking uneasy and only relaxes when the bus is well away from the airport and moving towards the centre of the city. The roads and rooftops are shimmering in the November heat. Mirages of an urban summer.

Eliza asks Josie where they are going.

'To my sister's house. We told the truth for once.'

'Does she know that we are coming?'

'She doesn't know that we've been in New Zealand. But she will take us in, don't worry.'

Eliza asks nervously, 'How long before I can go home?'

Josie says that it's not up to her. Now that they are back in Sydney they are under the guidance of Madeline. She will tell us when and if it's safe to return.

'Are you coming back with me?'

'Impossible.'

'But what about your studies?'

Josie confesses that she no longer cares. She had deluded herself for a while, about the possibility of finishing her thesis. But now it seems irrelevant. 'Don't you feel the same? That everything has gone too far to go back?'

Eliza is silent. She has spent the past week going over the events of the past few months in order to make connections between her own actions and those of Ivan's group. If she had not allowed him to make love to her would the killings still have happened? Yes. Did she contribute to the deaths of the feral people? No, she is not responsible for the murderous intent of the group from the Triple M.

But if she had not met Ivan, she would not have been there in the bush to witness the events. If she not left the land, if Sarah had not left the land, they both would be safe now. They would be in the vineyards to see the pale green tendrils racing along the supports to replace leaves and branches lost to the autumn prune. They would be working in the pastures and gardens, watching the birth of foals and lambs and young birds testing their wings.

She broke the rules of her community, she escaped through the border fence and this lead to her witnessing a terrible event. What should she do? Break her silence? But if that lead to violent retribution, then she would be directly responsible for causing pain to others.

They arrive at Circular Quay. There are crowds of people waiting at the bus shelters. They sit on their suitcases to wait for the next bus to Ryde. Buses come and go every minute, flooding the air with diesel fumes, but there is no sign of their bus.

'To hell with this,' says Josie. 'I've had it, let's take a cab.'

The driver is chatty, wanting to know where they'd come from today. 'On holiday girls? Sydney's the place for you then...' He spends the whole journey pointing out the sights as he drives like a maniac through the heavy traffic.

Josie answers him in monosyllabic grunts but Eliza is glad of his chatter. The motion of the car and the flow of his voice have helped to still her mind. Out of the mess of grief and indecision, one persistent desire has emerged. She will meet with Ivan one last time. To ask him to give himself up, make a confession, admit his crime. She has no idea what his reaction will be or what she'll do if he refuses. All she knows is that she must confront him. She owes this to the memory of Sarah.

They arrive at the house in Ryde. A screeching sulphur-crested cockatoo is sitting on the top of a lamppost. It almost drowns out the taxi driver's parting shot, 'Have a happy day girls. And don't do anything I wouldn't do...'

Josie hurls an insult at the back of the moving car. The cockatoo continues its raucous rave. Josie rings the doorbell. Nothing happens. Joe tries the bell again and this time keeps her finger on it for almost a minute. They hear a loud buzzing noise inside the house but no one comes to the door.

'Shit,' says Josie. 'She must be out. We'll go around to the back and wait there.'

They pull their suitcases along a path at the side of the house and Josie opens a high wooden gate. They find some shade at the edge of the lawn. The big white bird is now sitting on the roof of the garden shed, watching them. Eliza whistles softly to it. Josie lights a cigarette. The bird preens its feathered armpits. Minutes pass. Eliza takes off her shoes and lies full length on the spongy carpet of buffalo grass. Then the bird opens its beak and blasts their eardrums with a final harsh cry before flying away.

THE KEY TO LIBERTY

The first night in Ryde, Eliza and I sat on the buffalo grass lawn until after dark. Buses laboured up the hill and planes flew low overhead. The yellow street lamps looked down with indifferent eyes and houses darkened behind summer drapes and screens. I was just about to suggest that we go back into town, when Megan turned up with lover boy in tow. She was both angry and relieved. Glad to see me safe and sound, furious that I had been missing for over a month leaving her to fob off persistent phone calls from my mother-in-law. And what about poor Jack? 'He turned up from Canberra, alone,' she said. 'Looking for you. I had to send him away with a flea in his ear. He's beside himself with worry.'

My beloved sister. She knows exactly how to get to me.

But everything is changed now that lover boy has taken up my cause. His name is Cedric Power and he's a journalist. He's a freelancer, works for print media, radio, and television. We talked through the night and he is very excited about getting an exclusive story. I suggested that we go to the site of the massacre in secret, just him and me, with a camera. He wanted Megan to come too, as a witness, but she refused.

'It sounds a little far-fetched,' she said. 'Surely someone

would have reported the victims missing by now? There's been nothing on the news.'

Cedric left at about ten o'clock the next morning. He told us that he wanted to check up on a few things. He promised to come back to take Megan out to lunch.

Madeline turned up soon after he left. I saw her on the front veranda with her hand poised to ring the bell. I opened the door and greeted her and asked her to come in. I wanted to get through the confrontation with her as quickly as possible. I had all my arguments and excuses ready, fuelled by a month of rage and fear and frustration.

We sat in the dining room next to the kitchen while Megan fussed over making coffee and heating up sesame rolls in the microwave. Eliza appeared in my dressing gown, looking half-asleep. She barely acknowledged Madeline's presence.

We sat around the table and ate buttery rolls and drank coffee. Megan smoked one of my cigarettes. My tension eased. Madeline had not accidentally discovered our presence here. She knew that we had come into Sydney the day before. She told us that Jones had informed her of our departure and that we had been watched throughout our journey. It had been decided that it was safe for us to return to Sydney. Things were almost sorted out, the danger almost over. The police were about to make a move. As long as I promised not to talk about it until the crime had been made public, we would all be safe.

'I wish I'd known this sooner,' I said. 'The trip was a nightmare.'

'We couldn't find you in Auckland. All we knew was that you were both booked on a flight to Sydney yesterday afternoon. You should have checked with one of us first. If things had been different, you could have got us all killed.'

Megan's eyes almost fell out of her head. Until that moment, I hadn't been sure if she believed my story or not.

'Okay' I said to Madeline. 'Now that you've forgiven us for leaving without permission, you must solve a mystery for me.

The story you told Megan over the phone. About me doing something sexual to Eliza, something in a bath.'

'I did nothing of the sort,' said Madeline.

'You hinted that I had seduced Eliza, forced her to run away with me.'

Megan cuts in, 'I didn't say seduce. That's your word.'

Madeline said some parts of it were true. Ask Eliza.

Eliza looked positively ill throughout this exchange. She would not meet my eyes. She mumbled something about feathers and blackened rosemary and blood.

'Not good enough,' I told her. 'Say it loud and clear. Josie is innocent.'

'Munna was forced to do it,' she said. 'By Joshua.'

I reminded Madeline that she had promised me on the steps of the Opera House that she would ring Megan and tell her that the accusations were a pack of lies. Madeline admitted that she had forgotten. She'd had a lot on her mind at the time.

'Who's Munna?' asked Megan.

'A handicapped girl in Digger Town,' said Madeline. 'Mental age of ten.'

I could see that Megan was about to ask Madeline questions about Digger Town. She'd been doing the same to me ever since we'd arrived last night. She was literally bursting with curiosity. I was not prepared to provide her with enough fodder for her dinner parties and gossip sessions for the next decade. I have already told her exactly as much as she needs to know, no more, no less. I had gone through a lot to collect my stories about Digger Town. They belonged to me, not her.

I put a stop to Megan's imminent interrogation of Madeline. 'That reminds me,' I said. 'What time is lover boy coming to pick you up for lunch?'

Days passed and nothing happened. I'm waiting to hear from Madeline about the police arresting the murderers. Cedric is hassling me to go to Mudgee with him before someone else gets the story. I have to be very careful to remember what I've said. About what I'm planning. I've told Megan and

Cedric one version, Madeline another, and absolutely nothing to Eliza. She's clammed up completely since we arrived back in Australia. I've tried to make her read the research about the Ranters and I've tried to engage her in a dialogue about her and Ivan. She refused.

Every morning she walks out of the house and goes to The Field of Mars, a nature reserve near Megan's house. She stays away for hours. Eliza told Megan that the same white cockatoo calls to her each morning and that she has personally greeted each tree. Some of them are strangers given that she is so far from her own land.

Sometimes I fear for her sanity. I made excuses on her behalf to Megan. 'She has had to cope with so many changes,' I said. 'She only feels safe in the bush. That's all she knows.'

'We all have,' said my sister. 'Had to cope with change I mean. Look at my life. Look at yours. Why is she so special?'

Then on the seventh day, Madeline comes to pick her up to take her back to Digger Town. Eliza gets into the big car without a backward glance to me or a word of thanks to Megan for allowing her to stay here. The last thing I see of Eliza is the back of her head covered with the scarf decorated with boxing kangaroos that I had bought for her at Circular Quay.

I apologise to Megan for Eliza's lack of manners but she claims she doesn't care. 'To be honest Josie,' she says. 'I'm glad to see the back of her. She gives me the creeps.'

It's late at night the same day and I can hear Megan and Ceddy as she calls him, fucking in the next room. He's not married although he has been, three times. I'm certain that Megan believes that she is soon going to be the fourth Mrs Power. He tried to come on to me today, just after Madeline left with Eliza. I soon burst his bubble and he had the grace to look ashamed. 'Our relationship is strictly professional,' I told him. 'For our mutual benefit. I get you as a credible witness and you get the exclusive story and pictures.'

Sometimes I wonder if he is losing faith in me. Or at least in my integrity. He asked me about Briony, about my attitude to her. 'You realise that she will be severely punished. She'll get life.'

I laughed at him. 'Ironic isn't it? She was always telling me to get a life and now she's going to get a life *sentence*.'

He didn't seem to appreciate my joke. Or maybe he didn't understand it. Megan has warned me that he is very serious and not given to flippant comments.

Megan is putting pressure on me as well. She keeps asking me what I'm waiting for. 'You should get to Mudgee as soon as possible,' she said. 'Someone else may discover the bodies and the story will break before we are ready to release it. Besides, Ceddy is getting restless. He wonders if you realise the serious nature of the allegations that you are making.'

Allegations? I ask her if she's heard the old joke. 'I deny the allegations and I spit on the alligator...'

She doesn't crack a smile. She should be careful of spending too much time with Ceddy, he's turning her into a killjoy.

Eliza has been back at Digger Town for three days. Last night she got the news that the council has decided to allow her to resume her teaching. She has been in the classroom since six this morning, preparing her lessons and moving posters and paintings back to their original positions on the notice boards. Hannah and the other relief teachers have changed things around. Everything must be exactly as it was before she left Digger Town. She cleans the blackboard, and restores the contents of the drawers beneath her table to their former state of neatness. She counts the double wooden desks. Fourteen. One missing. She is puzzled. She goes into the other three classrooms but she cannot find the missing desk. She checks inside the lids of each remaining desk in her room. Two at the back are empty. The books and belongings of the four children who sat here have been taken away. The children are related to Eliza, all are bloodwoods, second-cousins-once-removed.

By seven-thirty the room is ready. She sits at her desk, composed and ready for the day's work ahead. Since she returned, she has kept her head down, she has tried to follow every rule and instruction to the letter. Her uncle had been pleased to see her. He feared that she had run away with Sarah. She did not tell him that Sarah was dead. This must wait until after she has seen Ivan. It is difficult for her to be with the other unmarried women at night in the dormitory. They keep asking her about Sarah, about their adventures together. She can't get it through to them that she did not run away to be with Sarah, that she has been somewhere else quite different.

Last night, she told them about flying in a huge plane, over land and sea, tossed about in a storm of air. And how, by pretending that she was far below in a sailing ship, scudding along on solid water, she had overcome her fear.

This diverted them to some extent. That, and the sharing out of Eliza's clothes that she had brought in from the outside. Each woman chose her favourite things. Celia and Anne took the underwear and satin nightgowns and Martha took the skirts and a woollen jumper. They exclaimed over the fine wool of Eliza's coat, the style and the stitching. Eliza was glad to get rid of the clothes. 'Hide them away,' she said. 'Be discreet. Keep them as a reminder of my so-called adventure.'

Celia wanted Eliza to give the coat to Munna who had suffered terribly from cold this winter but Eliza thought that this was too risky. Munna would tell someone where it had come from. Not deliberately of course. But she, Eliza, had enough trouble at the moment.

Someone enters the classroom quietly. Eliza looks up, expecting to see a child coming early to greet her teacher. It's Anne. Sent by Sister Hannah. 'To bring you to breakfast. We have almost finished eating and Hannah is concerned.'

'I'm not hungry,' says Eliza.

'But she said that I should bring you.'

'Where are the Logan children? Their desks are empty.'

'They have been taken away, them and ten others from higher classes.'

'Taken away?'

'By their parents.'

Eliza walks slowly to the back of the room. 'But education is compulsory. What does my uncle have to say about this?'

Anne has a gleam in her eye. 'You've misunderstood me. They haven't just left the school, they've left the community. Four complete families disappeared. They stole from us too, tools and bottles of wine and seed potatoes. From the communal store. And one of your uncle's dogs went missing the same night.'

Eliza refuses to go to breakfast. Anne says that Hannah will probably blame her for Eliza's disobedience. Eliza doesn't care. Anne's news has disturbed her. She has the same sensation of unreality that she felt when Josie accused the winemakers of technological subterfuge. *All that is solid melts into air…*

Anne's parting shot is that some of the people blame Eliza's uncle for letting Mrs Tabel come into our community. They are saying that she brought in a whiff of liberty, a tainted notion of freedom that has created a hunger among those who were once perfectly satisfied. Eliza makes a mental note to take back the satin nightgown and the two tainted petticoats that Anne had so willingly taken last night. She can't have it both ways.

The morning wears on. The children are rather shy of her but she expected this. They must have heard whispered speculations about her lengthy disappearance. She gives them a pep talk about the dangers of gossip and reminds them that there is a Law against it. This is needed, because gossip can destroy the heart of a group. If someone says something untrue about someone else, just by speaking about it makes it into a sort of truth. It takes on a life of its own.

She hangs up a map of the world on the blackboard. She tells them to ignore the lavish use of pink that covers almost a quarter of the world. 'This map is old,' she tells them. 'The colour pink refers to the British Empire which no longer exists. But look down here, this is our country, Australia, and here is

New South Wales. Travel east, across the Tasman Sea, and you will find a small green place where I saw trees just like we have here. Hands up, those who knows what a *Callistemon* is?'

A cough from the back of the room. Hannah is standing in the shadows. Eliza had no idea how long she has been there. Hannah comes forward to the front of the class. 'I'm taking over,' she says. 'Brother Winstanley is meeting with the elders. He has called for you.'

Eliza gathers up her things. Hannah has already rolled up the map.

Eliza walks down the street to the council room. The cool air of the early morning has disappeared. The sun is blazing overhead. She rejoices in the feel of the hot dry wind on her face and the hard ground beneath her boots. Above her, an intense summer sky, clear of blemish, except for a dust haze blurring the outline of the hills.

The elders have left the council room. Her uncle is the only one there. He is gazing out of the window at the front of the shop. He looks troubled. 'Make sure that you protect your face,' he says. 'You will need to get a straw hat from the store and wear it over your scarf. The sun appears to be hotter than usual for this time of the year, already some children have been badly burned.'

She thanks him for his concern.

'The elders are worried,' he says. 'They believe that your disappearance and subsequent return has unsettled the unmarried women. They want you to leave the dormitory at once.'

Eliza is frightened. She asks him if she is being banished.

He reassures her. 'No, a temporary move, that's all.' He takes a piece of bread from a wooden tray and offers it to her. Her stomach is empty and beginning to rumble but she is too shaken to eat. She declines with thanks.

He puts the bread into his own mouth and chews on it, then washes it down with water. 'There have been reports of the women displaying an unhealthy curiosity about the outside world. Is that so?'

She agrees that they have asked her many questions. And that she is finding it difficult to answer them. They believe that she ran away with Sarah. And he already knows that this did not happen.

'The council are putting more pressure on me. They want to know where you went to and what you did. I can't protect you for much longer.'

Eliza promises him that she will tell him everything very soon. She begs for a few more days. There is something that she needs to sort out first.

He tells her that the council has decided that she should move into the hut vacated by Mrs Tabel. As soon as possible. For her own protection and that of the other women.

Eliza says, 'But she may return.'

'I doubt it,' he says. 'A Mrs Madeline Branson came to see me just after you disappeared. She works at the university where Mrs Tabel was enrolled in her studies. She told me that Mrs Tabel sends her sincere apologies to me for leaving without notice. Her daughter unexpectedly became ill and was calling for her.'

Eliza pretends to be concerned. 'Nothing serious I hope.'

'I have had no further news.'

Eliza agrees to move into the hut. She would like to arrange it now, while the women were out of the dormitory. Her uncle does not seem to be in any hurry to move. He is eating another piece of bread and drinking more water.

'I'm pleased that you have agreed with the plan,' he says. 'It makes things easier for me. There has been some dissatisfaction expressed.'

She is surprised at the intimacy of his tone. Is he confiding in her? She sits beside him and takes some bread for herself. He pats her hand. 'Even if Mrs Tabel wants to return, the council will never allow it.'

She risks asking him a question. 'Are they challenging your leadership?'

He jumps to his feet. 'Enough, enough. Move your things at

once and go back to your work. And don't discuss anything I've said with anyone else.'

She thanks him for everything. For giving her time to sort herself out before she faces the council, for not laying the blame on her for Sarah's defection.

He nods in acceptance. She kisses him on the cheek and opens the door to the street. The hot dry westerly rushes in, smelling of dust.

'One more thing,' says Gerrard. 'Warn the women not to flaunt their new finery outside the dormitory.'

She holds the door firmly against a gust of wind. He gives her a little smile. 'They can keep the clothes that you gifted to them.' He puts on his leather hat and adjusts the brim. 'It seems such a little crime. Compared with everything else that is happening. But do advise them to be discreet.'

She packs a few personal belongings and takes her share of clothes from the piles of communal skirts and blouses and scarves. She carries her basket to the store and asks for candles, tapers, and an assortment of linens. Mrs Nelson is on duty, handing out provisions to the married women. She packs Eliza's basket without comment when Eliza explains that she has been ordered to move to the hut.

Eliza inquires after the health of her aunt, Mrs Hilda Winstanley.

'Same as ever,' grunts Mrs Nelson. 'Poor thing could do with more visits.'

Eliza promises to try to see her tomorrow.

The hut is stuffy and smells of stale cigarette smoke. Eliza props the door open to get a flow of air through. Two women walk by with children clinging to their skirts. They stop and stare into the room. One of them points to Eliza and says something behind her hand to the other woman. Eliza shuts the door and opens the window.

It is disconcerting to be in here without Josie. Her presence is everywhere. Clean clothes folded neatly on a chair, a pillowslip of dirty laundry lying on the floor beside the bed, notebooks scattered across the table.

Eliza peeks inside. Some of the entries are written in black ink, some in red and some in blue. She flips through the pages. She can't understand the entries written in black. They are written in some sort of specialised language and have headings like *The Role of Invented Historiography in Contemporary Closed Communities and Religious Forms of Patriarchy in Rural New South Wales*.

The notes written in blue ink are part of Josie's analysis of the Digger community for Gerrard Winstanley. Eliza is fascinated. Some of the words are her own, taken from the recordings that she made for Josie. Here are her verbatim descriptions of their work, the assignment of tasks, the meaning of the clan names and the rules surrounding them. But Josie has added many comments of her own. For the first time Eliza begins to understand the links between her personal experiences and the structure of the community as a whole. She wants her uncle to read the unfinished report. Urgently. She is certain that it will help him to work out why, after fifty years of relative stability, people are leaving the group.

Eliza remembers that her pupils are waiting for her. Lunch must be over long ago. She stacks the books back on the table and almost runs from the hut to her classroom.

Hannah is still there, complaining of Eliza's lateness and the fact that she has skipped a second meal that day. Eliza offers no explanation. Except to say that she has been involved in important council business.

'When I came in,' says Hannah. 'I overheard you telling the children something about the presence of *Callistemon* in a foreign country. You are not permitted to mention your travels to the children. Or to anyone else.'

Eliza almost apologises. Then she remembers the report that she has just read. Ignorance is *not* bliss, said Josie. We are in the information age, like it or not. And no matter how you hide the young people from the outside world, their curiosity will lead them out. Every time.

She unrolls the map and puts it back on the blackboard. 'Now children, pay attention, and I'll tell you what I saw in a rainy island country…'

Last night I gave Madeline her last chance. I rang her on her mobile phone. She was eating out in some restaurant or other and sounded a little drunk. I could hear laughter and the clinking of cutlery on plates. I didn't get anything out of her about the progress of the police investigation or lack of it. She pretended that I was some long lost friend, and we had this ridiculous conversation about seeing each other soon, when things had settled, know what I mean? Meanwhile, she was enjoying her wine tour of the Mudgee district.

Now that Eliza has gone from my sister's house, I can make a move. I have made careful preparations. There are two parts to my plan. First, to get the evidence I need so that Cedric can publicise the murders. I'll watch the media with great satisfaction. I can't wait for those nazis to get a taste of their own medicine. Secondly, I must make Briony pay for what she did. Face to face with me, not in some anonymous courtroom. But the timing is critical. I must make sure that I get to Briony before the cops do.

Cedric and I left Ryde at four o'clock in the morning to avoid the Friday morning traffic. Megan refused to come with us even though she's almost certain that I'm telling the truth. Or so she says. Her excuse now is that she couldn't bear to see dead bodies. Especially those of children.

We're in a rental car. There are two videocams on the back seat. I had to pay for the car and the camera hire. Cedric claims that his own car is too much of a wreck to drive out of Sydney. He's too broke to buy a new one, child support keeps him poor. And his ex-wives. We travel through the Blue Mountains and Katoomba. We are treated to a spectacular sunrise, spoiled by Cedric's fatuous comment *red sky in the morning, sailor's warning…*

The sun is well above the hills when we come into Lithgow.

I slouch down in the passenger seat when we pass the Police Station. It's unlikely that Fran is on duty at this hour but I don't want to tempt fate by being careless. Cedric chatters on. He's making me nervous with his reckless driving and his non-stop talking. I request silence. He stares at me. 'Watch the road!' I snap.

He admits that he's tense. From what I've told him, the Triple M are very dangerous. 'Are you sure it's safe for us to go onto their land by ourselves? Maybe we should get the local cops to accompany us.'

'Stop the car!' I shout. He swerves onto the shoulder of the road. The car travelling behind almost rams into us. The driver gives us the fingers as he passes.

I'm angry and upset. 'If you want to chicken out, tell me now.'

He drives back onto the road, narrowly missing a truck. I offer to get another journalist to accompany me. If he really wants to pull out that is.

He claims that he's too broke. This story will set him up for months. That doesn't stop him feeling scared. 'What will happen to us if we're discovered?'

'We've been over and over this,' I say wearily. 'It won't happen. And even if it does, they wouldn't dare do anything to you.'

We drive on. After another hour I take the wheel. Mercifully, I seem to have put a stop to his chatter. We come into Mudgee just before eight o'clock in the morning. There is little traffic except for school buses, and utes loaded down with hay and sacks of stock feed and yapping dogs. I am dying for coffee and food and nicotine. Cedric would not allow me to smoke in the rental car. Which is a bit rich seeing I'm paying for it.

The café in Market Street is open for breakfast. Cedric suggests that we stoke up here before we do the deed. I am wary of going back into a familiar place. There is a slight chance that we might bump into Madeline or Gregory Sharpe. But there's nowhere else open so I decide to take the risk.

I sit at a table near the window so that I can watch the street. I light up a cigarette and Cedric goes to the counter to choose his breakfast. I had completely forgotten about my last encounter with Jennifer Waite the woman who runs the place. She comes out of the back and recognises me at once and rushes straight over to my table. 'Do you have any news for me,' she cries.

Oh shit. It's coming back to me. She asked me to find her birth mother in Digger Town. Somebody Bloodwood. 'I'm sorry,' I say. 'I went through all the records but I haven't been able to find out anything useful for you.'

Her face falls. 'Can you keep trying? It's very important to me.'

'I'm no longer there. My work is finished.'

Cedric is drumming his fingers impatiently on the counter. Jennifer attends to his order. He comes back to the table with his tray loaded. 'What was that all about?' he asks. I hiss at him to keep quiet. I go to the counter and get some coffee and some hot rolls. Jennifer wants to know where I've been. 'That friend of yours and that cop from Lithgow have been in here asking about you. Twice.'

I explain that I've been on holiday, overseas. And if they come in here again, tell them nothing. I don't want to have anything to do with either of them again.

'Okay,' she says. 'And thanks for trying to find my birth mother. I really appreciate it.'

I feel mean for deceiving her. But I've got more serious things on my mind.

We drive past the gate of the Triple M compound. I can see two flags flying from the top of the pole at the rear of the farmhouse, one with a black triskelion on a red and white background and the other sporting three green M's, joined at the feet. There is no sign of life. Cedric stops the car and takes some shots of the flags.

We park up a gravel side road about a kilometre away from the compound. The bush is thick here but I have calculated that this is the safest spot to access the ravine on the Triple M's land. I have taken the precaution of bringing a compass and a roughly sketched drawing to guide us to the spot. We change into our hiking clothes and boots. The videocams fit neatly into our packs.

It's almost nine-thirty. I calculate that it will take us about an hour and a half to find the right place and another two hours to do the filming and return to the car.

We move as quietly as possible into the thick bush. Cedric is already sweating either with tension or physical exertion or both. I'm surprised at how calm I feel. I have dreamt of this return, both in nightmares and in wakeful terror for over a month. Now that I am actually here on this perfect summer morning, breathing in the astringent smell of eucalypts and listening to the shuffle of lizards and the flap of birds disturbed by our presence, I am much more in control.

We climb and climb. We arrive at the top of a ridge. I recognise some landmarks. Here is the rocky outcrop where I sat after I had seen Briony with the skinheads. I remember my shock at the change in her appearance; the camouflage gear, the shaved head, the rings in her ears. And I remember that Eliza had come up behind me so quietly that I had almost fallen off the rocks in fright.

I check the compass. The ravine lies in an easterly direction. And it will take us half an hour to get there. I decide to rest on the rocky outcrop in exactly the same place that I did before. Did I smoke a cigarette? I can't remember. Cedric is restless, he wants to move on. He warns me against smoking, the bush is tinder dry.

We move slowly along the ridge. The air is heating up. I drip some water from my water bottle onto a strip of cloth and tie it around my neck.

We arrive at the ravine. 'Is this the place? Are you sure?' whispers Cedric.

Last time I was here the air was cool and the sky was lower over the tops of the trees. Today the bush is hot and dry and still. But I'm certain that this is the place. Yes, here is the dry waterfall and the deep sharp-sided ravine. I lean over the edge. It does look a little different. The heat of the last few weeks must have dried up the water holes because there is no glint of black water at the bottom, just a dry dusty bed.

'Isn't there an easier way to get to the bottom?' asks Cedric. 'You didn't tell me it was so steep.'

I'm impatient. I throw off my pack and take out a video-cam. 'I'll go down alone then.' I turn clumsily and catch the toe of my left boot in an exposed root. Crack! Something in my ankle snaps. I let out a stream of abuse at the root and at myself for being so stupid.

'For god's sake keep quiet.' Cedric is looking really worried now. 'Have you broken anything? What the hell are we going to do now?'

The pain in my ankle is severe. I decide to leave my boot on to keep the swelling down. 'You go,' I snap at him. 'I'm not bloody giving up now.'

'But how are we going to get you out of the bush?'

'We'll work that out later. Now go.'

He goes down over the edge. I can hear him puffing and panting and once in a while, the sound of dislodged rocks falling. Then silence. I change my mind about removing my boot. I take the cloth from around my neck and soak it in cold water and tie it tightly around my swollen ankle. I move my toes carefully. I can't hear any noise of bones scrunching together and I can turn my foot both ways without too much difficulty. Obviously just a bad sprain. If I can find a heavy stick to lean on, I'm sure I can walk out with Cedric's help.

I open my backpack and take out a bag of raisins and nuts. I drink the last of my water. It's been over two hours since Cedric went down into the ravine. Where the hell has he got to? Another hour passes. I risk a careful cigarette, I doze a little.

I'm hearing voices now, and the thud of an arrow in a feral throat and the choking cry of a falling child. Grief as perpetual motion. I can see red rain falling from trees, and birds with singed feathers rushing past me. I pull the ripcord with a desperate hand, going down down down in the fiery flying air.

Since Eliza came to live in the hut, she has experimented with Josie's clothes. At first she paraded about wearing bits and pieces randomly selected; a scarf, a belt, a single item of underwear. Then, she found herself wearing outergarments, whole outfits, and once even Josie's nightdress. She doesn't understand why this happening. When she was forced to live far away from her home, she had longed for the comfort and protection of her familiar clothing. Perhaps her secret entry into Josie's interior world through the reading of her notebooks has transformed itself into a desire to take on her outer skin as well.

Eliza tries on a pair of Josie's jeans. They are a little tight around the waist and she has to roll up the bottom of each leg into thick cuffs. There are shirts hanging from a rope strung across a corner of the room. She chooses a bright red-checked one but is unable to fasten the buttons across her breasts. The white bra that she found this morning under a pile of Josie's clean clothes helps a little. But she cannot bear the restriction to her breathing so she removes both the bra and the shirt and puts on a long loose t-shirt instead. She crushes her broad feet into a pair of Josie's ankle boots and covers her short hair with one of Josie's caps.

She notices that the left cuff of her jeans has fallen down. She takes a pair of scissors from Josie's desk and cuts a piece from the bottom of each leg so that the raw edge fits exactly over the top of the boots.

She packs a small backpack carefully. The packets of cigarettes that she found hidden in the wall of the hut are fastened together with twine. She checks once again that she has everything she needs, then quietly closes the door behind her.

This is the third time since she returned that she has made this journey up into the bush at the top of the Digger's land. She has not yet made contact with Ivan but she hopes and prays that he will be there today.

Each time that she left the town she had become more open in her movements. She is sure that she has been observed but there has been no reprimand from her uncle, no snide looks or pointed comments from the other women. The people appear to be distracted, thoughtful, turning in upon themselves. There were murmurs about the growing number of families who had left and speculation about who would be next. She had noticed small but significant rebellions against the rule of law in the dining room and out in the fields. A woman working without her head covered, others coming late to meals, a group of children quarrelling over the ownership of a rubber ball in the street.

It's a hot Sunday afternoon. Wagon loads of strangers are arriving at the wine and produce shop but instead of reporting to work, she walks boldly down the main street of Digger Town dressed in the clothes of an outsider. Maybe today she'll be lucky, he'll be already waiting for her at their meeting place in the bush, wearing his brown and green soldier's clothes and carrying his tobacco pouch.

She goes to the barn to borrow a horse but to her surprise the stalls are empty. The Clydesdales are out working, pulling the wagons from the perimeter fence to the store. But where are the others? And where are the foals? The breeding mares should have given birth months ago. She notices that the floor is swept clean and that most of the bridles and saddles have been removed from the racks.

She begins the long walk to the edge of the flats. The ground is hard beneath her boots. There has been no rain this spring and the sections of pasture beyond the range of the monsoon irrigation sprinklers have already died down to a tangled mat of brown roots. She raises Josie's black umbrella against the burning rays of the sun. Flies molest her eyes and nostrils and feast on the moisture on the back of her cotton top.

She arrives at the firebreak between the vineyards and the bush and begins to climb. It is cooler amongst the trees and the flies have mercifully disappeared.

She climbs to the top of the ridge and finds the place where she saw Ivan for the very first time. She left a note tied to a bush last time she was here. It's gone, but she's not sure if the wind has stolen it or if he came here to look for her and took it away with him.

She sits in the shade beneath the brittle gum where months ago she had gathered botanical samples for her class. She had instructed them to write the name down in their books. *Eucalyptus mannifera*, a gum that reveals the changing seasons by the colour of the skin beneath the bark.

She settles down beneath the tree and removes Josie's tight boots from her feet. There is a noise in the undergrowth and then he's there, looking down at her, exactly how she had pictured him, dressed in camouflage clothes and black beret, carrying a rifle, and wearing a thin belt around his waist with canvas packets of ammunition attached to it.

'Thank god you're safe,' he says. 'I've been going out of my mind.' He sits down beside her and takes off his beret. She is surprised to see tears streaming down his face. 'Whose clothes?' he asks through his tears.

She takes the packets of cigarettes from her pack and hands them to him. 'A present from Josie,' she says. 'Like the clothes.' She puts the cigarettes on the ground between them. He does not pick them up immediately.

'You looked better in your old gear,' he says. 'And with your beautiful long hair.' He attempts to take her in his arms but she resists him.

'Why are you armed?' she asks him. 'Are you hunting cats?'

He begins to cry again saying sorry sorry sorry. Not for the cats but for losing it so badly. Strange things have been happening to him, he can't understand it. It's been hard to keep staunch in front of the others.

She waits until he has composed himself, then says, 'I had no choice.'

'What about?' He tears the cellophane from a packet of cigarettes.

'Losing my hair. And being taken from my home.'

He keeps his head down and smokes furiously. She notices that his hands are shaking and that he has lost a lot of weight. His eyes seem to be sinking back into his head. 'Are you ill?' she asks.

'I've failed,' he answers. 'It's the voices Lizzie, they won't leave me alone...'

She tries to tell him that she hates being called Lizzie but he's not listening. He's complaining that he can't sleep or eat and he breaks down over the stupidest things and the men are making fun of him about his visions of skulls boiling and bones burning and disembodied mouths speaking in tongues, coming at him through the walls day and night...

She tells him firmly to stop, right now, and he obeys her, in mid-stream, his mouth half-open. 'Now,' she says calmly. 'Why are you here?'

'You asked me to come. On the note.' He fumbles for another cigarette. 'Besides, my life is falling to pieces, I need you to help me.'

'I will.'

He manages a smile. 'So you're still my honey girl then.'

'Not exactly,' she says. 'Not yet. It depends.'

'What do you want me to do?'

'Admit that you have committed an evil act.'

He jumps to his feet and throws his arms up into the air. 'It's too late.'

'I've agonised over the meaning of Sarah's death,' she says. 'And whether I'd played any part in it. I've gone over every day, every hour, every minute that lead up to her murder.'

'It makes no difference now.'

'Sarah was my friend and my responsibility. Did you know that she hid a small child under her clothes? I am here to witness for her.'

He stares at her without speaking, stricken.

'You once told me you have a problem with unexpected moments of compassion that arise from nowhere.'

He admits that this is true. Even more so lately.

'It does not come from nowhere.'

'It's too late for me.'

'You must swear that you will never cause harm to another person. Swear that you regret your actions. Go at once to the police and give yourself up. Tell them exactly what happened. Then accept your punishment.'

'No point. The others will deny it.'

'You must admit to your crime.'

'But the evidence has been completely and utterly obliterated.'

'Then there's nothing more that I can do for you.' Eliza puts on her boots and lifts the backpack on to her shoulders. 'You will become sick to death with remorse.'

He holds onto the back of her t-shirt and begs her not to leave him.

'Goodbye,' she says. 'And don't ever come near me again.'

He whimpers and sinks to his knees. It wasn't all his fault. He didn't want to cover up what had happened to the ferals, he didn't. Terry made them do it, he went wild at them for going off and doing something without permission. Oh yes, they had plans, big ones, very hush hush. A political act. In Canberra, right in the heart of enemy territory. A booby trap in the caverns beneath Parliament House. To be defused in exchange for the promise of the restoration of the rights of all citizens to carry arms. All their plans are on hold now because of what had happened in the ravine. He shouldn't be telling her this but it's too late now. Too late for everything.

An unlit cigarette dangles from his wet lips. He pleads for her forgiveness, keening and weeping on his knees in the drifts of dry gum leaves.

Eliza watches him for a few minutes. Then she adjusts the straps of the pack across her shoulders and walks back the same way that she had come without a backward glance.

It has taken over a week for the swelling and pain to subside.

Megan is being very kind to me. Suspiciously so. She took me to the medical centre and arranged the x-ray. She has brought all my meals to me on a tray. She has arranged for a television set to be brought into my room so that I can lie with my ankle elevated while I watch news and movies and infomercials. I watch it for hours on end without taking anything in.

Cedric is barely speaking to me. I understand his disappointment. I couldn't believe it either when he told me there was nothing at the bottom of the ravine. No bodies, no scraps of clothing, no crushed or broken plants. Not a single sign. Fire had come through a small area of bush further along the creek bed but it did not look very recent. Probably an old camp site. Either I had taken him to the wrong place or I had invented the whole thing. I tried to tell him that Madeline Branson would support my story. If nothing terrible had happened, why had she arranged for me and Eliza to go to New Zealand? Why all the subterfuge?

'You underestimate me,' he said coldly. 'I have already made inquiries. She is a liar and an impostor. The police denied all knowledge of any woman of that name working for them.'

I struggled to my feet. 'Then take me to Gerrard Winstanley. He'll believe me. And Eliza. She saw the bodies flung into the ravine, just as I did.'

He shook his head and gave Megan a meaningful look. They've been doing a lot of that sort of thing since that terrible night when Cedric drove me back from Mudgee, driving like a madman, almost throwing me out of the car when we got back to Ryde.

I've heard the whispers, I've observed how they stop talking when I hobble into the living room on my crutches, I know that they think I'm becoming unhinged.

I tried to ring Madeline on her mobile phone. A recorded voice informed me that the number is no longer in service. Whoever or whatever she was, it's clear that I can expect no further help from her. Briony is my last hope. When I have done with her, she must tell the truth. There's no other way.

Chapter Twelve

Megan put on a cheerful front last night. I am always wary of her when she's in this mood. She brought me a cup of milo in bed. 'I know that this is a difficult time for you,' she began, 'but I have to speak to you about Ceddy.' She was smiling so hard her face almost cracked wide open. 'He told me that you've been flirting with him and that he has to keep reminding you that your relationship with him is strictly professional.'

'You've got lipstick on your teeth.'

The false smile vanished. 'I believe him. It wouldn't be the first time.'

'What the hell does that mean?'

'You've always been jealous of my boyfriends.'

I couldn't be bothered arguing with her. I promised not to do it again, cross my heart and hope to die. She seemed very relieved, she even kissed me goodnight. But I wondered why lover boy was stealing my words and claiming them for himself. Revenge? Sexual fantasy? I didn't have the energy to work it out.

I've been concentrating on healing. And planning my next move.

Tonight's the night. It's nine o'clock and the house is dark. Megan and Cedric have gone out to dinner. She showed me her new dress, a fancy frothy thing with flecks of gold woven into the fabric. She twirled around in it, and asked me if she looked nice. I assured her that she looked good enough to eat. And I meant it. She did look beautiful. And I felt sad too because I knew that Cedric would never be able to give her what she wanted. I thanked her for looking after me so well this past week. What are sisters for, she said and left in a cloud of perfume and a clatter of high heels.

I call a cab and arrive at the bus station. The ticket clerk informs me that the late-night service to Mudgee is fully booked. 'But there may be a cancellation. Wait over there.' I've almost resigned myself to spending the night in the bus station when he calls me over again. 'Must be your lucky night. Someone just phoned in. One way? Forty bucks please.'

I pay cash for my ticket. I've got plenty of money, courtesy of lover boy's wallet. Serve him right for leaving it lying around unattended. And for trying to cause trouble between me and Megan.

The bus is packed. There is one place left on the back seat. I have to squash myself in between a teenage boy who is noisily devouring potato chips and a frail old man who has somehow managed to spread himself across two seats like an unhinged scarecrow. The boy offers me some chips. 'Thanks a lot,' I say. 'But I'm not hungry right now.' He reminds me a little of Jack except that he is much taller.

The trip is slow and the night is hot and humid. The air conditioning is either on the blink or ineffective this far back. The smell of diesel and the swaying motion make me feel nauseous. The boy seems to have an endless supply of junk food. He eats the night away; chocolate bars, peanuts, sweets, washed down from time to time by cans of coke. Each time he opens a new packet of food he offers me some and each time I decline with thanks. The old man is snoring with his mouth wide open. I envy him his ability to sleep on a hot night while twisting and turning along country roads.

The bus stops to let passengers alight at almost every town and settlement. I have the back seat to myself by the time we get to Mudgee. I walk down Church Street wheeling my suitcase and carrying my backpack. It's two o'clock in the morning and the town is deserted. The night is fine and warm and thick with stars. A half moon is riding high. I'm careful on the rough pavements. I can't risk another fall.

I make my way to the empty house in Mealey Street. It is exactly as I remembered it except that the front fence has now fallen over completely and taken the padlocked metal gate with it. I check out the houses on either side. Good. No lights burning. I push the front door open and make my entry as easily as before.

My suitcase is packed full of essential items that I've borrowed from Megan's house. A pair of new sheets with matching pillow cases, a small rug, one plate, one mug, a knife fork and spoon. Tomorrow I plan to hire a car and go shopping. I need to prepare everything carefully for Briony, I want her to feel welcome in her new home.

The house feels much drier than before. The smell of mould and dampness has been replaced by stifling hot air. I don't want to force a window open and make a noise so I decide to endure it until the morning. I make a nest on the kapok mattress. Wrapped up in a sheet, and with my pack for a pillow, I fall into a deep sleep.

Day five. I've been very busy getting the house ready and haunting the road outside the Triple M compound, watching for any sign of Briony. I have driven slowly past the gate many times, night and day, but there's no sign of life. The flags are still there and the gate is secure. But although I sometimes sit and watch the road, no one comes in or out. I wonder if they have abandoned the property. If so, finding Briony is going to be more difficult than I anticipated. But I'm not ready to give up yet.

I've had two scares. The first one happened when I hired the car. The woman behind the desk asked me if I could tell her the opening hours of the shop in Digger Town. I said I'd never heard of the place, I'm just a tourist, a stranger. She apologised, said she's sorry, she thought I looked a bit like that woman researcher who had exposed the goings-on in Digger Town, a local religious commune. It had been the talk of the town a few months ago. The papers had been full of it.

I pretended to be interested. Luckily, I had taken the precaution of using Megan's licence to hire the car and luckily, the photo on it was an old blurred one that looked something like me if I had been ten years younger and had fake blond hair. I made a joke about it. She agreed that old photos can be a shock. Makes you realise how much you've deteriorated. From youth to middle age in a few short years. It's the harsh sun she tells me earnestly, that's our problem.

The second scare was a disturbance on the front veranda

yesterday. I peeked through a torn lace curtain and I saw the old woman with blue hair, the one who had told me I was wasting my time on my first visit to this house. She was trying to peer through the window on the other side of the door. Her big dog was pulling at his lead and barking his head off. Maybe he could smell me inside the house. She tried to shush him but he took no notice. I sank down onto the floor and kept very still until she left with her slavering hound in tow.

Otherwise, all is in order. I've concentrated on the kitchen and the room where I sleep. There are coloured candles and incense and cushions next to the mattress. The floors are washed, the cobwebs are down. I've boarded up the bedroom window against prying eyes. I've scrubbed out the enamel sink and polished up the brass tap. There's no stove and the electricity has been disconnected so I've bought in a primus and good supplies of kerosene. I have spent hundreds of dollars on items of hardware that are essential for my plan including a kettle for hot drinks and a cutting board and a set of sharp knives. All I need now is the missing guest, the one in whose honour I have made these expensive preparations.

Day six. I drive for the last time to the Triple M compound. This time the gate is wide open so I turn the car into the driveway and drive right up to the farmhouse. The flagpole is empty. I look through the window of the big room where Eliza and I were taken after witnessing the murders in the ravine. The pictures are gone and so has all the furniture. It's clear that they moved the whole operation to parts unknown. This makes me all the more determined to find Briony. And quickly. Before she leaves the district altogether.

Day seven. I'm driving near the site of the historic village of Eurunderee when I see her walking along the road. She's dressed in black and carrying a large pack with a sleeping bag rolled across the top. She sticks out her thumb. I slow down and pull over. I watch her running up to the car in the left-hand mirror.

'Thanks,' she gasps, 'thanks a lot.' She throws her pack

onto the back seat.

I'm wearing big sunglasses and a scarf wound around my head and throat and a sunhat with a large floppy brim. She doesn't recognise me until she's in the passenger seat and by then I've taken off with a roar and it's too late.

Day eight. Things are working out very well. She was angry with me at first for suggesting that we spend some time together. But I was conciliatory and kind. Just one night I begged. And then I'll drive you to wherever you want no questions asked. There are bridges to be healed between us. We'll manage, you'll see.

She wanted to know why I parked the car a street away. I reminded her that people in small towns are very inquisitive. I got her though the gate and the door. I apologised for the state of the house. I told her that I'm squatting here illegally. She approved of this. Made the comment that I would have never done anything this radical in the bad old days in Balmain.

I made two bowls of green salad and raw fish followed by chopped fresh fruit. She really enjoyed her food. I did too. I was careful not to ask her any questions. I wanted to lull her into a false sense of security.

She's not so bright this morning. I waited until she fell sound asleep on the mattress before I chained her to the bolts in the wall. They're working quite well. I had been worried about the chains. The man in the hardware shop had assured me that they would hold a big dog, no worries. And he's right. She can't get away. She can move around a little on her bed and turn over. I don't want her to be uncomfortable. I have no desire to hurt her physically.

She shrieks and yells at me when I take her in her breakfast. Accuses me of being crazy, sick in the head. I just smile at her and spoon muesli and milk into her mouth. She spits it right back at me. 'This is fun,' I say. 'Like feeding a toddler again.'

She asks me over and over, why why? Why are you doing this to me?

'Eat up,' I tell her. 'Don't go anorexic on me.'

Day ten. She's much quieter now and sleeps a lot. She seems to have accepted the situation. We've got into a useful daily routine. I feed her raw food and cereal and fresh bread three times a day and heat up water for hot drinks on the primus.

The first time I tried to wash her she fought like a tiger. But now she submits to the washer and the soap and the tepid water. She wouldn't lift a finger to help me when I pulled the stainless steel studs from her tongue and navel and the rings from her eyebrows and ears. She refuses to do anything for herself. I even clean her teeth for her. She's a good girl. She spits out dutifully for me.

In the afternoon and night I read to her. The same things over and over. From *Ranters Redux* and the *Stuff* file. At first, she was argumentative and stubborn and continually inter-rupted me. I warned her not to do this but she wouldn't listen to me so I've had to tape her mouth up during her re-educa-tion sessions. I remove it after I've finished my reading and lecturing for the night. Gently, so I don't tear away the dry skin in the corners of her mouth.

Day twelve. I made her smile today. I went shopping and I bought her a gift. I had noticed that she had CD's in her pack but nothing to play them on. So I bought her a portable CD player with batteries and ear phones. She lay there for hours with her eyes closed. Listening to her music and dreaming. I felt so happy for her.

Day fourteen. At last. A breakthrough. She talked to me this afternoon, rationally, without contradicting me. In exchange for having her mouth free. I'm happy to do away with the tape. I've been concerned at the raw and bleeding cracks in the corner of her mouth. All of her other wounds are healing well. The hole in her tongue has almost filled up with healthy pink flesh.

Day fifteen. She talked even more today. About the Triple M and how she fell for their ideals. Seemed to be just what she was looking for. A sense of shared purpose. I leap in. And now?

And now? She clams up again. I must be patient with her. There's still plenty of time.

Day seventeen. Another breakthrough. She told me that she loves me. This happened when I was washing her head in the basin. Her shaved hair is growing back nicely, quite a thick fuzz. A tribute to the good food that I'm feeding her and my tender loving care. I wish she'd eat more bread though. I noticed this morning that she's getting thin. Especially her arms and legs.

Day eighteen. She told me today that the Triple M is no more. There was conflict within the group. Some of the people blamed Terry for being weak, for not controlling his men. Some of the members left of their own free will. Others were sent away. Briony herself was asked to leave. And Ivan too. All because they had pleaded for me and Eliza to go free even though we had trespassed on their land. She hung around for a while hoping that things would blow over. But things got worse. Everything crumbled so quickly in the end, nobody would take orders from anybody else and fights broke out.

I give her a drink of orange juice. I have to help her to lift her head to take the straw in her mouth. I hold her in my arms and sing songs from her childhood days.

Day nineteen. She's too tired to eat her breakfast so I eat it for her. Then I break the news to her that our time together is almost over. She manages a weak smile. The money is almost gone, I tell her. The rental car has to be returned. I've enjoyed looking after her but I can't do it any more. Not without a car.

I tell her to be vigilant. The Triple M are probably regrouping elsewhere under a different name. Be wary of labels like National Front, or anyone claiming to be the One or the First of anything.

She promises that she will. She's learned her lesson oh yes, she'll be strictly a loner from now on. No more groups, no more communal living.

I take off one of her chains. She sits up and stretches her back and tries to stand up but the remaining chain is too short.

'You may as well lie down,' I say. 'I can't let you go just yet. There's still the matter of the murders to be resolved.'

She sinks back on the mattress. 'I don't know what you mean.'

'I know that the evidence has been removed from the bottom of the ravine but that does not solve the problem of your punishment.'

'For what, for what?'

'Don't play the innocent with me, I was there.'

She's shouting now. 'For god's sake! All we did was play a game, a war game. Why the hell do you think we had bows and arrows? They shouldn't have been on our land stealing our firewood and fouling our water. We wanted to give them a fright so we chased them off. No one got hurt. Except you, when you got a thump on the head for trespassing.'

I sit with her through the long morning and afternoon until darkness falls but I can't get her to budge from her version of events. I light the candles and go into the kitchen to chop some raw salad. Outside, a brisk southerly brings a threat of rain.

Briony refuses to eat. She accuses me of hallucinating, seeing things that were not there. How could I do this to her? How can a mother believe this terrible thing of her own daughter?

She is so convincing, so sure of herself, that I start to doubt what it was that I actually *did* see in the ravine. Were the ferals unknowingly taking part in some sick military game? Or is she in the grip of a powerful form of denial?

When I finally release her, she's listening to a CD with her eyes closed. She's got it turned up so loud that I can hear the thump thump thump of the base coming through the earphones. It takes a minute or two for her to understand that she is free to go.

I help her with her pack and give her my last fifty dollars to help her on her way. I stand on the veranda and watch her walk slowly away, limping a little. She's half way down Mealey Street before she turns to see if I'm still standing there.

I wave goodbye to her. I hear a choking cry, almost like that of an animal in distress. I can't tell if it's a human sob of relief or remorse or simply the call of a barking owl, one of Lupa's many cousins who come to hunt the mice in the long grass at the front of the house.

Large spots of rain begin to fall. I almost run after her to make sure that she puts on her hooded parka or at least takes shelter beneath a tree.

Instead, I enter the house and close the door against the long wet night to come.